STALKING GHOSTS

ALEXANDER C. JUDEN

5points press

STALKING GHOSTS

CONTENTS

1

____

Under the Weather

I sat alone at the café La Rotonde. I was less likely to be discovered there. My friends would find me eventually, but it would take them a little longer than if I were at Le Dôme.

I needed separation from the living. The demands of those who actually existed couldn't compete with the dead voices rattling around in my head. It seemed I didn't have enough mental capacity left for reality. The hallucinations caused by the goddamn Krauts were driving me crazy.

Dr. Richardson, the American army doctor who had treated me for my mental fatigue, had released me from Military Hospital No. 1 in Neuilly. I'd pretended to be in perfect health. Well, as perfect as one can be with old gunshot and shrapnel wounds, lungs flayed by phosgene, and a recent brush with five days of drug-induced hallucinations courtesy of German military intelligence. I wasn't sure I'd fooled the doc, but I think he realized there was nothing he could do for my fractured mind.

I had been released from the very same hospital just over two months before. I'd been there recovering from gunshot wounds. Wounds suffered when I distracted Sarah Willoughby, my lover, at the moment she intended to assassinate French Prime Minister Georges Clemenceau. In diverting her attention, I had given French marksmen time to shoot us both. They killed her and wounded me. The French thought I was a hero for delaying her shot. I thought I was a traitor.

My beer sat before me untouched. The condensation on the glass long gone. Bubbles no longer drifted to the top. I had watched them for a long time, riding with them as they rose up from the bottom of the glass.

In November 1918, recovering from wounds suffered while serving with the US Marine Corps, I had returned to the United States for the second time from the war in France. The bland, gray world to which I returned was devoid of life as I had come to define it. After nearly four years of fighting, the hard, vivid truths of war were gone. I had grown used to—addicted to—the vibrant colors of violence and the carnival ride of emotion that was a life in war.

A mirthless laugh escaped me. I recalled a family vacation to Coney Island. I couldn't have been more than twelve or thirteen. There'd been a ride called the Roosevelt Rough Riders. A roller-coaster. It was billed as the "funniest, fastest, and most fascinating ride" on Coney Island. Those were lies. It was terrifying. My sisters refused to ride it. My father reluctantly agreed. The cars raced around the track snapping our heads and bodies up and down and back and forth. I begged to ride it a second time, and my father refused to go. I rode it alone three more times. No other ride at Coney Island could compare. Rough Riders had ruined the rest of the park for me.

The war had ruined the rest of life for me, or me for the rest of life. I had been unable to turn my hand to peace. As a result, several months ago, I had accepted Harry Armistan's job to find his daughter. The job had given me the danger I craved, where each second mattered, where choices determined life and death, not in decades but in moments. I really should thank Harry. For the past few months, he saved me from civilization and delivered to me a dead friend, a dead lover, and the grinding wear on my soul of the blood I'd spilled.

My existence was becoming unendurable. The nightmares now bled into the day. In the morning when I'd wake, Tippy Frederickson, a friend from before the war, would be sitting at the end of my bed, goddamn him. He'd been shot in the head by a sniper, and I'd been there when it happened. We were in a frontline trench near his dugout, having a cup of tea. Most of the right side of his head was gone. He was dead, and I knew it. But each morning, there he'd be. His maimed and smiling face watching me from the foot of my bed. His arms ending in paws would be crossed, and he'd whisper my name in the obscene parody of a lover.

"Come on, Jack, join me. The grass is greener. It really is, sweetheart." And he'd laugh.

"Fuck off, Tippy," I'd growl, and he'd go for a time though he wouldn't leave until I acknowledged him.

A nod, a word, or a snarl, and he'd laugh, and off he'd go. "See you soon, Jack."

Before he left each morning, he made sure I knew he was real. And he was. It was a problem.

Since the war, I'd had nightmares. I was not alone in that. Thousands who'd been exposed to the violence and fear of battle had horrors locked inside them. The horrors would visit at night.

Since Basel, where Dr. Elsbeth Schragmüller,[1] Karl Fuchs, and German intelligence had imprisoned me in a cellar and injected me full of mescaline, a barrier in my head had splintered. The drug created powerful hallucinations. Combined with electric shock, the Germans succeeded in warping my reality. After five days of dogmen, lizards, a deformed, demented Woodrow Wilson, imagined gore, and real feelings of unspeakable terror, the nightmares bled into the light. Awake and aware, I now saw

---

1. Elsbeth Schragmüller. August 7, 1887–February 24, 1940. Professor and German intelligence officer.

things that could not be real, but they *were* real. It was impossible to ignore the twisted images I confronted daily. I was certain my friends knew I was broken. I started at imaginary sights and sounds. My companions—many who served as soldiers, nurses, or ambulance drivers—must have noticed the twitches I couldn't suppress.

Still, I thought the fact that I didn't jump out of my skin every time I was confronted by reptilian French grand-mères[2] miraculous. It was hard not to cry out at such sights.

During my hallucinations in Basel, somehow my brain pulled Harry Armistan, the financier who'd tried to sponsor the restart of the war, and Morgan Reynolds, his assistant, into the basement with me. Into the visions that tortured me there and after. They continued to haunt my sleep and my waking. Unless I put a bullet in my own head, my solution for their haunting was to put a bullet in theirs. The choice was easy. Long before the cellar in Switzerland, I had already promised Patricia Armistan I would kill her father for his attempt to restart the war, an attempt that resulted in Sarah's death. If that alone wasn't reason enough, Armistan had joined the ghosts in my head, haunting me both sleeping and waking. My sanity required him dead. I knew their deaths wouldn't banish them entirely. They would still live inside my brain. But knowing they were dead in the *real* world would make dealing with them inside my skull easier.

I was, as my particular friend William Mitchell noted while rescuing me, "out of my head."

He'd found me in Basel. Actually, Marie Masson, a French spy and unwilling double agent for the Germans, had found me. During the war, thinking she was staying in touch with her friend and former professor, Marie had joined Elsbeth Schragmüller in Basel, Switzerland—a neutral country where two old friends on the opposite sides of a horrid war could meet in peace. Marie didn't know Schragmüller worked for German

---

2. Grandmothers.

intelligence. Marie recalled meeting her old professor outside the house where I was held in Basel. Schragmüller had told her it belonged to a friend who was an instructor at Basel's university. Once Marie realized that Schragmüller was a member of German intelligence and that I had gone to Basel to meet her, Marie told Mitchell of the house.

Walt Disney,[3] one of our new friends in Paris, who also happened to be the driver for General Pershing, stole the army staff car he used to transport Pershing's son. The three of them drove ten hours to Basel to find me. I had no doubt that if they hadn't arrived when they did, I would have ceased to be. Not dead. My body would live, but the Germans would have succeeded in destroying my mind. Whether they could have replaced it with a simulacrum that could function well enough to ultimately assassinate Wilson, as they hoped, I did not know. I did know the Germans had come damn close to erasing whatever was in my head that was me.

So my friends saved me. I was still amazed that when I first came to Paris, I had made friends. Sure my pal William Mitchell had enchanted many of them first, but they were my friends too. Marie, Disney, Rachel Eisen, Kiki, and Eugene Bullard. They'd all helped me in one way or another to escape Germany. Madeline Moore, another friend—and briefly lover—had left for the States before I'd been captured.

Two months ago I'd been brokenhearted. The loss of Sarah had seemed overwhelming. Now, with a broken mind, I still felt Sarah's death, but the heartbreak was gone. Too much had been crammed into my head and heart for it to remain. And when ghosts, including Sarah's, haunted my waking hours, I didn't feel the old heartbreak quite as deeply.

I wasn't sure I could function when I didn't know what was real. With each improbable vision, a bullet became the more

---

3. Walter Elias Disney. December 5, 1901–December 15, 1966. Cartoonist and entrepreneur.

rational course. The heft of the pistol seemed significant, both for its physical bulk and its lethal potential. The possibility of ending the corrosive, spine-chilling visions was just six pounds away. A squeeze of the .45's trigger, and the specters and phantasms would be gone.

Of course I had no illusions. I had seen enough gruesome death to know what a bullet in the head would look like. I saw it in Tippy every day. But I wouldn't know or care. I'd be dead.

I knew it would be cowardly to kill myself. To leave William and my friends to wonder what they could have done to help me. To save me. I told myself they would be better off without me. It would still be a lousy thing to do. Running away had been a favorite option of mine since 1916.

In 1914, I'd been a visiting American attending university in England. When the war came, I had volunteered to serve along with my friends from school. By 1916, most of them were dead, and fear had eaten away any decency in me. It changed me into a man I couldn't respect, much less love. I was loathsome. All because of the fear.

Blind dumb luck saved me from the need to desert. A German sniper was my Christ. He shot me in the head. I know that doesn't sound like luck, but it was. His shot wasn't clean. The bullet spiraled through sandbags and the wooden parapet where I stood watch. The Boche bullet shards and wood splinters tore my face, fractured my skull, and blinded me. As I said. Good luck.

I'd been evacuated to England. I was out of the ghastliness of the trenches. My betrothed, elegant, dewy-eyed Evelyn, sister of my friend Bertie Wilson, tried so hard to love me when I came back to England to convalesce. But she had no use for a scarred blind man, and I had no use for her. Family, status, and complacent comfort had no place in my life. I had pursued a lie, but the war had set me straight. With my vision returning, I feigned continuing blindness and left England and Evelyn. I was back in the States just after Christmas 1916. It was the best gift I could have gotten.

Other than the ugly scar caused by the sniper's shot, I should have been free of the war, the trenches, and the death. Unfortunately, my ignominious exit gnawed at me. I'd abandoned my mates. Not the university men I'd joined with, for they all went on to be officers. Instead, I'd abandoned the men I'd served with. The middle- and working-class blokes who wanted out just as bad as I. Many of them never got a blighty. Never got home. Instead, they got one of a thousand awful wounds or one of a thousand hideous deaths. Not me. Because I'd run.

I became a sullen, angry drunk. In 1917, with the United States entering the war, my self-loathing drove me to enlist in the Marine Corps, an opportunity for redemption, or at least death.

I survived. I shouldn't have, but I was lucky in war. Killing came to me easily even if the price weighed on my mind. And now I found I had to pay the price, not just in sleep but while awake.

I threw some money on the table, leaving my untouched beer. I wouldn't kill myself today. I had things to do. Since my friends hadn't found me, I'd had a nice long wallow in self-pity. Now I needed to find them. Over a week before, Patricia Armistan had gone to London with Morgan Reynolds. Somehow he had convinced her of the need to resolve some undisclosed problem with both her murdered husband's estate and her US citizenship. I would find Mitchell. He needed to go to England and rescue his lover, Patricia. I needed to go to England to kill her kidnapper, Reynolds. Maybe then Reynolds would stay out of my goddamn head.

I FOUND MITCHELL AT LE DÔME. THE WEATHER HAD TURNED colder, and he was at an inside table surrounded by blue cigarette smoke. Eugene Bullard[4] sat across from him, and the two were so

---

4. Eugene "Jacques" Bullard. October 9, 1895–October 12, 1961. Boxer,

deep in conversation that they didn't notice my approach.

"...evil bitch screwed him up good," I heard Mitchell say as I arrived at the table.

With his back to the wall, Mitchell saw me first. Bullard was still shaking his head at the comment when Mitchell jumped out of his seat to welcome me and hide his embarrassment.

I saw no point in pretending I hadn't overheard.

"That she did, Mitch." I wasn't angry. He was right. I looked at Bullard. "Gene, thanks to Elsbeth Schragmüller, I've got more worms squirming in my head than a goddamn corpse. It's crowded in here," I said, tapping my skull with my forefinger.

"Mitchell was filling me in. I'm sorry, Griff. It's hard enough keeping the shit we've seen boxed up tight without the damn Boche drugging you to squeeze it out."

"That's true, but I don't blame Elsbeth. She was just doing her job. Karl too. They're patriots. But I do believe I'll get a chance to kill them."

"Faith is an important thing to have," Bullard said with a trace of humor. "And knowing you, John, I believe it too."

Mitchell was frantically waving for a waiter. As a former Navy corpsman serving with the Marine Corps during the war, he believed that the right medicinal tincture could fix even an invisible illness of the brain. In this instance, he was sure the right medicine was a whisky, which he ordered without consulting me.

He was wrong, but I appreciated his concern and didn't want to disappoint him by declining the drink. From the corner of my eye, I caught the flash of Sarah's sandy hair. When I looked directly at her, she had the courtesy to disappear.

Maybe the drink *would* help.

"Gene, when I left for Switzerland, you were still gathering the equipment on our list. If I'm going to kill Armistan, I'll need it. How's that coming?" I asked. Mitchell and I had provided

---

musician, club owner, war hero.

Bullard a laundry list of weapons and equipment to procure via the illegal underground markets in Paris.

"We. We are going to kill Armistan," Mitchell said, correcting me.

I glanced at him. "Sure. That's what I meant." It wasn't. I didn't want him coming with me. I wanted him to stay safely in Europe. I wasn't sure how I was going to keep him away.

"Oh, that's been done since before you got back. Mitchell knows," Bullard said.

"Sorry, Gene. I should have asked Mitch before now. My mind has been elsewhere," I said with a straight face.

Mitchell tried to choke down his laugh, and Bullard couldn't.

"It sure the hell has!" Mitchell said with passion, and I laughed too.

With my instability out in the open, it was okay. If they thought they had to walk on eggshells because I was a crackpot, we'd never get anything done.

"Yeah, in goddamn Dante's inferno…," I said under my breath, but they heard.

"Sorry, Griff." Bullard was sincere in his regrets. "I can't imagine."

"Sure you can, Gene. Just take the shit you dream at night and move some of it to the day, and you got the picture," I said.

"Nobody gives a shit that you're more crazy, John," Mitchell said bluntly. "You've always been crazy. You really aren't that much different from before. Just make sure shit really exists before you start shooting it."

I gave Mitchell a raised eyebrow. My drink had arrived, and I took a healthy sip. I ignored the blond woman who was back at the edge of my vision.

"When's the flight to London, Will?" I asked. Before I'd disappeared, Mitchell had arranged an airplane to fly us to London. He was to have reserved another now that I was out of the hospital.

"Two days."

"Nothing sooner?" When we'd first returned from Switzerland, he hadn't been concerned by Patricia's departure to London with Morgan Reynolds, but now, several days later, I knew he was. She should have returned to Paris by now.

"Nope. It'll be okay," he said with a pretense of his habitual optimism. "Drunk tonight, recover tomorrow, fly out the day after. The schedule is all set."

"I'm surprised you built in the extra day."

"Age. And you've been under the weather. I didn't want you to feel too much pressure given your fragile mental state," he said. "And I didn't have a choice. That's what the goddamn airplane schedule required. And a train ain't any faster." He was indeed worried about Patricia.

2

<hr>

Complications and Rewards

We lifted off as planned from Le Bourget aerodrome northwest of Paris. After two and a half hours, we landed at Waddon just south of central London. During the flight, I was the most relaxed I'd been since before Basel. Apparently, my ghosts did not like the noise and the cold of the airplane. I didn't either, but the price was worth paying.

Mitchell had booked a motorcab to collect us at the aerodrome and drive us into London. We had reservations at Claridge's. It was the same hotel where we'd stayed when we'd first met Gavin Kingsbury, Patricia's dead husband. He was dead because Patricia murdered him during a gunfight outside of Paris. Mitchell had no idea Patricia was the murderer, and I'd promised not to tell him. Despite myself, I liked her, and he seemed so damn happy with her. I didn't want to spoil it. Like us all, he'd had a hard time with the war. He buried it deeper and hid it better, but he deserved a measure of happiness. I kept my silence for him.

We brought only our pistols, which Mitchell insisted we pack in our bags. We had left the steamer trunk of weapons, tools, and ammunition that Bullard had collected on our behalf in Paris. Mitchell didn't want to set me loose in London to hunt Morgan Reynolds while wielding a BAR.[1] I felt badly for Mitchell. He had to balance his concern for his girl and my questionable mental state. His decision to leave the heavy weapons was likely a good one. Unfortunately, with our recent history, I expected the worst. It didn't help that I was afflicted with daymares and going to a place that had been at the heart of my nightmares since I'd taken the job to find Patricia in the first place. I remained terrified of being identified in England by a former classmate at university, a soldier from my regiment—hell, a doctor or nurse who had treated me. Such recognition shouldn't matter, but it did. It would tip the delicate balance in my noggin.

⁕

WHEN WE ARRIVED, CLARIDGE'S WAS BURSTING WITH ACTIVITY. With the war won and the peace treaty signed, the rich were out in droves. My room wasn't ready. The staff was expecting Mitchell and gave him a key to Patricia's suite. I told him to go up, and I waited in the bar. He was happy to go and happy to go alone. I didn't need to be around for his joyous reunion with Patricia. Of course, I didn't believe she was up there anyway.

As I entered Claridge's bar, I couldn't help but think about that first night with Sarah. We'd both been staying at the hotel. While I was there by chance, she was there as part of her and her brother's plans. It felt so long ago. We'd had dinner, and later that evening, she'd knocked on my door, came into my room, and slipped through all my emotional defenses. I knew I was lost to her then.

But now my memories of her had been swamped by more recent ones, real and not. The experiences with Marie Masson in Germany and the horror in Switzerland had simply

---

1. Browning Automatic Rifle.

overwhelmed my grief at her loss. If I were honest, I would admit that my brief love affair with Madeline Moore had helped as well.

Although it was early in the afternoon, the bar was stacked two deep. Many of the patrons were Australians, some in uniform but many not. A few Americans were scattered about.

I thought about the dinner with Sarah again, and I remembered Morgan Reynolds had been there. This recollection triggered a surge of paranoia. I carefully checked to make sure he wasn't lurking in the bar. Thinking about him caused my stomach to churn and my heartbeat to accelerate uncomfortably.

My reaction brought to mind a feral cat I'd once tried to capture for my sister Eleanor. She was the younger of my two older sisters and wasn't as pragmatic as my oldest sister, Margaret. But Elle was more wily, and she always found a way to manipulate me into doing what she asked even when it wasn't in my best interest. She had wanted me to get her the cat because she thought it was cute. It was small, cute, orange, and male. He was also agile, careful, and skittish. I'd managed to corner him under the back steps outside our house. I had him trapped, and he was terrified. When I poked my head under the steps, he arched his back and hissed a warning. I'd stretched out my arm to grab him by the scruff. Not one of my better ideas. He slashed my hand bloody quicker than I could follow. I fell back from the opening, and he shot past me and was gone.

When I thought of Reynolds and Armistan, I felt like that cat. Trapped and terrified. Feral. Unless I learned to control the horror born in the Basel basement, I would react just like that cat. Just as viciously. Just as quickly.

I managed to get a beer from the bartender, and I took it to a table away from the crowd. I set it down in front of me and watched the bubbles for a time.

"Hey, Griff." Mitchell surprised me. I had been absorbed in watching the beer. "She's not in her room. Her clothes and suitcases are. The staff expects her back tonight."

"Good. That's good." I decided I needed to warn Mitchell about my irrational fear of Reynolds and my reaction to that fear. "Mitch, we might have a problem. Well, I might have a problem."

I hadn't told him any details about what the Germans had done to me. "When the Krauts had me in that house, they didn't just drug me."

"I know, Griff. I helped Marie pull you off the dissection table. I disconnected the electric switch on your back. Marie broke the projector. They were forcing you to watch looped newsreel footage of Woodrow Wilson. Not what I thought would have been the worst of tortures, but there's no accounting for Germans."

"Between the drugs, the shocks, and the moving pictures, they screwed up my brain, Mitch," I said. "You need to know how badly so you can keep an eye on me."

He watched me intently, waiting for me to continue.

"The drug, mescaline, it made me hallucinate. From the pictures, Wilson transformed. Into a dogman of all things. I saw the bastard bounding along the Champs-Élysées in a top hat. And somehow my brain pulled Harry Armistan and Morgan Reynolds into the show. Like Wilson, they became dogmen. Rabid, slathering canine versions of the men I know. And Mitch, they terrify me. It terrifies me to think of them. It's not rational. I feel like I have to kill them just to protect myself. It feels like the only solution. If Reynolds walked through that door"—I nodded at the entrance to the bar—"I genuinely worry I'd blow his head off."

I decided not to tell Mitchell of my thoughts of suicide. This was a difficult enough conversation.

"Well, that's not *so* bad," he said with a slight smile. He was going to try to make me feel better. Not feel so crazy. "You wanted to kill Morgan before Basel."

"Yeah, that's true, but before Basel, I wasn't afraid of him. Now I am. And my fear makes me angry. I don't think I can be trusted to act reasonably."

"Okay. I'll keep an eye on you, but if you decide to kill Reynolds, I'm not sure there is much I can or want to do."

"There will be a time and a place for it, Mitch. I just can't spontaneously erupt and execute the bastard in Claridge's bar."

"No. You can't, but it would make a great story."

Mitchell got a whisky and came back to the table.

The Aussies became progressively more boisterous. They had a way of making Claridge's feel like Le Dôme. Hoots of laughter and the occasional spilled drink made me almost homesick. I expected a fight soon. More women worked their way into the bar. Maybe they expected a fight too.

"I'm going to see if my room is ready," I told Mitchell. The bodies surging across the room were taking unpleasant forms.

"I'll be here for a while and then head upstairs to wait for Tricia," Mitchell told me. "Hey, leave your gun in the suitcase."

I nodded and hurried to the lobby.

My room was ready.

When I got there, I sat quietly on the end of the bed. Alone. No dogmen. No lizards. No Tippy Frederickson. I lay back and closed my eyes. Jumbled and chaotic images flickered behind my eyelids as if projected there by the jerky, winking lights of a motion-picture projector. After a time, the confused impressions of explosions and monsters accompanied me into a fitful sleep.

When I woke, it was dark. The luminescent hands of my watch told me it was nineteen hundred hours, seven o'clock in the evening.

I sat up, rubbed my face, and realized that I had fallen asleep wearing my suitcoat.

I went to the bathroom and splashed water on my face. I looked bleary-eyed and haunted.

I came out to a knocking on the door.

It was Mitchell. He looked worried.

"She's not in our room. She should have been back by now. Everything is closed. Government offices, shops. Only the restaurants and bars are open."

"She could be at dinner," I said hopefully. I was still groggy from the restless sleep.

"She'd come back and change for dinner," he declared, dismissing my optimism.

"Let's go find her," I said.

I went to my suitcase and took the Colt from its holster, checked the magazine, and slid it back into the pistol. I made a show of handling the gun because I needed Mitchell calm. When he thought I might do something crazy, he became the responsible one. I was reminding him that I was crazy. It worked.

"I don't think we'll need that, John," he said seriously. "I'm sure she's fine. I'm just a little anxious."

"Yeah, me too." I left the pistol for the time being. "Let's get dinner first. Then we'll do a little scouting before we hunt down Reynolds."

He rolled his eyes.

"Sure. We'll eat here. Maybe she'll come back while we're at dinner."

<hr>

Our dinner table gave us both a view of the entrance to the restaurant. We ordered and then ate in relative silence.

As our after-dinner coffees arrived, I looked at my watch. Eight thirty.

"Where would she go for an evening out?" I asked Mitchell.

Mitchell signed for the bill, and we decided to take an evening stroll down Brook Street to Grosvenor Square and beyond. Just as we exited the hotel, we ran into Patricia. She was hanging on Morgan Reynolds's arm, taking a drag off a cigarette as they ambled toward the entrance of the hotel.

I felt nauseated at the sight of them. Seeing Reynolds whole and hale knotted my stomach. No dog ears or paws at least. A vein in my temple throbbed. Patricia was laughing at something

Reynolds had said. Seeing her with Reynolds felt like a betrayal to me. I glanced at Mitchell, and although his eyes narrowed briefly, his expression quickly changed. His face lit up and he smiled.

"Tricia," he called as he walked toward her.

She slipped free of Reynolds and, despite blocking the rotating door into the hotel, gave William a hug. Mitchell kissed her on both cheeks, and she held on to his arms while studying him.

"Oh, I am so glad you're here," she said. "I was worried you were still in Germany."

"We're back, safe and mostly sound," Mitchell told her.

She turned to me, and I gave her a quick peck on the cheek. Her perfume reminded me of Sarah.

"You look like you're ready to kill someone, John. Are you all right?"

"I'm fine, Patricia. Just a difficult few weeks."

Reynolds was watching the three of us. Sweat beaded on my forehead. I dashed it away with the palm of my hand.

"We need to get out of the doorway," I said and walked a few steps away from the entrance without greeting Reynolds.

"Where have you been?" Mitchell asked Patricia. "I checked the suite. Your clothes are there. We got in this afternoon, and I was sure we'd catch you when you came back to the room to change for dinner." The questions sounded slightly accusatory to my ear, but Patricia just laughed.

"The theater. A musical revue called *Bran Pie*. It was very good, wasn't it, Morgan?"

"Yes, it was quite gay. Each song more cheery than the last. Just the type of entertainment we need to put the war behind us," he said with poorly hidden meaning. He wanted to put Mitchell and me behind him. He looked at Patricia. "But we still need to grab a bite to eat, Trish."

"Of course. Poor Morgan. Always worried about your stomach." She looked at Mitchell and then me. "Join us?"

"Wouldn't consider doing anything else, my dear," Mitchell answered.

She turned to enter the hotel. Both men followed her.

I studied the back of Reynolds's head, watching to see if his ears pivoted to listen as I moved behind him. It was hard following him through the door. Like going up the assault ladder after the whistle blew. I was scared, and fear made me sore. Despite what my broken brain wanted me to believe, he was just a man. A mortal man.

"I'll meet you in the dining room," I called to the three of them once we were in the lobby.

Mitchell waved a hand in acknowledgment.

I hurried to the men's lavatory. It was empty as far as I could tell. I hunched over the sink and stared at myself in the mirror. The beads of sweat were back on my forehead, and my pupils looked huge. I needed to manage myself better than this. I needed to force myself to be around Reynolds. I would grow accustomed to the nausea and fear. Yeah, sure I would. Just like I'd grown accustomed to the terror of the trenches.

"Shut up!" I snarled at the mirror. I stood, straightened my tie, and took a deep breath. I'd faced worse. I would be fine. I went to find them in the restaurant.

<hr>

WHEN I ARRIVED AT THE TABLE, THEY WERE STILL BUSY ORDERING drinks. Reynolds and Mitchell flanked Patricia, leaving me the seat across from her. Her skin was flushed by the attention of two men, both who clearly wanted her.

The waiter was just leaving them, and I ordered a whisky before he could go.

"Tell us about your trip here, Patricia," I said. I didn't want to talk about Germany or Switzerland in front of Reynolds. I had no doubt Mitchell would share my problems with Patricia, but I'd be damned if I'd do it.

"Well, there is so much to tell. Some good and much infuriating." She smiled at William. "I'll start with the good. I've acquired a house here in London. I would have done the same in Paris, but the French just make it so hard. It's not far from here. Not large, but comfortable. I've bought a few things that I keep there. That's why I didn't need to come by the hotel to change."

The drinks arrived, and Patricia and Reynolds ordered dinner.

"That's all the good news." She smiled again at Mitchell, letting him know that his arrival was also good news though she didn't mention it. "Unfortunately, there are complications with Gavin's estate—really, my estate—and thanks to Morgan, I've discovered complications with my nationality."

"Your nationality?" Mitchell asked.

"Yes," Reynolds answered for her, and I didn't like it. "When she married Gavin, she lost her American citizenship. She became a citizen of Great Britain, which at least means she's not stateless. But she is no longer an American."

"That's ridiculous," Mitchell said.

"Perhaps, but it's the law," Patricia answered. "The Expatriation Act of 1907. Section three. 'That any American woman who marries a foreigner shall take the nationality of her husband.'"[2]

"So you're British now?" I asked.

"Yes, she is," Reynolds said. "This complicates her return to the United States, though it might help with some of the probate difficulties related to Gavin's death. But the authorities here still need reams of documents. A death certificate with a notarized translation. The marriage certificate. Since he had no will, they also need to confirm exactly what assets resided in his estate. Specifically, what European assets did Harry transfer to him?

---

2. The Expatriation Act. H . 8.24122. Fifty-Ninth Congress. Sess. II. Ch. 2534. 1907. Section 3.

Much of the statements and other information are in New York. I've contacted Harry, but he's being difficult."

Armistan was being difficult because he wanted Patricia back under his control. He would do nothing to promote her independence.

"We've got solicitors working on these issues day and night," Patricia added. "And Morgan has hired some of the very best lawyers in New York to address the American citizenship and probate issues."

I didn't think having Reynolds involved was a good idea, but that might have been because he made my skin crawl.

"It's made my situation very complicated," Patricia continued. "Fortunately, I have direct access to much of the cash that Gavin had when we came over. I've simply moved it into Barclays in my name."

"Clever," I said. I avoided looking at Reynolds entirely.

"With Sarah dead"—Patricia looked at me sadly—"Gavin has no other relatives to contest my claims, not that they would succeed anyway."

"Well, that's a relief." I shouldn't have said it, and the comment drew a sharp look from Mitchell. I shrugged my shoulders. "Sorry, Patricia. I've been a bit snappish lately."

"You need a good long rest, John. Maybe back in the States where no one is shooting at you."

The drinks arrived relieving me of the need to answer.

"Well, we'll certainly need to go back to the States eventually to fix Patricia's citizenship," Reynolds interjected.

"And William and John will come with me. I loathe the idea of leaving William in Paris with the pretty young women I've seen around him."

"You need have no fear of any other woman, I promise you that, Patricia." Mitchell's smile couldn't have gotten any wider, and Patricia's mirrored it. For a moment, I felt like an eavesdropper.

"We can't go back until the probate issues are on track here,"

Reynolds said, interrupting the lovers' moment. Despite myself, I wanted to thank him. "Cigarette?" he asked Patricia, offering her one from his gold cigarette case. She took a long, thin cigarette, clearly handmade with a blue ring around one end. Reynolds offered one to Mitchell as well with a gleam in his eye.

"I'll stick with my smokes, thanks," Mitchell told him, taking a Camel from the crumpled pack in his pocket. Patricia was oblivious to the implied rebuke.

"What do you need from us?" Mitchell asked Patricia as he beat Reynolds to lighting her cigarette.

"Just your company. We should be done here in a few days." She looked at Reynolds for confirmation. "And yours, of course, John."

I didn't want to stay in England, but I also didn't want to leave Mitchell and Patricia with Reynolds.

"Of course."

I left them shortly after. My drink remained untouched.

As I passed the hotel desk, the concierge raised a hand to catch my eye.

"Sir, I am sorry to bother you, but I know you are an associate of Madame Kingsbury. I wanted to be sure you had seen this." He handed me a sheet of paper. "We wouldn't want any problems for her. She is a valued guest. Obviously, we have not contacted the authorities."

My stomach clinched when I looked at the paper.

Under the heading "Metropolitan Police: £1000 reward for information leading to the detention or arrest of a man operating under the alias John Smith," was the picture of a man wearing a hat low on his head. He had a thin, hungry face and piercing eyes shadowed by the hat. A scar ran through his eyebrow and covered much of one side of his face. It was an ugly scar. Just like mine. Under the picture, the sheet read, "American wanted for questioning in murder of three."

"Looks a bit like me, doesn't he?" I said, looking up at the concierge.

"Indeed, sir. I thought you should know."

"Thank you for telling me." I handed him a pound note. "Can I keep this? Mrs. Kingsbury will enjoy teasing me about it."

"Of course, sir. We have others."

"No doubt."

I folded the leaflet and stowed it in my pocket. I went directly to my room and packed my bag.

<hr>

I waited until I was certain Patricia and Mitchell would have returned to their suite. Reynolds would not have escorted them there as much as he might have wanted to. While there was a risk I would interrupt their lovemaking, I didn't particularly care. The worst was happening. I should have expected it. In fact, it was laughable that I hadn't.

Mitchell answered my knock. His tie was gone, his shirt unbuttoned, and he had lipstick on his neck.

"Sorry, Mitch," I said, pushing past him into the room. "Something's come up, and you both need to know about it."

Patricia was in the sitting room sprawled on a couch, looking undisturbed by my interruption. One of her dress straps had slipped off her shoulder, and she tugged at it half-heartedly as I came in. She failed entirely to replace it. She reached a languid arm for her drink instead, but her glass was empty.

I dropped my bag on the floor and handed Mitchell the circular. He looked grim and passed the flyer to Patricia. She glanced from the picture to me and back.

"Not a good likeness." She giggled. I knew she had been drinking at dinner and after. Now I was certain she had been drinking before as well.

"Thank you, Patricia. That's the best news I've had since seeing this."

"Did you murder three men in London, John?" she asked.

"Remember when we first met at Le Dôme I told you that

since arriving in Europe I'd had to kill five men. I killed three of them in London, in my room at the Savoy. Gavin had sent them to kill me." And Sarah, but I didn't say that because I still didn't want to believe it. "They wanted to make sure I didn't spoil their plot."

"Then the police must have your name as well as your description!" The realization seemed to sober her up.

"No. I registered as John Smith. It's in the flyer."

"Well, Gavin's cabal was certainly right to hunt you, given the mess you made of their efforts."

My face dropped at her comment.

"I'm sorry, John, I didn't mean Sarah. She wasn't a Bolshevik. She wasn't part of Gavin's plot. I didn't mean to include…"

"Don't worry about it, Tricia," I said brusquely. "It's okay, and I didn't murder anyone. It was more like a knee-jerk reaction when they started the shooting. It really was self-defense, but I don't know if the bobbies will believe me. I did run after all." I didn't mention the wounded Englishman begging for his life or the bullet I'd put in his brain. It was his bad luck he'd known my name. And my bad luck too.

"Maybe you should head back to Paris, John," Mitchell suggested, looking at my suitcase.

"I'm not leaving you two with Reynolds. I think all three of us should go back to Paris. Let Reynolds do his magic here. I don't see why you're needed, Patricia," I said.

"Oh, I can't leave. Morgan will need my direction. And the lawyers will need me for the probate. Make me another drink, dear," she said to Mitchell, holding up her empty glass.

There was no point in arguing. She wanted to be in control. Perhaps she didn't trust Reynolds. I certainly couldn't blame her for that.

"Fine, but I can't stay here," I said. "I've got to find a place where the police haven't left a copy of my picture."

"That's not your picture," Mitchell said. "Lots of guys got shot in the face in the past few years, and it's not all that hard to pretend to be an American. But you are going to need a story if you get picked up."

The possibility of confronting the authorities was frightening. They would connect me with my wartime service. Perhaps they wouldn't call me a coward to my face, but they would know that I had left. I wasn't sure I could handle the accusation that I knew I would see in their eyes. Once the police knew about me, what was to keep soldiers I'd served with from knowing? What was to keep the few from my university crowd who survived from discovering me?

I took a deep breath. I was creating problems that didn't exist. I feared being identified as a coward. Why? I wasn't the only one who had returned from the front shattered by the experience. Yes, I'd left, but no one would blame me. I was already punishing myself for my scrimshanking. Anyone who'd served wouldn't condemn me for leaving. They knew that society's shackles—God, patriotism, glory, even morality—were fabrications of the prewar world that had duped an entire generation into agreeing to stumble meekly to the slaughter.

It was only the dead who blamed me, and that would not change no matter who knew I was in England.

"Yes, John." Tippy Fredrickson was perched on the arm of the couch where Patricia lounged. "We do blame you. Do the right thing, mate. Join us."

"Griff, did you hear me?" It was Mitchell.

"What?"

"I said you need to know what you'll tell the bobbies if you get picked up."

"No," I said to Tippy. He shrugged. The demons in my head were leaking out. Better to be recognized as a coward than to surrender to Tippy. I would take the offensive. I would go to the English police.

"What do you mean no?" Mitchell asked.

I realized Mitchell thought I had been talking to him. I was certainly not going to correct him.

"I have a better plan," I told him, doing my best to look earnest and intelligent. When I glanced back at the couch, Tippy was gone. "I'll go to the police. I don't wait for them to pick me up. I tell them I work for Colonel Edward House and the State Department. It's more or less true. As long as I can account for where I was the morning of the Savoy shooting, I should be fine. I just need an alibi."

"That sounds remarkably rational for a man who was willing to kill to remain unidentified," Mitchell said with a thoughtful look.

"Yeah, well, I've changed my mind," I said with a straight face.

Mitchell barked out a laugh. He handed Patricia a fresh drink and sipped on one he'd made for himself.

"Well, your mind sure as hell has been changed."

"William, what are you laughing about? John is at risk. We should be helping."

"Sweetheart, he's doing a pretty good job helping himself. But I do think we can help him a little. I'll be your alibi. The night of your gunfight, I stayed in a hotel in a town just down the river from Weybridge, Walton-on-Thames. The hotel was named the Swan. Old. Charming. Exposed beams on the outside. Small room. Low roof. We'll say we shared the room and you left early to see Sarah."

"That could work. I can use the plot to kill Clemenceau. Tell them I was investigating the Bolsheviks then." Briefly I felt guilty about abusing Sarah's memory, but I was certain she would have happily joined my efforts to dupe the authorities.

"Don't go to the police. Go to the military intelligence pooh-bahs," Patricia said. "They'll be less interested in the death of a few Bolsheviks and more interested in information about the French and the Germans."

"And any live Bolsheviks," Mitchell added.

"I don't know any intelligence pooh-bahs," I said flatly.

"Leave that to me," Patricia said. "I'm sure my solicitors can point us in the right direction."

I liked that she said "us." I was feeling panicky. Being haunted by dead men and people with dog paws was wearing on my confidence.

"And in the meantime, go to my new house," Patricia continued. "I'd love for you to see it. Of course, it still needs a great deal of work, but I think you'll enjoy the space. Lie low there until we can get you a British intelligence contact. It would be a shame for you to be arrested just when you're back from Germany."

"What's the address of your new place? I'll go there now. Having this picture out there"—I nodded toward the window—"has me worried."

"Number 2, Aldford Street. Just a ten-minute walk if your case isn't too heavy."

"I'll be fine. How do I get in?"

"Just ring the bell. The staff will answer."

"The staff. I should have known. What do I tell them?"

She looked confused.

I tried again. "When I arrive, what do I tell your *staff*?"

"That I sent you, of course."

I opened my bag and took out the Colt pistol from its shoulder holster and put it on a nearby coffee table.

"As long as I'm wanted by the police, I think it would be wise for me to leave my pistol with you, Mitch." I didn't tell him that Tippy was openly haunting me and urging me to shoot myself. He wouldn't want to know it, and I wouldn't want to say it.

"Patricia, don't tell Morgan about the wanted poster or the police. I know you trust him in some things, but don't trust him in this. Whether you believe it or not, if he knew about my problems, he'd turn me in quicker than a cat lapping chain lightning."

She thought for a moment. "Fine. I don't see any need for him to know."

"Thanks. I'll leave the two of you to your evening."

3

The Business of Distrust

Patricia's new house exceeded even my inflated expectations. I had fooled myself into thinking it would be a house appropriate for a new widow. A rich one, with a lover, but just one woman. This belief overlooked the fact that the house required a staff. When I arrived in front of Number 2, I was confronted with a townhome with two other houses flanking it and sharing common walls. By the style, it was likely built toward the end of the last century, no doubt around the time I was born. By London standards, it was a new dwelling. The four floors of red brick were broken by numerous windows with white frames and exposed stone borders. A black iron railing ran along the inside of the sidewalk in front of the house. Below the level of the sidewalk, arched windows testified to the existence of a lower floor. A basement. My stomach knotted at the thought.

Up five shallow stone steps, I came to a heavy wrought iron and glass door. I pushed the button for the doorbell and heard it buzzing inside the house. Even in the dim lights of the streetlamps, I was impressed by the polished brass of the plate framing the button.

I waited patiently. It was late, and the staff would be sleeping. A light in the entryway came on and the door opened.

"May I help you, sir?"

Even at this time of night, the man who answered wore black trousers with gray stripes, a black waistcoat, a double-breasted, black swallowtail coat, and a black four-in-hand tie over a stiff white shirt with a standing collar. He was older, but he stood very straight. His accent was one I had learned from my time at university to associate with the English upper class. He'd likely cultivated it carefully for his job. Despite his age, I was certain he had served in France, and I didn't think he was a draftee. He wore no facial hair and shaved his scalp. From the look of him, I suspected he had no time to waste caring for his hair. In the dim light of the doorway, his nose twitched, like a dog sniffing something new.

I nearly stepped back, but I managed to control myself.

"Mrs. Kingsbury sent me. She told me I could stay here while she is concluding her business in London."

"Of course, sir." He stepped out of the doorway to allow me to enter.

"I'm John Griffin." I held out my hand, knowing it would take him off guard. If he held out a dog's paw, he was a dead man even without my pistol.

He hesitated, and then his innate politeness forced him to take it, with a hand not a paw.

"I am Hackworth, sir. May I take your bag?"

"A pleasure to meet you, Mr. Hackworth, and no, I'll carry it." I didn't know how long he'd have hands, and I didn't want him to drop it if his appendages transformed.

"It's just Hackworth, sir. Have you eaten?"

"Yes, thank you. I'm just tired."

He nodded. No further conversation was needed. He led me through the entryway, up the stairs, and down a hallway. He held the door open for me to a room that looked like it had been waiting for me.

"Breakfast is at nine, sir. Shall I wake you?"

"Thank you, Hackworth, but that won't be necessary."

"Good night, sir." He pulled the door closed behind him, and I was alone. Safe from all but the demons in my head.

⁂

I WAS AWAKE EARLY. NOTHING IN PARTICULAR WOKE ME. No nightmares, no kicked-in doors.

However, I wasn't alone. Tipton Frederickson stared at me morosely from the foot of the bed. He didn't speak, which was new. There was something disturbing about his demeanor. He had been so cheerful in his encouragement of my suicidal urges that something felt wrong.

"Cat got your tongue, Tippy?" I asked.

His shattered face took on a look of hatred so stark and unmistakable that I sat up in bed.

"I wish the cat would take yours," he said. "There aren't enough lashes that could be laid on your back to erase what you've done," he growled with an anger that was new to our relationship.

"Why so hot, Tip?" I said, trying to mollify him. "I haven't deserted again. Nothing's changed since yesterday. You're still the ghost of a dead man, and I'm still a coward with hallucinations."

He stared at me so intently I began to fear he would attack me. I carefully drew my legs up so they wouldn't get tangled in the bedclothes when he did.

"You'll always find a way to avoid your comeuppance, Griffin." He never called me Griffin. Something was different with my personal apparition. I glanced toward my jacket but recalled that I'd left my pistol with Mitchell. Looking for the Colt was an irrational thing to do anyway. I knew the pistol couldn't stop him, but I couldn't help it. When I looked back, he was gone.

"Shit!" I said with a loud exhalation of breath.

I got out of bed and dressed quickly. I didn't want to face

Frederickson in my skivvies, but he didn't reappear. When I was done, I opened the curtains. It was still dark outside. I could just make out the weak glow of the hands on my wristwatch: 5:35. Too early for breakfast. Paranoia caused me to search the room for Frederickson. He wasn't lurking under the bed or in the wardrobe.

I quietly opened my door and went down the stairs to look for some coffee. I failed to find any, but I did find Hackworth. He was in the kitchen at the back of the house. He was dressed in his butler togs, sitting at the table and drinking tea. He didn't hear me, and as a courtesy, I scraped a foot on the tile floor. He still jumped in surprise.

"Sorry," I said. "It's a difficult time of day."

He looked up at me for a moment deciphering my meaning.

"Yes. Dawn rarely brought good news at the front, did it?"

"I don't recall it ever bringing good news," I said but then corrected myself. If I were to go to the authorities, I would need to start being honest with myself. I would need to open the Pandora's box of my wound and recovery. "Well, that's not strictly true. It did give me this." I touched the side of my face.

Hackworth nodded. "Nasty, that. Lucky you weren't killed, sir."

"More lucky than you can know. It got me out of it."

He raised an eyebrow in question and waited for me to continue. My stomach turned at the thought of his reaction to the truth or a modified version of it. I knew I needed to pass this first simple test of a working-class Englishman's judgment.

"I was here at university in '14," I said. "All my mates were joining up. I got swept up in the emotion. I told the recruiter I was Canadian and enlisted. The Artists Rifles, of course. But the Rifles became a training regiment, and my friends all went to be officers. I thought that was a fool's game and volunteered to serve in a different regiment. I was in a hurry to see some action. Transferred from the Twenty-Eighth to the Twenty-First. The

First Surrey Rifles.[1] I was with the Rifles until late '16 when I got this." I tapped the side of my head again.

"Lucky they didn't send you back once you recovered." I thought I heard an accusation in the comment.

"I was blinded. I went back to the States. By the time my vision returned, the Americans had entered the war. I volunteered with them and came back over."

This story sounded very good. It was so close to the truth as to be nearly inseparable from it, yet it failed to be true at all. Still, I was impressed listening to it as it spilled from my mouth.

"Very gallant to come back after that, sir."

"I don't know. The war had changed me, and I couldn't stay away. And you, Hackworth? You have the look of a man who served." I was taking a chance. If he hadn't done his bit, he would likely be embarrassed. Of course, I wouldn't judge him. I'd applaud him.

"Cavalry. The First Life Guards. I'd managed the stables for a senior officer in the Guards, and when war came, he was kind enough to make sure they had a place for me."

I wasn't sure that was a kindness but didn't say so. The Life Guards were as prestigious as British regiments got.

"And you ended up in service with Mrs. Kingsbury."

"At the start of the war, I was a batman for the major. He trained me up well enough to serve as a butler in a small household. With the casualties, promotion was inevitable. I was mustered out as a sergeant."

"Well, Sergeant, it's good to know you."

"It's just Hackworth, sir. Please."

I nodded and asked, "Is there any coffee?"

"Of course. I'll brew up a cup. It will take just a moment. Cook won't be up for a while."

The coffee came quickly. Other than learning how he was hired, I really had no need to speak with Hackworth to learn

---

1. FSR or Rifles.

more about him. I was positive I knew him all too well. He was a brave man who was fooled into fighting along with the rest of his nation. He would believe in God, the King, and the British Empire and his place in it. He would disapprove of Americans generally and womanizing Americans, in particular. I didn't think he would like William. He would likely be fine with a few dead Bolsheviks. I knew that he would have seen his beloved horses slaughtered along with his friends and possibly his sponsor in the Life Guards regiment. That was plenty to know about a man.

He was a good choice for Patricia. I felt better knowing he was about, but that thought prompted one last question as I put my cup and saucer in the sink.

"Did Mrs. Kingsbury hire you personally, Hackworth?"

"Of course, sir. She knows the major. He recommended me."

Good. Reynolds didn't hire him. "That's a relief."

"Sir?"

"You will find I am not the trusting sort. It is not my place to comment on Mrs. Kingsbury's associates, but I am always careful around her advisers from New York. I find them to be grasping." It was never too early in the morning to use English prejudices against Americans to undermine Morgan Reynolds. Anything I could do to hurt him was worth Hackworth's raised eyebrows.

"I see, sir."

⁂

PATRICIA AND MITCHELL ARRIVED AT THE HOUSE NOT LONG AFTER breakfast. She introduced Mitchell to the staff, and then they explored the house with me following along after them. I had met the rest of the staff earlier, but I had spoken only a few words of greeting to them. With Patricia and William at the house, it was as if the Windsors had arrived. Of course, prior to King Edward's name change in 1917, it would have been as if the Saxe-Coburg and Gothas were visiting. That would have been a

Kraut mouthful that just wasn't on. The thought made me chuckle, which earned a disturbed look from Mitchell.

Unsurprisingly, Mitchell charmed them all. The housekeeper and her staff of one, the cook, and even Hackworth. I was moderately disappointed that Hackworth seemed to like him. I had thought Mitchell's relaxed informality in all things would put him off. Hackworth's approval seemed to be an impeachment of my judgment, which I was already questioning.

Patricia insisted on showing Mitchell the full expanse of her new home. She explained that she bought it at auction fully furnished. I followed for most of the tour, but I waited in the study when they descended to the basement.

"Nothing down there but Hackworth's rooms and the furnace, Griff," Mitchell said when they joined me.

I nodded, unconvinced.

"We identified the man you need to meet," Patricia said without preamble. "Lieutenant-Colonel Kell.[2] His role in the government is not particularly clear, but it seems he is involved in tracking and the policing of foreign spies and subversives."

"Which means he won't like Reds," Mitchell added.

"Where did you get his name?" I asked.

"My solicitor. Well, actually, my barrister, who works with my solicitor. Both men are very well connected."

"Do you trust them?"

"For Christ's sake, Griffin, they're lawyers!" Mitchell interjected.

Patricia gave Mitchell a cross look.

"I do, John," she answered.

"Did Reynolds hire them?"

"No, he identified various firms for me to consider, one of which was Willis, Weeks & Co. They are a very well-regarded

---

2. Major-General Sir Vernon Kell. November 21, 1873–March 27, 1942. Soldier, linguist, and head of the domestic counterintelligence branch of the British Security Service Bureau. He headed this branch, later named the Security Service or Military Intelligence 5, MI5, for thirty-one years.

firm. All the firms were impressive, but I chose Mr. Willis after meeting with him. He is an expert on the laws regarding estates and probate. It was his suggestion that I retain a King's Counsel as a precaution in the event there is a trial. It is the KC, Mr. Bayford,[3] who gave me Kell's name."

"Why Kell?"

"Mr. Bayford has connections with Scotland Yard, and he understands through them that Colonel Kell was responsible for the apprehension of several German spies early in the war. He is, apparently, trusted by the government and the Metropolitan Police. If the colonel believes you aren't the man in the flyer or if he doesn't care if you are, you should be safe," Patricia said.

"How do I meet him?"

"You start by meeting with Bayford," Mitchell said.

"The lawyer?" I asked. My heart sank.

"It will be fine, and he's not just a lawyer, he is a King's Counsel," Patricia told me.

"Yeah, and that makes all the difference," I said sarcastically.

"John, in this country, it does matter. You must be patient."

"And what happens if I get picked up by the bobbies before I can meet with Kell?"

"Well, it won't be the first time you've been in the hoosegow, Griffin," Mitchell said with a smile.

"That was just a flimsy stockade in the French countryside, and those were just soldiers pretending to be policemen. No one really cared that I'd broken curfew."

"Still got to see the old man though," Mitchell elaborated, enjoying my predicament. I'd gone to Neville[4] for punishment when he was still the colonel of the Fifth Marines. Despite that unfavorable experience, somehow Neville still had enough regard for me to recommend me to Harry Armistan.

---

3. Robert Frederick Bayford, O.B.E., K.C. September 24, 1871–June 5, 1951.

4. Wendell Cushing Neville. May 12, 1870–July 8, 1930. Commandant of the Marine Corps. Congressional Medal of Honor winner.

"An English jail will be a lot different, Will."

"You won't be picked up. We have an appointment with Mr. Bayford this afternoon," Mitchell assured me.

"Good. The sooner the better," I said.

"And John, please have a shave," Patricia remarked.

⁂

I WAS SHAVED, PRESENTABLE, AND SITTING IN THE STUDY WHEN I heard Patricia breeze down the steps from the floor above.

"The car is just outside, Mrs. Kingsbury," Hackworth declared from the hallway in response to her arrival.

I came out of the study and found Patricia looking petite and beautiful holding Mitchell's arm. They were a handsome couple. A shadow flitted behind them, and I thought it might have been Sarah coming down to meet me. My heart jumped, and then I was afraid. I didn't want to see Sarah as I'd last seen her, shattered and bloody.

"Are you ready to beard the British lion in his den, Mr. Griffin?" Patricia asked me.

"Funny girl, Patricia, and yes, I am, but I thought we were seeing the lawyer first."

"We are, but you must convince Mr. Bayford of your need to see Colonel Kell. He won't squander his goodwill with the security services if he thinks you will be wasting the colonel's time."

"Fair enough. I hope you brought the wanted poster," I said irritably. I was afraid of being detained by the police, and fear always made me angry.

The weather was cool and a smog hung in the air, which carried the smell of the coal smoke causing it. I could feel my lungs tighten, and I tried to take shallow breaths. A fancy deep blue automobile waited at the curb with its black top up. Hackworth handed Patricia into the back seat, and Mitchell climbed in after her. I slid onto the front seat next to the uniformed driver. Something about the tufted black leather upholstery inside put me on edge.

"Did you buy this too?" I asked over my shoulder.

"It's for our use while we're in London," Patricia said not answering my question.

Despite the cooling weather, wagons, motorcars, and people crowded the streets. As a result, the drive to the barrister's office took nearly forty minutes.

We exited the car on Fleet Street in front of a tall office building. An old pub stood next door. I considered simply going there and drinking my problems away. Unfortunately, a doorman already had the door open for Patricia and Mitchell, and I was forced to follow.

The elevator was waiting, and the operator closed the Bostwick gate after us, shut the glass-fronted door, and shifted the operating lever to three. We all stared at the door until the lift jerked to a stop, and the operator released us at our destination. The painted black and gold letters on the office door read the LAW OFFICE OF THE INDEPENDENT BARRISTER, R. F. BAYFORD, K.C.

We went in without knocking and found ourselves in a small reception. A young woman occupied a desk stationed in front of a second door on the far wall. She stood as we entered.

I was surprised to see a woman in the office. With so many men dead and injured in the past four years, she must have been the only assistant the lawyer could find.

"May I help you?" she asked.

"Yes, Patricia Kingsbury for Mr. Bayford."

"Of course. One moment."

The girl opened the second door and spoke in a voice too low for me to hear.

"This way please."

We followed her into the adjoining office, which was at least three times the size of the first. Two men rose to greet us.

"Mrs. Kingsbury, a pleasure to see you again." A middle-aged man with a receding hairline took Patricia's hands in his and kissed her on both cheeks.

"Mr. Bayford," Patricia said with a warm smile.

Bayford turned to the second man. "Mrs. Kingsbury, I asked Mr. Willis to join us this morning. I thought his input might be valuable for our discussion of the issue." His eyes cut to me quickly and then back to Patricia. I was the issue.

The second man was older than Bayford but had a headful of wild gray hair and a thick mustache. Willis nodded to Patricia but did not offer his hand in greeting. He was an old-fashioned gentleman.

Patricia introduced Mitchell and me, and Bayford arranged for his assistant to bring tea and coffee for those who wanted it. Then Patricia got right down to business.

"As I mentioned briefly, Mr. Griffin is an associate of Colonel House of President Wilson's staff. I suggest he lead the discussion."

Both men turned to me, with measuring eyes. Before I could begin, Mr. Bayford said, "First, Mrs. Kingsbury, as a matter of form, both Mr. Willis and I need to be clear that, for the purposes of legal representation, we represent you. We do not represent Mr. Griffin."

"Do you anticipate a conflict between my interests and those of Mrs. Kingsbury," I asked, allowing some of my annoyance to show.

Bayford was not bothered by my tone.

"Well, no, Mr. Griffin, but I don't want there to be any confusion."

Patricia came to my rescue. "So you refuse to represent Mr. Griffin?" she asked calmly, but her implication was clear. If they refused me as a client, they would lose Patricia. I was pleased by her support.

"No, no. We just don't know if there might be complications." Bayford heard Tricia's message clearly.

"Please let us know if such *complications* should arise at the time they arise." She turned to me. "John?"

"The poster?" I held out my hand to Mitchell for the flyer the Metropolitan Police had left at the hotel.

"Colonel House retained me to assist with the security and protection of America's treaty partners, particularly Prime Minister Georges Clemenceau. In that capacity, with the help of Mr. Mitchell and others, I exposed a Bolshevik plot to upend the treaty. I also thwarted two attempts on the French prime minister's life." The story rolled off my tongue so smoothly it felt like another man was speaking. Both attorneys raised an eyebrow at my claims.

"You can confirm this information through Préfet Fernand Raux, head of the Paris Police Préfecture, and General Bliss and Mr. Gordon of the American Commission in Paris," I said in response to their doubts.

Now both men nodded, if not impressed, at least listening.

"We are staying at Claridge's hotel, and the concierge showed me this." I unfolded the poster and spread it on Bayford's desk.

"I am not the man the police seek, but I am concerned that I will be picked up and detained as the English police conduct an investigation."

"Aah," Willis said. "I see your concern. This certainly could be a picture of you, and it could lead to your detention."

"Exactly," I agreed. "I would like to go to the English authorities, preferably the counterespionage representatives of the British government, before that happens. I understand from Mrs. Kingsbury that you have some thoughts on whom I might approach. I don't want my work interrupted, and I don't want there to be any misunderstandings. I am more than willing to meet with the police, but I cannot have my work for the United States hindered."

"And you did not murder these men at the Savoy Hotel, Mr. Griffin?" Bayford asked. I disliked him for the question, but I found myself respecting his intelligence.

"I did not," I said without hesitation. I've heard that you shouldn't lie to your lawyer, but given my situation, that seemed like silly advice. I tried to close my mind to the Englishman lying on my hotel room floor with a shattered leg, begging for help, but his pain-wracked face peered at me from over Bayford's shoulder.

"And in France did your *work* result in any deaths?" Willis asked.

"I suggest that, to the extent the English authorities want details of my activities in France, they speak to the French. It is not for me to discuss," I said.

I said no more. Patricia, Mitchell, and I waited for their response.

Bayford and Willis looked at each other, and Bayford took the lead.

"There are two men we could try to reach. Lieutenant-Colonel Vernon Kell, whom I mentioned to Mrs. Kingsbury. His role with the government is not clear, but he is well connected in the espionage world. The second would be Sir Basil Thomson.[5] He is in charge of the Criminal Investigation Department[6] of the Metropolitan Police, and he has also been appointed as the director of the various intelligence services by the Home Office. He's a bit of a self-promoter but very highly thought of as a spycatcher. Meeting these men will be difficult. They are both very busy and powerful, and they may not agree to see you."

"In addition," Willis added, "they may not believe you. The war has made these men even more suspicious than they were before it began. They are now in the business of distrust."

"I have found that, since the war ended, that remains a healthy attitude to have," I said.

---

5. Basil Home Thomson. April 21, 1861–March 26, 1939. Colonial administrator, novelist, chief of Criminal Investigation Department of the Metropolitan Police, Director of Intelligence of the British Home Office until 1921.
6. CID.

"What should he do in the event he is taken up by the police before we have spoken to either of these men?" Patricia asked.

It was a good question and one I hadn't considered.

"Well, let's hope that doesn't happen, but if it does, if the police suspect you, they are obliged to caution you about making any statements.[7] Don't speak with them except to ask that they contact us."

We agreed that Bayford would approach Kell as the most likely to see the value in an additional connection to America, particularly one with a direct link to Colonel House. He would advise us when a meeting had been arranged.

When we left the office, both Patricia and Mitchell were buoyed by the possibility of my meeting Kell. I was not.

Even if Kell believed everything I told him to be true, he might still view me as a foreign agent on English soil. He could easily believe the best course for the security of the empire would be to let his friend, Thomson at the CID, grill me for a few weeks in some hellhole of a prison just to see what I revealed.

---

7. Judges' Rules 1912 and 1918.

4

Hounds Circling

When we arrived back at Patricia's house, I retired to my room and left Patricia and William to each other.

I sat on the bed, staring at the walls and imagining the worst outcomes of any meeting with Kell. As the shadows lengthened, the dead decided to visit. Frederickson did not speak. He brooded and watched me. Sarah hid her disappointment at my willingness to use exactly the type of men she loathed to solve my legal problems. She did, however, keep reaching for my hand, which did nothing to calm my nerves.

Finally I tired of the imaginary company and went downstairs. Hackworth told me Patricia and Mitchell had gone back to the hotel. I was left with the choice of returning to my room and the certain company of the dead, following Patricia and Mitchell to the hotel, or walking the smoggy London streets as evening came, hoping the dead did not follow.

I chose the haze and the wished-for solitude.

Hackworth sent me to the park. He hadn't been informed about my issues, but he sensed that I needed to be alone. Within two blocks, I stood on the edge of Hyde Park. The mist hung over the trees as darkness settled on the city. Hackworth had promised dinner when I returned.

I walked slowly, for I was going nowhere, and kept my head down, hoping to avoid eye contact with those hurrying out of the park for home. Despite the lamps stationed along the path, the darkness could not be entirely broken. I kept my eyes on my feet rather than on the shadows surrounding me. I didn't want to see the dogs lurking at the edge of my vision. Elsbeth Schragmüller and Karl Fuchs really had done their best to break my mind.

"Sir, can I help you?"

I didn't realize I had stopped walking. I raised my head and found a uniformed young woman standing in front of me. She was dressed like a bobby, but instead of pants, she wore a long skirt and laced boots. Sergeant's stripes decorated the sleeves of her tunic. A London cop. She carried no truncheon, but she did have a whistle on a cord through a buttonhole.

"I'm sorry?" I asked. My brain was having trouble comprehending her existence.

Her eyes widened briefly. "I asked if I could help you? You seemed somewhat lost." She was charming in her dark blue uniform and broad brimmed helmet. She was tall with strong, even features and intelligent eyes. She reminded me of my sisters.

"No. I'm fine. Thank you," I said.

"American?" she asked. She recognized me from the poster. My hat was pulled low just like the drawing on the circular.

The worst had happened. I stood frozen in this hazy London park confronted by a young woman with knowing eyes and a calm manner.

"Are you a police"—I searched for the right term—"woman?"

"I am."

"I didn't know the English had female officers."

We were alone on the path. I could overpower her. Beat her senseless and run. I wouldn't do that. I needed to find a way to escape without running and without hurting her. I was trapped.

"New initiative. Among other things, we patrol public spaces." She was watching me carefully.

"No chasing down criminals?" I didn't smile. I didn't want to scare her.

"If needed, but one hopes it's not." She didn't smile either. She was telling me not to run.

The shadows pressed around us. The dead and the dogs. Hounds circling. She didn't see them.

"Well, I appreciate your offer, but I'm fine." I prayed she would move on. She didn't oblige me. She just stood motionless in front of me.

My heart began to pump harder. It wanted me to flee. So did my brain. Whispers made demands from the darkness.

"Knock her to the ground," Frederickson said from behind my shoulder.

That wasn't the plan. The plan was to meet with the British authorities in the light of day with lawyers around me. The bobbies weren't supposed to find me. And certainly not a female copper.

"A quick shove, and you can be gone, mate," Tippy promised me. He had roused himself from his cold silence and was pretending to be helpful.

I wouldn't hurt this girl.

"Ah," I said. "You've seen the poster of the Savoy murderer."

Now she stepped back. I'd frightened her. She'd hoped I hadn't realized she recognized me from the police flyer.

I raised my hands in a calming gesture as she fumbled for her whistle.

"I'm not your man, but I can see why you would think I was." I was very careful not to step toward her.

"I'm going to need you to come with me, sir," she said. The tremble in her voice was hardly noticeable.

"Of course. Do you need to handcuff me?" I asked with what I hoped was a reasonable tone.

"I am not empowered to arrest. I have no handcuffs."

"How 'bout I walk in front of you, and you tell me where to go?"

"That would be helpful, sir." She was afraid of me but was doing her best to hide it.

"John Griffin. Please call me John. I suppose I'm going to miss my dinner."

"I'm afraid so. That way, sir." She wasn't going to call me John. She'd pointed me west, deeper into the park.

"What's your name, Sergeant?"

"Wyles."[1]

"Sergeant Wyles, I hope the station is not far."

"The station is just a few minutes' walk. You know your ranks, sir. Were you in the service?"

My heart skipped a beat. Well, hell! In for a penny in for a pound. If I were going to meet with the British authorities, I saw no point in delaying the inevitable.

"Yes. Twice. Once with your lot and then with the Americans."

"You've got the look," she told me.

That made me laugh. This woman was certainly direct.

"That I do!" I gestured to the side of my head.

"That's not what I meant, sir. I was a nurse during the war. I saw wounds like that, and worse, obviously. Lucky it didn't kill you. But that's not why. You've got the air about you."

"How long have you been a policewoman, Sergeant Wyles?" I was impressed by her insight.

"Just this year. As I said, female officers are a new endeavor of the Met."

"Well, you've been promoted pretty quickly to be a sergeant within a year."

"There're only three sergeants and only twenty or so girls in the Met in total. So it's not so impressive."

"Well, you've certainly got the courage for the job."

____

1. Lillian Wyles. August 31, 1885–May 13, 1975. Nurse, constable, sergeant, chief inspector, and author.

"And why do you say that, sir?"

"I've seen the police flyer, Sergeant Wyles. If what I read is correct, you think you are detaining a triple murderer. In an empty park." I gestured to the dark expanse of Hyde Park lit only by a few pools of inadequate light from the gas lamps along the path. "Without a weapon."

I heard her steps slow behind me.

"It's the job, sir."

"Helluva job." I kept walking.

We continued single file for a few more minutes and came upon a three-story brick building that stood along the path. It looked like a stately country home. Not too fancy but big with a slate roof, dormers, and large windows, which were filled with light. The only clue to our location was the wrought iron lamp that sat atop a tall post across the path from the front door. It glowed blue with white letters reading POLICE STATION. Just my damn luck.

"Who would have guessed it?" I said under my breath.

"It's not too late," Tippy noted.

I turned my head to look for him, but he was nowhere to be seen.

"Sir?" Officer Wyles asked.

"Sorry. Just thinking out loud. I wouldn't have thought to find a police station here."

"The park can be dangerous. Particularly at night. Thieves, bullies, and their paramours."

I wasn't sure what she meant at first.

"Aah, pimps and whores, Sergeant Wyles?" I asked, turning to look at her over my shoulder.

"Yes, part of the Women's Police Service charge is to try to lead the unfortunate from that life."

"I see. A difficult task. Through there?" I asked, pointing to the heavy wooden front door.

"Yes, sir."

With Wyles behind me and my stomach in my throat, I

walked into the English police station. I tried to stand tall. That was how my bravery would be judged, I thought inanely. I wouldn't cringe or curl up as I faced what I had so long feared.

I didn't bother to hold the door for Sergeant Wyles. I knew she would want me to walk through first. So I did. I went straight to the front desk, which looked not so nearly as grand as the front desk of the Paris Préfecture of Police. The English didn't raise their desk sergeants higher than those who entered. I stood slightly to one side and kept my head tilted down. Despite my growing terror, I wanted Wyles to get the credit for bringing me in. She seemed dedicated to her new job as a policewoman, and there was no doubt she was brave.

The desk sergeant looked up at me briefly, and I pointed a thumb at Wyles.

"What's this then? Why it's *Sergeant* Wyles. Finished your knitting already, lassie?" the sergeant asked.

"Sergeant, I have detained a suspect in the Savoy Hotel murders."

"Of course you have, lass. And where would this devil be? Out on the path running away toward the river?"

"He's right here, Sergeant," Wyles told him.

I took off my hat and looked down at the desk sergeant. As frightened as I was to be standing in the station, it gave me an undeniable jolt of joy to see his eyes widen at the sight of me.

"I'm not your man, but Sergeant Wyles did see that I bear an unwelcome resemblance to the fellow you are searching for, and the suspect and I also apparently share the same nationality. The sergeant and I thought it best for me to come in and have a chat with you."

"You certainly are unsightly enough to be the bloke in the flyer," the sergeant opined. He stood. "Where did you find this man then, Wyles?"

"Walking in the park, Sergeant."

"Not very clever police work, that. Walking in the park, you say. And you think the Savoy murderer was just out for a stroll? In the park? A few steps from this station?" he asked sarcastically.

Wyles reddened. It was immediately clear that her male counterparts didn't want her in their ranks. She was doing a man's job, and she certainly couldn't expect to be welcomed by men who didn't think she should have it. I felt sorry for her. I respected her pluck and her diligence, but if the sergeant's prejudice would get me out of the station, I wasn't going to complain. In fact, it was time to stab Wyles in the back.

"That's what I told her, Sergeant, but she had difficulty understanding the illogic of a murderer peacefully escorting an unarmed young woman, police sergeant or not, to a police station. New to the work and a little emotional, I suppose. I didn't want to argue and cause a scene." I felt bad, but if it got me out of the station, I'd survive.

"Quite right you were, sir!" The desk sergeant had made his decision, and it wasn't to support Wyles. "Thank you for your consideration. I'm very sorry for the waste of your time."

"Please don't worry about it. I enjoyed my conversation with Sergeant Wyles, and it was interesting to see the experiment of women policing in person."

The desk sergeant nodded. He was embarrassed by the experiment.

"You're free to go, sir."

"Sergeant—" Wyles's face hardened, and she lifted her chin.

"Lassie, you'll be lucky if I don't report this!" the desk sergeant snapped.

"Perhaps I should leave the address where I'm staying?" I suggested as if trying to ease the tension. I was starting to enjoy the situation. Poor Wyles knew she was in the right, but it would do her no good. I was certain that the desk sergeant had no interest in taking my address.

"No need, sir."

"I'd like that address, Mr. Griffin. I'd like to send you a written apology," Wyles said to me with an angry glint in her eye.

I smiled. I liked Wyles and her gumption. Of course I was an idiot for suggesting leaving the address. If I really was going to meet with the authorities at some point, it would be a risk to give a fake one.

"That's not necessary," I said.

"I insist," Wyles said with narrowed eyes. She withdrew a pen and pad from her pocket.

I didn't want to look to the desk sergeant to save me again. I had his support, and I didn't want to raise any suspicions. "Of course. I'm staying at Number 2, Aldford Street, but an apology isn't necessary."

Thirty seconds later, I was walking up the path away from the police station, alone.

———————

I DID GET BACK TO THE HOUSE IN TIME FOR DINNER.

We sat in Patricia's large dining room crowded around one end of the table in a very American manner. Patricia sat at the head, and Mitchell and I sat across from each other on each side of her.

I told them about my adventures with Wyles and the police as we ate lamb prepared by Patricia's English cook and drank wine made by the French. The wine was excellent. The lamb was not. I didn't comment for fear Patricia would fire the poor lady, but neither she nor William noticed the food. They were too engrossed in my story and my luck.

"Griffin, only you could have walked into a police station a murderer and come out a beloved foreign national," Mitchell declared.

"Only I could get captured by one of the twenty female police officers operating in this entire damn city," I retorted.

"Hardly captured, John," Patricia said. "But I will need to light a fire under Bayford and Willis. The sooner you meet with the

British chiefs, the better. I do wish you hadn't volunteered my address."

"Sorry, Patricia. I was sure the desk sergeant wouldn't want it, and he didn't. But Wyles is clever. We'll just have to hope she can't find support from anyone else."

Unfortunately, that hope was in vain.

5

———

A Fraying Plan

The next morning as we sat around the same table, drinking coffee and eating a fry-up of eggs, streaky bacon, sausages, beans and tomatoes, the front bell rang.

Shortly after, Hackworth appeared and whispered in Patricia's ear. She raised an eyebrow and gave me an I-told-you-so look.

"The police are here, John. To see you."

My stomach knotted, but I had committed to this course the night before. It was too late to run.

"No, it's not," whispered Frederickson.

"Don't interrupt your breakfast. I'll go speak with them," I said, standing.

"Nonsense, John. I don't let my friends face trouble alone," Patricia said.

"Me neither," Mitchell added.

Hackworth led us to the front door where I found Sergeant Wyles looking sharp in her police uniform. Another sergeant and two uniformed constables accompanied her.

"Sergeant Wyles, a pleasure to see you this morning," I said with a false cheer. "How can I help you? I hope you didn't write a note to apologize."

Wyles nodded a greeting, but before she could speak, the other sergeant said, "Sorry to bother you, sir, but we need you to accompany us to the station to answer a few questions." He was heavy and wore a short beard, which did its best to hide his jowls. The buttons on his uniform tunic strained to hold him in.

"Might have been easier if we'd done all this last night, eh, Sergeant Wyles?"

"Sorry for the interruption of your day, Mr. Griffin."

"Not just my morning?" I half joked. She was certain I was the man they were looking for, and it didn't help that she was correct. I could feel Frederickson's happiness just behind my shoulder. I shrugged. "Let me get my hat."

"These officers will accompany you, sir," the sergeant said.

I looked at Wyles. "You did tell them that you managed to walk me across Hyde Park to the station there without me running away."

"I did, sir, but it's procedure." She wasn't apologizing.

I stepped into the entryway, took my hat from Hackworth, who had already collected it. He didn't look surprised to find the bobbies at the front door.

I turned back before the two constables were even in the house.

"Where will we be going?" I asked.

"Bow Street Station," the sergeant answered. He wanted it to be clear that he was in charge.

"I'll call Bayford and Willis and have them meet us at the station, John," Patricia said.

"Just have them meet me, Patricia. You and Will won't be able to do anything by waiting around a police station. Better to finish up your business here so we can get back to Paris as soon as possible. Let the lawyers deal with the law."

She nodded. "Good day, Officers," she told the coppers as she turned to make the call.

The four hustled me into the back seat of a motorcar parked at the curb. The sergeant sat on one side of me and one of the constables on another. Wyles sat in the front seat.

My breakfast had been interrupted, and I was hungry. I was irritable when hungry, and I needed to keep that in mind while dealing with the police.

In twenty minutes, we were at the station, which was not far from Covent Garden. I had wandered through the neighborhood when I'd returned from my first meeting with Sarah at her house in the country.

The station sat behind a courthouse, which faced Bow Street. Not a promising location. I had no plans of ending up in the courthouse. The thought of all my surviving mates reading about me in the *Times* made my stomach clench. That would only happen over my dead body.

Once in the station, the two constables took my arms to guide me to my destination. A pressure began to build in my chest. The British authorities had me trapped in a goddamn police station. I would be found out. My heart began to pound, and the constables' claws dug into my arms.

"He's not been cautioned," I heard Wyles say behind me.

"Have Morrison ring Scotland Yard. We need the CID blokes who are investigating the Savoy murders here," the sergeant said.

They escorted me to an interview room, sat me at the table, and left me there. I was alone but for the dead who crowded around me. Thankfully, they remained silent.

"This is what you've waited for," I said to them.

Frederickson sat across from me.

"So have you, John," Sarah said in my ear.

Sarah was right. I had been waiting for this. I'd dreaded it, of course. I tried to avoid it. In fact, I'd murdered that man in the Savoy to prevent it. But here I was. Back in England. I'd chosen to come for this reckoning. I'd chosen this. With that realization, the dead—Tippy, Sarah, Gavin, Horace, Shed Bean, Bertie Williams, and so many others—who gathered in the cell to keep me company, no longer felt threatening to me. I was on a path that must inevitably reveal the truth. Faced with that reality, the dead held no menace at all. It was now the living that I must face.

I tried opening the door to the interview room and found it locked. Oddly, I felt safe. Of course, that was irrational, but I was certain the door prevented any of the living dogmen from reaching me. Armistan and Reynolds were trapped on the outside. I sat down and stretched my legs out before me. I tilted my hat over my eyes and pretended to sleep. All I could do now was wait.

"They're going to find that you ran, Jackie. They're going to learn that you're a coward. Everyone will learn," Tippy said.

"Hush it, Tippy!" I answered sharply. His malevolence had returned, but he was losing his power to evoke any fear in me at all.

He was right, of course, but I had chosen this.

<hr>

THE DETECTIVES ARRIVED AN HOUR LATER. BOTH WERE DRESSED IN worn dark suits, still wearing dripping mackinaws, which told me it had started to rain while I waited.

A constable showed them to the room.

The older of the two, likely too old to have served in France, was thick, like an aged heavyweight boxer. His nose supported my assumption. It was mashed so badly it must have been repeatedly broken. The red veins decorating it also testified to the man's fondness for a drink or two.

I stood and removed my hat so they could take a good look at what they'd caught.

The second detective was younger. He had the aspect of a man who had fought in France with the dark shadows under his eyes and his heaviness of spirit.

He studied me and nodded to himself. He understood why I had been detained. Even so, he wasn't impressed by what he saw. Triple murderer or not, he saw things more frightening than me in his sleep every night.

"That's 'im," the constable pointed out unnecessarily.

"Obviously," the older of the two said sarcastically. "You can go."

The constable left, shutting the door behind him.

The two detectives remained silent. So did I. They were professionals, and they wanted the quiet to work for them. They were going to be disappointed. The dead had left me when the two detectives arrived. No shadows danced in the corners or behind my shoulders. I felt more calm than I had since taking the first sip of Elsbeth Schragmüller's goddamn coffee. These men felt like protectors.

"Sit," the older detective directed.

I sat back down, and they sat across from me. The younger detective took a short pencil and a notebook from his inside coat pocket.

"What's your name?" The older man was taking the lead.

"John Griffin." The pencil scribbled.

"Mr. Griffin, this is Inspector Norton," the older detective said, nodding to the serious younger policeman. "And I'm Detective Inspector Fair. We have a few questions for you. You are not obliged to say anything to us unless you wish to do so. But what you do say may be put into writing and given in evidence at any trial."

Reading upside down, I watched Inspector Norton write "10.20: caution given" in his little book.

"I understand. I'm not the man you are seeking, but I can certainly understand why you might think so. I'd appreciate if you could contact my barrister, Mr. R. F. Bayford, and my solicitor, Mr. Willis of Willis, Weeks & Co."

The two men looked at each other briefly. They had expected the denial, but they had not expected me to be armed with lawyers. The uniformed officers must have neglected to tell them.

"Also, I would like to commend Sergeant Wyles. She saw me in the park, recalled the picture from your flyer, and asked that I accompany her to the Hyde Park station. She was very professional. And believing me to be a murderer, very brave as well."

They had me talking, which is what they wanted, but other than the denial, they hadn't expected anything I'd said.

"So you are saying you were not detained by police constables as you walked through the park?"

"No. If that's what you were told, you've been misinformed."

"Why don't you tell us what happened?" Fair suggested in a reasonable tone.

So I did. I split my attention between the two of them so I could watch Norton take notes. I was trying to read his writing upside down without being too obvious. For some reason, his failure to record Wyles's name annoyed me. The whole situation annoyed me. I reminded myself that I hadn't eaten, but it didn't calm me.

"W-Y-L-E-S," I said slowly as my story ended just to make sure he got it. "Wyles. I want to make sure you get her name right."

Norton gave me a dead-eyed glare. I gave it right back.

"So you weren't detained in the park. You went to the station voluntarily."

"Are you going to record her name, Inspector Norton? She did a good job."

"Not for you to worry about, Mr. Griffin," Fair interjected.

"You don't like women on the force, gentlemen?"

"Again, not your worry. Why don't you tell us where you were the morning of the sixth of May of this year?"

"I don't like to see work that is shoddily done. I like working with professionals. Why don't we pretend you are both professional? Go ahead, Inspector," I said to Norton, "pretend you care about your job. Write down Sergeant Wyles's name. Maybe she'll get a nice commendation."

Now I'd done it. If they weren't sympathetic before, now they were downright hostile. I was sore about their hostility toward Wyles, my interrupted breakfast, and the fear bubbling under my skin, and I was taking it out on the coppers. They'd eventually get back at me, but I couldn't help myself.

"Why do you care?" Fair asked, as his face flushed with anger.

"I just like to see people rewarded for good work, but I'm done talking now. And I'd thought the French police were bad."

Now I'd really gummed up the works for them. It was a shame. Once they tucked me in a holding cell, the phantasms lurking in my head would reappear.

In large block letters, Norton wrote WYLES in his notebook. He turned it around so I could read it and raised an eyebrow.

"Too late. I'm done." I sounded like a petulant child.

"You're not making it easy on yourself, mate," Fair assured me.

"I don't often do, Detective Inspector."

"Fetch a constable, Cecil. Get his fingerprints and transport him to Brixton."

Shit! Fingerprints. I hadn't thought of that possibility when I made the decision to meet with the British authorities, and I certainly hadn't thought of it when I was fleeing the Savoy. I'd touched the doorknob to the room and the window frame I'd escaped through. There was also no doubt that I'd touched the handle of the Mauser I'd used to kill the Englishman. Any one of them and many other surfaces besides might hold a print well enough to identify me. It didn't help that the US military had my fingerprints from when I'd enlisted. I'd chosen not to run from Wyles or last night when I'd returned to Patricia's, but I never really thought I'd be convicted of murdering anyone. My plan to confront the English wasn't as clever as I'd thought.

Norton left the interview room to collect a constable. Tippy Frederickson appeared in Norton's chair, grinning like a loon.

My plan to remain free was quickly fraying away, and
Frederickson loved it.

Later that afternoon, I was put in a police transport and
moved to Brixton prison. No one told me if my prints matched
those of the Savoy killer, but I had the distinct impression that in
sending me to Brixton, the two detectives were sending me a
message.

6

Brixton

Brixton was a real prison, not some knocked-together stockade. Inspectors Fair and Norton were acting like they were sure I was the Savoy murderer. It didn't help that they were right.

It hadn't occurred to me to be frightened of a stay in an English lockup. That was unwise. Brixton was a real prison for real criminals and held the dregs of the city. There was a chance that Mitchell, Patricia, and the lawyers might never know I'd been transferred there.

I had not considered my scarred face an asset until I lined up with my fellow inmates for dinner that night. I didn't smile, and I kept my expression blank. I didn't know much about prison, but I knew a little bit about dogs. I didn't look anyone directly in the eyes. For dogs, it's a challenge, for criminals, I figured it was probably the same. Whatever the fellows around me saw, they left me alone. Despite the tension of being arrested and imprisoned, Frederickson and my other ghosts were absent. I sensed them just at the edges of reality, but it felt like those haunting me were waiting for something.

It didn't take long for me to find out what it was.

Fair and Norton returned the next day to question me again. We sat in a white-washed, high-windowed interview room. I was handcuffed to the table. That should have told me something.

"I've some bad news for you, laddie," Fair began.

I didn't react, but Tippy gave a small snicker from behind my left shoulder.

"Your fingerprints match those collected from the room at the Savoy. Three men dead, and you were there."

I didn't see any point in speaking. I needed those damn lawyers badly. That was a thought I never expected to have.

"What are you going to tell the man?" Tippy asked me. This was what he had been waiting for. Proof I'd killed those men. Any claims of my innocence were crumbling under the pressure of the new criminal investigation sciences. Tippy would resume his relentless pressure for me to kill myself.

"Inspector Norton and I examined the scene. It looked like a gunfight. Maybe self-defense?" He was offering me a sham escape from the murder charge, but I knew the dead Englishman wouldn't look like he was killed as part of a gunfight. I watched Fair and Norton in silence. I also saw no point in responding to Frederickson. I didn't need the coppers to know I was insane as well as a murderer.

"You're going to have to speak with us eventually," Fair assured me.

"No. When my lawyers get here, they won't let me do any talking at all." My statement infuriated the detective inspector, but his partner didn't seem bothered.

***

THE LAWYERS TOOK THEIR TIME LOCATING ME. BY THE TIME THEY did, I knew more about Brixton prison and London criminals than I wanted to.

At the midday meal, despite my best efforts, trouble found

me. I was eating with my head down, minding my own business, when I heard a voice behind me say, "You're an ugly bugger, aren't you?"

I thought it was Tippy speaking, and as had become my habit, I ignored him. It wasn't Tippy, and I got a shove between the shoulder blades as proof.

"I'm talking to you." The voice came from just behind my head. I'd always been a little short-tempered as a child; in my teens I learned to control it better, at least until the war. Since France, my temper had gotten damn hard to manage, and between Frederickson's constant harassment, the fear of being revealed as a coward, the murder investigation, and prison generally, I'd had enough. A rage boiled up from the back of my neck and overwhelmed my good sense.

I pushed off the table and snapped my head back toward where the voice originated. I was in luck. I'd found my tormentor. The back of my skull cracked against a half-open mouth. I supposed I interrupted another comment. Cracking teeth cut my scalp. I spun off the bench and got to my feet in time to see a bald man stumble back into his two mates. His mouth was a bloody mess. God only knew what the back of my head looked like.

Three men.

Well, fuck! I was in for a good kicking.

Since I saw no point in waiting to see what they decided to do, I waded into the three of them. The inmates from the nearby benches scattered, knocking me closer to one of the men. Fortunately, his hands were full with his bloody friend, so I hit him in the side of the neck. Not as hard as I'd hoped, but it snapped his chin down into his chest. I smacked the side of his head and felt my knuckle split. I followed it with an elbow to his face. My arm went numb, but his eyes rolled back in his head. I judged it to be a fair trade. He fell back toward his friends, and I let him.

The talker was recovering quickly, which was bad. He was a

big bastard. I felt a brief moment of fear, and then it was gone, consumed by my anger. I kicked his shin with the point of my toe. The point of a good leather shoe can do wonderous damage to a man's shin. It was a low-down, cowardly blow, but there were three of them, and I was in no mood to fight fair with three criminals. My kick drew a suppressed squeal, and he fell back again, which left me with just one man to fight.

I pressed forward and threw a jab. He bobbed his head away, and I only grazed his cheek. He knew what he was doing, I'll give him that. He'd boxed for certain. With a vicious grin, he twisted his hips and hammered his left fist into my gut, and from there, things went south. I backed off and tried to keep moving, but the first gent got back in it, and before you knew it, I was on the ground. That's when the kicking really began. I tried to cover my head, but the kicks still made unpleasant knocking sounds on my skull, and I couldn't do anything about the blows to my kidneys. I was just a few minutes from being dead. Where the hell were the guards? It was a useless thought that did nothing for my chances of surviving.

"That's enough, boys." I wasn't sure I'd actually heard the command. The sound of the blows striking my arms and head and the grunts of my attackers made it difficult to be sure, but the onslaught mercifully stopped.

I took the risk of peeking through my forearms. My nose was bleeding from a kick that had made it past my guard. A fourth man stood among my attackers.

"Aah, salvation," I gasped out with a small laugh. It was hard to talk. I hadn't completely recovered from the punch that had dropped me to the floor.

The comment drew a laugh from the new man.

"A Yank! Well, welcome to Brixton prison, Yank. What brings you to our humble bit o' Rome?" He held out his arms to encompass the prison cafeteria in all its glory.

I rolled onto my back and let my bruised arms fall to my sides. I didn't understand what he was asking, but I could guess.

"Murder."

"Hear that, boys? You introduced yourself to a bloke who's in the nick for murdering some poor bastard."

"Three," I said.

"Whasat?"

"Three. Three poor bastards. I didn't murder them though."

"Of course not. I wouldn't think a bloke like you could hurt a fly."

I rolled to my side and tried to stand. One of my former attackers took my arm and helped me up.

It was the boxer.

"Thanks," I told him.

I turned to my savior and got my first good look at him.

He wasn't a big man. In fact, all three of his "boys" were taller, but he was thick with muscle, and he had an undeniable charisma.

"Wag McDonald,"[1] he said, offering me his hand. I was better off with him friendly than not. I took it.

"John Griffin." I looked around at the other inmates. They all had their heads down over their food, doing their best to be invisible. I couldn't blame them for not stepping in during my beating. My back and sides were battered. I had a split lip and possibly a broken nose.

"So the guards don't step in to break up fights?"

"Not much of a fight, was it?"

"No, I guess it wasn't," I answered honestly.

"For the time being, they leave discipline to me. As long as no one is killed, things run smoothly," McDonald said.

"And if someone is killed?"

"A little more paperwork for them and bad news for one of these blokes here." He nodded at the tables. "Lots of witnesses willing to say one of them did the killing."

"You have that much sway?" I was impressed.

---

1. Charles "Wag" McDonald. February 5, 1877–October 1940. Gangster.

"Oh, I do indeed," McDonald said confidently.

"How did you manage to end up in here then?" I thought I might have touched a nerve, but he answered.

"Oh, this 'n' that. Sometimes the coppers got to bring you in to show they can. It's like a reminder of the balance of power. They have the power. Don't want us to get too cocky, do they? I get out of here tomorrow morning. My visits to Brixton are a bit like bank holidays at Brighton: short but sweet." He smiled when he said this, and his boys chuckled.

I must have been slow from the beating. It took me a while to catch on. He ran a gang.

"Which part of London?" I asked.

He raised his eyebrows in question.

"Which part of London do you control?"

"We're from Southwark. South of the river. But I like to think we have a healthy influence beyond our neighborhood," he answered with confidence.

"And how did kicking the crap out of a tourist like me help with your influence?"

All four men laughed at that, even the one with the broken teeth.

The question was a risk, but I figured he'd already achieved whatever he'd intended from my beating. I was thinking about the value of an ally in the London underworld. I knew Reynolds was up to something, and I could use the help. I knew that any help would come at a price.

"Well, several reasons, really. First, you looked like you needed it."

"Guess I've got one of those faces folks want to punch."

McDonald laughed. "It's not that, so much as you've got a face that says you're not afraid of dying. Can't have some tough guy, who's not afraid and who doesn't work for me, right under my nose, now can I?"

"I suppose not."

"Also, it's always a good reminder for these other fellows. And most of all, I wanted to see what you had in ya."

"And why would that matter?"

"I need help now and then from men who are able, but I didn't know you were a Yank, now did I?"

"So a Yank can't help you?"

"Don't have many connections in America," McDonald told me. He looked at me closely. "But maybe I could use some."

"Well, then despite my nationality, we might be able to help each other, Mr. McDonald."

"Oh, *mister*. I like that. You must need help badly."

"Not yet, but I am sure that will change."

"Already lying to your new friend," Tippy commented.

A commotion at the barred door to the cafeteria drew my attention.

"Griffin!" a custodian called from the open door. Behind him, inspectors Norton and Fair turned away and disappeared down the hallway.

"Yup, already changing. If I can get out of here, how can I find you?" I asked McDonald.

"The Wellington Pub near Waterloo Station. Leave word there."

"If you happen to have any contacts outside, I'd appreciate it if you could let a Mr. William Mitchell know that I'm here. He's staying at Claridge's. Also, a Mr. Hackworth at Number 2 Aldford Street would be interested in my current location. If you can get word to either one, I'd be in your debt."

McDonald nodded.

"I'll see what I can do. Might need a favor in return," McDonald said.

"I understand, and you won't ask me to do anything worse than either my country or yours has already asked me to do. I am certain of that."

He guffawed along with his men.

I nodded to the four of them and walked toward the waiting custodian.

<hr>

THE INTERVIEW ROOM IN BRIXTON PRISON WASN'T NEARLY AS TIDY as the one at Bow Street. Decades of grime and despair had settled on every surface and permeated every pore of all the poor sods who occupied the same seat I was in. I was handcuffed to an eyebolt on top of the table. Inspectors Fair and Norton were already in place when I arrived. Norton had his little book out ready to take notes.

"You look like you're having a bit of a hard time, Mr. Griffin," Detective Inspector Fair said with a satisfied air.

"Just getting to know the town a little better. As a tourist in your city, it's always nice to become acquainted with the locals. I didn't get to do that much in France. Met a lot of other tourists though."

Norton smiled grimly.

"You do understand that there is a real chance you will be beaten to death in here?" Fair asked, hoping to make clear exactly how desperate my circumstances really were.

"Not by the other inmates. This was just a bit of fun." I tried to smile, but my face hurt, and a stab of pain in my jaw prevented me from succeeding. "If I'm beaten to death, I suspect it will be by men like you."

Norton shook his head, and Fair's face hardened. He wasn't amused by my resistance. Of course, there was no profit in baiting the detective.

"Any success finding my lawyers?" I asked, hoping to move the discussion along.

"Let's talk about the sixth of May and your activities on that day," Fair said.

"Nope. Find Bayford or Willis."

Fair reached across the table and slapped me. He moved so

fast I was surprised. I didn't think he had that much speed in him, and I really hadn't expected the English police to beat me. The pain of the blow wouldn't have hurt so bad if my jaw hadn't already been knocked about.

"Goddamn it!" The oath escaped before I could stop it. I didn't want to give them any satisfaction, but I had. Fair at least. Norton wouldn't meet my eyes. He kept his on his notebook.

"So that's how you do things in this country?" I said with as much disgust as my bruised mouth could muster.

"That was nothing!" Fair promised.

"Get Bayford and Willis," I said again.

I was ready for the second blow and swayed back and turned away as it came. It still hurt but not nearly as much as the first.

Fair was out of his seat, leaning over the table.

Norton put a hand on his arm, and Fair sat back in his chair.

"Your fingerprints match those in the room at the Savoy. The bed was shot to pieces and so were the men. Three men." Norton was speaking now. "It looked like they kicked in the door and started shooting."

I wanted to ask if they'd identified the men. If they knew that two were German, but I refused to be drawn in.

"If they shot first, you could lawfully defend yourself. That is the law here in Britain." Norton was trying to coax me into conversation about the shootout.

I looked at my knuckles, which were cut and bruised from my encounter with McDonald's boys.

"They were Germans," he said.

That admission did cause me to look up.

"Sounds like you should be giving a medal to whoever killed them," I said. I knew I shouldn't have spoken, but I was weary of the conversation and of waiting. I had no problem waiting to ambush German soldiers, but I was damned if I could outwait the police.

"Good for you," Sarah said approvingly. "You shouldn't be ashamed of what you've done. Talk to them."

Her voice surprised me, and I looked around the room. I wanted to see her, but she wasn't there.

Fair and Norton watched me closely. They knew something was happening in my head.

I wanted to tell Sarah that she was wrong. I'd shot the English bastard in the forehead as he lay helpless on the ground. I *was* ashamed, and I wasn't going to tell anyone about it.

"It's fine, John. You had a hard choice to make," Sarah said soothingly.

Was it really Sarah? I started to worry that Tippy was masquerading as Sarah, the bastard.

"Perhaps we will give you a medal," Norton said. "We just need to know what happened."

"Have you spoken to Colonel Kell or Sir Basil Thomson?" I dredged their names from my recollection of the discussions at Bayford's office.

My question caused an involuntary glance between the two men. It was a brief look, but I saw it. They knew Kell and Thomson were involved. For the first time since I was picked up at Patricia's house, I felt some optimism. Bayford and Willis were out there somewhere working for me.

"If you find my lawyers in the next couple of hours, I promise I won't tell them you gave me the beating I'm wearing," I said, looking as smug as my battered face would allow.

I was ready for Fair to leap across the table, but instead, he leaned back, looked at Norton, and nodded.

TWENTY MINUTES LATER, MR. BAYFORD SAT ACROSS FROM ME IN the very same interview room.

"My God, you look a sight!" he exclaimed when he first came into the room.

"Mr. Bayford, I'm afraid I always look a sight. I suspect that the bruising looks worse than it feels, and the blood will wash off."

Bayford nodded. "Well, it is shameful that this should have happened."

"To be fair to the police, they didn't actually do it," I clarified.

"Still, you were in their care! In any case, I am working to get you free."

I was very pleased to hear that but tried to control any hope from gaining purchase.

"What have they asked you, and what did you say to them? Tell me everything."

I recounted to Bayford my limited conversations with Fair and Norton. I mentioned their claim that my fingerprint impressions matched those at the Savoy. The prints worried me more than I was willing to admit. I didn't understand the science of fingerprinting, and I didn't know if it could really tie me to the Savoy.

I didn't mention my discussions with McDonald.

"Fingerprinting is ridiculous mumbo jumbo. Judges don't like it, and I'm not concerned with it. It sounds like you acted correctly during your detention. Just a few more hours and you will be out."

He stood and knocked on the door to the interview room. He looked back at me as a custodian entered the room.

"Mr. Griffin, please try to keep to yourself. Prison is dangerous, and I'd hate to see you hurt again," he said in a patronizing tone. The image of my fingers wrapped around his neck flashed through my head. It had to be Tippy who put the thought there.

7

Outside Channels

I did manage to keep to myself, and by that evening, I was back at Patricia's house with a drink in my hand, talking with Mitchell and Patricia. I told them of my adventures, and Patricia was wonderfully solicitous of my injuries. I could feel Sarah nod her approval at her sister-in-law's concern. Mitchell was less sympathetic. Instead, he wanted to hear all about prison, my beating, and Wag McDonald. He was not particularly impressed with my fight against McDonald's three henchmen.

"There were three of them," I said for the third time.

"I just thought Gene and I had trained you better, that's all," Mitchell said in a tone laced with disappointment. He was referring to the boxing lessons Bullard and his friend, Georges Carpentier,[1] had given me before my trip to Germany.

"William, I am sure John did his best," Patricia said coming to my defense. Her comment brought a satisfied gleam to Mitchell's

---

1. Georges Carpentier, January 12, 1894–October 28, 1975. World champion boxer, pilot, French war hero (Croix de Guerre).

eye. He knew any defense by her would be a thousand times worse than anything he might say.

I looked from her to him and back again.

"You do realize you are encouraging him, don't you, Patricia? 'He did his best,'" I mimicked. "Honestly, the two of you should spend a few days in Brixton before you criticize me for a few bruises."

"John, I'm not criticizing…," Patricia began.

I held up my hand.

"Stop. You're going to say something sympathetic, and Mitchell will translate it into something simply pathetic. I don't need to hear it. Or any more from you, Mitchell," I said, glowering at them both. "Bayford seemed to think he could get me a meeting with Kell."

The change of subject cleared the nascent frown from Patricia's beautiful face. She didn't like criticism, but she wasn't my girlfriend.

"Yes, in the next few days," she agreed. "He is optimistic about the outcome. It sounded like the British have been in contact with the US commission in Paris and with the French. He did suggest that you stay in the house until the meeting."

"Fine by me. I could use the sleep."

The next day crawled by. It turned out it was hard to sit in the house doing nothing. Mitchell and Patricia went out to see the sights. I sat in Patricia's study with a book in my lap and my ghosts around me. I tried to ignore my predicament and figure out what Reynolds was up to. My stomach still clenched at the thought of him. I didn't believe for a second that he was genuinely trying to solve Patricia's legal problems. I just knew he was up to no good. After a few hours in the study, I got restless. I paced around the room, pulled musty-smelling books from the shelves, rifled through the desk, and tried to ignore a murmured conversation between Sarah and Gavin just at the edge of my hearing.

The desk held nothing of interest. An inkwell and pen, a few court papers, a shockingly high fee invoice from Willis, Weeks & Co., some stationery, and a couple of Reynolds's fancy blue-ringed smokes.

Bastard! He was like an infection that spread everywhere. Just like the damned Spanish flu.

A flash of light from the window caused me to look up. My heart leaped at the thought that it was the sunlight reflecting off a lover's hair. Sarah was dead and Madeline gone. It wasn't either one of them.

Patricia's car had stopped on the street in front of the house, and light off the car door window had caused the glint I'd misinterpreted. It wasn't either girl. I was surprised at the depth of my disappointment.

Patricia and Will climbed from the car. They were clearly happy together. I slid the desk drawer shut, irrationally hoping the action would protect the young couple from Reynolds.

They found me sitting quietly in the study.

"What the hell are you doing in here all alone?" Mitchell asked. "Surely you're not reading a book."

"You know I don't know how to read, Mitch."

He laughed.

I didn't bother telling him that I was rarely alone. It doesn't pay to let folks know you're hearing people in your head and seeing ghosts.

I could tell they both were a little tight. Not only had they seen the sights, but they'd stopped for a few drinks as well. They did bring good news though, which softened my annoyance at their tipsy animation.

"You meet Colonel Kell tomorrow morning," Patricia exclaimed excitedly.

"Bayford is downright giddy about the meeting," Mitchell added. "It sounds like Kell wants to offer you a goddamn knighthood."

"Why would that be?"

"According to Bayford, Kell talked to the French via telephone," Mitchell answered. "To Préfet Raux, specifically."

"Great, that's just great," I said unenthusiastically. Damn telephone! I hadn't considered that the English would be able to speak with Raux. I had figured they would listen to my story, and it would be enough. I was an idiot.

If Kell had talked to Raux and had a positive impression, it meant that Raux had shared elements of either the Clemenceau assassination attempts or my mission to Germany or both. Chances were good that he highlighted a bunch of dead Reds, which meant the British would be interested in my purported ability to sniff out Bolsheviks and spies.

"Better than the alternative, Griff," Mitchell assured me. Frederickson nodded his shattered head in agreement, and if he agreed, it couldn't be good.

They explained that Bayford had been very clear that neither of them were invited to the meeting with Kell. It was to be Bayford and me, and Bayford would leave after the introduction. I had a knot in my stomach thinking about it. I would be left at Kell's mercy. Just like I had been at Colonel House's after the assassination attempt on Clemenceau. I had lied to the French and told them I was House's agent. As a result, I became his agent in reality. All because of my lies. More lies promised more manipulation, this time at the hands of the British, but I had no choice. The Met and Inspectors Fair and Norton wouldn't suddenly decide to leave the Savoy case unsolved unless someone in power forced them to. The detectives would continue to investigate and find another reason to bring me in. I needed protection.

Patricia's limousine took me to Waterloo House, 16

Charles Street,[2] Haymarket, the headquarters of the Military Intelligence Division Five. The building was an imposing white stone affair with six floors. Both Waterloo House and His Majesty's Theater, which stood directly across the street from it, looked to my eye to have been built in the same self-assured, arrogant style that seemed so common in London. Despite the stains of coal smoke and smog, the premises had an imperial air that promised an intimate connection to the powers that controlled the realm. I did my best to be appropriately impressed.

The only sign of welcome was Bayford standing on the sidewalk, waiting for me.

"Mr. Griffin, it is good to see you out of custody. You are looking hale despite that ghastly bruising."

"I am sure it will go nearly unnoticed on this face, Mr. Bayford," I said as I shook his hand.

He gave me a grim smile of understanding. "Come. The colonel is eager to meet you."

After a few words with the doorman, Bayford led me to a raised reception desk. A self-important young man, who'd never seen the inside of a trench, looked down on us as Bayford explained that we had an appointment with Colonel Kell. That was significant enough that an escort was called. Another youngster arrived, and we followed him up a broad staircase to the floor above. He led us past offices occupied by men bustling about looking busy. At the end of the hall, closed double doors signaled our transition from the common rooms of the security service to Kell's inner sanctum.

Without knocking, the escort opened the doors. A secretary stood waiting by his desk. A second set of doors stood open behind him.

"The colonel is expecting you," he told us and took us directly through to the office.

Kell immediately rose from behind his desk as we entered. He

---

2. Renamed Charles II Street in 1939.

came around it and studied me closely. He was of medium height but thin, which made him look taller. Despite the rank attributed to him, he wore a civilian suit. He was at least fifty, but he had a mustache that made him look younger. Small round glasses gave his eyes a piercing look he might not have had without them. A cigar burned in an ashtray on the desk. The smell reminded me of my father.

"Colonel, it is good to see you again," Bayford said, shaking Kell's hand. Bayford turned to me. "Colonel Vernon Kell, allow me to introduce Major John Griffin. He is the man we spoke about."

The colonel's sharp eyes took in the bruising and the scar on my face, and he nodded. Whether in acknowledgment of Bayford's introduction or in confirmation of some unvoiced opinion, I could not tell.

"A pleasure to meet you, Major," he said.

"And you, sir." I decided not to correct him for addressing me by the fictitious rank the French had manufactured for me.

"We have much to discuss. Please have a seat. Tea? Coffee?" he asked, looking from me to Bayford.

Bayford waved away the suggestion on his part. "I do not want to waste your time, Colonel. I should go and let the two of you discuss the matters that bring Major Griffin here. Please let me know if there is anything I can do for you."

"Of course," Kell answered.

Bayford turned to me. "Let us speak later today." I nodded, and he left, shutting the door behind him.

"Please sit," Kell said, directing me to a chair facing his desk. He returned to his seat.

"He doesn't want to know," I said, referring to Bayford.

"Nor should he. These are dangerous times. I understand that you are under investigation for murder. Tell me about it. Oh, and Major, I don't care about crimes other than espionage against Britain. I can assure you that you can tell me the truth, and it will go no farther than the walls of this room."

He had an earnestness and intensity that was magnetic. I liked him, but I didn't trust him. I considered how much to tell him.

"Please, Major, you are weighing what to say and what to leave out. Let us start with what I know, and perhaps that will put you more at ease."

I nodded.

"In 1914, you were a Canadian volunteer in His Majesty's services. You claimed Canadian citizenship because you didn't want the fuss being the citizen of a neutral nation would cause. A clever ploy but likely unnecessary. While you joined the Artists Rifles, you left that regiment to serve with the First Surrey Rifles. Not clear why you did that. You would have been commissioned had you stayed with the Artists, but you'd likely be dead as well."

He spoke without referring to any notes.

"You fought in numerous engagements, quite bravely, I might add. You were even awarded a Military Medal for your actions during the attack on High Wood during the Somme offensive. Remarkable. In late 1916, you were blinded by wounds received on the line and returned to England. You did not remain in England to recuperate."

My stomach knotted at those words. He knew. Somehow he knew I'd run. I could feel sweat prickle on my brow.

"You returned home, to the United States, not Canada," he said the last with a small smile, showing his sense of humor. "Breaking off your engagement with your fiancée, Evelyn Wilson."

My heart skipped a beat. His probing eyes studied me closely.

"A miracle that you recovered your sight."

I wanted to stop his words, but I couldn't. Tippy was sitting on the edge of Kell's desk, watching me. All the war dead crowded around. Sarah stood by a window overlooking the road, beautiful but remote. I would not find support there. I would face my cowardice and my madness alone.

"Tell him, Jack. Tell him how it was," Tippy said softly. "You know you want to."

"Yet the most exceptional part of your story was yet to come," Kell continued. "You joined the United States Marines and came back. Most men would have stayed home after what you had been through, but you came back. That is the part of the story I don't understand."

He looked at me as if waiting for an answer, but I couldn't speak. The dread of discovery locked my throat like a vise. The feeling might have been irrational, but that was irrelevant.

"Again, you served bravely. Some might say suicidally. You were awarded the American Distinguished Service Medal and three wound chevrons. And even the French decorated you individually with a palm for the Croix de Guerre you earned as part of the Second Division. What drove you to do this, I wonder?"

He asked the question with such intensity that I was certain he knew the answer. I started to open my mouth to say something. To make an excuse. Anything was better than listening to him label me a coward.

"And then you came back, because, while the fighting was done, the peace was not. You came back, without expectation of recognition, behind the scenes to protect those laboring to deliver the final peace. You have shown yourself to be devoted, not just to the preservation of the English-speaking world but to the hopes of the entire fraternity of peace-loving nations."

"What the fucking hell are you saying?" Tippy roared at Kell, who was unable to hear him. He then grabbed his shattered head with both his hands in amazement, his body vibrating with rage at Kell's obliviousness.

I managed not to jump at Frederickson's outburst, and as the meaning of Kell's words penetrated the dread that had gripped me, I leaned back in my seat. I hadn't realized that I was crouched forward readying myself to flee.

"I have spoken to Préfet Raux. He is most impressed with you. He explained that not only did you save the French prime minister, but you also performed certain duties on behalf of the French that he would not specifically describe."

I tried to adopt an air that combined humility and nonchalance. He didn't realize I was a coward. He didn't understand that guilt and self-loathing had driven me. He didn't know the truth at all.

"I believe that you have been performing duties on behalf of the United Kingdom as well. I have not spoken with your embassy because I am certain they would dissemble. I don't want to put them in that position."

"What do you mean, sir?" With the fear of discovery ebbing, I found I could speak.

"My job is to protect the United Kingdom from foreign interlopers. Spies. Anarchists, nationalists, Bolsheviks, villains of every stripe. I have believed for some time that with the war's end, Britain would face more foreign interference. Not less. Before the war, it was clear who our allies and enemies were. Now with Germany broken, it is not. The framework that existed before the war is gone. There are more competing and dangerous interests, not fewer. Thanks to your president, there are more countries and more peoples with unrealistic, unmanaged, and unmanageable expectations, not fewer. The established order is at risk. With the peace treaty signed at Versailles, the Empire is more at risk. Not less."

I hoped he wasn't looking to me to commiserate. In my view, the British Empire was just as much to blame for the past four years of slaughter as Germany. The fact that the Empire now had to face the unrestrained aspirations of the millions it ruled hardly aroused my sympathy. Also, I wasn't sure that Britain's allies and enemies had been all that clear in June of 1914. The emotions and pressures of the moment had overcome all rationality in July of that year. My recollection was that, prior to the declaration of war on August 4, my British friends had detested the French with a finely aged and cherished loathing that had been cultivated for centuries. They'd also found the Tsar's regime to be brutal and archaic. Until Germany refused to leave Belgium, they saw neither France nor Russia as a worthy partner of the British Empire.

"Of course we didn't," Tippy chipped in. "Can't sympathize with the frogs, and the Ruskies are brutes."

Kell didn't bring me to his office to argue politics, and he wouldn't find Tippy's opinion persuasive.

"I have warned the government of the risks I see," he continued. "But most of the current cabinet is intent on demobilizing the army and dismantling all our wartime counterespionage efforts. When your attorney contacted me about your situation, in addition to researching your background, I did some investigation into the murders at the Savoy Hotel. I have contacts with the Metropolitan Police and the Criminal Investigation Department, specifically, the chief there, Sir Basil Thomson. He was reluctant to share the details about the Savoy, but I have sufficient understanding of what occurred at the hotel in May to believe that it is an example of the continuation of foreign, nefarious activity in Britain."

I nodded my head as if following along.

"I need to know what happened there. I give you my word what you tell me will remain within these four walls. The police are eager to find the killer or killers from the Savoy. I am eager to know why two German nationals were shot dead with a large caliber pistol, and one anarchist from Fulham was shot dead with a German Mauser. As you know, they are searching for a man, likely an American, who looks like you."

"I am familiar with the police investigation." I wasn't sure that Kell heard the sarcasm in my response. My stay in Brixton should have made it obvious. He was a serious fellow, and I didn't think his sense of irony was particularly well exercised.

"Can you help me?" he asked. He wasn't quite pleading, but there was an urgency in his voice that I couldn't ignore.

"Mr. Bayford did explain to you that I'm not the man the police are looking for, didn't he?"

"Yes."

"What makes you think I can help you then?"

"You are the man who was in the room at the Savoy. I don't know if you are the killer. I don't care. There are no coincidences in my line of work. There are many men in Britain who suffered facial wounds during the war. But there are not so many who are Americans and were in London in May. And only you were empowered by Woodrow Wilson to investigate threats to the peace treaty negotiations and to act outside established channels. I don't mean to be insulting, but frankly, I am surprised the Americans have such an agent. I hadn't thought your lot would be so clever. So ruthless. I suppose Colonel House has worked behind the governmental curtain long enough to understand the need for such security."

"He certainly is a clever one," I said dryly.

Kell looked at me sharply. He was not accustomed to a dogsbody mocking his better. I was happy to expand his understanding of Americans. "Well, but for his foresight, Prime Minister Clemenceau, Lloyd George, and your president might be dead."

"Yes. It is a good thing he took the precaution of putting some additional security for them in place." I was scrupulous in my effort to eliminate any of the scorn I felt from my tone.

"You did the work, and you resent my crediting others," Kell said. Apparently I failed.

I stayed silent. I knew I couldn't keep from being brutally honest if I answered, and he sensed my reluctance to speak.

"Major, please. I need your help. Most of all, I need your honesty. The Empire is in peril, and very few are willing to see it now that the war is over."

"All right, Colonel. I can tell you what I know. I told the French, and they still choose not to believe what is right under their noses. I told House, and as long as the French are happy, he doesn't care. I don't expect you English will be any different. But I'm happy to tell you too. I won't talk about the Savoy, but I can tell you some of what I found. I don't think Colonel House or the French would think I'm sharing information they wouldn't want you to have."

"That is certainly a good start," he answered.

"I stumbled onto a plot here in London. I didn't understand the full scope then. It originated with British Bolsheviks, who intended to block the Treaty of Versailles and to prolong the war by assassinating Prime Minister Clemenceau. The plan was likely to kill Wilson and Lloyd George as well. But with help, I managed to complicate things for the Reds. Their final plan was to kill Clemenceau as he left his house one morning. I stopped them. Clemenceau and Raux insist that the attackers were German. They weren't. They were Reds. The French refused to believe it since it was more convenient for the plotters to be Germans."

Kell nodded his head in confirmation and said, "When I spoke with him, Préfet Raux told me you had helped the French discover a plot to assassinate the French prime minister."

"The French didn't *discover* anything. The first they knew of the plot was when Bolshevik assassins fired a Maxim gun at Clemenceau's front door. Fortunately, I was there and managed to drive them off." I was conscious of Horace Merchant's shade slipping past my shoulder. "The French were late to the game when it came to the Bolshevik plotting."

"Préfet Raux did say you had been involved in gun battles with German assassins and Bolshevik revolutionaries." He shook his head. "Remarkable. In the middle of Paris! I have been worried about the Russians and Bolshevism in the United Kingdom since well before the war ended. It is certain that both would love to see the empire disappear. Not even the Germans genuinely hoped for that."

"You are right to worry," I said. "Préfet Raux and the French see Germans under every rock, and they're convinced the Germans fabricated the Bolshevik threat. They may be right that the Germans support the Reds outside of Germany, but they are wrong to think that the Reds are a threat only because of German support. Bolshevism beyond Russia is real. I don't know what the Russians want, but I do know that Bolsheviks, no matter their nationality, want to bring revolution to Europe. All of it."

I might have been overstating the facts, but I didn't care. It was nice to have a government official listen for a change, and Kell seemed to like hearing what I was saying. If singing my Bolshevik song meant he would help me, I'd keep singing.

"I have someone you must meet," Kell told me. "He is in Lloyd George's current cabinet and is the secretary for both air and war. He is, perhaps, the most farsighted of those serving in the government."

"If I'm not back in Brixton, I'd be happy to meet him," I said, hoping to remind him of my situation.

Kell stood so quickly that I was surprised.

I stood as well.

"I think I can keep you out of Brixton. I will speak with Thomson immediately and arrange a meeting with the secretary. We should be able to find a way to convince the Met that they don't need to arrest you."

His secretary arranged the calls while I sat on a wooden bench near the entry.

Kell did not keep me waiting long.

"We have an appointment with the secretary this afternoon at two. Where should I collect you?"

I gave him the address of Patricia's house on Aldford. He shook my hand, and I left his office. Apparently, with my credentials as a Bolshevik killer established, I no longer needed an escort.

8

———

Sinister Blackguards

Tippy and I waited in Patricia's study, watching the road. Hackworth brought little sandwich squares and coffee. I ate the squares and left the coffee. I was already tense at the thought of meeting some nabob at the War Office. Tippy didn't eat. He just stared out the window sullenly. We didn't talk. Tippy was angry at the thought of me avoiding my comeuppance, and I didn't have much to say to a phantasm who hated me.

Instead, I considered my predicament. I really had no choice but to get help from Kell and his contacts. I needed the police to leave me alone. That was the only way I could hope to avoid discovery by the families of my dead English mates. I also needed to get the hell out of England, bringing Mitchell and Patricia with me, and I couldn't do that in police custody.

At 1:40, a black four-door limousine with whitewall tires pulled up in front of the house. I left the study and arrived at the front door before the driver could knock. Together we walked back to the car, and he placed me in the passenger compartment next to Kell.

"Sir Basil will meet us at Whitehall," Kell explained.

In short order, we were driving down the Mall toward Trafalgar Square. From there, we turned onto Whitehall, and I felt the same dread I'd felt when Préfet Raux had dragged me to the Hôtel Crillon to speak with Colonel House. I could only hope that, like my first visit to the Crillon, I would not be exposed as a liar. Of course, the disadvantage of securing the help or even the notice of the secretary of air and war meant he might try to use me as the French and House had.

The motorcar stopped in front of an imposing, white, baroque building directly across from the Horse Guards' barracks. Domed towers capped the two corners of the structure that I could see. The War Office. It could be nothing else.

After a desultory security check conducted by two bored civilians, Kell led me through the entry hall across a black-and-white-checkered stone floor and up a majestic marble staircase. At the first landing, he could have gone either left or right because the staircase split and turned back on itself to reach the floor above. Light streamed down through the dome above reflecting off the marble and gilt. The whole space conveyed a sense of celestial power, which was, of course, the point. I was apparently mounting Olympus. I found myself disliking the British, their empire, and whoever the secretary of air and war might be.

Kell hurried up the right set of stairs and along the high-ceilinged corridor to the secretary's office.

"Colonel Kell for an appointment with Mr. Churchill,"[1] he said to a mature woman sitting at a desk in the anteroom.

"Of course, sir. One moment please." The secretary picked up a telephone receiver, spoke quietly, and said to us, "Please go right in."

Before we could reach the door, a tall, fit man opened it.

---

1. Winston Churchill. November 30, 1874–January 24, 1965. Politician, soldier, author, painter. Served on the Western Front from January 1916 to May 1916.

"Colonel, Major Griffin, please come in," he said, raising sharply pointed brows in an odd welcome.

I didn't know who this fellow was, but I knew of Winston Churchill. Another one of the old men who caused the damn war. The architect of the failed invasion of the Gallipoli Peninsula in Turkey. Booted from Asquith's cabinet as a result, but like a bad penny, he came right back. He was in thick with Lloyd George. To his credit, he'd served on the Western Front. Most damn politicians hadn't, and his service counted for something with me. Even if he did it to preserve his political aspirations, which I was sure was the case.

Cigar smoke hung in the air, and Churchill had a stogie in his mouth as he rose from his desk to greet us.

"Ah, Kell, come in." He came around the desk and studied me intently.

"Secretary Churchill, this is Major John Griffin of whom I've spoken."

"You are so welcome, Major. Welcome indeed," Churchill said as he pumped my outstretched hand. He was shortish, round, and middle-aged with a lopsided smile and a disturbing glint in his eye. There was something of the zealot about him.

His assistant shut the door while remaining in the room.

"Gentlemen, Edward Marsh,"[2] Churchill said, introducing him. We turned back to the door to shake hands again. Perhaps Marsh wasn't an assistant. He couldn't have been much younger than Churchill even though he looked like he was. It was probably because his longish hair, although receding, gave him a more youthful look than Churchill, who was losing the battle for his.

Churchill gestured us to a sitting area with a couch and three overstuffed leather chairs positioned before his desk. Although crowded with papers, the desk itself was remarkably tidy. Each

------

2. Edward Marsh. November 18, 1872–January 13, 1953. Civil servant, scholar, patron of the arts.

pile of papers was squared and clearly separated from its neighbors. Books sat on nearly every horizontal surface around the office, and many had markers in their pages, indicating that books were for reading and not decoration.

"Eddie, please arrange some tea and coffee for our guests. There will be two more joining. Then come back and sit in please," Churchill said to Marsh. Marsh nodded and left for just a moment before returning and sitting at a round table just to the right of Churchill. Not an assistant so much as a right-hand man. I felt Fredrickson at the back of my chair. My right-hand ghost. I was growing accustomed to his presence and didn't react. It was hardest when he spoke.

"You present us with an interesting opportunity, Major Griffin," Churchill declared. "While the prime minister certainly has the ability to communicate directly with your president, he is not eager to abuse that privilege. And it is difficult to convey diplomatic nuances and dangers via telephone, cable, or even through an ambassador. And in these most uncertain and perilous times, the British Empire needs a less obvious and more intimate channel to the president."

I didn't comment, but I knew my problem was House. I told one lie to stay out of French prison, and now everyone and their dog thought I was House's man, and through House, a conduit to the president. They were all wrong, but I needed them to keep the Met from tossing me back in prison.

"I will be direct with you, sir," Churchill said, looking me sternly in the eye. "There is no greater threat to the peace and stability of the world than Bolshevism."

He waited for me to comment. I thought that ambitious, grasping men like him were probably a greater threat to peace and stability, but I needed to stay out of the pokey. So I kept my mouth shut.

"Bolshevism is the worst tyranny in history. It is far worse than German militarism."[3] He added with undeniable approval, "You, sir, kill Bolsheviks."

I waited for him to stand and applaud. He certainly seemed to want to.

"I have spoken to Raux in Paris. He told me of the *German* attack on Monsieur Clemenceau. He also told me you claimed at the time it was a Bolshevik plot, but once the French had reviewed the situation with you that you understood it was a German one."

I shook my head. "It was Bolsheviks. Oddly, it was led by a former British army officer, who served honorably in the Royal Welsh Fusiliers. It wasn't a German plot. I just got tired of arguing with the French and with Colonel House. House wanted to support the French viewpoint, so I clammed up." I saw no point in lying to Churchill, and I had just told Kell the same. It was also what he wanted to hear.

"Obviously, it was Bolsheviks!" Churchill exclaimed. "They are as sinister a bunch of blackguards as to ever stalk in human form."[4]

"Sir, I must admit the ones I've met were idealists disillusioned by the old imperial power games. They simply wanted to make the world a better place. Misguided certainly, but not evil." I couldn't resist challenging him. It seemed like he wanted to backslap me for my willingness to gun down Reds, but I wasn't going to stay mum while an imperial gasbag told me what kind of people plotted against Clemenceau and the treaty. Not that I owed Gavin Kingsbury and Horace Merchant anything, but I couldn't stomach Sarah being painted with the brush he was wielding.

"Nonsense," Churchill declared hardly listening. "Every British and French soldier killed in the final year of the war was

---

3. "The Quest of Peace." *Civilian & Military Gazette.* Lahore, p. 3. April 20, 1919. Through Reuters Agency. From a speech at the Aldwych Club.
4. "Russia's Agony." *The Globe*, p. 11. December 14, 1918.

killed by Lenin. By Trotsky. By the treacherous desertion of Russia at the height of our need."[5]

I raised my head and gave the impression of nodding without actually nodding. I wasn't going to change his mind, and they were dead. And I did need him. No point in sacrificing his goodwill defending Sarah, Gavin, and Horace any further.

"Of course. Too timid to even defend your lover," Tippy noted.

"I have not forgotten this truth, Mr. Griffin." Churchill gave me a stern look telling me I had. "And I can do something about it. I have responsibility for the British military resisting Bolshevism in Northern Russia. Mr. Wilson withdrew the American troops supporting Kolchak and Denikin there in July."

I'd never heard of Kolchak or Denikin, but I didn't let on. Fortunately, the coffee and tea arrived and saved me from comment.

"I have had to reinforce the contingent in Northern Russia to make up for America's withdrawal. I've sent additional British battalions, but we need to do more. America needs to do more. I suspect Mr. Wilson withdrew your soldiers because he wants fewer *foreign entanglements,* which your President Washington so feared. He knows he must argue for ratification of the Treaty of Versailles in your Senate, and troops in Russia make that more difficult. But Russia teeters on the edge of a precipice. Bolshevism must be stopped now before it infects the whole of Europe and the globe. You have seen how its tendrils have penetrated France, Germany, and even Britain. I know you believe me. I can see it in your eyes. Stopping Bolshevism is more important than ratifying the Treaty of Versailles."

He spoke passionately and with conviction. I didn't know what he saw in my eyes, other than dismay at his hysteria, but I'd be damned before I'd say anything else to alienate him. He was a fanatical crusader seeing Bolsheviks in the shadows just like the

---

5. Gilbert. *Winston S. Churchill.* Vol. IV: *1917-1922*: 278. Paraphrased.

French saw German boogeymen everywhere. Unfortunately, even a fanatic can be right from time to time. There *were* Bolsheviks in the shadows. At least that was where I'd found them in Paris.

"I am not certain President Wilson would agree. He has all his eggs in the treaty basket," I said carefully.

"You are very likely right, but it is important that these truths are given voice in Washington, whether in the White House, the Senate, or Congress as a whole."

It was clear that he wanted me as a clandestine go-between with the powers in Washington. I was a terrible choice, but he didn't know that yet. I decided now was the time to nip his enthusiasm in the bud.

"Mr. Churchill, I'm not sure what you know about me, but I'm a former enlisted man, who became a trumped-up major to work, very briefly, for the French. While I worked for the French, German intelligence tortured me and very possibly ruined my health. I would be of questionable use in any effort to convince the powers in Washington of the Bolshevik threat in Europe. I'm just some hapless doughboy who got in over his head."

Frederickson's ghost nodded in agreement.

Churchill laughed at my comments. He looked very merry and much less grim when he smiled and waved his cigar about.

"I do like you, Major. Your face looks like that of a boxer who has gone fifteen rounds with Jack Johnson. To earn bruises and a split knuckle like that in Brixton, you had to fight some toughs. I am sure your health is perfectly fine."

I didn't correct his impression that I was talking about my physical health. I didn't want to tell the secretary of air and war that I was a lunatic.

"You insist you are of no use," Churchill continued, "yet Préfet Raux swears by you, claiming that you are the most efficient and effective American agent with whom he has ever dealt. No small praise."

"He can't have met many," I said sincerely, which caused Churchill to laugh again and both Kell and Marsh to smile.

"Colonel Kell told me I would like you. When he suggested this meeting, I wasn't sure what would come of it, but now I know. I don't need you to do much, sir. Britain doesn't need much. Less than you gave her in the trenches in '15 and '16," he said, glancing from my eyes to the scars on the side of my face.

I hated the fact that he knew about my service and that it fooled him. But his ignorance might protect me.

"I just need a trusted messenger," Winston Churchill said to me. "I will write a detailed letter for your president, one for Colonel House, and finally one for the republican leader in the Senate, Henry Cabot Lodge. I need them delivered with the utmost discretion and haste."

"And what will these letters say?" I asked. My stomach knotted at the thought of facing Wilson. I wasn't sure I could separate the dog from the man. I really wasn't sure which was reality. That thought prompted Tippy, who had been glowering at the thought of me escaping England blameless for my desertion, to choke out a good laugh. No one but me heard him.

"President Wilson and Senator Lodge know me and have some small respect for me. They will listen. They must. The ties between the recent terrorist attacks and the current massive labor strikes are undeniable evidence of the workings of Bolshevism in the United States. These are not the arbitrary, isolated events directed by a few uneducated immigrant anarchists. These are coordinated efforts promoted and guided by Moscow."

I wasn't aware of any bombings in the States or strikes for that matter, but I'd been away. If Churchill thought he could convince the powers that be that Bolshevism needed a good stomping, that was fine by me. I wasn't sure what he expected Wilson and the others to do. It sounded like he wanted America to send soldiers back to Russia. I didn't see that happening. And while I was against it, I was in favor of escaping England, murder charges, and more importantly, my past.

I quickly learned that the last was not to be.

The telephone on Churchill's desk buzzed, and he answered. "Yes, send them right in."

The door opened.

"Sir Basil Thomson and his man," Churchill told us.

I knew the CID chief was joining, but I didn't know who the additional guest would be. It was Churchill's party, and he could invite whomever he wanted as long as he and his cronies kept me out of Brixton.

Thomson led the way into the room. He had a long, narrow face and a mustache that turned up ever so slightly at the ends. He also had sharp, inquisitive eyes and a slight smile on his face, as if he knew more than everyone else in the room. When I saw the man who followed him, I knew that he did.

A cold terror seized me around the throat, and an unseen pressure pushed me back a step from the smiling newcomer. It took all of my will not to bolt from the room. My heart thundered in my chest, and I struggled to breathe.

Billy Jones. My old friend. My best friend during my time at university in England. We'd looked enough alike with our brown hair and muddy eyes that I could have been his less charming doppelgänger. When our friends spoke of the two of us, we were the *cousins*. One English. One American.

He'd been blown to bits in France, and yet here he was standing tall and whole before me.

Ghosts of the dead now walked with the living. It was clear that the men in the room could see him. Tippy Frederickson was gone. Nowhere to be seen or felt, but Jones stood right before me with a grin on his dead face.

Churchill was speaking. Gesturing to Thomson, Jones, and then me. I couldn't hear him. My overwhelmed mind refused his words.

Here was my punishment. The dead would speak to the living and all would know I had run. I took another step back.

The men were staring at me. They must already know. They had brought me here to trap me with Jones.

My pistol was with Mitchell. I wished for it desperately. A bullet in my head and Jones and the horror haunting me would be gone.

"I say, Griffin, are you all right?" Churchill asked me with nearly sincere concern.

"Jack, don't you recognize me?" Billy Jones's apparition asked.

"You look like you've seen a ghost," Kell chimed in. I wondered if he was taunting me.

Thomson just watched me. His face wore a look of detached fascination like that of a child watching ants consume a beetle.

"What do you want, Billy," I said. My voice was barely a croak. "You're dead. You've been dead since '16."

Jones laughed. He was enjoying my terror. I considered attacking him, but what was the point? I couldn't hurt him. The other men studied me. No doubt they were considering what to do with me now that they had me trapped.

"No," Jones said, interrupting my careening thoughts. "I was knocked about by shellfire. That's all. I got a good blow to the head. Terribly concussed. And mustard gas burns. Damned painful but not fatal. When they got me back to the aid station, I didn't even know my own name. They stuck me in hospital. The burns healed quickly enough I suppose, but it took a few months for my wits to return."

He touched a barely noticeable scar on his forehead at the edge of his hairline. He then reached the same hand out to me, and I backed away.

"Are you all right, Jack? I'm not a ghost. I promise." He gave me a small, encouraging smile. Not a ghost. Jones was alive? I considered the possibility that he was real. Hesitating, I took his hand. It was warm, living flesh. I squeezed it hard, and his smile broke into a grin. "I'm alive, Jack, really!"

"My God, Billy! You made it through. So many dead, but you're here!" Relief washed through me, and I beamed at Billy Jones like an imbecile. He wasn't a ghost at all. He wasn't like Tippy. He lived. They hadn't found me out. They'd simply found someone who knew me. Someone I thought was dead but wasn't. Billy Jones was alive!

Churchill and Kell smiled uncomfortably at my joy. After my response to Billy's appearance, they must have suspected I was unbalanced. Thomson did not smile. He sensed something more behind my reaction. And he was right. I was glad Jones was alive. I was glad he'd survived. But I was happiest for myself. I might be mad as a hatter, but my secret betrayal was safe today. Instead of being unmasked as a coward, I was reunited with an old friend.

I started to laugh. It sounded hysterical to my ears, but I didn't care. The tension of the past few moments fled with the sound.

Billy Jones living and breathing. Tippy Frederickson could go fuck himself, the dead bastard. Out of caution at the thought, I searched the room for any sign of Frederickson, but he had made himself scarce in response to my good fortune.

I pulled Jones into an embrace that embarrassed everyone but me.

"Damn I'm glad you're alive, Billy!" I said sincerely.

"Americans," Thomson said under his breath, with more than a little distaste.

I could sense Churchill getting impatient with the reunion, and since no one was going to call me a coward or a deserter, I was happy to get the meeting back on track.

"My apologies, gentlemen. I never expected to see Mr. Jones again. So many were lost, and I was sure he was one of them. The shock of seeing him. Well, it is just so hard to believe," I stammered.

"Of course! We completely understand," Churchill said insincerely. "But we should continue our discussion. Time is short, and as I've said, we need your help, Major."

The men moved into the room. Churchill gestured Thomson and Jones to the couch, and the rest of us resumed our seats.

"Before you arrived, Sir Basil, I was telling Major Griffin that we needed him as an emissary to America. Someone who can speak directly and discreetly with the president on our behalf." Churchill spoke to Thomson, ignoring Jones.

I wondered if he thought Jones's attendance was unnecessary, but Thomson had brought Billy for a reason. He was a tool to provide insight into my character, my motivation, my capacity for mayhem. Thomson believed correctly that I was a murderer. Unfortunately for him, Billy Jones wouldn't learn anything from me about the Savoy, and he had no conception of my affinity for violence. The last time Billy saw me, I was a shallow, selfish boy. He never served with me in the trenches. He knew nothing of my service in the Marine Corps or that the past four years had turned me into a killer. Killing was what I knew best. It was what I was good at. And, God help me, it was what I enjoyed. He would never know how easy it all had become for me.

"And if he's a murderer, Mr. Secretary?" Thomson asked.

"Well, I am sure he's not. As you told me yourself, no usable fingerprints were found." Thomson looked sharply at Churchill for divulging this important bit of information. Inspectors Fair and Norton had told me the exact opposite. I should have known. Cops trying to trick me. Why should that be a surprise?

"The lack of clear prints does not determine the major's innocence, Mr. Churchill."

"Well then, let's assume he did kill those fellows at the Savoy. Which I am sure you did not," Churchill said to me as an aside. "What of it? Two were Germans and all were Bolsheviks. Good riddance to bad rubbish."

"I cannot be so cavalier about the peace and safety of the realm," Thomson said firmly. "It is my job to investigate and apprehend their killer or killers. I am no less concerned with Bolsheviks and Jews than you, sir, but we can't have murderers walking our streets. Even if they happen to appear to be allies." He said the last directly to me.

I wasn't sure what Jews had to do with Bolsheviks, but Thomson clearly felt there was a connection.

Churchill turned to me. "Major, would you mind stepping outside for a moment? Colonel Kell, Sir Basil, and I need a few minutes to discuss the proper course of action."

"Of course. Please let me know if you have any questions for me," I said to Thomson.

He nodded noncommittally.

"Certainly," Churchill said, rising with me and patting my arm as I moved toward the door.

"Mr. Jones, why don't you accompany the major," Sir Basil said. "It will give you two old friends a chance to catch up."

It seemed it was time for Billy Jones to earn his keep. He would report whatever I told him to Thomson and possibly Churchill. He might have been my friend in '14, but a lifetime had passed since then. He was a stranger now. A stranger who wanted evidence I was a killer.

The door shut behind us, leaving the two of us standing in the anteroom with the disinterested secretary. Marsh had remained with Churchill and the others.

"Jack, it is so good to see you." Jones clapped me on the shoulders. "It feels like a miracle. By the time I had recovered, you'd been wounded and had gone back to America. I'm damn glad your sight came back. Evelyn told me how horrible it was for you."

"Evelyn?"

"Yes. I know you two were close," he said. He sounded like he was apologizing, but I couldn't imagine for what. "The gas burns on my legs kept me in England. I had some time, and I went to see her. You were gone. It was clear that your engagement had ended. We spent a great deal of time together, and, well, there's no easy way to say it, but we're married." He wore a rueful look, as if he were embarrassed.

Evelyn married? Of course, it made sense. She was an attractive woman. She wouldn't have gone unwed. I supposed Jones was as good a husband for her as any. I decided that I was happy for her and him.

"Billy, that is excellent news. Evelyn deserved better than me. Especially after I'd been wounded. I am happy for you both," I told him.

"I'm glad to hear you say that," he answered. "I remember how fiercely all her brother's friends, including the two of us, competed for Evelyn's attention."

"I'm glad she married you, Billy. Really." I meant what I said. He was welcome to her. The sooner I was away from them both and England, the happier I would be.

"You should have dinner with us, Jack. Evelyn would love to see you."

"I appreciate the offer, Billy, I do, but I am not sure I'll be free. It seems like your boss wouldn't mind seeing me back in Brixton. And as you can see," I said, pointing to my face, "it can be a pretty tough place."

"Oh, I'm sure we'll work out his concerns," he said with certainty. "I told him on the way here that the Jack Griffin I knew was no murderer."

"I appreciate your confidence, Billy, but I am sure Sir Basil reminded you that you haven't seen me in a very long time."

"He did, but I am not worried about that. You've always been one of the most noble fellows I know. Nothing would change that."

I struggled not to laugh in his face. Had he fought in a different war than I had?

"Of course, I wasn't at the front as long as you were," he continued. "I was delayed in completing officer training because of my father's death, and then I hadn't been with my unit more than a few months when I was diagnosed with trench fever.[6]

____

6. Quintan fever (caused by lice).

Honestly, I think the fever saved my life. I was out of the line for three more months. I missed most of the Somme as a result."

The Somme. A slaughterhouse of men. I remembered it all too well. The Forty-Seventh Division, of which the First Surrey Rifles were part, had not been in at the start. We were held in reserve until the beginning of August 1916, but it was bloody enough when they'd finally put us in the line. And we'd certainly seen our share of action before the Somme. Billy Jones was right. He had been lucky to miss most of the monthslong battle. If his regiment was part of the original attack in July, as an officer, he probably wouldn't have survived the first day of the battle.

"When I finally did get to the front, it was bloody awful, as you know. The lads in my company were wonderful. I'd do anything for them and they for me. The camaraderie was the only light in an otherwise hellish darkness. When I was wounded, it was the lads in my company who found me. They searched no-man's-land. It was a miracle, but they never gave up."

I nodded in understanding. He was right that the bonds forged between men in that otherworldly hell really were the only good. Unfortunately, I knew those very connections drove my guilt in 1917 and my decision to return to the war. They likely conjured the ghosts in my head as well. Of course a double helping of German mescaline didn't hurt.

"Before we came over from Scotland Yard, Sir Basil gave me your military record to review," Jones said. "My God, Jack, you went through hell with the Rifles. What on earth made you join up when America came in?"

It was clear Jones didn't see me as a coward. He was fooled just like so many seemed to be. Tippy Frederickson was a still shadow in the doorway. He wasn't fooled. Tippy, my dead FSR mates, and my conscience knew my heart.

I decided to tell Billy as much of the truth as my fear would let me. He had been my friend after all, and perhaps he could help me out with his boss.

"It's not too complicated. My vision came back. I started to feel guilty about being out of the fight. When America entered the war, I felt like I had no choice but to join up. All I could think about were my mates in the battalion dying in the mud while I was sleeping safely on clean sheets an ocean away. I was ashamed to be out of it. Hell, Billy, I still feel ashamed," I said with more honesty than I intended.

"Well, that's just absurd, Jack! You'd done as much as any man. And if what Churchill seems to think is true, you're still fighting for King and country."

He was feeling me out, trying to get information about the Savoy. I was sad and glad at the same time. Sad because he had once been my best mate, and he was using our past relationship as a means to question me for his boss. Happy because it told me where I stood. Jones wasn't my friend anymore and hadn't been since 1915.

It was time to produce the alibi. It had made sense for me to keep mum with the two inspectors. I hadn't wanted to seem desperate. Telling Jones in confidence would be different. If Thomson thought Jones coaxed the information from me via our old relationship, he would be more inclined to believe it was true.

"I'm not fighting anybody, Billy. Well, except for some thugs in prison, and they left me no choice. And gave me a good beating besides. I'm an investigator for Colonel House." I liked the sound of that. "I wasn't in London the day of the Savoy murders. I was in Surrey following up on an investigation for House. I had come across some information that Bolsheviks were planning to interfere with the treaty. As I told Mr. Churchill earlier, it turns out my information was correct. The night of the murders, I was staying at a hotel in Surrey with an associate of mine. We were both there to question the sister of one of the conspirators." Briefly I felt guilty about using Sarah as my excuse, but I felt her breath in my hair as she snickered at my misleading of the imperial authorities she loathed.

I could tell my statement surprised him, but he hid it quickly.

"Well, that's good news, Jack, but it would help if we could speak with your friend to confirm this."

"William Mitchell. He's staying at Number 2 Aldford Street with his girl. It's her house. Patricia Armistan Kingsbury. A very rich widow. If he's not there, he'll be at Claridge's." I wanted to make sure they talked to Mitchell and got confirmation. Unfortunately, no one at the Swan would confirm I'd been there, but I hoped our story that I came in late and left early would be enough.

"Let me share this information with Sir Basil. If we can confirm what you say, you should be free to go."

"He won't believe me. He doesn't want to. And I don't think he likes Churchill interfering with his investigation. You don't want to be in a farmyard where two big dogs are fighting, Billy. And those two are big dogs."

Jones laughed. "Ah, I missed your Americanisms, Jack. Listen, I am sure Sir Basil won't send you back to Brixton. Which means you will be free tonight. You must come to dinner with Evelyn and me. I won't take no for an answer. It will be grand for the three of us to be back together."

I didn't want to see Evelyn. She represented all I had surrendered when I'd run: my self-regard, a career, and a future spent with a loving wife and children. I had abandoned all of that —my humanity most of all—but I needed Billy Jones.

"Sure, I'd like that. Just tell me where and when, and if I'm not in prison, I'll be there."

"And I'll be there too," Tippy Frederickson told him, but I was pretty sure Billy Jones couldn't hear Tippy. And I wasn't going to pass on that message.

Jones excused himself to join the men in Churchill's office. He wanted to share my alibi with Thomson and the others.

"Don't leave me alone out here too long, Billy. I might run away!"

"You'd never run away, Jack."

Yeah, sure I wouldn't.

9

_____

A Goddamn Hero

I paced the waiting room for what must have been an hour. The secretary ignored me. I looked out the windows. I studied the books on the shelves. Then I sat in the one chair only to stand and pace again.

The door to Churchill's office opened, and Billy emerged.

"Come in, Jack."

He did not accompany me back into the room. Apparently, what was to follow was too delicate for someone of his seniority, which was curious because, after he'd told them of my alibi, he had listened as they'd discussed my future.

They sat me back in the overstuffed chair, my cold coffee still before me.

The four men studied me for a moment before Thomson started the conversation.

"We've made a few calls. And I've instructed my officers to expand their interviews to include your associates. It appears you were not in London on the day of the murders. It might have saved us all a great deal of time if you had bothered to tell the investigating officers that you were not in the city during your initial questioning."

I didn't respond. It looked like they might let me go, and I didn't want to spoil that possibility by angering Thomson.

"We are continuing our investigation, but you are no longer a person of interest in it," Thomson said.

That deserved a nod and a glance at Churchill. The look was enough for him to clear his throat and take over from Thomson.

"You are free to go. Free to return to the United States."

"I do plan on returning to the States eventually, but I have some business to finish in Paris," I told him. Specifically, I needed to gather a steamer trunk stuffed with weapons. I would need them for my discussion with Armistan.

"I thought you might say that. But I very much need you to take a quick trip to America before you do so." Churchill was not negotiating. He was telling me the price for my freedom was a trip to Washington as Britain's tool. Somehow my desperate lie to Préfet Raux in the aftermath of the gun battle on the rue Franklin had transformed into reality. I really did work for House and Clemenceau, and now I would work for the goddamned English. At least they weren't sending me to Germany. At worst, I would waste a few weeks delivering Churchill's messages.

I considered balking at Churchill's demand. I wasn't sure they really had any proof that I'd killed the men at the Savoy. Unfortunately, even if they didn't, they could make life difficult. A nod from Thomson, Fair, and Norton could have me back in Brixton in the blink of an eye, where I could waste a lot more time than just a few weeks. I guessed they wanted Jones out of the room just in case they had to strong-arm me. It would have been awkward for everyone but me if he'd taken my side and urged them to leave me be. The obvious course was to agree. Even I could see that.

"When do you want me to leave?"

ONCE I AGREED, IT WAS JUST A MATTER OF CONFIRMING HOW LONG it would take Churchill to write his letters. The three men decided I would depart for New York City from Southampton on the RMS *Adriatic* in three days with a ticket paid for by His Majesty's government, money in my pocket for my expenses, and three envelopes containing Churchill's letters. They even promised me a ride to Southampton the morning the ship departed.

I didn't ask whether Lloyd George was aware of Churchill's plan to contact the president and key decision-makers in America outside of ordinary diplomatic channels. I didn't care, and Churchill didn't care either.

"Please keep the details of your travels to yourself, Major Griffin," Sir Basil instructed me. "I know you were friendly with Mr. Jones in the past, and he is the best of men, but I think it wise to limit those of us who know when you will be returning to petition your government."

I wasn't planning on petitioning anyone. I was just a mailman, but I had no reason to argue with him about keeping my departure date to myself. I didn't want to involve Billy, and if I could avoid Evelyn and him, I would.

That was not to be. With my assent to Churchill's plan, Jones was invited back into the room.

"Give me a few days," Churchill told me. "We may need you to speak with the prime minister." He had no intention of having me speak with Lloyd George. He just wanted to make sure Billy Jones didn't know how soon I'd be leaving for America. For some reason, Churchill and Thomson didn't trust Jones, or more likely, they were playing fast and loose sending me without the prime minister's blessing. They were worried that Jones would be too honest not to report what he knew if questioned.

As we departed the air and war secretary's office, Billy reminded me of his invitation to join him for dinner. He was so happy at my freedom and eager for me to see Evelyn that I couldn't retract my earlier acceptance. After being manipulated by Churchill, I had no fight left to argue with Jones. We agreed that I'd join the Joneses at seven that evening at Bentley's in Mayfair not far from Patricia's new home.

I stopped by Bayford's office to let him know what had happened with Kell, but he was out. I left a message and returned to Patricia's house where I found Mitchell in the study. He was smoking and reading the newspaper.

"Well?" he asked. "You don't look like a murderer on the lam."

"Just a murderer," I said gloomily.

"Tricia and I will take you out on the town tonight. You'll forget all your worries."

"Sorry, I can't go with you. Tonight I have dinner with my old fiancée and her new husband, who was my best friend when I lived here in England. Maybe tomorrow."

At the news of my dinner with Evelyn, Mitchell started to laugh. Tippy cackled as well.

"Oh my God, Griffin! I'd accuse you of making all that up except the expression on your ugly mug confirms every word of it. You've got to tell me what you've been up to today. No! Wait! Let me get Patricia. She'll want to hear this." He jumped from his chair and started calling her name before he was out of the room.

He found her quickly, pulled her into the room by the hand, and sat her in his chair. He was too excited to sit himself and practically crackled with energy. Patricia, on the other hand, wore a heavy-lidded look, as if she'd been asleep.

"I'm sorry Mitch woke you, Patricia. My news isn't really that urgent."

"Nonsense, John. I wasn't sleeping. I was having a relaxing smoke when this juggernaut barreled into my room shouting," she said, nodding at Mitchell, who just grinned back at her.

"Now tell us about your day," Patricia demanded.

I described my visit to Kell and the appointment at the war

office. I hadn't gotten to the fact that Churchill required my services when Mitchell interrupted.

"So they let you go? That is excellent. Morgan came by earlier, the little rat, keeps promising that the citizenship business is in hand and the probate's on track. The trouble is, he's doing all the talking to the lawyers. So who knows what the truth is?" He said the last with a disapproving glance at Patricia.

"William," Patricia said with a sniff, "you don't want me spending my days with a bunch of lawyers in their dusty offices. That is what Morgan is for. I direct. He does. There is progress. He has reported the details, and I believe him."

Mitchell wanted to argue, but I cut him off. Their quarreling over Reynolds would resolve nothing.

"Well, that at least is good news. You both should go back to Paris as soon as you can," I said. "I can't. I now work for the English. Churchill wants me to deliver letters to the president, House, and Senator Lodge."

"Jesus Christ, Griffin, you must be the most employable leatherneck in Europe. How did that happen?"

I told them about Churchill's fear of Bolshevism and what I assumed about his negotiation with Thomson and Kell.

"Churchill doesn't care about three dead men in the Savoy. He cares about preventing the worldwide Bolshevik revolution," I explained. "Sending me to Washington is part of his plan to do that."

"Well, if it will keep you out of prison, John, I think working for the British is a positive development," Patricia said.

"I'm not sure why Churchill thinks I'll persuade anyone in Washington of anything, but I have no choice. It seems like the French and the British all think I have some sort of backdoor access to Wilson and House."

"That's because you do, you dope," Mitchell said. "But enough about the Brits drafting you as their carrier pigeon. Tell Tricia about your dinner tonight."

I scowled at Mitchell. He enjoyed my discomfort more than

was healthy. He wouldn't have been so delighted with my misfortune if he understood how terrified I was when I thought about the dinner.

Tonight I would face Evelyn, who had lost her brother and friends we shared. I would dine with Billy Jones, once my friend, who had served honorably and didn't seek an escape from the horror through deception. I wasn't sure how I would react to them and Tippy and any other phantoms who might join dinner. With my broken mind and the old gnawing fear, the dinner could be cataclysmic. Unfortunately, I was committed. Perhaps seeing Evelyn with Billy would be the catharsis I needed to escape my past. More likely, it would be the straw that broke the camel's back of my sanity.

I would visit Mitchell's hotel room and retrieve my pistol. With it tucked securely in its shoulder holster, I would carry an immediate solution should the pressure become too much.

I arrived at Bentley's at the appointed time, my heart racing. I didn't know how I would react to Evelyn. She was the personification of all my prewar hopes. She was the future I had sacrificed. My palms were clammy. Jesus. I needed to get control of myself. Tippy and Sarah were both just at the edge of my awareness. Tippy was there to see me crack and finally shatter completely. I didn't know why Sarah was there. Curiosity, perhaps? She didn't tell me.

I hadn't really laid eyes on Evelyn since before I was wounded. At first I couldn't see her at all. My head was swathed in dressings. When those were removed, and I was hiding the truth that my sight was returning, I still couldn't really see her. She was just a hazy, sympathetic shadow. By that time, I knew I was deserting England, my friends, my honor, and of necessity, her too. Nearly three years had passed since then. I was walking toward a terrifying confrontation created by my splintered mind because I felt I had no other option. That was why my pulse was pounding and I had a handgun under my jacket.

I told the maître d' that I was part of the Jones party.

"Right this way, sir. The other guests have already been seated."

I suddenly had a horrible premonition.

"How many guests?" I asked.

"Four. Two young men and two young women."

"Four," I repeated, my mind scrambling for an exit that didn't exist.

I followed him, trailing along with no more choice of direction than a pig trapped in the maze of an abattoir's pens. He wound his way through the other diners, and I caught sight of Jones seated at a round table. White linen and crystal promised an expensive meal. Jones leaned back in his chair, laughing, and I saw Evelyn beyond him.

My heart skipped a beat.

Evelyn. Brown hair, large expressive eyes, translucent skin. While her face had thinned and matured, she remained beautiful. In fact, she was more beautiful than I remembered. Four years of war, rationing, and loss had polished her to an elegant peak of womanhood. She was everything I had ever wanted—when I was nineteen.

The other man at the table had his back to me, and a woman with light hair sat next to him.

It was clear that my seat would be between Evelyn and the unknown woman.

"Your table, sir."

Billy caught sight of me.

"Jack! So glad you could come!" He jumped up and grabbed my hand. "You remember George Moore, of course."

Moore also stood. He was tall with thinning hair and a mustache he didn't used to have, but I recognized him. I recalled that the younger me hadn't liked him. He laughed too hard at his own jokes, and he had been in competition for Evelyn as well.

"Of course," I managed to say as I shook Moore's hand. I could feel Evelyn's eyes on me.

"And Evelyn."

I turned to her. I stopped thinking. My social reflexes took over, which was lucky because my brain couldn't keep up. Tippy was overjoyed at my floundering.

"Evelyn," I said as I moved around Jones to lean down and kiss her cheek. She smelled exactly as I remembered. The lavender perfume mingling with the same captivating, singular scent of hers. I felt dizzy. Like I might collapse.

"And Lily Blakely. A friend of ours from here in London."

Miss Blakely studied me. I watched her take in the scar, the bruises on my face, and my split lip. Her candid and unflattering assessment showed on her face and brought me to my senses. I appreciated her good taste.

"I just got out of prison," I said with a grin that would have scared a child.

She gave a small laugh as did the others. She was a pretty girl with wide-set eyes and a nice smile.

"Unfortunately, he's telling the truth," Jones supplied, shaking his head as I sat between the ladies. "He was wrongfully arrested by the Met and spent a few days in Brixton."

"How perfectly terrible that must have been," Lily said.

Evelyn didn't say anything. She just watched me with a knowing curl to her lips. She knew I'd run. I could see it in her eyes.

In response to this certainty, I reacted as I'd been trained. I took the offensive. I had to keep her from sharing the truth.

"Not the best part of London I've visited. But enough about my sightseeing," I said. "Evelyn, I must hear about how you've been. Your parents? And George. I haven't seen you for years."

And with that, I opened the floodgates of reminiscence and news, most of it about those who died, but all of it diverting attention from me.

Jones ordered champagne, and as it began to flow, the

conversation became easy. Evelyn seemed in no hurry to reveal me as a coward. In fact, our conversation, while stilted at first, settled into the comfortable banter of old friends long parted. Lily, too, was interesting. Inevitably, we spoke of our part in the war. She had worked in an ammunition factory for a time and then trained as a nurse. She'd never been sent to France. Instead, she had remained in England, working with amputees fitting their prosthetics, of which devices there had been all too few. I tried diverting her questions about my service, but Jones, overhearing from across the table, was unwilling to let her queries pass.

"Don't let him put you off, Lily," he said. "I've seen his record. It's bloody astounding!"

"Billy, you are not Eliza Doolittle. There's no need to curse," Evelyn said, fondly chiding her husband.

"Well, it's a miracle he survived."

They all looked at me. This was the moment I had dreaded since returning to England. The moment the dead waited for. The living wanted to know why I lived. So I told them.

"I ran away. That's how I survived. If I'd stayed in the trenches, I'd have been killed. You know how it was," I said, looking at Jones and then Moore. Tippy nodded his agreement with my admission of cowardice. I ignored him. "No doubt about it. I'd be dead. The best thing that happened to me was getting shot in the head."

"That's ridiculous," Evelyn said. "You stayed and fought for us and were horribly wounded. You hardly ran away. And Billy tells me you came back after going home."

She was baiting me, which was fine. She knew the truth. Suddenly I wanted the whole thing to be done. I wanted the truth out. I wanted to get their disgust out in the open and put it and them behind me. It didn't matter anymore. The dead in my head were the real worry.

In anticipation, all my dead university chums had joined Tippy Frederickson around the table. Cecil Thomkins, John

Franklin, Tony Beecham, and even Evelyn's brother Bertie Williams, were crowding up against me. Worse than the university boys were my mates from the First Surrey Rifles. They were the ones I'd really abandoned. Sergeant Cooper, Artie Gwen, Terry Caldwell, and another ten or so besides. They all wanted to hear my confession.

"The blindness saved me. It got me out of the trenches. After I got out, there was no way I was going back." As I said it, I realized the objective absurdity of the claim. After all, I had gone back. "I wasn't going back to the trenches. I ran from those as far and as fast as I could." I couldn't quite bring myself to tell them that before I left England to recuperate in the States, my vision had already started to return. The timing was irrelevant, I told myself. My sight had returned, and I had not. I had no way of knowing what joining the Marine Corps would bring, but I knew damn well what a return to the British Army would have.

"Can't say I blame you. I was on General Wilson's staff, and every time I had to go up to the line I was terrified," Moore said with a glance and a smile at Evelyn. He was still interested in her. I hoped Jones could see it.

"And you did go back," Jones said approvingly. He turned to the others. "He was an American marine."

The shades of the men around me weren't pleased by Jones's comment or those of the others. The dead men all wore uniform looks of disgust.

"I didn't do anything," I said to the dead, hoping they wouldn't blame me for the reaction of the living, but it was Jones who answered.

"That's hardly true, Jack. After all, you did volunteer. Again." He shook his head as if amazed. "You had certainly done enough, but you still came back. Remarkable! I'm afraid, in the same situation, I would have kept mum and stayed home."

"Nonsense," Evelyn told him.

The waiter brought a third bottle of champagne, briefly halting this undeserved praise.

"And now he is a confidant of Colonel House and President Wilson and friend to prominent men here in Britain," Jones said, bragging on my behalf.

Evelyn bobbed her head at her husband's comments. Was she fooled as well? She was. I had been certain she knew the truth about my desertion, but here she was, acting like I was a goddamn hero. She didn't realize I'd hidden my returning vision. She didn't know that I'd run. It would have been sickening if it hadn't been such a relief.

I looked at Tippy, Bertie, and the other dead and shrugged. I had tried and failed to convince the living. Tough luck, Tippy.

"And friends to you all as well. To old and new friends," I said to the table, raising my glass with a nod to Lily. They raised theirs, and we drank.

I had faced the nightmare returning to my English friends and come out the other side. A weight lifted off my chest, and Tippy and my dead friends were gone. At least for a time.

10

———

Natural Child

I enjoyed the dinner immensely.

True, I was still insane. I had ghosts in my head and feared that at any moment dogmen might attack me. But I had lost my terror of the living. The acceptance by Evelyn, Billy, and George had lanced the swollen boil of dread that I had carried with me since my decision to run. I felt light. So light I could float away.

The dinner contributed to my sense of weightlessness. We enjoyed raw oysters along with chilled lobster and grilled dover sole. I laughed at everything, funny or not, and found myself flirting with Lily just because I could. Also, she had come to the dinner with George Moore, and I had realized, as dinner progressed, I didn't like him any better in 1919 than I had in 1914.

I was giddy with relief, and it made me as engaging a companion as I was capable of being. Billy, George, and I shared stories with the ladies about our time at university. The mood was gay as we reminisced about the summer of '14, which had taken on an idyllic veneer. I found it easy to be at the table with the four of them. It was comfortable and comforting, despite the dead at the fringes of my perception. My dinner companions' acceptance of me and my explanation of my war record robbed the dead of their power. To my surprise, I found that I was among friends.

As we ordered after-dinner drinks, Evelyn leaned over conspiratorially and asked, "John, why do you have a gun under your jacket?"

I was so elated at the extraordinary absence of terror that I had forgotten about the pistol. Still, I didn't hesitate in answering.

"I work for Colonel House and President Wilson. Unfortunately, the job can be"—I hesitated dramatically—"dangerous."

She smiled at the melodrama, unsure if I was being honest, but I couldn't very well tell her that I had it handy to shoot myself or everyone else depending on my mental state.

"My goodness. I thought when the war ended, life would return to normal. I suppose that was naive of me," she said.

Naive didn't begin to describe it, but her absurd optimism didn't bother me. She believed me. She believed it all. I was so sure she knew my heart, and I was so wrong. I nearly burst out laughing at my change of fortune.

"Oh, don't be concerned about it. I am sure things will improve now that the treaty's been signed." I was sure of no such thing. I had just returned from the impending disaster that was Germany after all, but I wanted Evelyn to be happy. At least this was one thing that hadn't changed since 1914.

"John, I would like you to have tea with Billy and me tomorrow afternoon. I know you will be returning to America sometime soon, and it is possible, if not certain, that we won't see you for some time. It would be nice for all of us to have a few more hours together."

I decided that I would appreciate more time with them as well. They were happy, and I liked seeing them so. An hour or two at tea and then gone forever with fond memories of them and England. This was the exact opposite of what I'd expected when I'd first returned here.

"I'd like that," I answered, "but won't Billy have to work?"

"It appears that Sir Basil has asked him to learn more about you, so tea with you is Billy's work. He'll go back to the office after," Evelyn assured me.

"Of course."

"We'll see you at three," Evelyn told me. "Twenty-One Hans Road."

"I look forward to it."

Dinner ended with empty promises to George and Lily to do it again soon, and I walked back to Patricia's house on Aldford Street with a lightness of heart I hadn't felt since before that damned archduke had been assassinated.

<hr>

At breakfast, I described my evening to Mitchell and Patricia. As I did so, I realized Mitchell was bored. He was living vicariously through me, so the more miserable or outrageous the events surrounding me, the happier and more engaged he became. Patricia, on the other hand, was apathetic. She tried to pretend, but it was clear to me she was uninterested and lethargic, and when she went to her room to rest, I mentioned it to Mitchell.

"She's not feeling well. Not poorly, just not well. I'm not sure what's the matter, and she refuses to see a doctor. At times, she seems fine," he told me. He was worried but not so worried to press the point with his strong-willed lover.

"Keep an eye on her, Will. Maybe when we get back to Paris, we can get a doc lined up to take a look at her without her even knowing. I'll bet Gene Bullard knows somebody. I'm just worried that Reynolds is responsible."

"Keep your hat on, Griff. I don't trust the bastard either, but I haven't seen much of him since we found Patricia outside

Claridge's. He's supposed to come by today with Willis to get some signatures, but he's not doing anything to Patricia. I just don't trust that he's doing right by her with the lawyers."

I didn't like that Mitchell wasn't taking my worries seriously, but I was the one with a mescaline-addled brain.

"Well, I have to leave for the States in a couple of days, so I won't be here to keep you two out of trouble. You need to get back to Paris as soon as you can. Okay?"

"John, without you around, the probability of anything bad happening to us drops off a cliff," Mitchell declared with an uncomplimentary scoff. "And don't worry. Tricia loves Paris and will be happy to return as soon as we can. We should be back there not too long after you leave."

"When you get there, send me a cable at the Pennsylvania."

"Will do. I'll let Patricia know that's the plan."

Satisfied that I had done what I could to hurry Patricia and Mitchell back to Paris, I went out to buy some new shirts and a couple of ties. I was going to be seeing House and Senator Lodge, and I figured I should dress for it. God forbid I should see the president. I wasn't sure I could face him, but I might have no choice.

I returned to Patricia's house to drop off my purchases before leaving for the Jones's flat. It had been raining intermittently all day, but I'd managed to avoid it. As I prepared to head for the Joneses', heavy drops began to fall in earnest. My trench coat was upstairs in my room, and I didn't want to be late. Mitchell's brand-new, buff-colored mackintosh, a gift from Patricia, hung from the stand in the entry, drying from an earlier trip he must have made. I slipped it from the rack and took a guilty joy from borrowing it for the afternoon. Mitchell would be annoyed, which made me smile as I put it on.

The bus ride down Knightsbridge was short. I exited the double-decker in front of Harrod's department store. The rain pelted down, and I hurried to Hans Road, which bordered the west side of Harrod's massive food halls. A row of charming, yet identical, red brick Victorians promised refuge from the rain. Only the numbers over the arched entryways distinguished one from another. I went up the steps to Number 21 two at a time and turned the handle on the mechanical bell.

Evelyn answered the door. She wore a light white summer dress, and her hair was down. I was surprised, but I supposed she and Billy thought of this tea as an informal occasion. That was fine with me. I was still a little fidgety about getting reacquainted with my old English friends, and I hoped for a drink to steady my nerves.

"Jack, come in. Here! Take off that dripping coat." She hung Mitchell's raingear from a peg holding similar coats just inside the door. "I'm so glad you could come. Billy is in the sitting room. I'll get the tea, unless you'd like something stronger?"

"I'd welcome a whisky."

"Of course. We'll join you."

She led me into a spacious sitting room. Tall windows looked out onto the street, letting in the thin, gray afternoon light.

Billy jumped up and grabbed my hand as I entered.

"Jack, come in. Have a seat. Thanks for coming."

"Jack's having a whisky, dear."

"I'll have the same," Jones declared.

"Well, I won't have to put on the kettle," Evelyn said, joking. "I'll have a whisky as well, Billy."

Billy showed me to a seat and went to a drinks cart against the far wall. He poured three whiskies and handed one to Evelyn and one to me.

For the next hour, we sat in their living room and continued our warm, effortless conversation from the night before. In short order, Billy and I were laughing about George Moore still carrying a torch for Evelyn, despite his obvious connection to Lily.

"Well, I'm glad you two can see it, but I hope Lily doesn't," I told them.

"It would be difficult to miss," Billy explained.

On her part, Evelyn just shrugged as if to say "What's a beautiful girl to do?"

I sipped my whisky.

"And don't worry about Lily, John," Evelyn said slyly. "She is just friends with George. I suspect she found you more interesting by the end of the evening."

Her comment caused me to nearly aspirate my whisky. As I coughed, both Billy and Evelyn laughed.

"I am sure that is *not* the case," I finally managed to choke out.

Billy tossed back the remains of his whisky and looked meaningfully at his wife.

"Evelyn, dear, could you give Jack and me a few minutes?"

"Of course. I'll be upstairs," she said. I watched her glide from the room and managed to avoid coveting my friend's wife.

I took a cautious sip of my drink and waited.

"Jack, I have a tremendous favor to ask of you." Jones was uncomfortable. His face was flushed, and he seemed to be embarrassed. "And I'm not really sure how to ask."

"Well, Billy, you know I'd be happy to do anything I could for you and Evelyn."

"I know. I know that. But this is exceptional. You see, Jack, I have a problem. Evelyn and I have a problem."

Money. It was always money.

"Billy, I've got a few quid to spare. More than a few, really. The job I just finished for the president really did pay very well. I'd be happy to help you out." Between the money I'd squeezed from Armistan and Patricia, I figured I had more than enough to give two old friends a hand.

"No, no!" Jones exclaimed, holding up his hands. "It's not money. We're fine. The job for Sir Basil pays more than enough. We both have family money as well. That's not the issue."

Now I was confused. If it wasn't money, what was it? Something to do with Wilson or Churchill? I had no idea. I decided to shut up and wait.

"I told you I was wounded."

I nodded.

"An artillery barrage. High explosives and a few gas shells just to keep us honest."

I could easily imagine what had happened to him. I and thousands of other men had endured shelling like he described.

"I'm not exactly sure what happened," he said. "I should be dead. Lungs seared out by mustard gas. I must have been knocked half in and half out of a shell crater. Somehow as the gas settled, it did so over my legs. Heavier than air, don't you know? It never really reached above my waist. The burns were bad, but the gas likely had drifted. Thinned. So that by the time it settled into the shell hole I shared with it, it was weaker."

"That's a blessing," I said sincerely. He was right. He should have been dead.

"Yes, and no," he answered. "I lived, but the sulfur mustard affected me in ways you cannot see."

I frowned, waiting for him to elaborate, dreading that he would.

"It appears, Jack, that I am sterile. The gas did something to my insides, and the doctors tell me that I cannot father a child."

"Good God, Billy. I am so sorry. Are there any other continuing risks from the exposure?" I supposed being sterile was bad news, but dying a slow, painful death would be worse. I really didn't want to know what Jones was insistent on telling me.

"No other medical issues that the doctors know of."

"Thank goodness."

"We want a child, Jack." He studied me intently, willing me to understand how important this desire was. "Evelyn and I want a child."

"I'm sorry, Billy. I can't imagine. It must be terrible for the both of you." I took a gulp of my whisky, hoping my words were the right ones.

"It has been. It was only when we tried having a child that we realized…" He had difficulty finishing. "It was the gas. We've tried everything."

"Have you considered taking a ward? Maybe a relative in need has a child that they can't support."

"Goddamn it, Jack. We can't advertise our problems to our families or outside the family for that matter."

"I'm sorry, Billy. I know it must be difficult. I'm sure anything I'd suggest you've already thought of." I didn't understand what any of this had to do with me, but I felt bad for Billy and Evelyn. Even though the damned war was over, it continued to claim victims.

"I apologize, Jack. I don't mean to snap at you. The whole predicament has got me on edge. We've considered everything we could think of, but there's no way I can get Evelyn with child."

Suddenly I understood what I was doing in their sitting room.

No! This couldn't be. This was more horrible than any reckoning I had contemplated. Surely I wasn't right. I couldn't be!

"Seeing you again, knowing you and the man you are, knowing our past, knowing what you mean to Evelyn and me, it got us thinking."

"No! No, Billy," I exclaimed, jumping up.

"Jack, please. I know about you and her. She's been honest with me, and I don't fault you or her for your intimacy. It was war, you were in love, and you were to be married. She needs you again, Jack. I need you."

"Jesus Christ, Billy! You can't want that! And you don't know me anymore. You've seen me for a total of a few hours since 1915. You don't know what I've become, who I am. You can't be serious. Evelyn can't be serious."

"We are very serious," Evelyn said, coming into the room. She went to the drinks cart, poured herself a second whisky, and brought the carafe over to me. Without asking, she poured more into my glass.

"Billy, why don't you go back to work. I'll talk to Jack," she said calmly.

Jones put his glass on the side table and stood.

"Please just consider it, Jack," he said. "You really are the best man I know, and I understand this is a tremendously difficult decision. But it would literally mean the world to Evelyn and me. The war has taken so much. Please don't let it take our child too."

It was as if he'd crawled inside my head.

Tippy Frederickson began to laugh.

Evelyn sat down in the chair Billy had vacated and sipped her whisky, watching the cogs in my brain click through the ramifications of what they were asking.

"I know your sight had started to return before you went back to America, Jack," she told me with complete conviction.

Her statement shocked me. How did she know? Why didn't she say anything then? Did she just want to end the relationship too?

"It was the little things. As it started to come back, your eyes would move toward motion and almost seem to focus, and then they'd stop. You tried to hide it, but I knew. You don't have to admit it. I wanted you to escape. I knew if you stayed and went back to the front you would die. Like my brother. Like nearly all the others. It was a miracle that you survived as long as you did. I didn't want you to die. Not you. If the price for your survival was losing you, that was a small price to pay."

A tear ran down her cheek.

She knew! She'd known all along.

"I couldn't have gone back, Evelyn." I was surprised I spoke, but once I started, I couldn't seem to stop. "Just as I said last night, I wouldn't have made it through. No doubt about it. I'd be dead. Or in pieces. Instead of dead, I'm just a coward."

"Don't say that! You did more than most in a war that wasn't even yours."

"I joined to get you, Evelyn. I'll always remember the look you gave George Moore when you first saw him in uniform. I wanted you to look at me that way."

"I always looked at you like that, Jack. You just couldn't see it.

You didn't have to join to get me. I was there waiting for you. But ultimately it was the war, that awful war, that gave you to me and then took you away."

I was stunned by her admission. I had misjudged her. I had been sure she wanted me gone because she didn't want to be stuck with an angry, blind man, and I didn't blame her for that. I wanted to be gone too. But she had known! She had still loved me, and she let me go knowing it was the only way I could survive. I shook my head in amazement, but learning the truth didn't change anything. The man she had loved didn't survive the war. He was dead and gone. I still couldn't give her the child she so very much wanted.

"I'm sorry. Very sorry. But Evelyn, I can't do what you and Billy are asking. I'm not the man I was. It wouldn't be right for me to father your child."

"Why wouldn't it be right, Jack? Why? You've been with me before."

"I'm broken. My mind is fractured. You don't want a child with me. And you're married to Billy, goddamnit!"

"And he will be a fine father."

"To my child! Assuming it even works."

"It will work. I know. It will be your natural child, but I won't be having a child with you. I will be having a child with Billy. He will be the real father."

My stomach roiled.

Wild cackling echoed in the room. "I couldn't have planned this on my best day," Tippy Frederickson said, dancing a jig in front of the windows.

"I've found a girl! A girl I care about. It would be wrong." I threw Madeline out before me to shield me from her desperation. As I spoke the words, I realized they might even be true.

"We're not asking you to leave her. We're asking for help. A brief moment in a lifetime that will mean the world to us and cost you nothing."

Cost me nothing? My head told me that this would cost me plenty. My heart told me that they were my friends begging for my help. But I knew I would likely lose any remaining shreds of my self-respect.

"Please, Jack. Please."

Surely they didn't want this. This wasn't right. My stunned mind swirled, unable to hold on to any thoughts other than dismay and denial. This was a nightmare. It couldn't be real. Oh God, it couldn't be.

"Please," she said so softly I almost wasn't sure she had even spoken.

I hung my head.

I would do it.

"It won't be so horrible," Evelyn said, sensing my surrender. She rose and crossed the room to me. She cupped the scarred side of my face in her hand and leaned down.

The first kiss brought back a rush of memories and emotion that nearly overwhelmed me. The feel of her. The smell. The same eagerness and need, but she was no longer the girl I had known. She was a woman, and she was no longer my lover. I was a tool to an end, and she used me for that end.

She was right though. It wasn't so horrible.

BILLY JONES HADN'T RETURNED HOME BY THE TIME I LEFT Knightsbridge. The rain had stopped. As I walked the long block past the Harrod's department store, a depression unrelated to the ghosts in my head overwhelmed me. I sank into a funk of self-doubt and disgust. The war, disfigurement, Sarah, and now this. It all piled on, crushing me. I was a puppet mindlessly stumbling from one demand to the next, never choosing my own path. I was the shell of a man who had lost his way and all his dreams.

"You've earned every bloody groat of that self-loathing, you bastard!" Frederickson said with satisfaction. He was right. The dinner of the night before seemed like a thousand years ago.

I shuffled along the streets in the direction of Patricia's house. The fear of discovery I'd felt since returning to England was gone. It was replaced by an emptiness. Desolation. The war and its aftermath had sucked everything decent out of me.

And God help me, but I felt a guilty, secret joy of having had the forbidden fruit. I had stumbled into Evelyn's arms one more time, and I'd liked it.

Goddamn me! Hell, he already had.

I sensed the warm glow Tippy Frederickson felt at my thought.

In their dealings with me, the English saw what they expected to see. What they wanted to see. Murderer, criminal, agent, messenger, and ultimately, stud horse.

I choked out a bitter laugh standing in front of Patricia's house.

I went in and put Mitchell's borrowed coat back on the peg in the hallway.

I didn't know what to make of what had happened. I had no one to go to for guidance. There was no possibility I'd tell Mitchell what I'd done. I couldn't imagine his reaction to any description I might offer.

I wouldn't tell a soul what had happened. The one solace was that any child would be raised well and loved by two people I cared about. That would have to be enough.

It was time to leave and never return. I would go to Washington, do as the English demanded, and then face Reynolds and Armistan. With any luck, we'd all kill each other.

That night, Mitchell invited me to dine with Patricia and him. I declined. I wasn't fit to be in the company of friends. He sensed something wasn't right, but he didn't press me. Instead, we made plans to meet for breakfast.

I went to my room and took a scalding hot bath. I hoped to

wash away the smells and the memories of the day. I was only partially successful. The memories weren't going anywhere.

11

An Unnatural Angle

I was up early. Disgust at my conduct of the previous day made sleep impossible. Worries about the trip to Washington compounded my restlessness. Washington was the final hurdle before I confronted Armistan in New York. Part of me was eager for our meeting while part of me was terrified of it, but all of me wanted to be out of England.

Tippy was up with me, and he whispered abuse in my ears to tear at my confidence.

"You're just a gadfly, Frederickson," I told him. "Nattering on about cowardice, fear, and dishonor, but there are only two people in this country who believe I'm a coward. You and me. And only one of us is alive. And if there is one thing the war taught me, it's that it doesn't matter what I believe. It's all just goddamn luck anyway. And I'm lucky, you bastard."

"Luck runs out, Griffin. And you are still a loathsome scoundrel who took advantage of your best friend and his wife."

"I've forgiven myself, Tippy," I lied. "I helped them, and they're happy. The guilt is just in my head. Just like you are."

I *had* done what they asked. I might be ashamed of it, but I wasn't going to tell that bastard Frederickson. The best way to deal with the whole episode was to forget about it. That was what Evelyn and Billy would want.

I got a cup of coffee from Cook and went into the study to wait for Mitchell to come down. Despite my decision of the night before, I considered telling Mitchell what I had done, but Mitchell's good opinion meant too much to me. It certainly meant more than my own. I knew his perspective would help, but I wouldn't take the chance.

It was raining again. I needed a raincoat, and mine was still upstairs. This time I wouldn't be able to steal Mitchell's since he would be going with me. I went up to retrieve my own.

"It's raining. I'm getting my coat," I told him as I passed him as I went up and he came down the stairs.

"It's always raining," he answered over his shoulder.

We walked to Claridge's for breakfast. The restaurant was just busy enough that the hum of conversation covered the sound of our discussion as we ate.

"I hope you didn't disturb Patricia this morning," I said. I was still worried about her, and I was gently fishing to see how she was doing.

"Naw. She was still sleeping when I left." Mitchell stared into his coffee for a time. He knew what I was doing. "Griff, at times she seems fine and at others tired and almost beaten. It's got to be all this legal business: the citizenship question, Gavin's estate, her lack of control. She hates not having control. It does seem like the lawyers are making some progress, but it's all filtered through Reynolds. It's all so slow it's wearing on her."

"Did Reynolds come by yesterday?" I asked. I remembered he was supposed to bring some papers for Patricia to sign. My skin crawled at the thought of him.

"Yeah. But I was out when he came. If I didn't know better, I'd say Patricia tells him when I'll be gone. She knows I don't trust him."

"It's got to be tough for you too, Mitch. Look. Let's talk to her after breakfast. You both should go to Paris while I'm in the States. I'll be back as quick as I can. I'll meet you in France, and if things aren't resolved with her citizenship and Gavin's estate by then, we can all return to London together."

"You keep playing that same tune, but she's not leaving here until it's all straightened out. She seems to think it's all close to being resolved."

That prompted a snort of humor from Frederickson, who had joined us uninvited. Even he didn't believe Patricia's legal problems were any closer to resolution.

Once again, I considered telling Mitchell about my tryst with Evelyn if only to divert him from his problems. But I didn't have the courage.

"Of course you don't," Frederickson agreed.

We finished breakfast. I stopped by the head, and Mitchell went to the lobby.

When I came out, he was outside smoking and talking to the Claridge's doorman. Both men were chuckling, standing under one side of the hotel marquee, watching the crowds of scurrying pedestrians stream by with heads down and umbrellas clutched tightly.

Mitchell saw me, said something to the doorman, and patted him on the arm. He pulled up the collar on his coat and tugged his hat down to shield his face from the rain, which had taken on a decidedly horizontal slant. Mitchell stepped out from under the marquee to flick the stub of his cigarette into the gutter in front of a taxicab pulling to the curb at the hotel entrance.

Just before the taxi came abreast Mitchell, a man, flowing with the passing mass of bodies, stiff-armed him hard in the shoulder, knocking him into the street directly into the path of the cab. Mitchell twisted like an acrobat, but it did him no good. He was still off-balance and falling when the black automobile struck him. It flung his body into the back of a motorcar parked at the curb, collapsing its fabric top. The sharp bang of crumpling metal and the tinkling of shattered glass overwhelmed the sounds of traffic. A woman let out a horrified scream. Mitchell rolled off the back of the car onto the pavement.

By the time I pulled my horrified gaze from Mitchell back to the pedestrians, the attacker was gone, but I'd seen him. We'd locked eyes, just for an instant. I'd recognize him if I saw him again, and he knew it. His fear showed in his face as he hid in the passing crowds. I wavered between helping my friend and pursuing his attacker, but there really was no choice to make. I ran toward Mitchell, shouting for help. Claridge's doorman reached him first and knelt by his unmoving body. Blood was everywhere, but I told myself that was a trick of the rain. A gash ran across Mitchell's forehead, and his face was dripping crimson. His left arm was bent at an unnatural angle.

"Goddamn it, don't you be dead!" I heard myself hiss. I checked his neck for a pulse. A flutter against my fingers confirmed he lived. I pressed my handkerchief to the cut on his head and gently ran my other hand under his body, looking for more bleeding. I didn't find anything obvious, but God only knew what his insides looked like.

"We need a doctor!" I shouted to no one. I was screaming now. I was helpless and close to panicking. He would go into shock soon. I needed to get him out of the soaking downpour.

I took off my raincoat and laid it on the road next to his body.

"Help me carry him inside," I said to the doorman. Together, we carefully bundled Mitchell onto the coat and used it as a makeshift stretcher to carry him into the lobby. By then a doctor had been found and the ambulance service called. I was pushed out of the way by those more capable than I.

I collapsed into an overstuffed chair in the lobby. As I watched the volunteer doctor work on Mitchell, terror began to build in my gut.

"God, don't let William die," I whispered.

I almost laughed aloud at the prayer I knew had no power. Prayer had never done me any good. I'd said plenty over the past four years, but I meant this one more than all the others.

He was too good a man to die, but I knew that was an empty thought. Good had nothing to do with it.

If Mitchell died, I would be lost. Of that I had no doubt. It was a selfish thought, but I couldn't help it.

"You'd still have me," Tippy whispered in my ear with just the hint of a smile.

"Shut your fucking gob!" I snarled. A passing guest was shocked by my outburst, but my glare hurried him on. Mitchell's blood was still on my hands.

The doctor seemed to have the bleeding under control, and an ambulance appeared outside the hotel. Four attendants bustled in with a stretcher, and I hurried over to find out where they were taking him. They were all women, but I didn't have time to think about that. The lead attendant told me that they were transporting Mitchell to Endell Street Military Hospital in Covent Garden. She said the hospital was staffed by very experienced wartime doctors, who'd seen a lot of traumatic wounds. She was very calm. She spoke clearly with her hand on my shaking arm. She pulled Mitchell's personal information from my frantic brain. Name, address, next of kin. I was terrified they might need his father's address. They'd only need that if he died or was so horribly injured that he would not recover quickly. She could see my dismay and patted my arm.

"I've seen worse," she said. "He'll be fine." Her confidence reassured me, and I appreciated the lie. She must have been at this type of work for a while. Likely since 1914. It wouldn't surprise me if she'd worked in France like Maddy and Rachel Eisen had. I didn't have the presence of mind to learn her name.

She did, however, refuse to let me ride in the ambulance. She explained, with great sympathy, that they needed to focus on their patient and not his worried friend. I was grateful for her commitment to Mitchell.

I hurried back to Patricia's house on Aldford. She needed to know about Mitchell. Together, we would find a way to help him. To protect him. Someone had tried to kill Mitchell. Not someone. Reynolds. And the son of a bitch might have succeeded. The man who pushed him might be a stranger, but Reynolds was responsible. Patricia must have told him I was leaving for the States, and without Mitchell in his way, he could figure out how to convince Patricia to return to America and her father.

"Hackworth!" I bellowed as I burst through the front door. "Where is Mrs. Kingsbury? There's been an accident. Mr. Mitchell has been hurt. Hit by a motorcar."

Hackworth appeared in an instant, unflustered by the emergency, a Guards noncommissioned officer in butler's garb.

"Which hospital, sir?"

"Endell Street."

"A good choice, if unconventional," he said with reluctance. I didn't understand his comment, and it didn't matter anyway. Mitchell needed care quickly, and he was getting it.

"Where is Mrs. Kingsbury?"

"She is still in her chambers, sir. She asked not to be disturbed after you and Mr. Mitchell left for breakfast."

I started up the stairs two at a time. Hackworth, in his wisdom, left me alone.

I rapped twice on the bedroom door and was already opening it when I heard her soft call to enter. Still in her nightgown, Patricia was relaxed in bed. She was propped on her pillows and smoking.

"You need to get up. William's been hurt. Hit by a taxicab. Reynolds tried to kill him. We need to go to the hospital. Now!"

"What do you mean? William's hurt? What does Morgan have to do with it?" She tried to rouse herself, but she moved as if she were underwater.

"Patricia, what the hell's the matter with you? Get up! Mitchell's badly hurt. He's at the hospital. A man shoved him into traffic. I saw it. I'm sure Reynolds is responsible."

"John, that makes no sense." Reluctantly she put out the cigarette. "How badly is William hurt?"

It had taken longer than it should have for her to start to

show concern. Mitchell was right. She did seem beaten down. Sluggish. A word I'd never thought would apply to Patricia Kingsbury.

"Patricia, are you all right?"

"What? Yes. We're talking about William. How badly is he hurt?" she asked again with some of her old spirit coming through.

"I don't know. The ambulance service took him to Endell Street Military Hospital." I decided not to tell her about his head or his arm or about the grotesque *thump* his body made when it struck the motorcar.

"Let me get dressed, and we'll go to the hospital." Finally she threw her legs over the side of the bed. I chivvied her off the bed toward her closet.

"I'll be in the study," I said as I left the room.

I went back down the stairs and found Hackworth.

"Don't let Reynolds in this house. I am sure he's responsible."

"Really, sir? Should we call for the police?"

I didn't know if he was mocking me or serious. Had Mitchell or Patricia talked about my mental issues within his hearing?

"Course they have," Tippy told me with certainty. "Can't have a crazy man in the guest room without the lady's gentleman knowing about it, can they?"

"I saw a man push him into the road in front of a taxicab. I'll talk to the police at the hospital. If I have to wait for them here, I'll go crazy."

"Of course, sir. Did you apprehend the villain who attacked Mr. Mitchell?"

"What? No, I had to help Mitchell. He was bleeding and unconscious."

Was Hackworth criticizing me, telling me I should have pursued Mitchell's attacker? I started to get angry.

"He certainly is," Tippy told me.

Frederickson's comment stopped me from reacting. Anything Tippy said, I could safely assume was a lie designed to undermine me. He wanted me to destroy myself and would say anything that would advance that end.

"I'll be in the study when Mrs. Kingsbury comes down," I said.

I could feel the butler's eyes follow me down the hallway. Only when I was behind the closed door of the room did I feel safe from his gaze.

It didn't matter if Hackworth or anyone else thought I was crazy. I knew what I had seen. It wasn't a dogman or Woodrow Wilson who had pushed Mitchell. It was just a man. Average, about my age, medium height, brown hair. Ordinary. But not so ordinary I wouldn't remember him.

Surrounded by the quiet insulation of the books, I sat in a wingback chair, put my head in my hands, and let panic take me.

I felt like I had failed Mitchell because I hadn't taken the threat of Reynolds seriously enough. I'd thought the problem was just inside my head, but it was not. Mitchell had carried me to safety at the Meuse-Argonne, saved me during the Paris gunfight where Shed Bean had died, and rescued me from the basement in Basel, yet I couldn't do the same for him in London. Anger and fear boiled inside my chest.

Oh God, don't let him die.

He was my one and only friend, undemanding, always steady.

I thought of his crooked smile and the wicked twinkle in his eye.

Unexpectedly, I began to shake. Just a quiver at first, but in a few seconds, violent, uncontrollable trembling overcame me. I was shaking worse than I had when cold and bound to the dissection table in Basel. My mind raced. The images from the cellar danced before me. Wilson loping, Reynolds prancing, Armistan growling. All dogs, and not dogs. I could command neither my thoughts nor my limbs. I don't know how long I was locked in the battle to regain control of myself. Eventually the convulsions eased. My body relaxed, and my mind cleared. I didn't know what caused the attack or my recovery. My cheeks were wet from tears I didn't know I'd cried.

I was coming apart.

Frederickson nodded.

That nod enraged me. The anger burned away the lingering images of Wilson and Reynolds. It focused my mind.

I took a deep breath and roughly wiped my face.

I would kill Reynolds for his attack on Mitchell. I would kill Armistan for his part in the plot to restart the war. I just needed to hold on to my anger, to use it as a shield to keep the panic and terror at bay. And to keep Tippy away.

Mitchell would be fine. The ambulance attendant had told me so.

He was too smooth, too confident to be killed by a goddamn taxicab. Men like him weren't killed by the ordinary. Despite having seen good men, kind men, the most decent fellows in the world dead from disease, infection, and violence, I was comforted by the self-deception. Mitchell wasn't immune, but I needed the delusion because I needed him. I needed his friendship and, lately, his presence tethering me to reality. My reality was haunted by the bizarre and the unreal. He managed to keep me from spiraling too far into the fantastical hell in my head. He kept Tippy and Woodrow Wilson at bay. Mitchell wouldn't abandon me. He wouldn't desert me as I had deserted my mates. He was a good man, a better man. That thought, more than any other, allowed me to bring myself under control.

Damn Morgan Reynolds to hell.

12

A Favor in the Future

Hackworth had Patricia's car waiting in front of the house when she came down. Her staff was concerned, and they all saw her off on the way to the hospital. They all liked Mitchell.

"John, why do you think Morgan is responsible for this?" Patricia asked once her driver pulled away from the house.

"Who else wants him dead, Patricia? Who? The Krauts don't care about Mitchell. The Bolsheviks are all dead. There's only one person I can think of, and that's your close friend *Morgan Reynolds*!" I put all my fear and anger into his name. I wanted to hurt her, both for refusing to see the obvious and for not seeming to care enough.

"I'm sorry, John. I'm so sorry. I haven't been myself. I know it, but I just can't seem to help myself. The citizenship issues are so vexing, and nothing moves quickly in the law." She began to softly cry.

I stared fixedly out of my side window. I wouldn't let her manipulate me like she did Mitchell.

"Please, John. Don't be like that. I love William. I am worried about him too. I didn't attack him. Please don't blame me."

I turned away from the window. I was afraid and peevish, and I was going to take it out on her.

"Why not? You're the one who keeps Reynolds hanging around. You know he moons after you, and you let him, despite the fact that you're with Mitchell. I guess you're so used to men wanting you that you don't even notice it anymore," I said cruelly.

"That's not fair!" She was sore now. It was better than crying. I could deal with anger. "I haven't given Morgan any reason to believe he has a hope with me."

"It didn't look that way outside Claridge's when we saw the two of you coming back from the theater!"

"Don't tar me with that brush! Just because you thought that doesn't mean Morgan does. I can be kind to a man without leading him on. And I have to keep Morgan by my side. He's willing to assist me. And no one else has offered to help me manage my legal issues. Not William and not you. You two are great at gunfights but useless in the real world! Of course I rely on Morgan. I have no one else."

"The real world! You don't live in the real world. You live in a fucking fantasyland created by your wealth and your family. In the real world, people don't have millions of dollars, and they don't get away with murder!" I knew raising her murder of Gavin meant the gloves were off between us.

"Really? Well, I guess you don't live in the real world either. You've killed half the population of Europe, been interviewed by the police, been locked up, yet here you are. Free as a bird, and instead of *you* being in the hospital or the morgue, it's William. Some friend you are."

The driver was listening in, but I didn't care. I was sick of Mitchell treating her like a princess.

"And some girlfriend you are," I snarled the pitiful rejoinder as I turned back to the window. At least she wasn't crying.

After that, we didn't speak. The ride felt interminable, but neither of us would apologize. Perhaps this break had always been coming. I was sorry it would pain Mitchell. If he lived.

The hospital seemed to cover an entire city block. It was housed in a gloomy four-story early-Victorian building. The once red brick was now stained and streaked by the smoggy London air. The motorcar stopped at a heavy iron-faced gate. A stern-looking police constable stood before it. On one side of the gate, painted in large white letters, were the words MILITARY HOSPITAL and on the other ENDELL STREET, W.C.

"We're here about a patient who just arrived," the driver told the policeman.

"Pull on in, but you can't leave the motorcar in the courtyard. You'll have to leave it elsewhere." He pushed each side of the gate open. The driver pulled up behind an ambulance, which was parked near the main hospital entrance. The rain had driven everyone inside, and other than the ambulance and Patricia's automobile, the yard was empty.

I was out of the car before it had stopped.

I passed through the door into a receiving area that immediately reminded me of the police station in Hyde Park. A desk sat in the middle of the space, but instead of an overweight aging copper, we found a young woman in some sort of blue uniform.

"We're here about William Mitchell. He was struck by a taxicab and was just transported here," I said.

"Actually, I'm Mr. Mitchell's fiancée, Patricia Kingsbury, and this is his brother, John," Patricia said with a quick glance at me. I wasn't going to argue. She was more clever than I. As family, we would get as much information as they had as soon as they had it.

"He was just wheeled into the surgical theater. There are some benches where you can wait, but it may be some time." She gestured to wooden pews on two sides of the walls.

We sat silently on the hard wood. Patricia smoked, and when I got tired of sitting, I paced. Tippy walked with me, as if he were sympathetic. Sarah was nowhere to be seen.

Patricia was right. I didn't like it, but she was. I *was* only good for fighting. It was no surprise to me that she found me to be useless in helping with her *real-world* problems.

Mitchell, on the other hand, was clever and thoughtful. He could have helped Patricia. For him not to offer meant he must have felt that his contributions weren't needed or welcome. He was all too aware that she was a beautiful, rich, and capable woman. He wouldn't want to horn in where she didn't want him. He was being careful. She didn't see that. Instead, she felt abandoned.

I was being unfair to her, but I'd be damned if I'd apologize while Mitchell was on death's door. Mitchell was my concern, my only concern. I needed to find a way to protect him from Reynolds while he was in the hospital and I was in the States.

I'd contact Wag McDonald at the Wellington Pub.

"I'm going out," I said to Patricia abruptly. "I'll be back as quick as I can."

She shrugged as if my abandoning her during her vigil was to be expected. I considered explaining to her why I had to go, but I was still sore. She also wouldn't understand the need for Mitchell to have trustworthy men monitoring his safety since she didn't see Reynolds as a threat. She thought he was in her thrall. A man who was both obedient and perfectly happy under her thumb. I knew differently.

I walked up Endell Street and flagged down a taxicab on Shaftesbury Avenue. I arrived at the Wellington just as the publican was unlocking the doors. Inside, tables and benches filled the wood-paneled space and attractive arched ceilings curved overhead. It was a comfortable place for a drink, but I wasn't there for a beer.

"Help you, sir?" the publican asked once he was behind the long bar.

"I need to leave word for Mr. McDonald. I need to speak with him as soon as possible." I passed him a five-pound note.

"Mr. McDonald. Well, there's more than one now isn't there?"

"Wag."

"Ah. And what would your name be, sir?"

I told him.

"Rory!" he called through a doorway at the side of the bar.

An eight- or nine-year-old boy appeared.

"Yessir?"

"Run to Mr. Wag's and tell him a Mr. Griffin needs to speak with him. And be quick!" The little boy shifted scared eyes toward me, nodded, and ran out the front door as two workmen came in.

"Don't know if the boy will find him. Drink while you wait?"

"Sure. A pint of bitter."

He pulled the beer, and I took it to one of the cushioned booths.

The boy returned in a few minutes. He glanced at me as he hurried over to the bar. He stood on the footrail and leaned onto the bar top to report to the proprietor in a whisper.

Three more men entered and ordered drinks. I had to force patience while I waited for the barman to serve them. When he finished, he came around the end of the bar to my booth.

"Mr. McDonald's on his way. Should be here shortly."

I nodded, sipped my beer, and did my best to wait calmly.

As I drained the last of my bitter, Wag McDonald pushed through the doors. He was dressed in an expensive suit and might have been a banker from the City of London. He looked to the publican, who nodded toward my booth.

I stood as McDonald approached.

"Aah, my favorite Yank," he said with a smile and a hand thrust toward me.

"Know many Americans, Mr. McDonald?" I asked as we shook.

"No. You're the only one. And of course, the little fella who found me mentioned the devil hisself was waiting for me at the Wellington. He was surprised to discover that Satan was a Yank. I told him you just looked like the devil," he said, laughing.

I was too worried about Mitchell to join him, and he noticed.

"Something bothering you then?"

"An associate of mine, a good friend, was attacked this morning. Pushed into traffic. He's at the Endell Street Military Hospital. I saw the man who pushed him, but he got away. He's still out there, and I am sure he will try again."

"That's a shame," he said. I couldn't tell if he was sincere.

"I leave for the States tomorrow, and I need men to go to the hospital to guard him."

"It sounds to me like maybe you should postpone your trip to America."

"I have no choice. I have to go. The authorities here require it."

That got his interest.

"Authorities?"

"To be blunt, I'm an errand boy for your secretary of air and war. I either do a job for him or the Met will toss me back into Brixton."

He laughed again.

"You are a marvel, you are! You're running errands for Winston bloody Churchill?"

I nodded.

"What the hell could he want from you?"

"I need to deliver some letters." I didn't want to tell him the recipients. I needed McDonald's help, but I also knew he was a gangster. He would manipulate me for his benefit, and he wasn't going to help me without getting something in return. Not so different from House, Clemenceau, and Churchill.

"You're to be a postman. Perfect. Well, Mr. Postman, what do you want from me?"

"I'd like a few of your boys, like the ones who introduced themselves to me in Brixton, to keep an eye on my buddy."

"I might be able to arrange that, but they won't be able to get into the hospital. The women who run that place are worse than the King's Guards. Few men are allowed access without good reason."

"Women run Endell Street?"

"Course. Many think it's the best hospital in the city, but the old horses there won't let just any bloke wander into the hospital. Very protective, they are."

"Good. That's good." I didn't know that women ran Endell Street. It seemed odd to me, but then the British had women coppers too. I was happy for the women at Endell to guard Mitchell as well as Wag's men. "The man who attacked my friend was ordinary. Medium height, brown hair. I'm sure he'd been a soldier."

"Weren't we all? I'll get a couple of boys there this afternoon."

"What'll it cost me?" I asked.

"Happy to do a favor for an ally."

I snorted. "Sure you are. I should be back in a month or so. I don't know how long he'll be in the hospital, and chances are good once he's out, he'll go to a house on Aldford to recuperate. Can your people watch him that long?"

"Of course. I might have to put some youngsters on him, but they won't be far from help, if it's needed. Keep in mind they're not going to get killed to protect your mate. They'll look intimidating, but I won't have my boys killed."

"I understand. Just having them watching will be a relief. You'll let me know when you decide what you want for payment?"

"Sure I will. A favor in the future maybe. A fellow who knows Winston Churchill. Well, that fellow could be valuable."

That's exactly what I was afraid of, but I had no choice.

———

AFTER THE MEETING WITH MCDONALD, I TOOK THE TUBE BACK TO Leicester Square and walked to the hospital. Patricia was still sitting on the bench when I returned. She looked like she hadn't moved.

"Look how pathetic she is. She looks terrified," Tippy said unsympathetically.

And I did look. Across the lobby, Patricia Armistan Kingsbury sat huddled in on herself. Her bleak, vacant gaze passed over me without any sign of recognition as I entered the hospital. Her face intimately conveyed how desolated she was by Mitchell's condition. She appeared to feel friendless and frightened. Without Mitchell, she was more alone than I had ever been.

"Thanks, Tippy," I said under my breath. His disdain had helped me see her more clearly.

I had selfishly been worried about what Mitchell's loss would mean to me. I was consumed by the thought of losing my only friend, but Mitchell wasn't my only friend. Yes, he was certainly the closest, but I had others who cared about me. I had the entire café-crawling menagerie in Paris. I had Madeline. I still had a family who loved me. True, I didn't see my sisters often, but I never doubted that they loved me.

Whom did Patricia have if Mitchell died? Not her father. He was a perverted monster who sought to use her for his own ends. Reynolds? Me? She was right to be so devastated.

I stopped in the middle of the lobby when another thought struck me like a blow.

Patricia had already lost her best friend. She had lost Sarah. Sarah, who was as close to her as Mitchell was to me. I had never even thought about how Sarah's death affected her. Patricia had just seemed so impervious to pain and vulnerability that I hadn't genuinely considered how she felt about Sarah's death. I faced that now with Mitchell, but I was infinitely better off than Patricia. This thought was both comforting and damning. Patricia had no one. Not Reynolds, who wanted her for her money and her body. Not me. I'd made no bones about the fact that it was Mitchell who was my friend, not her. Yet when Sarah died, Patricia had tried to comfort me. She had sat beside my sickbed. She had supported Mitchell when he rescued me from Switzerland. She had tried to be a friend to me, but for some reason, I couldn't get past her murder of her husband even though he needed killing.

Standing on the checkered tiles in the middle of the Endell Street Military Hospital lobby, I realized how hypocritical I had been. How selfish. She was right. I had murdered half the population of Europe. All she had done was kill one deluded Red. She'd killed Gavin Kingsbury to be free. Free of him. Free of her father. One dead Bolshevik, who sought to restart a horrific war, and I couldn't forgive her for killing him.

I felt sick to my stomach at how I had behaved. She needed a friend. We both did.

I crossed to her bench and sat down next to her.

"Patricia."

She looked up at me. She took a moment to refocus on the present. I gave her the time.

"I am sorry," I said. "I am sorry I blamed you for what happened to Will. Sorry I didn't think about how little help I have given you. Sorry I didn't consider you or your feelings with Sarah or with Will. I'm sorry I didn't think about what you'd gone through with your father and Gavin. I'm sorry. I've been a very poor friend to you."

She pulled my hand into her lap and began to cry. It was a hard cry. She tried to suppress it, but deep sobs shook her small frame. I didn't know how to comfort her, so I held her hand tightly as if that would help. I'd had no idea that so much emotion was trapped inside her icy exterior. We sat together hip to hip as her body quaked from the emotions that she'd bottled up for months, if not years.

She stopped crying after a time, but she held on to my hand and rested her head on my shoulder. We remained on that bench, not speaking. We probably hadn't resolved our differences and misunderstandings, but I felt closer to her. I felt like maybe she was my friend as well. She certainly wanted to be. I was glad. Mitchell would be happy.

A middle-aged woman came from a corridor leading into the foyer. She appeared to have emerged straight from the operating theater, for she still wore an operating gown over a blue uniform. The receptionist looked up, recognized her, and immediately stood.

"Dr. Murray?"[1] she said.

"Sit, Constance, I'm here to talk to our patient's family," she said just loudly enough for me to hear. Scottish accent. I found myself hoping that Scotland gave birth to doctors as good as her infantrymen.

Unfortunately, the doctor's serious face under her operating cap made my heart sink. She was a thin, stern-looking woman, and the red marks on her cheeks where the surgical mask had dug into her skin did nothing to soften that impression.

My dread built with each step she took across the floor.

Tippy's joy at what was coming washed over me. He knew, and I nearly howled my denial at the woman. This female Scots doctor with Mitchell's blood on her operating apron was going to tell us he was dead.

I jumped up, and Patricia stood with me. I still held her hand.

The doctor could see the tension radiating from the two of us as she approached. She tried to soften what was to come with a smile. Her severe look eased, and a small seed of hope took root in my chest.

"Mrs. Kingsbury, Mr. Mitchell, I'm Dr. Murray. I have been taking care of William." It took me a moment to remember that she thought I was Mitchell's brother.

"Thank you, Doctor. How is he?" Patricia asked.

"He's out of surgery and in recovery. His body was severely injured." She looked us both in the eye to make sure we understood exactly how dire his condition was. "A compound

---

1. Dr. Flora Murray. May 8, 1869–July 28, 1923. Physician and suffragette.

fracture of the leg and a broken arm, but he is young and strong. I have seen worse both in France and here at Endell Street. Barring infection, his body should recover."

"Oh thank God," Patricia said, squeezing my hand tighter.

"He did receive quite a blow to the head," she continued. "It is this that we are most concerned with now. We had to relieve the intracranial pressure. We'll remain alert to any excess swelling, but the procedure went well."

It sounded like the doctor had fished around inside Mitchell's skull. I was afraid to ask, but I felt like I had no choice.

"Surgery on his brain, Doctor?" I asked. It felt odd to call this woman *doctor*, but she carried herself with a professionalism that eased the awkwardness.

"Not on the brain itself. He had a good crack on the napper, and we just needed to set that right," she said, using the slang to minimize what they'd had to do, and I was willing to let her for both Patricia's sake and my own.

"As I said, he's out of surgery now. We have fewer patients since the war is over, and we are able to put him into a private room. Once he's settled, I'll send someone out to get you. You can sit with him for a time. Hearing your voices should be good for him, but don't expect him to respond."

"Thank you, Doctor," Patricia said fervently.

The dread I had felt as the doctor approached threatened to return. I'd known far too many men who had made it to the aid station or even the hospital only to die from infection or disease.

"That's right, Jackie boy, he's still going to die," Frederickson promised me.

I closed my eyes and took a deep breath and focused on Dr. Murray. On her confidence. Her apparent ability. He may still die, but he was in the doc's hands now. She exuded competence and toughness. I disregarded Tippy and put my faith in her.

After a short time, a female orderly, also in what I came to realize was the Endell Street uniform, brought us to Mitchell's room. He lay on his back with his head swathed in bandages.

Cuts and scrapes covered much of what we could see of his face. His left leg was raised and in traction; his left arm was in a cast. He looked awful, but his breathing seemed steady.

I pulled the one chair in the room next to the bed for Patricia. I put it exactly where she had placed the chair when she sat next to me after I'd been shot in Paris. She sat and gently placed a hand on Mitchell's undamaged arm.

"Patricia, it looks like William will be here for a few days." I was trying to sound optimistic.

She glanced at me, then went back to watching Mitchell.

"It's almost as if he knew there was a hospital run solely by ladies." She looked up at me. "You have to admit he has a way with women. I'm just pointing out that if anyone could figure out a way to get sent to a hospital full of ladies, it would be Mitchell."

That comment got a smile. "Even William wouldn't go so far as to leap into traffic," she said.

"No. He had help."

"What happened, John? Tell me what happened. I know you blame Morgan, but tell me everything."

I did as she asked as dispassionately as I could. I described our breakfast and Mitchell waiting for me outside with the doorman. I closed my eyes and did my best to recall the attack exactly as it happened. The passing crowd. The unexpected shove. I didn't describe to her what I had seen of the motorcar striking Mitchell. She wasn't asking about that and didn't need to hear it.

"And the man who pushed him?"

"Ordinary, Patricia. Ordinary. He looked like a thousand other men in London. Maybe tens of thousands. Dark eyes. Dark hair under his hat. Medium height. Easily swallowed by the crowd." The bland picture of the attacker I delivered convinced me I had done the right thing to go to McDonald. Even if I told the police everything. They would never find Mitchell's would-be assassin.

I needed to protect Mitchell, but unless I could get a reprieve from Churchill, I would be leaving in the morning. Once

Mitchell was out of the hospital, he would be a target again. Maybe even before then. I hoped the women of Endell Street would guard him closely. I knew Wag McDonald's boys would do so from outside.

"Patricia, once William is recovered enough, you both need to go back to Paris." She started to speak, and I held out a calming hand. I didn't want to fight again. "I know you have to resolve the estate and your citizenship, but there are people here who want Mitchell dead. In Paris, we have friends. Both of you would be safer."

"John, I don't have any real friends in Paris, and I can't get my problems straightened out there. I have to be here. William could go back without me if he wants."

"He would never do that," I said with certainty. I remained quiet for a moment, considering whether to tell her about Wag and his men. I decided I had no choice.

"Patricia, I've arranged for a few men to watch over Mitchell while he's here and when he gets out."

"How on earth did you manage that?" She was surprised. "Kell and Churchill?"

"No. Nothing so formal as that. I asked a fellow I met in Brixton who's part of a gang here in London. Hell, I'm sure he's the leader. He agreed to help me, and I'll owe him a favor or two."

"John, was that wise? A gangster. You might have jumped us out of the frying pan and into the fire."

"Maybe, but I'm pretty sure it will be me in the fire and not you or Will. And we have no choice. If I'm gone, Mitchell injured like this"—I gestured to the bed—"would be easy pickings for anyone who wants to hurt him."

She thought about what I'd said and finally nodded. She might not believe it was Reynolds who directed the attack on Mitchell, but she couldn't deny that someone had attacked him.

As the afternoon wore on, I went out and found Patricia's driver and agreed on a place to meet when we left the hospital. When I returned, I borrowed a chair from another room. Patricia and I talked about Paris and the days I'd spent with Sarah at the Hôtel de Vendôme. It was less painful now to speak of Sarah. It all felt like a long time ago, and the sting of her loss had faded.

As five o'clock neared, an orderly warned us that visiting hours were ending. Patricia kissed Mitchell on his cheek, I patted him lightly on his uninjured arm, and together we walked toward the lobby. Part of the way down the corridor, Patricia looped her arm through mine. I didn't say anything, and I didn't look at her. We both seemed to value the contact.

We confirmed with the attendant at the reception desk that we would return in the morning, wished her a good evening, and left. It was still light and promised to be for another hour or so, but we were both knackered.

Upon returning to her house, Patricia quickly reported on Mitchell's condition to the staff. We agreed to leave for the hospital at nine o'clock in the morning. She then retired to her room. She wouldn't be coming down for dinner, and I wouldn't either.

13

An Airless Scream

The next morning, I was waiting in the study for Patricia to appear while contemplating the likelihood of delaying my trip to the United States by a few days. While I might not be able to postpone it long, if I could just miss the sailing of the *Adriatic*, I might get a few more days to watch over Mitchell and to investigate the attack. At least I'd have time to have a chat with Morgan Reynolds if I could find him.

But I knew I couldn't count on any delay. I went to Patricia's desk and sat down. I pulled open the drawer where I knew her stationery was stored. Along with the paper and envelopes, the pen and inkwell were still there. Reynolds's fancy cigarettes that had been there before were not.

I took three envelopes and three sheets of paper and laid them on the desk. I would try to secure more help. McDonald and his men were better than having no one at all, but I wanted some friends I could trust.

The first letter I wrote was to Eugene Bullard. I told him Mitchell had been attacked, that I had to return to the States for a time, and that I believed someone might attack Mitchell in the hospital. I asked him to send help. It was unfair of me, but I had no choice.

I then made a second copy. I addressed one envelope to "Eugene Bullard, Zelli's Club, rue de Caumartin, Paris, France." The second, I addressed to "Eugene Bullard, 15 rue Mansart, Paris, France." Unfortunately, I had no better addresses. I couldn't remember Zelli's street number at all. I hoped the French postmen were diligent enough to deliver at least one of the letters to Eugene.

I wrote a third letter to Stanton Simms at the Hôtel de Crillon, the headquarters for the American mission to France. Simms had been an assistant to House, and he remained in Paris with House's return to the United States in late June. I advised Simms of the attack on Mitchell and my mission to Washington. I requested that he send a telegram to House advising him I was coming. My letter to Paris should arrive sooner than my steamship from Southampton to New York City.

A discreet tap at the door pulled me from my half-baked plans for protecting Mitchell and avoiding returning to America.

"Two policemen are here for you, sir." Hackworth had slightly opened the door to deliver the message.

I stood and ran my hands through my hair. What the hell could they want?

"Show them in please."

I wondered where Patricia was. I had hoped we could have left for the hospital earlier.

In a few moments, Inspectors Fair and Norton stood in the study with me.

"What can I do for you gentlemen?" I asked.

"It's what we can do for you," Detective Inspector Fair said with false cheer. "We're here to drive you to Southampton. We're your chauffeurs, if you like."

I'd forgotten that Churchill had promised to have me driven to Southampton. It never occurred to me that the two coppers would be my escorts.

"Gentlemen, something terrible has happened, and I have to delay my trip to the United States. My good friend, William Mitchell, whom I believe you interviewed, was struck by a taxicab yesterday morning in front of Claridge's. I'm sure you understand."

"We certainly understand, Mr. Griffin," Fair said sweetly. "But a traffic accident does not change our orders."

"Actually, he was pushed in front of the taxicab. I saw the man who pushed him, and I'd recognize him if I saw him again." I hoped if the accident appeared to be an attempted murder, that might sway them. "We need to find the man, and I can help you. I know you wouldn't want to leave a would-be murderer loose." I didn't mention my belief that Reynolds was responsible. Patricia's reaction had been enough to warn me that I needed some real evidence of his involvement.

"A murderer on the loose. It's almost hard to believe," Fair said with obvious sarcasm.

Norton glanced at him sideways and said, "That's terrible news, sir. We both found Mr. Mitchell to be a likable, honest bloke. Unfortunately, our orders from Director Thomson himself are quite clear. We are to pick you up and put you on the steamship at Southampton. No ifs, ands, or buts about it."

"I'm certain he'd reconsider. Let's call him. I'm the only witness to the attack, and I can't leave Mitchell injured and alone."

"He won't be alone." Patricia had chosen that moment to arrive in all her stylish glory. Her face was made up and her fatigue and distress of the day before just a memory. "I'll stay with him, and we'll get additional help to watch over him, so you needn't worry, John."

Detective Inspector Fair was delighted by her timing and her words.

Why was she undermining me? Did she want me gone?

"I saw his attacker. I'm needed here," I objected.

"It was a public street, sir. I'm sure we'll find other witnesses.

It'll just take a little leg work to find 'em, but that's the job, isn't it?" Norton said.

I shook my head. "Gentlemen, please. Just a few days. That's all I need."

"I'm afraid that's not possible. We have the authority to use whatever means are necessary to deliver you to the ship. Even arrest," Fair said with a grim smile, taking a step forward. "I trust you'll resist?"

"Stop," Patricia ordered. "John, it will be fine. You took some precautions yesterday, and I will take more today. We will keep William safe. You just need to hurry back. If you delay now, you'll delay your return."

She put her hand on my arm. She could sense my resistance and anger. "Please don't fight them. I need to go to the hospital, and I don't want to have to worry about you too."

"You never have to worry about me, Patricia. I can take care of myself."

"Oh, John, if only that were true." She turned to the door. "Hackworth is bringing your bag down now."

So much for remaining to watch over Mitchell. It made no sense to fight the Metropolitan Police, Kells, and Churchill. Even if I called Billy Jones to seek his help, he would be powerless against his boss and Churchill.

"Patricia, you can reach me at the Hotel Pennsylvania in New York. Please let me know how Will is doing."

I took my bag from Hackworth.

"Off we go. Don't want to delay aiding and abetting a murderer's escape from the country, do we?" Fair said, turning for the door.

I didn't bother to respond.

THE DRIVE TO SOUTHAMPTON WAS UNREMARKABLE. I SAT IN THE back of the noisy Model T and didn't speak. The coppers ignored me until they dropped me at the quayside. The smell of the ocean competed with that of the coal smoke from the vessel.

Norton handed me a leather packet. "Your tickets, money, and the letters you are to deliver."

"Can't believe the bloody toffs are paying you to run away," Fair said, spitting in disgust.

Norton turned back to the automobile, and Fair followed. I didn't think they ever expected to see me again. They left without a wave, but I did get one last glare from Fair.

I made my way to the gangway, which was crowded with other passengers boarding, and I heard a familiar voice call out to me.

"Hello, Jack! Hello!"

Billy Jones, who had clearly just exited a taxicab, waved his hat at me to get my attention. He had a broad smile on his face, and he collected his suitcases from the cab and hurried over.

My stomach turned at the sight of him.

"I've been ordered to go to Washington as well. Sir Basil dropped the news on me as we left the office last evening. The powers that be decided the letters alone aren't enough. Churchill wants me to coordinate with our embassy staff so that they will supplement the letters with in-person persuasion. Of course, I thought you weren't going for days. I'm to give you any assistance you might need. And I need to get to Washington to brief our people there so they are ready to follow up once you deliver the letters. So here I am. I've been packing and tidying up at home all night."

So Thomson and Kell had decided they needed to send a babysitter to keep me honest. Or perhaps it was Churchill. Trust had to be as rare as diamonds in the corridors of Whitehall. But to send Billy Jones! I would have rather they'd sent Detective Inspector Fair to keep an eye on me. With him, at least, I knew where I stood, but with Jones? What did he think of me now? I knew what I thought of myself. How could he think of me any differently? The thought of traveling with him made me ill, but I had no choice. He was my friend. I had done what he and Evelyn had asked, and it would be unfair to treat him poorly now. I'd agreed. It was my fault, not his for asking.

"Billy!" I forced a smile onto my face. "I'm sorry Sir Basil sent you to chaperone me, but I'm happy to have the company."

He dropped one of his cases and seized my hand.

"I'm glad to come, Jack. I hope I can help. And Jack, thank you. I know it was a lot to ask, but thank you. Evelyn sends her best."

I felt myself redden at his thanks and his mention of Evelyn.

"Billy, you and Evelyn are my friends. Please don't mention it." I said the last lightly, but I meant it with all my heart.

"Of course, of course." He patted my arm and led me up the gangway.

The RMS *Adriatic* was an enormous ship even if it was not as large as the *Mauritania*, which had brought me to Europe to chase after Patricia Armistan. The primary difference I could see between the two ships was that the *Adriatic* had only two funnels compared to the four of the *Mauritania*. I didn't know if that meant the *Mauritania* was faster, but I guessed it did. That was bad because I wanted my time with Jones to be as short as possible. I also wanted to get to the States as fast as possible.

To keep me friendly, the British provided a first-class berth. Jones was also in first class, which made sense if he was to keep an eye on me. With our bags in hand, two stewards showed us to our rooms. Unfortunately, our cabins were directly across the passageway from each other. Like it or not, I was going to be seeing more of Billy.

The ship was ridiculously luxurious. Not so different from the *Mauritania*. Patricia would feel right at home. I supposed Sarah would, too, were she not moldering in the dirt. Her shade nodded her agreement in my mind. Maddy, well, she'd be at home anywhere.

As we navigated the way to our berths, the senior steward described to us the extravagant amenities available on board. He had the younger, acne-plagued hand tailing behind us and carrying most of the bags.

"We've a full jazz band for dancing in the evenings, a swimming pool, and a Turkish bath," he said enthusiastically. "There's also a gymnasium."

A gym. Excellent, but that was for tomorrow. For the immediate future, perhaps a drink was in order.

"And the first-class lounge?"

"Of course, sir. It's forward on deck A and overlooks the promenade deck below," he said pointing toward the bow of the ship.

"Drinks in an hour, Jones?" I asked.

"That long?" Billy said, joking.

"I figured we could watch the departure from there," I answered as if I had really planned it.

"An hour it is."

"That would give you time to explore some of the other amenities of the *Adriatic*," the senior steward noted. He had stopped outside of a cabin door, unlocked it, and handed the key to Billy.

"And your bags?"

Billy identified his luggage.

The steward turned to the door across the passage. "And your stateroom, sir."

He gave me the key, and I put two shillings in his hand.

"Remember, gentlemen, the *Adriatic* will be making a brief stop in Cherbourg, France."

Now that was interesting. I could jump ship when we docked, but the only reason I would do so would be to return to England. With Jones across the hall, the English would know immediately, and I'd be arrested in short order if I showed up in London without completing Churchill's errand.

The pimply-faced steward settled my bag in my cabin. I told him I'd unpack my things myself but gave him two shillings as well. I wanted him attentive. I stowed my clothes, hanging my suits and dinner jacket in the en suite bathroom and running the water hot to steam out the wrinkles.

Even though it left me feeling vulnerable, I left the .45 in its shoulder holster buried under my folded clothes. I didn't want to wear it on the ship. There was simply too much opportunity for someone to see it and raise questions. I also didn't want Billy to know I had the pistol, which happened to be the same one that killed two of the men at the Savoy. Without Mitchell to watch my back, I was feeling very naked indeed.

I wondered briefly if Tippy would cross the Atlantic with me.

"Of course I'm coming. I wouldn't miss this shipwreck for the world," he answered, snickering at his pitiful joke.

"Bastard," I said under my breath.

His response reminded me that my major problem for the next few weeks was in my head and not in the first-class lounge. I could handle Billy, and Mitchell and Reynolds were out of reach. All I could do was work quickly to deliver Churchill's messages.

I sat on the bunk and took the letters from the packet. Three of them. All sealed and addressed just as Churchill had promised they would be: one for the president, one for House, and one for Lodge. I didn't even know how I would approach the president or Senator Lodge. I would start with House based on the letter I had sent to Simms. I had no better plan. I would take the train to Washington, likely side by side with Billy.

I went in search of the first-class lounge. I would establish a routine in the morning, but for the time being, sitting in a comfortable chair and nursing a whisky while I waited for Jones made good sense to me.

Deck A was close and the lounge staff helpful. Jones had not yet arrived. In a short time, I was seated with my drink before me, studying the other passengers. Many appeared to be English couples traveling to America likely to visit a country less affected by war than their home. I wondered briefly if any German agents might be hiding among them, and my skin crawled at the thought.

Frederickson was amused at my discomfort, but Sarah put a reassuring hand on my arm. Unfortunately, I found it difficult to be comforted by a ghost or a hand I could not feel.

I shook my thoughts free from the dead and considered the immediate future.

The British had forced this delay upon me. I would use it wisely. I would exercise as I had with Bullard in Paris. My mind might be cracked, but I could make my body strong. I would plan my confrontation with Armistan and Reynolds. Of course, my stomach knotted as I considered confronting the two. Fear was part of it, but the cellar in Basel had expanded my feelings toward them beyond what was normal. I did not think of them as men. I remembered them being in that cold, damp space with me. Taunting me. Part hound. Inhuman. Wrapped in a sinister shroud created by my brain and the mescaline.

It occurred to me then that perhaps Churchill had given me a gift if I could find a way to use it. I was working for the British and the American governments. As liaison between the two, I was the agent of both. I was going through New York City at their direction with an officer of the British government. I had an alibi, and if I could just be clever enough to use it, I could take care of Armistan in New York as we traveled through. Murder him now. My heart beat faster as I decided I would use the opportunity I'd been given. I wouldn't go to Washington right away. I would delay for a day or two. I would investigate Armistan, his routine, his friends, his habits. If the opportunity presented itself, I would kill him. If not, on my return to London, I would have to come back through New York. I would have a second chance to kill him, ideally in a way that did not implicate me.

Sarah, now sitting next to me, nodded in satisfaction.

"Of course you'd like the idea," I told her. "You hated Armistan."

"Yes, I did, and for good reason. I'd be glad for you to kill him. He's why I'm dead," she said.

Armistan was certainly to blame for the conspiracy to kill Clemenceau, but Sarah's stubborn love for her dead husband was the real cause of her death. There was no point in arguing. She looked hurt as the thought entered my head, and I shrugged. She was dead, and it wasn't wise to chat with her in the first-class lounge.

As I considered delivering Armistan's punishment for Sarah, a genuinely despicable thought occurred to me. I discarded it immediately, but the fact that it sprang into my brain was telling. I felt disgusted that it had wormed its way into my head. I had considered that, if push came to shove, I could blackmail Billy Jones into being my alibi in New York City. He would do whatever I asked of him. If he didn't, I could simply tell the world about Evelyn and me and their baby.

"Now that's a plan that's worthy of you," Tippy Frederickson said.

AT DINNER THAT NIGHT, JONES AND I HAD COMPANY AT OUR sitting. Since I was going to be around Billy, I needed to find a way to overcome the awkwardness of our relationship after the engineered tryst with Evelyn. Fortunately, I needn't have worried about it. Billy remained the same fellow I had gravitated to at university. The same biting sense of humor. The same unwillingness to suffer fools. He made it easy for me to forget that I had sex with his wife. Most of the time.

We were seated with an older Canadian couple, the Flavelles, and an American army lieutenant colonel and his wife, the Prescotts. The Canadians had been visiting their daughter and new grandchild near London and were traveling back to Toronto. The Americans were returning to the United States. He was leaving the service, and they were going home to Albany.

Since I was worried about Mitchell and uncomfortable around Billy, I was poor company at that first dinner. Jones carried the conversation for the two of us while I ignored the dead haunting the edges of my vision. Of course, the conversation came around to how we happened to be traveling together.

"Work. But we've been friends since 1913 when Jack came over from Texas for his education," Billy told the table. "Honestly, I'm not sure how he was accepted into Durham University."

"Low standards," I quipped.

"Everyone knows that while they can ride, rope, and shoot in Texas, reading is not a prerequisite for children there," Billy responded.

The two couples laughed.

"Fortunately, I had Mr. Jones to teach me my English ABC's. They're different from in Texas," I assured them.

"We lived along the same hall in Hatfield College," Billy continued. "No one liked the Yank, so I took pity on him. We've been friends ever since."

"It's funny. I don't remember it that way."

"Of course you don't. You were so befuddled by all things British that I doubt you remember much at all," he said teasingly.

"Well, there wasn't much to remember of the second year. It was 1914 after all."

"Did you remain at university after the war started, Mr. Griffin?" Colonel Prescott asked. "I'm sure most of your English friends would have joined the army in August or September."

"He did not remain at Durham," Billy said, jumping in. "As you would expect, all our school chums volunteered. All very patriotic. But Jack insisted on joining and signed up too. We were all very moved by his gesture." His voice cracked a bit, and he stopped speaking. I was touched by his emotion. I'll be damned. Billy Jones really did think the world of me.

"He's a fool," Tippy stated.

"Somehow Jack putting on the khaki meant America was with us," Jones finished.

"That's very noble of you," old man Flavelle said.

The entire table looked at me for some response.

I shook my head and told the truth. "I did it for a girl."

They all laughed, but Billy didn't. He looked at me and nodded.

I wanted to shift the conversation, and I turned to Lady Flavelle,[1] who was seated to my right, and asked, "Will you be in New York City long?"

I didn't fool anyone. They could tell I was uncomfortable, but Lady Flavelle was happy to talk about herself.

"Yes, for a few days. Sir Joseph[2] ran the Imperial Munitions Board for the Canadian government. He is close to many of the members of the American equivalent, some of whom live in New York. We will spend some time with them. Sir Joseph was awarded a baronetcy from the British for his work, and they have all insisted that we must see them so they can congratulate him."

"That's quite an achievement, but what did the Imperial Munitions Board do, ma'am? I'm embarrassed to say that I've never heard of it."

"During the war, the board ensured that war material, particularly artillery shells, were manufactured and delivered efficiently," she said with obvious pride in either her husband's work or his baronetcy.

Sir Joseph was listening in and nodded. "Helped you men kill a lot of Boche," he added, looking Billy and me in the eye.

"The Germans must have had a pretty effective munitions board too," I said cynically, recalling the seemingly endless German artillery barrages that our cannon could never seem to silence.

Sir Joseph didn't catch my sarcasm, but Billy Jones did.

"The Boche must have had a very good imperial poison gas board as well," Billy said seriously. I didn't know if he was

---

1. Clara Ellsworth Flavelle. March 1, 1858–February 8, 1932. Philanthropist.
2. Joseph W. Flavelle. February 15, 1858–March 7, 1939. Businessman and philanthropist.

thinking about his own gassing or just mocking Flavelle, but I liked him for the comment either way.

After dinner, Billy and I had a drink in the lounge with Colonel Prescott. He was not as impressed with Flavelle as Flavelle's wife was. Prescott told us that Flavelle had been accused of war profiteering in Canada. The numbers he'd been accused of pocketing were in the millions. Prescott said he'd been cleared of any wrongdoing, but it was obvious that Prescott remained unconvinced that Flavelle was innocent. I was sad to learn of the accusation because I'd liked the old fellow, but I wasn't surprised.

I recalled my father's depressingly accurate assessment of humanity that he was always all too happy to share. Beginning in grade school, he'd cautioned me by saying "John, people are no damn good." I supposed he was right. It was hard to argue differently based on my experience and my own behavior. Armistan certainly had sought to profit from the war. Hell, he wanted to continue the whole damn thing. I remembered that I had liked Armistan when I'd first met him as well. Perhaps Flavelle was just a more clever Canadian version of Harry Armistan.

That thought prompted a question for Prescott, who seemed like he would know such things. "Colonel, what was the American equivalent to the Imperial Munitions Board?"

"It was called the War Industries Board. The WIB, and I'm not sure ours shouldn't be investigated too. It was disbanded at the beginning of this year."

"I don't suppose you know who served on it?" I asked.

He laughed. "Not all of them. Hell, between the board itself and the divisions and sections within the divisions, I'm sure there must have been hundreds of rich old bastards milking the government teat for their share of the moneys spent on the war."[3]

---

3. American Industry in the War, a report of the War Industries Board, by

"Colonel, what makes you so damn cynical?" I asked, laughing.

"Me? How about the two of you? Damn it, Jones, I just about ruptured myself when you mentioned the German's imperial poison gas board. The comment went right past the Flavelles."

Billy smiled at the compliment.

"I came over to France on Pershing's staff," Prescott continued. "I was there from the beginning and saw plenty of fools and greedy bastards come through his headquarters. Civilians and soldiers both. If you'd seen what I'd seen, you'd be even more cynical than you are."

I nodded. Prescott was right. I knew I was plenty cynical, and Jones certainly seemed to be. I didn't share my view that Pershing fit right in with the gang of gasbags.

I considered Armistan's possible involvement with the WIB. The potential for profit must have been astronomical. Armistan and his cronies would have certainly sought connections to any entity that managed the manufacturing and distribution of war materials. They would have sought out members or friends of members in order to benefit from the decisions of the board. It was exactly the type of organization that Armistan would have insinuated himself into using Patricia as a tool. Instinct told me that the board and its former members might provide a way to destroy Armistan. I just needed to find that way.

Given Sir Joseph Flavelle's membership on the Canadian equivalent of the WIB, I hoped he might have some thoughts or connections I might use to ingratiate myself with the former members of the now-defunct US board. Having Flavelle available to quiz about war profiteering allowed me to think about something other than the sickening crunch as Mitchell hit the motorcab.

Bernard M. Baruch, chairman, March 3, 1921, lists more than seven hundred names of those who served on the board.

Unfortunately, Billy had other plans. I hadn't realized he'd taken a dislike to Lady Flavelle.

At dinner the second night, he learned from Lady Flavelle that Sir Joseph had made his fortune in the meatpacking industry.

"Meatpacking! How interesting," Billy said, gushing.

"Yes, it is. Quite a big business," Sir Joseph said.

"I can imagine. I've read about it. *The Jungle*? By Upton Sinclair? You've heard of it?" Billy asked Sir Joseph with an evil twinkle in his eye.

The Flavelles' smiles vanished and their faces became wooden masks.

"Surely you've heard of it," Billy continued, deliberately ignoring their reaction. "It's about meatpacking in Chicago. I'm sure things are different in Canada, being so much more civilized than America, but, my God, the book is damning!"

"That was written years before the war and is entirely fiction. Fabricated," Sir Joseph declared.

"Sinclair should have been sued for libel," Lady Flavelle added. Her cheeks were flushed in anger at the thought of the book.

"I'm glad to hear it was fictional, eh Jack?" Billy looked at me. "After having read that book, I can't tell you how many times in the bottom of a muddy trench I would open a can of bully beef and study the contents horrified at the possibilities of what was actually in that congealed lump."

I did my best to hide a laugh, but the damage was done with Lady Flavelle. After that, she took dinner in her stateroom. Sir Joseph insisted she found sea travel to be tiring.

Despite Billy's mockery, which Sir Joseph somehow failed to notice, the old Canadian eventually took a liking to Billy. The two would smoke cigars in the smoking room as Flavelle would lecture us on the wartime importance of regulating flavoring extracts, optical goods, and pneumatic tires, among hundreds of other items. Billy would roll his eyes behind Flavelle's back, but I learned that managing all aspects of industry closely was essential for any nation hoping to win a war. He also made it clear that managing industry was a very lucrative job. If there was any possibility for manipulation or abuse of the American WIB, I was certain Armistan was hip deep in it.

<hr>

THE FIRST FEW DAYS OF THE VOYAGE, I BREAKFASTED EARLY AND worried about Mitchell. At about ten a.m., I would take a turn around the deck with Billy Jones, then go to the gymnasium. Billy had no interest in the gymnasium, and I was there too early for others to be using the facilities, which allowed me the freedom to use the equipment without embarrassment. A grown man jumping rope is a silly picture, unless he's a boxer. After the exercise, I'd swim in the plunge pool. In the evenings, Billy and I would have a drink in the lounge, then go to dinner.

After a rubber or two of bridge back in the lounge, I'd go to bed. The Prescotts played cards, but the Flavelles did not. Billy Jones did, and we partnered frequently. He was competitive yet always courteous. Our pairing in bridge and the other social time we spent together reminded me why I had befriended Billy Jones in the first place. When he had questioned me on behalf of Sir Basil in Churchill's anteroom, I had concluded he was no longer my friend. His willingness for me to father his child and the time we spent together on the *Adriatic* proved me wrong. He had just been doing his job in London, and it was clear that he defended me with Sir Basil at no small risk to himself. Billy remained the same funny and irreverent companion he had been in 1914. It seemed that, despite his terrible injuries, the war had not damaged him as badly as it had me.

"Jack," he told me one night as we leaned on the rail on the promenade deck with the wind off the bow blowing in our faces, "no matter what happens with the baby, I want you to know that I love Evelyn more than life. I would do anything for her."

"I know you would, Billy. I'm very happy for you both. I really am."

I was glad for him and found to my surprise that I was not jealous. I really did want them both to be happy. His job with Sir Basil promised him a future in the imperial hierarchy, and the social standing that both he and Evelyn enjoyed from their family connections guaranteed them a status that could not be earned. The life he spoke of seemed so structured and preordained that no uncertainty or excitement remained. In truth, it sounded a little like hell to me, but it clearly made him happy.

A few days out from Cherbourg, I paid my first visit to the *Adriatic*'s Turkish bath. My concern about Mitchell kept me from sleeping, and I hoped the steam would relax me. The gymnasium and pool were in the same section of the ship, and I had felt the heat of the steam room when using the plunge pool. That morning, I decided to go in after my swim. The attendant told me it was closed to men until the afternoon, and so I returned after lunch. The bath cost four shillings, which was damn expensive, but I wasn't spending my money. The ship's boilers had no trouble generating a satisfying cloud of steam, and I found the heat and humidity eased my tension and did indeed take the edge off my worry.

After my first visit, I changed my routine. In the morning, I would read the old newspapers on the racks in the lounge, then eat a late and hearty breakfast. I'd walk the deck with Jones. After lunch, which I'd skip, I'd visit the gymnasium. Few passengers frequented the facility then, and I could use the equipment, the Turkish bath, and the plunge pool in relative solitude. I made a point of going every day. The attendant was very discreet. I tipped him to leave me alone. He would absent himself for long periods, leaving me alone in the cooling room, wrapped in a robe, dozing on one of the loungers.

Unfortunately, the staff was not the only ones who noted my habits. Two days from New York, I was lying on a lounger away from the entrance to the bath and plunge pool. I was relaxed after the steam bath, and my eyes were closed as I fantasized about Madeline. I heard motion in the room and dripping, but I couldn't be bothered to open my eyes. The attendant always tried not to disturb me whenever he had to enter the cooling room, so I ignored him.

Without warning, a wet towel slapped down across my face, and a hand snaked under my head, twisting the fabric tight. I tore at the towel and the hands I knew were holding it. My face and head were trapped in a saturated, inescapable death mask.

Reynolds had sent his assassin after me too! First Mitchell, now me.

I bucked my body up off the lounger, which was bolted to the floor and didn't move despite the violence of my action. Pain shot through my back where I landed on its edge. I twisted and thrashed trying to loosen the dense, wet gag over my nose and mouth. The bastard had it tightly knotted in his fists behind my head. I couldn't reach them. I flailed my arms behind me. The nails of my left hand hooked into my attacker's face. Maybe an ear or a jaw. I didn't know, but he grunted in pain as I raked them down, tearing his skin. He jerked me up and slammed me back down, stunning me, and dug a knee into my side, pinning me against the immovable lounging bed.

I couldn't pull in enough air through the soaked cloth. Whoever had me was strong. At least as strong as I. And he had leverage. He was above me pressing me down while I struggled for air, struggled for life. I was going to suffocate beneath a bath towel!

I was frantic now. I tried again to push off the lounger, but my attacker's weight held me down.

I'd seen men trapped and dying just like I was now. Hell, I'd been the man killing them.

The air in my lungs was gone, burned up in my useless struggle.

I remembered the German on the Rhine. The sergeant battling for life in the bottom of the rowboat. He had struggled and clawed just as I was. It had done him no good, and it did me none now. There was no air. I was a dead man. My time had come. With an airless scream of rage and fear, I was gone.

I RETURNED TO CONSCIOUSNESS FLAT ON MY BACK ON THE COOLING room floor. The attendant was bent over me, shaking me by the shoulder. He looked scared.

"Mr. Griffin, sir, are you all right? You collapsed."

"What? A man. There was another man here. Did you see him?"

"No, sir. There wasn't anyone else. Just you. Are you all right?" he asked again.

The wet towel was beneath my head. Water pooled on the tile under me. I struggled to sit up, and the attendant helped me. I studied him. Had he tried to kill me? Was he my attacker? He was small and didn't look like he'd been involved in a life-and-death struggle. There were no scratches on his face. He just looked worried about me and about his job. He was thinking he shouldn't have left me alone.

"I'm fine. There was no one else in here when you came in?"

"No. Just you here on the floor. You weren't breathing. When I shook your shoulder, you jerked and started breathing again."

"Help me up."

He pulled me off the floor. I sat down on the lounger. My body felt incredibly weak. The closeness of death had sucked all the energy from it. Another passenger or crewmember had just tried to murder me.

"More's the pity he didn't succeed," Tippy Frederickson said.

I glanced at him, but I didn't bother to retort. I didn't want to disturb the already worried attendant, and I couldn't really argue the point.

Once I felt able, I checked the exit of the cooling room. A ladderwell on the left led down to the deck below. A short corridor went to the plunge pool straight on. To the right was the entrance to the steam room. There was a doorway between the steam and the cooling rooms.

The attacker must have heard the attendant coming. He couldn't have fled down the stairs. He had to have gone into the steam room through the plunge pool and down the steps behind the attendant's back. I was saved by the timely return of the attendant.

I began to dress.

"What's your name?"

"Arnold, sir. Arnold Nibley."

I took a fiver from my pants pocket and handed it to him. "Thanks for saving me, Arnold."

"I didn't do nothing, sir. I just came upon you on the floor." He started to hand the note back, but I waved it off.

"Well, I very much appreciate you finding me, Arnold. If you hadn't come along when you did, I couldn't say what might have happened to me."

Of course, I knew exactly what would have happened. The attacker would have dragged my body to the plunge pool and dropped me in. It would look like an accidental drowning. I'd be dead. Then the field would be entirely clear for Reynolds. I wondered if my attacker was the same man who had attacked Mitchell. I doubted it. I hadn't seen that man on board, but then again, there were about four hundred first-class passengers and two thousand others. I'd be surprised if I'd even seen all of those traveling in first class.

As I finished dressing, Arnold remained with me. He watched nervously, hoping that if I collapsed, it would be somewhere other than the Turkish bath. I patted him on the shoulder and went down the ladderwell to my cabin.

I could make a stink and insist I'd been attacked, but I had no evidence. I'd look like a fool.

And I *was* a fool.

I'd put on a brave face for Arnold, but I was terrified. I'd been caught by surprise and was alive entirely by chance. There was a killer on board hunting me who was smart, strong, and had killed before. To stalk and nearly suffocate me on a crowded ocean liner required a cold, bloody-minded focus that I only hoped I could match. I'd been treating the voyage as a vacation from Armistan, Reynolds, and their hired killers. I couldn't afford to half step anymore. I needed to collect myself and focus. Despite what Tippy hoped for me, I needed to survive. If Mitchell still lived, I was the only hope to keep him that way.

I'd been stupid to think Reynolds couldn't reach me. I'd just have to find a way to return the favor.

14

Dancing and Cartwheels

As I sat in my cabin, I concluded I had to tell Billy Jones of the attack. Traveling with me put him at risk, and I had to warn him.

I found him in the first-class lounge, nursing a drink and playing solitaire. When he looked up and saw me approaching, he could tell something was wrong.

"Jack, you look ghastly. Has something happened?"

"You know I like the Turkish bath. Well, someone just tried to kill me there. They tried to suffocate me with a wet towel."

He gave a half laugh, as if I were joking, but the look on my face must have convinced him of my sincerity.

"My God. Did you get a look at whoever it was?"

"No. He came up behind me and damn near killed me. If the attendant hadn't shown up, I'm sure my body would be floating face down in the plunge pool."

"We need to tell the captain, the first officer, the ship's security," Billy said in a rush.

"There's no evidence. The attendant didn't see a soul. He just found me passed out. No one will believe it. I'm telling you because you need to be careful too. Whoever attacked me might attack you."

"Me? Why me?"

"Just because you're with me."

"But who would want you dead, Jack?"

I didn't want to take the time to explain my fears of Armistan and Reynolds. I had no real evidence, and I didn't want to admit to the torture in the Basel cellar. I didn't want Billy to think I was crazy.

"You *are* crazy, you stupid sod," Frederickson said.

I shrugged in response.

Billy thought I worked for House and as a messenger boy for Churchill, and I wanted to keep it that way.

"Bolsheviks. If they got wind of the letters Mr. Churchill wants delivered, it could be them. And the damn Germans have been after me since the mission I completed for the French. I don't know for sure, but we both need to be careful."

Billy finished his drink and swept his solitaire hand into a pile with the remaining cards. Attempted murder seemed to have sapped his interest in the game.

For the remainder of the voyage, we both gave full rein to our paranoia and caution. We did our best to remain in public spaces of the ship. I also spent more time in my cabin where the Colt and Tippy kept me company.

The attack left no outward mark on my face and neck. My back was tender to the touch, where I had slammed down onto the lounger, and I had a spreading bruise above my hip where the would-be killer's knee had driven into my side. Nothing that a drunken fall couldn't have produced. I had made the right choice to keep quiet about the attack.

The ship docked at the Chelsea pier in New York with no more excitement than a few temporarily lost children and missing luggage. Fortunately, neither of those issues were my problem. The weather was fair. Cool but not cold. Overcast but no rain. Good weather to return home to, I supposed.

Billy and I had left our cabins together.

"I'll get train tickets to Washington," he told me as we carried our bags down the stairs to the departure deck.

"I've got some errands for House here in town, Billy. They'll take a few days. Can you wait?" I asked him, praying that his answer was no.

"Colonel House? He gave you a task here in New York before we left Southampton?" he asked with a raised eyebrow. He clearly didn't believe me.

"Yes, his assistant, Stanton Simms, in Paris sent me a message before I came down to the port," I lied.

"Well, I'm sorry. I can't wait. I've got to get to Washington."

"I'll see you there in three days. Noon in Lafayette Square in front of the White House. Near Jackson's statue."

"All right then." He offered me his hand. "Thank you for everything, Jack. Good luck to you. I'll see you in three days."

Billy hurried off, and I dawdled so that we wouldn't share a motorcab from the port. He would take the train from Penn Station, and I planned on staying at the Pennsylvania across the street.

I encountered the Prescotts and Flavelles on the gangway as we all departed. Sir Joseph gave me a hearty handshake as did Colonel Prescott. Mrs. Prescott gave me a kiss goodbye on my unscarred cheek. Lady Flavelle gave me a sniff and a cold shoulder, which meant Billy's reference to Sinclair's damn book went unforgiven. I just didn't have Mitchell's way with women. Who was I kidding? I didn't have Mitchell's way with anyone. At the thought, my stomach knotted with renewed fear for my friend. My first stop would be the Hotel Pennsylvania to see if any messages had arrived telling me of his condition.

Pier 58, where the *Adriatic* was docked, was bustling with passengers, porters, hawkers selling food and drinks, and God only knew who else. There was a carnival atmosphere, and the slight ocean scent struggling up the Hudson was overwhelmed by that of trash, sewage, and hundreds of unwashed bodies. The voyage had erased these smells of massed humanity from my mind, but they returned quickly enough among the crowd.

The streets around the pier were an excellent place for me to be knifed or shoved into traffic as Mitchell had been. The price of a taxicab was worth the protection it brought. Also, I didn't relish the idea of carrying my bag the nearly two miles to the Pennsylvania.

Billy was long gone, and I found a taxicab easily. Fifty cents a mile was a steep price to pay for most people, but I had my own money and Churchill's.

The motorcab left me at the Pennsylvania's Seventh Avenue entrance. I turned my bag over to the bellman and hurried to the reception desk. They didn't remember me from my previous visit, but I didn't expect them to.

"John Griffin, I'll be staying for three nights," I told the desk clerk. "And there should be some mail or cables waiting for me."

With the possibility of news about Mitchell's condition, my heart began to race. I needed him to be alive.

"Of course, sir. Have you stayed with us before?"

"Yes."

"Do you have a reservation?"

"No."

"Well, with over two thousand rooms, we should have no trouble finding you accommodations."

He began to flip through a cabinet full of narrow drawers holding visitor cards.

"And I'd appreciate if you could check for any correspondence," I said, reminding him of what was most important to me.

He stepped back from the files with an aggrieved look. "My apologies, sir." He snapped his fingers for a bellhop. "Run to the mailroom and telegraph room. I need anything for John Griffin." He turned to me. "He'll be back shortly."

I nodded.

He pulled the registration card for my April visit from a drawer.

"Is the information all the same, sir?"

"Yeah."

"The room will be six dollars per night. It has an en suite bath. There are restaurants on the first two floors and one on the roof."

"I stayed here just a few months ago," I reminded him.

He tried to smile, but it was more of a grimace.

By the time the room key was in my hand, the runner returned with an armful of correspondence. I took the letters and cables and headed for the elevators.

The clerk on the eighth floor directed me to my room. Once there, I reviewed the mail that had been waiting at the hotel. I quickly flipped through the correspondence and pulled out the transatlantic cablegrams. There were three. Relief coursed through me. They might tell me that Mitchell was dead, but at least some communication had gotten through.

The first cable was from Simms assuring me that he had notified Colonel House of my impending arrival. The second was from Bullard. It said concisely, *Help sent to London Stop More to follow Stop EB.* I didn't know what that meant. More help or more cablegrams? In either case, I was relieved that one of my desperate letters had reached him. The cable was dated three days previously. Help should have already arrived in London. What kind of help was also a question, but anyone was better than Patricia alone, even if she did hire people to help protect Will and also had Wag McDonald's support.

The third cable was from Patricia. It read simply: *William's condition rapidly improving Stop Patricia.*

I took a deep breath and began to laugh. Tippy Frederickson scowled, and I laughed harder. Mitchell was alive. At least as of five days ago. He was a tough son of a bitch. A weight lifted from my chest. Thank God!

I still needed to get back to London, but with help on the way and Mitchell recovering, the urgency that had been clawing at me since I'd been forced on to the *Adriatic* eased. I could focus on finishing my business for Churchill and then on Armistan.

I gathered up the stack of letters I'd put aside in favor of the cables. There was a letter from Armistan dated in May. That one would be interesting. Likely old news. General Neville, my former commander in the marines, had also sent a letter. That was curious. Then there were two letters with return addresses promising they were from my sisters. A warm glow kindled in my chest. A thick letter from my parents' lawyer followed those, and the glow went out. At the bottom of the pile were two letters I had no reason to expect: one from France addressed in a woman's hand with no return address and a creamy envelope from the White House.

I realized I didn't have a pocketknife to open the letters. I'd given mine to Jean-Paul, Marie Masson's son. I looked again at the letter from France and narrowed my eyes. Could it be that despite all my warnings, Marie had actually written me? Surely not. How would she have found me? I recalled that she was a spy after all.

I worked a finger under the flap and tore open the letter.

My dearest John,

Jean-Paul and I have arrived in Biarritz. Madame Errázuriz has been a godsend, and I feel so fortunate to have found her. Yet one more thing I am indebted to you for.

Madame Errázuriz was an art patron and connoisseur, who had given Marie and her son shelter from those hunting them. She was unconnected to me or anyone from Marie's previous life.

I am sure the first question you would ask is: Are we safe? Yes. Yes, we are safe. I am laughing and maybe crying a little, because, as I write this, I remember Jean-Paul's priceless mimicry of you in Elsbeth's dining room. He was afraid of you then but still brave enough to tease you. He is not afraid of you now. He asks about you constantly, and Mr. William too.

It is unfortunate that we did not know Elsbeth was the leader of the plots that ensnared us, but in any event, Jean-Paul's grandmother would likely still be dead. We are not. We are alive and well thanks to you.

I will not share our address. I know you would be upset with me if I did. Of course, should you ever wish to contact us, you could do so through Madame Errázuriz. I am certain you will destroy this letter as soon as you are able. You wish to protect us even when we do not need protection. Instead of worrying about others, I beg that you take care of yourself. You are too headstrong, too brave, too quick to risk your life for others. Please know that if you were not in this world, it would be emptier for the three of us. (I include Anneli in our number because Jean-Paul insists upon it.)

With our love,

Marie and Jean-Paul Griffon

I carefully refolded the letter and put it back into the envelope. *Griffon.* She had threatened to adopt the surname. I realized I had a smile on my face.

Marie was right though. I did need to destroy the letter.

"You deserve to be happy, John," Sarah told me.

"Sure I do."

I weighed the second unexpected letter in my hands. The return address simply read: THE WHITE HOUSE. Why would the president write me? I could leave it unread. Claim I never got it. That might be awkward given that I needed to speak to Wilson or at least deliver Churchill's mail. If I did see Wilson, he might ask me about the contents of his letter to me.

The address was written in large, sprawling script that covered nearly the entire front of the envelope. Was it a feminine hand that scribed *John Griffin, care of the Hotel Pennsylvania?* I couldn't tell.

I tore the envelope open with no more care than I had Marie's.

The letterhead was that of the White House, and the writing inside was identical to that on the envelope. It was not a long letter.

Dear Major Griffin,

Please contact me at the White House at your earliest convenience. I cannot stress enough the urgency of my request. I can only hope that this letter reaches you soonest.

Yours faithfully,

Edith Wilson

The letter was dated just a week ago. Now I had no choice but to respond. I didn't have it in me to ignore the First Lady. After Basel, I could ignore President Airedale. Hell, I wanted to. But the First Lady? I couldn't do it. This letter's urgency scuppered my plan to kill Armistan before continuing on to Washington. I would take the train south in the morning.

I looked at the other letters. The one from Armistan conveniently reminded me of his address. I still had much of the day. I would walk by his brownstone. An opportunity might present itself.

I ripped the letter open.

It was dated May thirteenth. That was just after Mitchell and I had left London for Paris against the express instructions of Armistan, at least according to Gavin Kingsbury and Reynolds.

I snorted as I read. It was very short. It turned out Armistan really did fire me. The key sentence in the letter stated: *By this letter, I formally terminate your employment on my behalf. I also terminate the employment of any subcontractors operating under or at your direction.* I guessed that meant Mitchell. *All payments owed and not already made are canceled.*

Looked like Mitchell wouldn't get his five thousand dollars

from Armistan. That was okay. He got Armistan's beautiful but murderous daughter instead.

I took my pistol and holster from the bottom of my suitcase. I put on the harness and studied the hang of my suitcoat with the pistol in place under my left arm. Good enough. Out of habit, I dropped out the pistol magazine to check it and that the chamber was empty. With the magazine in place, I slotted the gun back in the holster. There still remained some payments between Armistan and me. I just didn't know when I'd be making them.

I left the remaining letters on the bed. The ones from my sisters I was saving because I looked forward to them. Neville's was a curiosity that could wait. The one from the lawyer annoyed me, and I hadn't even opened it. I'd read them when I returned. Right now I wanted to hunt.

⸙

I HAD NOT FORGOTTEN THAT A KILLER ARRIVED IN NEW YORK WITH me, so I was careful as I crossed the street to Penn Station. At the entrance, I gave a young newsie, who couldn't have been more than six, a nickel for a two-cent newspaper. He needed the extra pennies, and I hadn't seen the baseball scores for months. I was curious to see which teams would still be playing.

I bought a ticket for the express train from Penn Station up to West Seventy-Second Street. Instead of reading the paper, I waited well back from the tracks and studied those around me. Despite the grime and overuse that resulted from so many damn immigrants settling in New York City, the subway was still a marvel of effort, engineering, and artistry. Much the same as Paris, right down to the whipping grit and musty smells.

Once on the train, I took a seat against a window and examined the passengers in the compartment with me. Satisfied that none were about to murder me, I flipped open the paper.

The headline read: TROOPS SENT TO OMAHA; MOBS FIRE

175

Nearly Lynches Mayor; Steel Strike Test Today.[1] Bullard was right to stay in France. I hoped Henry Johnson was okay. And God only knew what the strike news was about. It couldn't be good. I realized I needed to study more than just Harry Armistan's habits. I needed to understand what was happening in Washington.

The headline of the first column was of more pressing interest to me: Wilson Returns to Washington Worn and Shaken. The article mentioned nervous exhaustion so severe the president was having difficulty controlling himself. It couldn't be a coincidence that Mrs. Wilson had sent me an urgent letter just a few days before and the president had now suffered a breakdown. There was clearly a connection to the treaty ratification.

I skimmed the rest of the paper and discovered that the White Sox were playing the Reds in the World Series. The paper made clear that the Sox were heavy favorites. I was horrified to learn that, in the interest of meeting the avid fan interest in the game, the officials at major league baseball had decreed that the Series would be nine games instead of seven. Somehow the old men that controlled baseball were as bad as those that controlled government. It wasn't about fan interest. It was about money. More games meant more money. Bastards. To take something sacred like baseball and cheapen it. It made me sick.

Neither Tippy nor Sarah understood my outrage.

I recalled Bullard's lecture to Mitchell and me on the terrace of Le Dôme. He had said "If you want to know why anything happens anywhere, follow the money!" He was right. It was happening in baseball too. Maybe my odd German friend Hans Richter had it right when he said "Baseball is a sport to divert the

---

1. *New York Times.* September 29, 1919. Page 1.

common man. It promotes distraction." And it earns money while doing it. I was disgusted by the grasping effort of major league baseball to squeeze a few extra bucks out of the Series. A nine-game Series? Ridiculous. Outrageous. And unsurprising after what I'd seen Armistan do for a few bucks.

Tippy shook his head in distaste at my inane thoughts. The English just didn't understand.

At Seventy-Second Street, I folded the newspaper under my arm and left the train. I walked from the station to Armistan's home, which wasn't far. Broadway was crowded with afternoon foot traffic. Once I turned east on Seventy-Fourth Street toward Central Park, the traffic thinned, but I wasn't worried about being recognized. My hat was low over my eyes, and no one would expect me to be foolish enough to be wandering around Armistan's neighborhood.

I studied his house from the sidewalk. It was the same stately brownstone I remembered. It cried money, power, and privilege. I continued past, walking with purpose.

Unfortunately, I learned nothing from my quick examination of the front of the brownstone. Armistan might be home. He might not. He would still have a butler, a cook, and likely more staff than his daughter had in London. After all, she would have learned how to run a household from her parents. There could be five or six innocent people in the house. I didn't intend to kill a handful of servants just to reach Armistan.

I was surprised at how easily I was contemplating murder. It was both unsettling and encouraging.

"You see, John. You are beginning to understand," Sarah said to me.

I didn't answer.

Perhaps I did understand better now why she couldn't let go of James Willoughby's death, but I didn't feel that I was hunting Armistan for her. At least, not her alone. It was for all my old mates. For all those who had died and had lost so much—their youth, their innocence, their health, their lives.

I stopped walking. The itching in the back of my skull that had begun in the Basel basement eased as I realized all my planning was, first and foremost, for me. It was as if this hunt was the culmination of everything that had happened to me since August 1914. This was my purpose. It promised to bring an end to my inability to live in the postwar world.

Briefly I wondered whether all of this was a delusion created by the mescaline the Krauts had pumped into me.

"Course it is, you half-wit," Frederickson confirmed.

Maybe he was right, but it didn't matter. I felt better.

I crossed the street and walked past Armistan's house again on the opposite sidewalk. I learned nothing new. My reconnaissance had been fruitless.

I turned south parallel to Central Park.

At Sixty-Sixth Street, I turned away from the park. There was a subway station at Sixty-Sixth and Broadway.

Once on the southbound platform of the station, I found it crowded with people waiting to go downtown. The platform clock indicated a train was due in three minutes, but the rushing sound of an approaching train came from the round black tunnel north of the platform. It wasn't slowing as it approached the station. An express train. It would rocket past the platform in a tornado of newspaper pages, dust, and trash.

Damn. A tourist's mistake. Only local trains stopped at Sixty-Sixth Street. I would be stuck on a slow train that would stop at every station between Sixty-Sixth and Penn Station.

As I turned to find a subway map to count the stops to Penn Station, an arm took mine like a lover readying for a stroll. For one irrational moment, I thought it was Madeline.

It wasn't. It was a balding, stocky man, older than me by at least five years. With his other hand, he seized my wrist.

I started to pull away, and a second, younger man appeared at my other side and twisted my wrist up behind my back.

"Hup," ordered the first. A waft of rotten breath accompanied the command. Together, they hoisted me between them and frog-marched me toward the tracks. The high-pitched sound of the approaching express train was upon us.

They were going to throw me in front of the train!

I dug in my heels. An image of Jean-Paul heading a soccer ball popped into my head. The angle was bad, but I mimicked his motion. I rocked away from the older man. My left shoulder strained from the lock on my arm, but I shrugged off the pain and rotated my head hard, snapping the side of my forehead into the older man's face. I missed his nose but caught him in the cheekbone. The blow was cushioned by my hat, which flew off, but it distracted him enough that I could wrench my arm free.

Then the train was in the station, whistling past faster than a motorcar.

The second man continued to press my wrist hard between my shoulder blades and pulled me toward the tracks. My dance with his companion had put him between me and the subway rocketing past. I went with his pull and dropped the shoulder nearest him. His eyes widened in surprise as I exploded into him, driving him into the cars flashing by. He flew against the blur that was the passing train. His hand was torn violently from my wrist, spinning me and wrenching my shoulder. The sounds of exploding glass and the wet impact of flesh hitting hard metal accompanied the howl of the racing train.

His body flew past me, and part of him, his arm or his leg, struck my thigh as he cartwheeled back onto the platform. From the screaming and shouts, his body must have struck others waiting for the local train.

I swung back toward the first man, but he was stumbling away from me. I wanted to follow, but the pain in my leg where I'd been struck by his flying companion hobbled me, and he was gone more quickly than my stumbling run could follow.

The platform was in chaos. The express train was gone and with it the roaring noise, but cries and shouts filled the air. A policeman's whistle from across the tracks punctuated the horror around me. My second attacker was dead. His head was a shattered pulp, and his limbs were torn and twisted unnaturally from the force of the speeding train, which had flung his body into the waiting crowd.

I didn't stop to help the injured. I picked up my hat from where it had fallen and walked to the far end of the platform. Standing close to the soot-crusted wall, I waited for the local back to Penn Station.

15

On the House

I spoke to the hotel concierge about travel to and accommodations in Washington. He arranged a first-class train ticket for the early afternoon the following day. He also reserved a room in the Washington Hotel, which he assured me was nearly as new as the Pennsylvania. He also noted it was equal in many respects, if smaller. At five fifty a night, it was certainly not much cheaper. The most important attribute of the hotel was its proximity to the White House.

Once I settled on the hotel, I also wanted to send cablegrams to Patricia, Eugene, and Simms so they would know where to contact me in Washington. The concierge organized this as well, and I was happy to leave him with a two-dollar bill for his efforts.

He commented on the limp I'd picked up during the attack in the subway and suggested I see the hotel doctor. I agreed, and he summoned a bellhop who took me to see the doc.

The doctor was in his early thirties, but he seemed to know his business.

"What's the problem?" he asked looking closely at the scarred side of my face as if he was trying to judge what weapon had caused it.

"I was knocked down by a taxicab."

"Damn motorcars are a danger," he said. "The dressing room is through there. There's a hotel robe on the hook."

I pulled the door closed and removed my jacket and then the pistol in its shoulder holster. I hung the harness from the hook that had held the robe and then covered it with my pants, shirt, and jacket. I draped my tie over the top for good measure.

The doc examined me from head to toe but spent the most time on my thigh and shoulder. He made no comment about the various scars I'd acquired over the past few years. He did note the yellowing bruises from my brush with death in the Turkish bath.

"You get knocked down by motorcars often?" he asked with a straight face.

"It happens more often than you'd think, Doc," I told him.

"Just bruising. You'll be sore for a few days. I strongly suggest the plunge pool on the third floor. Stay out of the heat. Just the cooler water and maybe some ice from the floor clerk tonight. It should speed the healing."

I followed his advice, but first I locked the pistol in my room.

A few men swam and lounged in the pool. I just sat on the steps soaking. Whether it really made a medical difference or not, I didn't know, but I felt better for it. I kept my eyes open the whole time. No one was going to sneak up on me.

The bellhop, who'd brought me to the doctor, had bragged that the hotel had a barber in the basement. After the plunge pool, I was so relaxed that I decided to get a haircut as well.

The barbershop was huge. There were at least ten barbers on duty, most of them working.

My barber wore a white jacket over a protruding belly. He was short and had to pump the chair down to reach the top of my head. He looked to be sixty and kept his thinning hair short. The broken veins in his nose reminded me of Detective Inspector Fair.

"You want your shoes shined?" he asked in a thick New York accent as he tossed the bib over me.

"Why not and a shave too," I said.

He briefly left the shop and returned with an old negro with woolly salt-and-pepper hair. The bootblack took my shoes with a smile. I sat in the barber's chair in my stocking feet, closed my eyes, and curled my toes in relaxation.

I doubted if the barber was on Reynolds's payroll, but if he was, I was a dead man. He could slit my throat before I got my eyes open, but the thought didn't bother me. Instead, the sound of him stropping his razor made me think of Marie. And then Jean-Paul. And the dog, Anneli. I couldn't help but smile.

"If only he would slice you from ear to ear," Tippy said.

"I've been out of the country the past few months, who do you think will take the Series? The Sox or the Reds?" I asked the barber in order to silence Frederickson.

The barber proceeded to rail against the White Sox, the Reds, and major league baseball. He was a Yankees fan, of course. In short order, he moved on to complain about wops, Greeks, micks, and immigrants in general. I grunted at the appropriate times in his monologue.

"And the darn Reds are everywhere," he said as he wiped the excess shaving cream from my jaw. "And I don't mean the baseball team. Bolsheviks coming out of the woodwork."

"Really? Here in New York?" I asked.

"Yup. And all over the country. A general strike in Seattle and now the steel workers. Hell, even garment workers went on strike here. You don't think strikes and coloreds rioting are just accidents do you? It's the Reds. In June, they set off bombs all over the country. Nearly blew up the attorney general. It's Wilson's fault. He's a friend to Lenin and Trotsky."

"I didn't know that," I told him as he removed the barber's cape and brushed off my shirt. I was happy to be freed from his chair. I was pretty sure he was full of shit, but I thought it was a bad practice to argue with a man who had a razor at my throat.

My shoes returned with a mirror shine, and I looked as clean-cut as I ever had in the Marine Corps.

Although I was still in pain, I felt much better than when I'd returned to the hotel.

I took the elevator back to the ground floor and went to the Men's Café for a bite to eat. On the way there, I picked up a newspaper from the newsstand in the lobby. I'd lost mine in the scuffle in the subway. Since the clerk had one from the day before, I got that instead of the current one, which I'd already skimmed.

As I waited for my steak and what was likely to be one of my last pre-Prohibition beers, I considered what had happened in the subway. Were the two men Armistan's? I didn't think so. That would be too coincidental, and while my luck might be running out, his men recognizing me on the street was too much to believe.

Reynolds's men then. They'd followed me from England. That was more likely. Could one of them have been my attacker on the *Adriatic* or Will's in London? I smiled grimly at that thought. I very much wanted the shattered body on the platform to belong to Mitchell's cowardly bushwhacker. A more appropriate end was hard to imagine.

My food arrived, and I ate mechanically, spending more time thinking than tasting.

I considered the older man who had gotten away. There was something about him that made me think he was English. I couldn't put my finger on why. His clothing? His teeth? That was unfair, but the thought made me chuckle anyway.

"Bastard," Tippy whispered.

No. It was the order to lift me he'd given his now-dead partner. It had sounded like a British Army command. It wasn't much, but it was enough to convince me that Reynolds had sent the same killers after me that had tried to kill Mitchell in London.

I emptied my plate, ordered a second beer, and opened the

day-old paper. While the strikes were in yesterday's news, the president's collapse was not. I read the paper closely looking for any additional clues as to the actual cause of Wilson's illness. One article indicated that the president was not willing to negotiate with the Senate any changes to the treaty, which was his baby. I thought it ironic that he had been all too willing to make concessions to the allies but refused to consider working with his own people. Hell, he needed the Senate to actually ratify the damn thing. Instead, he had traveled across the country bringing his case for the treaty to the American people. I wondered if this direct plea had caused an actual attack on his person by his opponents.

I flipped through the rest of the paper without reaching a conclusion about the president. I did come across an odd few lines hidden under a headline on another subject. The article noted that a reverend from San Francisco, who had lived in Ireland, believed that "the Irish situation viewed from an American standpoint was deplorable. The cities were full of soldiers and the prisons were full of sympathizers for the Irish cause." Nationalists in prison wouldn't do the Fenians much good. I'd met Churchill, and listening to his vitriol directed at the Bolsheviks was bad enough. Thank God I didn't have to hear him rail against the Irish too. He would have no truck with those pursuing an independent Ireland.

I folded the paper and set it on the table. The article gave me an idea. One that I was sure was diabolically clever, if only I could manage it.

I finished my beer and paid the bill. I asked the waiter for a comfortable Irish bar where someone sympathetic to Irish national aspirations might have a drink. He wasn't impressed with my desire to mingle with the Irish, but he promised to ask others on the staff. The maître d' came over to confirm what I wanted.

"I'd like a place where the ties to Ireland are close, where gentlemen yearn for an independent Ireland." I passed him two dollars, an outrageous tip for such information. It was important that I got the right sort of place. "One where the patrons would be unsympathetic to the British occupation."

"Ah, yes," he said, pocketing the cash. He was a tall, thick man with a shock of black hair and blue eyes. He looked like he might have a bit of Irish in him, but he had no lilt. Second generation? "There are several such places, but the most… militant would be Hanley's on East Eighteenth. The concierge might have a thought or two, but I know Hanley's. You'll find many devoted to an independent, united Ireland there."

"Excellent. I'm John Griffin," I said, offering my hand.

"Patrick McGowen. If you need anything during your stay, Mr. Griffin, anything at all, don't hesitate to ask. If the concierge seems reluctant or unable, I might be able to help."

"Of course, Mr. McGowen. I'll ask you first and save a bit of time."

The train for Washington departed Penn Station at twelve thirty p.m. the next day, and with McGowen's directions, I hoped to accomplish one important task before departing New York City.

⬥

There was a nip in the air as I stepped out of the hotel. The tavern was about eighteen blocks south and east of the hotel. The maître d' had said it was near Gramercy Park. While I didn't find the geographical reference helpful, the taxicab driver I hired did. I asked that he leave me at the south side of the park so I could walk the last few blocks to the bar.

I was taking a chance. If the men who'd attacked me weren't English, I'd be in for a rough time. I'd probably be in for a rough time in any case.

I intended to flush out the last of Reynolds's English henchmen. I didn't know how many men he'd sent after me, but one had been on the ship and two were in the subway. Chances were good one of the men in the train station had been my attacker on the ship. With any luck at all, there would be only one man left: the stocky man from the subway. He'd sounded and seemed English. My plan was for him, or them, to follow me to the pub and confront me there. They wouldn't know or particularly care that it was an Irish pub. Like all Englishmen, it wouldn't occur to them that some in this quaint New York neighborhood might hate the empire, resent the king, and wish for an Ireland free from Britannia's yoke. They also wouldn't expect the fervor for freedom to burn hotly in an out-of-the-way tavern in Manhattan. I was gambling that McGowen had steered me right.

Hanley's, which sat on a corner of the street, looked exactly as I expected it to. The bar itself encompassed the ground floor of a five-floor tenement house. At one time, the building was likely red brick, but it was stained dark now. Light spilled onto the sidewalks from the long many-paned windows. A few gas lights gave it a welcoming look.

Butterflies danced in my gut at the possibility of action, failure, and perhaps even death.

I pulled open the door. The rumble of conversation, the bark of laughter, pipe and cigarette smoke, and the smells of spilled beer and body odor embraced me. A long, carved wooden bar ran along the inside wall. Brass lamps glowed weakly making the bar dim but not dark. Nearly hidden by the patrons at the bar, I glimpsed a brass footrail running its length.

It could have been a pub anywhere in the British Isles, and here it was in New York City. I moved to the far end of the room and squeezed up to the bar. The men around me had dark beer in their mugs that could only be Guinness. When the bartender reached me, I ordered the same. He pulled the beer, allowed it to settle, and topped it off before placing it in front of me. I put a quarter on the bar, took a sip, nodded in appreciation, and began my wait.

The Tommies might try to kill me where I stood, but I didn't think so.

It wasn't ten minutes after I first braced a shined shoe on the footrail that the balding killer from the train station pulled open the front door. Three men followed him. All were his age or younger. All were veterans of the war. I didn't know how I knew, but I did.

They spread out through the dim, crowded room, and when the leader spotted me, he gave a sharp nod in my direction.

The butterflies were now at full flutter. Four. I hadn't expected four. I hoped to God the folks in this bar hated the English.

He came straight up to me, no hesitation, no worry, like he had everything under control. Like he didn't remember the man he'd lost that afternoon.

"We can do it here, but we don't want any of these innocent patrons to get hurt, do we?" he asked.

English. He was English. Tradesman by birth. Probably a sergeant by the war's end. An old hand at killing and dealing with fear. He had scratches on his neck.

"Are you English?" I pitched my voice to carry and pushed it out from my diaphragm. Just like my marine drill instructor had. Despite the noise in the bar, the near shout was distinct and carried through most of the room. Conversation subsided as the patrons grasped what I had asked.

"I asked you a question. Are you a damned Limey?" I snarled.

His three companions worked their way closer. All heads in the pub were turned to us.

One hand crept toward his waist, and the other tried to take my arm.

"You're going with me you cowardly shit or you'll die right here," he said with a hiss.

"It's about bloody time," Tippy said with satisfaction.

"I'll not go anywhere with you, you Sassenach bastard!" With that shout, I released all the rage I didn't know I'd bottled up within me. I'd felt helpless since the attack on Mitchell and since the attack on me on the ship. Now one of Reynolds's would-be killers stood before me.

I slammed my half-full mug into the side of the Englishman's head. The mug shattered splashing the beer in a tarry arc across the room and leaving only the stout glass handle in my hand. He fell to his knees, and his men rushed forward to protect him. The nearest swung an overhand punch at my head. I bobbed to the side, and it glanced off my scalp and into the face of the poor bastard behind me, who fell against the bar with blood bursting from his nose.

A collective growl spread through the tavern. The patrons didn't like one of their own getting socked one bit, and I didn't have time to rouse them further. The limey might have missed me with his first punch, but he was following it up with abandon. One or two blows struck my forehead, and I returned his attentions by hammering the broken mug handle into his gut, which bent him double. It cut him, or at least I hoped it did. I brought it down on the back of his head like a hammer. The glass of the handle cracked in my hand, and I let it drop to the floor.

With a roar, Hanley's customers decided to join in.

The first man put a hand down to try to stand. A fellow next to me stomped on his fingers, and I kicked him under his ribs with the tip of my very shiny shoe. He went back down curling around the blow. I kicked him once more in the head.

That was for Mitchell.

The bar was in a frenzy.

Tippy was rooting for the Englishmen, but they didn't have a chance.

I was tackled into the bar before I could finish kicking the first man to death, but by then, every occupant in the bar had risen against the English tyrants. It was beautiful. Young and old, men and a few women. It was a riot.

"Éirinn go Brách![1]" I cackled wildly as I kicked a second Tommy, who'd fallen to the ground.

My plan worked wonderfully. The American Irish sympathizers in Hanley's knocked the hell out of those Englishmen. All four men were beaten into unconsciousness or, at the very least, immobility.

I checked each of the downed men in turn, turning out their pockets and opening wallets. All I found was some American money, a leather cosh, and some knives. I found no British pounds. I considered waiting for one of them to recover sufficiently for me to question him, but I had neither Mitchell's talents for persuasion nor the time. Also, I knew exactly who they worked for. I didn't need to question them to know that.

I stole the blackjack but left the money.

In addition to his heavy leaded sap, the last man I examined had a sheathed trench knife belted at the small of his back. I unbuckled his belt and pulled the knife free. A trench knife like this one had only one purpose, and that purpose was made clear from the tip of its seven-inch blade to the spiked butt of its knuckleduster guard. It was made to kill men. The Brit had never managed to reach the knife. If he had, things would have gone badly for a few of the Hanley's guests.

These men had intended to murder me. I unsheathed the blade. There was some unpleasant but necessary work that needed to be done.

The bartender understood what I had planned.

"None of that in my place," he growled.

"How about you help me move them outside then, and I take care of them there?"

"No. It's bad for business."

Many of his patrons were listening to the exchange. None looked like they would complain about a few dead Englishmen

---

1. Ireland Forever.

on the sidewalk, but they also didn't look ready to become accessories to murder.

"I'll send a runner to bring the coppers and tell them your English friends started the fight. We've certainly got plenty of witnesses to support that story," he told me, waving an arm at the men and women setting chairs upright and dabbing blood from their noses and mouths. Those who heard his comment hooted at the thought of duping the police, and sending beaten and bloody limeys to the hoosegow was frosting on the cake.

Unfortunately, it wasn't as good as killing them, but they would be out of my way for a while. I'd see them again, so I tried to make a point of memorizing their faces. Most were so bloodied I wasn't sure I succeeded, but I'd remember their leader. I knelt down beside him as the barkeep watched me carefully. "Tell Reynolds I'm coming for him," I whispered in the prone man's ear. I didn't know if he could hear me, but I got satisfaction from the promise.

I stood and peeled three tens off the roll of bills from my pocket. "Here," I said to the barman. "For the trouble and the help."

He looked at me and then the bills. He shrugged and took the notes with a smile.

"Joseph Hanley," he said, introducing himself. We shook hands over the unmoving body of the trench knife-bearing Englishman.

"John Griffin, Mr. Hanley. This is a fine tavern you have here and a fine clientele. I would appreciate it if you wouldn't mention me when you speak with the police."

"Don't worry about that, Mr. Griffin. The folks at this tavern are more than happy to have beaten these boys within an inch of their lives without any help. This was as good a night as we've had in quite a while."

A few men nearby overheard the remark and laughed, calling out their agreement.

I left shortly after. I didn't want to be around when the police appeared. Hanley was pulling beers for all who wanted them.

"Beers on the house!" he called out to his patrons.

The thirty bucks I'd given him could buy a couple hundred beers, but I was happy for him to get the credit.

16

———————

The Messenger Boy

With nothing to do in the morning, I planned a leisurely breakfast in the dining room. On my way there, I bought a copy of the *New York Times* in the lobby. I also brought with me the four unread letters that had waited for me when I checked in.

With coffee on the way, I decided to get the lawyer's letter out of the way. It was the one I was least looking forward to. The letter was from the attorney handling my parents' estate. I'd met with Mr. Willard M. Swindell of Swindell & Fox only once. After I was released from the hospital in late 1918, I'd traveled at his request to San Francisco. After that meeting, I had believed it was just a matter of time until my parents' estate would be settled. Swindell seemed certain of it.

My father had retired in San Francisco before the war. It had taken me all of a week to be promoted to major as part of a French spy hunt. It had taken my father thirty years of honorable service to make that same rank. The irony was not lost on me. His last posting had been the Presidio. My mother loved California. The weather there spoiled her. She had sworn she would never return to the "hell that was Texas," where she'd spent much of her time as an army wife. Well, she never would get back to Texas. Neither of them would.

They died when I was overseas with the marines. The Spanish flu killed them. My father caught it, and my mother caught it shortly after, likely as the result of taking care of Dad. A strong, healthy, happy couple dead in a few weeks. It made no sense to me. But I'd learned that death rarely did.

Their much-loved city of San Francisco had the toughest mask ordinance[1] in the country, but it made no difference for my parents or thousands of others. Of course, it probably didn't help that some folks resented the masks, which they called *muzzles* and *pig snouts*, the ordinance mandated. When I was out there to see Swindell, I'd heard stories about some folks who'd cut holes in their masks so they could smoke their damn cigars. Others preferred jail time or a fine to wearing the confining coverings.[2]

Wilson and his propagandists told me I was going to war in Europe to fight for "freedom," and folks back home used that freedom to be selfish. Well, God bless America. The damn Anti-Mask League of San Francisco wouldn't have gotten away with its shenanigans in Kaisar Willy's empire. In any case, my parents were dead, and there was nothing I could do about it.

I slit the letter open with the dining room knife. I'd left my newly acquired trench knife in the room, which, given its size and lethal aspect, had seemed like the wise course.

As I expected, the letter was filled with condescension and legalese. Perhaps the lawyers didn't intentionally seek to befuddle and dupe the uninitiated, but I chose to believe they did. I might not believe in God, the president, or that the war I fought would end all wars, but I sure as hell believed that the lawyers were

---

1. "Masks for all San Franciscans." *New York Times*, October 25, 1918. Page 22.
2. Hauser, Christine. "A Raging Pandemic and a Resistance to Masks: Welcome to 1918." *New York Times*, August 3, 2020, updated December 10, 2020. *New York Times*. Aug. 4, 2020, Section A, Page 6.

trying to dupe me. I didn't know why, but it didn't matter. I
believed it.

Dear Mr. Griffin,

I trust this letter finds you and your lovely sisters in good health...

And so on and so on. Despite its length, I deduced that the
letter was simply asking for the signatures of my sisters and
myself on the enclosed documents. I wondered if we paid the
lawyers by the word.

Fine. I'd sign the documents and send them to my sisters.
Hell, I'd hand carry the documents to Eleanor, my sister in DC,
and get her to sign them before sending them on to Midge in
Texas.

Next, I turned to General Neville's letter.

Dear Sergeant Griffin,

*I hope you have recovered from the honorable wounds you suffered
in defense of our great nation.*

Ha! If only the general knew about the wounds I'd suffered
since. He likely wouldn't be surprised to know that women were
involved. I was sure he'd have kittens if he learned of my
manufactured promotion to major. I certainly didn't plan to
tell him.

I write you now to extend a most sincere apology.

*I recommended you to Mr. Harry Armistan of New York City based
on my regard for you and your abilities and not because of any specific
relationship I have with Mr. Armistan. I have learned from the
acquaintance that connected me to Mr. Armistan, Mr. Thomas
Reynolds (a great supporter of the armed services and a Christian man),
that your employment with Mr. Armistan did not go as smoothly as I'd
hoped. Mr. Reynolds's information was spotty and unclear as to the*

Thomas Reynolds. He had to be a relation of Morgan. In fact, given the fact that Thomas was of an age to know General Neville, he had to be Morgan Reynolds's father or uncle. It was too much of a coincidence to be otherwise.

In the event that your employment on Mr. Armistan's behalf was, in any way, unpleasant, please accept my apology. It was only my intention to give a deserving marine an opportunity.

Should you travel to the District of Columbia, please do not hesitate to contact me. If you leave a note at the Army and Navy Club, I will respond with alacrity.

Sincerely yours,

Wendell C. Neville

Brigadier General

USMC

Now that was an interesting letter.

Neville knew the senior Reynolds. I wondered if Thomas Reynolds served on the War Industries Board. According to Colonel Prescott from the *Adriatic*, service on the board would give a man like Thomas Reynolds the perfect position to manipulate strategic products to profit from the war. However, based on his letter, Neville respected Reynolds. Maybe even liked him, and Neville certainly felt guilty for connecting me with Armistan.

I would have to take the general up on his offer. I'd make a point of leaving a note at the Army and Navy Club, then I'd see what *alacrity* meant to a marine general officer. Neville might be the connection I needed to begin my destruction of Harry Armistan. It would be ironic if the man who introduced us unknowingly helped me put Armistan in the ground.

My breakfast arrived, and I put the letters aside. I would read my sisters' on the train to Washington, and with luck, I would be able to visit Eleanor, and her family in person. Elle sure would be surprised to see me, and I'd lost track of how old the twins would be by now. No doubt her husband remained just as devoted as I remembered him to be.

I SLEPT FOR MUCH OF THE FIVE-HOUR TRAIN TRIP TO WASHINGTON. The first-class seat the concierge at the Pennsylvania had procured for me allowed me the undisturbed rest and the peace to read my sisters' letters.

The contents of the letters were as different as the sisters who penned them.

Midge's letter shared that she was expecting a third child. Our family ran to twins, and I hoped she'd would be spared that burden in childbirth. She also damned the El Paso weather in language my mother would have appreciated and gave a gloomy account of her husband's prospects in the army now that the war was over. Her husband, Dodd, or Doddridge Emory Jr., had served in France as a captain in the tank corps, but with the war's end, he'd been returned home and his unit disbanded. He was kicking his heels on some general's staff at Fort Bliss, and Midge was worried he might be mustered out of the army. Yet despite the worry about Dodd's career, the risk of childbirth, and the sweltering desert heat of El Paso, her letter was cheerful and optimistic about the future.

We are healthy and the children are growing like weeds. Shelley turned nine last month and has yet to meet a math problem she can't whip, and Trey is five and has yet to meet a picture he can't draw. Or at least one he thinks he can't draw. They miss their uncle and would love to hear his war stories instead of their Poppa's. They keep reminding Dodd that you are a marine, which they know annoys him to no end. Please write!

I laughed at my sister's desire to play matchmaker. I was very sure that none of the girls she had in mind would be interested in me. She always thought I was better than I was. Midge was thinking of me, and it gave me a warm feeling.

It was clear that she and her family were happy.

Eleanor's letter had a different tone. She scolded me for not writing and then provided me with a detailed account of the Senate's debate of women's suffrage and the vote to grant it in June. Elle had always felt the need to find a good fight, and women's suffrage was the perfect one for her. For one horrible moment, I worried that the next subject in her letter might be her fervent support of the prohibition of ardent spirits, but it was not.

There was terrible rioting here in July. Soldiers, sailors, and marines swept through downtown Washington hunting for any poor negro they could find and beat them mercilessly. Several coloreds were killed. The newspapers claimed that the attacks were in retaliation for a series of assaults on white women,[3] but I think some people will just always hate black folks. It makes me sad. I worry that the attack might spread to Brightwood. Any rioter who stumbles into my home, I will shoot dead like a dog.

Brightwood was Eleanor's neighborhood in Washington. It seemed Omaha wasn't the only city with a race problem. I thought again of Bullard and Henry Johnson. It was no wonder that they were reluctant to return home when they could be attacked on the street by soldiers for the misfortune of their skin color.

---

3. "Service Men Beat Negros in Race Riot at Capitol," *New York Times*, July 21, 1919. Page 1.

After sharing the national news, Elle's letter cataloged her twin daughters' recent accomplishments with the piano and their fists, and she seemed equally proud of both. She reminded me that they were eight years old, and I couldn't help but think they would like Jean-Paul if they ever got to meet him.

God help him, if they ever did.

Finally, she mentioned her husband, Burton, had returned safely from France and was busy at the hospital. She thanked God that the influenza had passed. Despite the combative, emotional tone, her letter still conveyed the impression that she and her family were happy as well. I looked forward to seeing her.

The thought of my sisters being content brought a smile to my face. Maybe I had fought for something. Sitting across from me, Tippy Frederickson narrowed his eyes and sneered. "Don't bet on it. Death will come for them too."

I closed my eyes and pretended to sleep.

<hr>

THE TRAIN PULLED INTO UNION STATION IN A SWIRL OF STEAM. I gathered my bag and hurried down the crowded platform with the other passengers. The station was filled with uniforms, which surprised me. I supposed many men were going home after being mustered out.

A line of motorcabs stood waiting outside the arrival hall. I marveled at their number. It was just a matter of walking up to the first in line and calling my destination through the window to the driver. He told me the ride to the Washington would cost a quarter, and within twenty minutes, I was at the hotel.

It was likely too late to present myself at the White House, but I didn't want to delay. I left my pistol in my room. Armed with the letter from the First Lady and Churchill's letters to the president and Colonel House, I left the hotel and crossed Fifteenth Street. I passed the impressive bulk of the Treasury building on my left. Two soldiers stood at the top of the steps leading to the entry of the building.

I was certain a few soldiers would guard the entry to the White House as well. After all, the attack on Clemenceau was just a few months before, and President McKinley had been assassinated not twenty years ago. Given the bombings, the rioting, and the suffragettes my sister mentioned, I assumed the area would be teeming with doughboys and Secret Service agents, but I was wrong.

I turned south down the path between the Treasury building and the White House because I saw a small guardhouse at the east gate onto the White House grounds. My hope was that a guard there could guide me to the proper entrance.

A lone policeman with his thumbs tucked in his Sam Browne belt stood in front of the shack, watching me as I approached.

"I'm here to see the First Lady," I told him.

He looked me up and down. "Sorry, bub. You need a pass to get in."

"I have one." I handed Mrs. Wilson's letter to the copper.

He eyed me and then the letter. "Wait." He turned in to the guardhouse, which had a telephone box installed on the wall.

I wondered about the security of the president. If this policeman was the standard of quality for his protection, the First Lady was right to worry. One inattentive man didn't seem adequate to guard an entrance to the White House. The copper gave the phone a couple of cranks and held the earpiece close as he spoke softly into the mouthpiece. The only word I overheard was "Griffin."

He turned back to me. "Someone will be out for you in a minute."

It looked like I was actually going to get into the White House. The thought caused my stomach to roll at the possibility of seeing Wilson. Edith Wilson I could face. Seeing the president worried me. I hoped that after his breakdown, he'd be too tired or weak to take canine form.

A bespectacled, bow-tie-wearing man hurried out the glass-paned door of the White House, past the columns of the portico, to the gate where the policeman and I waited.

"Major Griffin? Ronald Wood," the man said, thrusting his hand at me. I shook it as he said, "I'm sorry. The First Lady sent me. As you would expect, caring for the president is occupying her energies presently. She does need to meet with you, but she just can't do so now. Please come the day after tomorrow in the morning."

He turned to the policeman. "Please tell whoever is on duty the morning of the second to expect the major at eight a.m. sharp."

"I'll be on duty, sir," the policeman answered, returning the First Lady's letter to me. "I'll look for you then, Major."

"Mr. Wood, before I go, I have a quick question."

"Yes?"

"Is Colonel House available? I am supposed to report to him as well."

"The Colonel no longer has an office at the White House. He offices in the tempos. Building A, I think, south of B Street near the National Mall." He pointed in that direction.

How the mighty had fallen. I shouldn't have been surprised given the tension between President Wilson and House when I saw them together in Paris.

"Tempos?" I asked.

"Yeah, the temporary buildings between the Capitol and the Natural History building. You can't miss them. Just look for the two smokestacks. Building A is the first on the north side, but they'll be closed this late in the day. Tomorrow morning would be better."

"Okay, thanks. I'll try to find him there, and I'll see you the day after tomorrow. Officer, thanks for the help. I guess I'll see you too." My comment caused the policeman to smile. I had a feeling he wasn't used to appreciation from the White House staff.

THE DELAY IN SEEING THE FIRST LADY MEANT THAT I HAD THE entire following day to search out House and Senator Lodge. I also decided that when I saw the First Lady, I would deliver Churchill's letter for Wilson to her. Churchill would be none the wiser, and I could then avoid the president entirely. Since I wasn't meeting Billy Jones until noon the following day, I would be able to report to him I'd delivered all the mail. We could pack up and take a ship back to England.

In the morning, I collected Churchill's letters and tucked them in my coat pocket. I left the letters from Mrs. Wilson, my sisters, and Neville neatly stacked on the corner of the bureau in my hotel room.

The weather was fine, and rather than take a taxi, I decided to walk to the National Mall and try to find the temporary building where Colonel House officed.

I was in no particular hurry since it was still early. The streets were crowded with motorcars, carts, and horse cabs, and the sidewalks teemed with men and a few women on their way to their work. Soldiers and sailors dotted the throng. The high, piercing calls of children hawking newspapers competed with the rumble of the other street noise. The smell of horse manure was ever present despite the bags rigged on most carts to catch the droppings. The number of people increased as I approached several long utilitarian concrete structures that had to be the temporary buildings I'd been told about.

A soldier manned the reception desk inside Building A, which was indeed the building nearest Avenue B on the northside of the mall. He sent me to the second floor, where I found House's suite of offices with no trouble. He might have been booted from the White House, but he'd found a decent enough substitute.

House seemed genuinely glad to see me.

"Major! Welcome home. Simms has kept me abreast of your successes on America's behalf. In Germany this time. Amazing."

Simms knew I'd been captured by German military intelligence and escaped, but he didn't know about the torture I'd endured in Basel at the hands of Schragmüller and Fuchs's minion Dr. Plöchner. House wouldn't be so impressed if he knew how badly my head was cracked.

"As you can see, my break with the president is complete. He has not seen me since we returned from Europe. Mrs. Wilson's maneuverings have successfully isolated me from her husband."

I made what I hoped was an appropriately consoling grunt, but the Colonel didn't seem to think it was sufficiently biased toward him.

"I tell you, Griffin. She poisoned the president against me, and I have been shouldered with all the blame for what we had to concede to obtain assurance that the League of Nations was in the final treaty…."

I let him talk and nodded when it seemed right. Even Tippy lost interest, vanishing shortly after House's tirade began.

"So you see, our efforts preserved the heart of the treaty and the peace," he said in summary.

"Indeed, sir, but I am afraid there may be a greater threat to the peace than the failure to ratify the treaty." I took Churchill's letters from my coat, separated out the one to House, and returned the remaining two to my pocket.

"What is this?" he asked as I handed him Churchill's missive.

"A letter from the Secretary of Air and War, Winston Churchill. Whether he is writing as a representative of Lloyd George's cabinet, I don't know. I just know he felt the delivery of these letters to be most urgent. In short, he believes the greatest threat to our collective way of life is a Bolshevik Russia. Given my work for the French and for you, sir," I said with some irony, "he believed I would be the ideal messenger to deliver a letter on his behalf to you, Senator Lodge, and President Wilson."

House used a silver letter opener from his desk drawer. The missive was two typewritten pages. I sat quietly while House read. He seemed to reread certain sections of the letter. When he finished, he placed the folded pages on his desk and examined me with his clever, piercing eyes.

"We should go see the president together."

"The First Lady sent for me, and I have an appointment with her tomorrow morning. She is going to accompany me when I speak to the president." I told the lie with complete conviction. No one would benefit if Colonel House accompanied me to the White House. Mrs. Wilson wouldn't see me if I were with him, and of course I didn't actually want to see the president.

"Aah. I see. Well, do you have an appointment with Senator Lodge?"

"No, I don't."

"Well, perhaps I can arrange a meeting with him."

I almost felt sorry for the poor bastard. He just wanted to matter again. He'd been at the center of a world power since 1912, and now he was out of the spotlight. He must have found it painful to be an irrelevant nobody once again. Welcome to the party, Colonel. My visit offered an opportunity for him to reclaim some of his former importance. Well, if he could get me in to see Senator Lodge without having to wait around, I'd let him.

"That would be very helpful, sir," I told him.

"Let me make a few calls and see what I can do. Come back after lunch. I'll know something by then."

I promised him I would.

I USED THE TIME I HAD BEFORE RETURNING TO COLONEL HOUSE TO find the Army and Navy Club. I didn't expect to see Neville, but I did hope to leave a message for him. I had considered asking House where the club was located, but I didn't want him to sink his paws into any meeting I had with Neville. My discussions with the general wouldn't involve the treaty or Churchill. I needed to see Neville to find out about Armistan and the War

Industries Board. I could ask House about the WIB, but I didn't trust his discretion. If it turned out I had to gun down board members—the older Reynolds and Armistan—I certainly didn't trust that House would have any loyalty to me.

Despite the regard that seemed to have grown between us, I was sure I remained a tool to be used and, if necessary, discarded. And so was he for me.

I walked back past the White House and asked the policeman in the shack where the Army and Navy Club might be. A different copper from the one I'd met earlier was there, but he was helpful enough. He told me I'd find the club on Farragut Square, a couple of blocks north of the White House.

I walked past Lafayette Square and crossed H Street. The club was an impressive multistory brick building at the corner of Seventeenth and I Street. Red-and-white-striped awnings shaded the many windows, and a colored doorman in a top hat and tails guarded the wrought iron entrance.

"Good morning, sir, how can I help you this morning?"

"I received a letter from General Neville asking that I contact him through the club."

"The general is not presently in attendance; however, if you would like to leave him a note, the club can provide you some writing materials."

He allowed me to enter the ornate foyer and directed me to a small standing desk designed for the express purpose of allowing visitors to leave messages for the membership.

"Just leave it at the front desk when you're done," the doorman told me. He left me to return to his post outside.

Sheets of creamy paper bearing the Army and Navy Club crest of crossed cannons atop an anchor stood in a stack on the desk. I wrote a quick note to the general with the fountain pen provided and sealed my request for a meeting in an envelope, which also bore the club's crest.

I addressed the note and carried it to the club's reception desk.

"We'll see that the general receives this as soon as possible, sir," the dignified, gray-haired attendant told me.

House was waiting for me when I returned to his office.

"I have a driver downstairs. Senator Lodge is expecting us shortly, so we need to hurry." I didn't argue. I followed the bustling House out of his office building and into his motorcar.

Once we were in the automobile and moving, House explained what he had accomplished. "Senator Lodge is eager to meet you. We spoke briefly on the telephone. I must warn you, he is no friend to the president. But he does love this country, and he will do what he believes is right for her. At present, he is opposed to the Treaty of Versailles. He has certain reservations he would like included in the treaty before he's willing to vote for ratification. He is enormously influential in the Senate. Don't say anything that might damage the president or the treaty."

I nodded. I didn't know what I might say that could hurt Wilson or the treaty, but I suspected Churchill's letter wouldn't help either one. He was more interested in rolling back Bolshevism than seeing the treaty ratified. I was certain House knew this, yet he was arranging my meeting with Senator Lodge. It seemed inexplicable. At least it did until we were in the meeting with the senator.

The Senate office building was straight down B Street from House's office in the tempos. We disembarked from the automobile directly in front of the broad steps leading up to a grand building at the corner of Delaware and B Street. Marble columns over large arched windows marched down the side of the building that faced B Street. It was at least as grand as any government offices I'd seen in Paris and London.

No soldiers or policemen stood guard, and we entered with no fanfare. The inside was even more impressive than the outside. We walked through a high-arched door into a rotunda circled by identical arches. The marble-faced columns and floors glowed with the warm sunlight pouring from a skylight in the domed ceiling above. I felt like I'd stepped into a church.

If the owners of my baseball team, the Senators, spent money on the team the way the US Senate spent money adorning their office building, we'd win the World Series every year. But other than sharing a name and a city, the paupers of baseball had nothing in common with the men working in this building. As my father used to tease, quoting his favorite sportswriter, "Washington: First in war, first in peace, and last in the American League."[4] He would then laugh wildly, and my sisters would join in. Not because they understood how bad the Senators were at baseball, but because they enjoyed my discomfort.

"His office is this way," House said, leading me to the stairway beyond the arches. We climbed to the second floor and passed a few doors to one labeled SENATOR HENRY CABOT LODGE, SR., MASSACHUSETTS. The door was already open. An assistant rose as we entered.

"Colonel House. A pleasure to see you again. Please follow me, gentlemen." He didn't bother to get my name. He understood the pecking order, and I wasn't in it.

Senator Lodge, for it could have only been the senator, stood from behind his heavy wood desk as we entered. He had curly salt-and-pepper hair cut short, and he wore a white beard long in the mustache and chin and short on the sides. He looked exactly as a US senator should, which made me dislike him, yet he produced no fake smile as he came around his desk to shake our hands. There was no smile at all. Just a serious, intent look, and I decided that I might have to reserve judgment before deciding to loathe Senator Lodge.

"Major Griffin, the colonel explained that you carry a letter for me from the British government."

"I have a letter for you, sir, but I would not claim it comes from Lloyd George's government. I don't know with what authority Secretary Churchill writes, but he was very eager that I

---

4. *Washington Post.* June 27, 1904.

deliver this letter to you promptly and in person." I handed him his envelope.

"Excuse me, gentlemen. If Mr. Churchill is eager that this be delivered, he would be eager that I read it. Please have a seat." He gestured to a couch and chairs in front of his desk, and he sat back down.

We sat, and neither of us spoke as we waited for Lodge to read Churchill's letter. His was two pages as well.

Lodge finished the letter quickly. He didn't bother rereading sections as House had.

"Are you aware of the contents, Colonel?"

"If the contents of your letter are similar to mine, the bogeyman of Bolshevism has Churchill by the throat," House answered.

"Indeed. It is the same. But I am not sure Bolshevism is a bogeyman, Edward. Did Churchill mention in your letter that he believes defeating the revolution in Russia is more important to peace and world order than ratification of the Treaty of Versailles?" He was speaking to House, using his Christian name. I had thought that because he was hostile to the president, he wouldn't get along well with House. It was clear that I didn't understand how politics worked. The men apparently liked and respected each other.

"Churchill's arguments are compelling," Lodge continued. "And you must admit that anarchist and Bolshevik activities here in America are worrisome. If they weren't, the attorney general wouldn't be on the warpath against dissidents of every stripe and religion."

I didn't know that there were Bolshevik dissidents associated with any religions, but I had a sneaking suspicion that they were talking about Jews in the same way Sir Basil had in London.

"I am not sure you should use Attorney General Palmer as your measure of the danger associated with the Red threat," House answered. "Mitchell Palmer is an ambitious man and knows that the best way to generate followers is to create enemies for them to fear."

"I'm not using him as my measure of the Red threat. He's in the president's cabinet, which means the president does or should be using him as his measure of that threat."

"You know the president spends very little time consulting with others."

"Yes, I know that all too well."

"Please, Henry. Don't let Churchill's letter divert you from the work on the treaty. It must be passed."

"We must have a peace with Germany, but it doesn't have to be this treaty. And I am beginning to think it shouldn't be. It seeks to deal with the world as the president wants it to be, not as it is. A war to end all wars? Peace without victory? These are nonsensical fantasies that endanger the American people." Lodge turned to me. "Will you be returning to England and Churchill?"

"I'll be going back to England to report to the minister that his letters successfully reached their destinations, Senator," I said carefully.

"Good. I would ask that you deliver a response to him on my behalf."

I saw no way to gracefully avoid continuing my duties as messenger boy, and so I agreed.

"Where can I have it delivered?"

"I'm staying at the Washington Hotel for at least the next few days," I said.

"I'll have it there tomorrow morning."

House glared at me as if I had betrayed him, but I had no idea what else I could have done. I took my leave without asking about the War Industries Board. I would have to learn about the board from others. I didn't want to run the risk that Lodge or House would draft me into their competing schemes.

It took me until I was at the bottom of the marble steps exiting the Senate office building rotunda to realize I had already been drafted by Lodge. As with Churchill, I was to be his pet postman as well. I was becoming inured to submitting to the demands of the powerful, and it disgusted me.

Tippy laughed at me all the way to the cable car stop on Delaware Avenue.

17

Throbbing Drapery

Although no one else waited at the stop, when the streetcar arrived, most of the seats were filled. I paid the conductor a nickel and moved to the middle of the car. I found an empty bench by a window where I could watch the city pass. The car had no signs declaring it to be segregated, but the negroes on board mostly populated the section I occupied.

Tippy muttered damning comments about me in my ear as I tried to focus on the city's activity beyond the window. At the next stop, I felt a passenger take the seat next to me. I turned to nod a welcome, and my heart stopped.

"Hello, John."

Karl Fuchs was sitting next to me.

Fuchs. Hatchet man for Elsbeth Schragmüller, who masterminded the German plot that manipulated me and ultimately broke my mind.

I couldn't speak. I couldn't move.

"You look pale. You should get some sun, John," Fuchs said with a barely perceptible smile.

The two of us sat on a bench surrounded by negroes in the

middle of a Washington streetcar. We couldn't have been more isolated in my room at the hotel. Nausea washed through me, and for a moment, I felt like I was about to vomit.

Tippy retreated back into my head, where he didn't think Fuchs could find him. Tippy's terror at Fuchs's presence helped me recover from some of the shock of seeing the German intelligence officer.

"I'm not here to hurt you." Fuchs reached out a hand and patted my leg.

It took all my strength not to jerk away. Thank God it wasn't a paw, or I would have failed.

"How did you find me?"

"Oh John, you are such an innocent. You were under Dr. Plöchner's care for five days. We had plenty of time to explore your conscious and unconscious mind. We know of your unhappy affair with Sarah Willoughby, your hatred of Harry Armistan, and your preference for the Hotel Pennsylvania in New York. You are not so hard to track. You are not a very clever fellow."

"What do you want from me?" I asked hoarsely.

"I am here to remind you of what you learned in Basel."

"You have no idea what I learned in Basel." I spoke in barely a whisper.

"You are an American hero. You love America," he said. I'd heard these phrases before. Schragmüller had said them to me. Fuchs leaned closer, our shoulders touching. I was wedged against the streetcar window.

"Woodrow Wilson has betrayed America. Wilson is a traitor to America." He was reciting back to me the script Schragmüller had used in Basel. He seemed to think the mescaline-induced hallucinations and torture still had their hold on me.

Snakes writhed in the back of my head. Maybe they did.

"I'm not naked in a basement now, Karl." I made the claim as much for me as for him.

He straightened, no longer pressed against me. He didn't seem disappointed at my resistance.

"No. You are not, John. But it does not matter. Wilson should not be allowed to betray America. You still care about your country. And you have a sister with a beautiful family living in Brightwood just a few kilometers away. She should remain safe. Only you can make sure she remains safe."

He stood quickly. The cable car was coming to a stop.

How did he know about my sister? I grabbed his arm.

"Don't do anything foolish, John. Even you wouldn't risk a gunfight on a busy streetcar." Two men were working their way down the aisle toward us. Fuchs wasn't alone. Of course he wasn't. The men had the look of former soldiers, and Germany was teeming with willing squareheads like these two. God only knew how he'd gotten them into the country. Whether he was bluffing or not didn't matter. I didn't know if they were armed, but I knew I was not. I wanted to threaten him. Rail that hellfire would rain down on him if he even thought about my sister, but I didn't believe in empty threats. I would look weaker than he already thought I was.

Instead, I pulled him close, forcing him to bend toward me. I saw a flicker of fear in his eyes, and it gave me strength.

"You're right, Karl. No president should be allowed to betray America," I said with urgency. "Where can I find you? What you want done will not be easy. I may need help."

He studied me for a moment. His men moved closer. They were worried about him. They were right to be. I could try to finish him right here, but I had no doubt it would be the end of me too.

"I will find you, but if you are in a great hurry, contact me through the Swiss embassy. I am now Swiss," he said. "We are all Swiss. I work for the Swiss ambassador, Herr Sulzer, in the Department of German Interests. Germany has no embassy in the United States, and Switzerland has the protecting power mandate for Germany. You can get a message to me through his office."

I let him tug his arm away.

"We will be watching with great anticipation, John. I know the president is exhausting himself urging the benefits of the treaty to the American people. It seems as if he is meeting with some success. His success would be unfortunate for us all. *Klar?*"

Fuchs and his men were off the car and swallowed by the traffic before I thought to ask him the address of the Swiss embassy. The train restarted, rattling along the tracks passing other streetcars, automobiles, and pedestrians, putting distance between me and my enemies. All I could think about was the threat to my sister. I believed Elle could take care of herself, but I needed to warn her. Despite my agitation at seeing Fuchs, I remembered that my sister needed to sign the damn lawyer's papers. Once in my room, I put on my shoulder holster and picked out the legal letter from those scattered on the top of the bureau. Fortunately the WR&E[1] train serviced most of the District of Columbia. I hurried back out and took another cable car north to Brightwood and my sister.

ELLE'S HUSBAND, BURTON, WAS BASED AT WALTER REED GENERAL Hospital. He was a relaxed, mild-mannered man with a sharp intelligence and a sharper wit that I enjoyed when it wasn't aimed at me. The prewar army had been a small, incestuous organization. My sisters, both pretty girls living on army posts, were necessarily courted by my father's fellow officers, but my dad made it clear that no one who served with him in the infantry was welcome to call on his daughters. As a result, one sister married a cavalryman and the other an army doctor. Burton, the doctor, although temporarily assigned to a military

---

1. Washington Railway and Electric Company.

hospital in France during the war, had been stationed at Walter Reed since 1914. Their Brightwood neighborhood was near the hospital.

I walked from the streetcar stop to my sister's home on Fourteenth Street. All the houses on her block sat on a slight rise above the road. Her two-story, wood-sided home looked cozy but in need of a coat of paint. I knew it was drafty as hell in winter, but my sister had been there for years. She would be disappointed when Burton was transferred out of Washington.

Her girls should be home from school, and I looked forward to seeing them. The last time I'd visited, just after returning from England in late 1916, they had been five or so. Small whirlwinds of noise and emotion bouncing through Elle's house.

I climbed the stepped path to the front door and pushed the button for the electrical doorbell. The abrasive ringing set off a series of shouts, barks, and running around inside. The girls were indeed home, and my sister now had a dog. The thought made me smile. I was still smiling when the front door opened, and my sister looked at me through the screen door. Her reddish hair was pulled back in a bun, but much of it was trying to escape. She wore no cosmetics yet didn't look much older than the last time I'd seen her.

I took off my hat and watched recognition, relief, and affection flood my sister's face. Her look made all my problems smaller even if just for a moment.

"Hey, beautiful sister," I said.

She whipped the screen door open and seized me in a bone-breaking hug.

A black-haired mutt jumped and yapped around my knees.

"John! Oh God, John! It's so good to see you!"

"Momma!" I heard from behind her. "Don't swear. It ain't ladylike."

"And neither is saying 'ain't,'" my sister answered.

"No! It isn't," another girl's voice said.

She released me from the hug but kept hold of my arm as if I might fly away.

"Girls, this is your Uncle John. Do you remember him?"

"Of course, Mother," a smaller version of my sister said as Elle pulled me into the house.

"But last time we saw you, you had your head wrapped in a scarf," the other miniature of my sister said. "And you couldn't see too well."

"Very well," interjected my sister.

"Yes, that's true," I said. "I prefer to think of that scarf as a bandage, but it did look an awful lot like a scarf." Both little girls laughed. They shared their mother's coloring: pale skin, light curling strawberry blond hair. With each other, they shared skinned knees, which I could see below their identical plaid dresses, and mischievous smiles.

"Will that red patch on your face go away, Uncle John?"

"Clara!" My sister scolded her daughter.

"I don't think so, Clara." I tried to record the differences between her and her sister so I wouldn't confuse them. "It might fade a bit, but I'm pretty sure it's here to stay."

"Well, I think it makes you look fierce, and so does Doughboy," her sister said.

The dog was still yapping at me.

"Enough!" my sister barked back at the dog. "Doughboy! Stop!"

The dog backed up for a moment, then barked again.

"Anna, Clara, go outside and play with Dumbboy."

"Momma, she's not dumb and that's not nice," Anna said, scolding her mother.

"Then maybe she should stop barking."

The girls ran to the back of the house, the dog turned in a circle once and followed them, barking on the way.

"Sorry, John, she'll settle down in a bit."

"She?"

"The girls wanted a dog. We got her just after you joined the

Marine Corps. They wanted to name it Doughboy, because of you. They didn't care that she was a girl. She was always going to be named Doughboy. After seeing the shape you were in when you came back from France the first time, none of us thought we'd see you again."

She had tears in her eyes, and I did my best to ignore them. "Well, it's good to see you and the girls, Elle. They seem great. How's Burton?"

"He's well. Busy army doctoring his way into the textbooks. New procedures for all sorts of surgeries. He says the war taught him a lot, but he won't talk about it. Coffee or I could make you a drink? Prohibition *is* just around the corner."

"Coffee is fine. Maybe when Burton gets home we can all have a drink together." I could understand why Burt didn't want to talk about the war, and I didn't blame him.

I followed her into the kitchen where four chairs surrounded a table that showed evidence of Roman numerals and fractions homework.

"You look tired, John," she said as she poured me a cup of coffee from a pot on the stovetop. "Are you okay?"

"Tell her about me, my friend," Tippy suggested from behind me.

"Fine. I'm fine," I answered. "But I needed to see you." I took the lawyer's letter from my coat and laid it on the table. "Mom and Dad's estate. A few more signatures, but that isn't why I needed to talk to you."

She had removed the contents from the envelope. My tone caught her attention.

"Does it have anything to do with the gun under your coat?"

She must have felt the pistol when she hugged me.

"It does. I hope you have time for a story, and I hope you still have grampa's old cavalry pistol."

"In the trunk upstairs under our bed. It's unloaded," she said with concern.

"You need to have it handy."

"I'll talk to Burt. He's got his bird gun too. We'll keep them both handy. Is there romance in your story?" she asked, joking to ease her fear at my gravity.

"Yeah, there sure is and some heroic derring-do on my part," I promised her. She laughed, and for the next hour, I told my sister about my job for Armistan, the Bolshevik plot, the attempted assassination of Clemenceau, my lies to House and the French, the trip to Germany, and my messenger duty for Churchill and the planned meeting with Edith Wilson. Despite how outrageous some of the story sounded, she didn't doubt me. She believed me.

I tried to minimize my relationship with Sarah, but she pulled the truth out of me. She actually teared up and took my hand when I told her Sarah had been killed. I didn't mention Madeline at all, which felt a little disloyal, but I didn't want my sister to catch the scent of another girl she could grill me about. I also didn't include Marie Masson. That relationship was just too complicated. After all, the point in telling her the story at all was to warn her about Karl Fuchs, Elsbeth Schragmüller, and the German plot to kill Wilson. I didn't tell her about the Basel basement or the ghosts following me. My sister loved me, and she probably still would even if she thought I was crazy. I just didn't want to find out.

"Elle, the Krauts are here. The worst of them is here. I saw him on the streetcar. And he knows you live in Washington with your family. I don't know how, but he does."

"It doesn't matter, John. We've got the best guard dog on the block. She barks anytime a stranger comes near the house. We've also got good neighbors. I'll tell them to keep an eye out for foreigners. That's sure to keep them on their toes."

"He's got Swiss papers, and his men probably do too. Don't take any chances. I saw him murder a woman at a dinner table, and I couldn't do a damn thing about it."

"My God, John. It seems your life has only gotten more dangerous with the end of the war. You need to come home. Find a nice girl and settle down."

"Sorry, did she say 'you need to find a bullet in your head and fall to the ground?'" Frederickson asked innocently. "That's what I heard."

Burton came home not long after, and the three of us sat on the back porch with soon-to-be-illegal whiskies in our hands, catching up. We finished our drinks, and as the sun set, Eleanor went in the house to make dinner. I told Burton an abbreviated version of my adventures of the past few months, and my sister shouted uncomplimentary commentary about my intelligence and decision-making from the kitchen.

When I described the attack on Clemenceau, she stepped onto the porch and relistened while shaking her head at either my luck or my stupidity.

"Burton, honestly, what sort of dope charges a machine gun on a Paris street."

Burton rolled his eyes at me in apology.

When I got to Sarah's death, she retreated to the kitchen with tears in her eyes. As I relayed the attack on the Mangin family in Mainz, she called through the screen door, "See? A dope."

I never mentioned Basel to either of them. Fuchs and Schragmüller had done plenty without the need to mention the torture.

The girls returned from wherever they had gone with the dog. At some point in the evening, Doughboy decided that I wasn't a stranger anymore. She was dozing at my ankles by the time I had to leave.

Burt remained a solid, congenial foil to Elle's unrelenting intensity, and despite their physical similarities, the girls were as different as my own two sisters. Both were sharp as tacks but uniquely so. I said my goodbyes on the porch, with hugs and kisses for the girls, a handshake for Burton, and a final ear scratch for the dog. The time spent with my sister and her family was a balm for my troubled mind. Tippy and the others left me alone on the way back to the hotel. Unfortunately, the warm glow seeing my sister and her family had created would not last.

THE SENSE OF CALM MY SISTER'S FAMILY HAD GIVEN ME SO distracted me that I missed my stop and ended up leaving the streetcar on Pennsylvania Avenue near the Capitol. I retraced the route the train took, crossing Ninth Street. From where I stood on Pennsylvania, it was clear that Ninth was the place to be in the evenings in Washington.

The time with my sister and her family left me hungry for more companionship, and I decided to have a final drink. The next day promised to put an end to my obligations to Churchill, and I hoped I could swiftly address whatever the First Lady wanted.

I turned up Ninth Street. It was past nine p.m., and while the high-class theaters were closing, the burlesque shows and bars along the street were in full swing, hell-bent on squeezing the last few bucks from a soon to be dry America. I passed the ornate and gaudy Gayety Theater with its flashing lights designed to lure in those passing. It looked to be the beating heart of Washington's entertainment district. The cafés that flanked the theater looked like the type of places my old mates from the Rifles or the marines would go to drink cheap beer, get in fights, and meet the wrong kind of women.

I kept walking. I'd either find a more sedate place or I'd have a drink at the hotel bar. I didn't want to risk losing the glow I had from Eleanor and her family in such haunts.

At F Street, I took a left toward the hotel, and just before reaching the Washington, I came upon two bars, side by side and sharing a single entrance. They looked like they catered to the more well-to-do theatergoing crowd that had just let out.

I pushed through the door and was given the choice between a Dutch room and an English room. I thought it serendipitous that I could return to England, so I did. The pub had a mirror-backed bar stretching the length of the room. Tables occupied by tuxedoed men and their bejeweled women indicated that I had found the place for the silk-stocking crowd.

Indifferent to the fact that I probably didn't fit in, I took a seat near the far end of the bar.

While I waited for one of the bartenders to notice me, I watched the white-jacketed waiters carry trays of oysters from the kitchen to the crowded tables. The patrons were laughing and drinking champagne and what looked like French 75s as they ate their late-night fare. They all knew Prohibition was coming.

I ordered a whiskey neat and caught a glimpse of myself in the mirror. It was dim, but there was enough light to see the scar and the shadows under my eyes. I looked gaunt and fragile.

The bartender placed my drink before me without a word.

A young woman pushed up to the bar between me and the couple next to me.

She was pretty, with lively eyes, an easy smile, and a pert air that assured me she wasn't alone.

She felt my gaze and glanced at me as she waved a hand at the nearest bartender. He noticed her a lot quicker than he noticed me.

"A French 75," she said. Champagne and French 75s. Not so different from Paris.

I looked back at the mirror and caught the eyes of the girl at my side watching me.

I turned to face her squarely. She didn't flinch at seeing my scarred face.

"Looks like you should have used a safety razor, mister," she said.

I couldn't suppress a laugh. "Not sure that would have made a difference."

The bartender set her drink before her.

"Well, here's to modern innovations even if some of us don't use them," she said, raising her glass and her eyebrow.

I lifted mine in acknowledgment of her toast but didn't drink. She didn't care and took a healthy sip of her own.

"You one of the government drudges working on the Hill?" she asked.

Maybe she was alone. For some reason, that disappointed me.

"Just in town visiting."

She tossed back the remainder of her drink and waved a hand at the nearest bartender.

"Another, please," she ordered.

"Where you from?" She was talking to me again.

I glanced at her and answered, "Here and there. My father was in the army."

I turned back to my drink.

"You're supposed to ask me where I'm from. That's what normal folks do."

I looked at her, wondering why she was bothering me. "Are you meeting someone?" I asked.

"No. I just stop in here for a drink now and then. I'm from Massachusetts," she volunteered.

I grunted.

"And you? Were you in the army?" she asked.

"Marines."

"*Semper fidelis*," she said.

"You know a marine?"

"My dad, but he was a real bastard. I figure he went to so many shitty places filled with bugs, snakes, and little brown people trying to kill him that the springs in his head just got too stretched. It was probably not his fault."

"You may be right about that."

"Yeah, well, it sure didn't make growing up around him easy."

"Sorry to hear that. Those old-timers were tough as nails."

"How about you finish your drink, and you buy us two more," she suggested. She had finished her second drink.

"You're a brave woman, but I don't think so."

She shrugged. "Broken heart, huh," she declared with certainty.

"I'm just here for the drink, miss. Not the company."

"A sentiment I can understand. Well then, cheers." She lifted her empty glass and clinked it against mine. She then swiveled on the barstool to study the room.

I liked her for her irreverence and indifference, but her presence made me uncomfortable. It was time to go back to the hotel and hit the rack.

"Is the ladies' back there?" she asked. She pointed to the back of the bar. There was a hallway there that was the only possible location for the toilets.

"Must be," I said, turning back to her. "Enjoy your evening." I finished my whiskey, put a dollar on the bar, and left.

The short walk along F Street to the hotel was enough time for the drink to turn sour in my stomach. Briefly I worried that my sister's dinner had somehow poisoned me. She was a wonderful sister, but her cooking was not the equal of her personality.

By the time I reached my room, I understood that it was the interaction with the woman in the bar that had knotted my stomach. I felt physically nauseated from the encounter. It depressed me.

I left the lights off and sat on the end of the bed considering the meeting. I might have sat there for five minutes or an hour. I didn't know.

"Broken heart," the woman had declared.

That was it.

That comment was eating at me.

It reminded me of Mitchell lying broken on the wet street in London. Marie and Jean-Paul turning to leave my room at Military Hospital No. 1. Madeline promising to see me soon and then disappearing. Sarah professing her love for me and stepping to the window with a rifle at her shoulder.

I did have a broken heart.

And a broken mind.

The curtains framing the windows fluttered as if in a breeze.

The lights from the street below cast shadows into my darkened room.

A broken mind. That thought and the now throbbing drapery warned me that something was coming.

The woman at the bar had asked me where the toilet was. I'd turned away from her to look where she was pointing.

She had put something in my drink.

I was horrified. My current depression wasn't natural. She'd caused it, and I suddenly understood what was to come.

The crown molding framing the room undulated in time with my pulse, and that same beat pounded like a bass drum inside my head, vibrating my eyes. Vibrating all my senses.

Tippy was suddenly with me on the bed, sitting right beside me. He wore a jubilant grin.

"Here we go, Jack!"

He was right. Here we go. At least this time I wasn't strapped to a dissection table.

Goddamn mescaline. Goddamn Fuchs and Schragmüller.

I fell back on the bed and was consumed.

The shapes in the shadows on the ceiling reveal themselves to be soldiers huddled together wearing Brodie helmets: ranks of men topped with inverted metal salad bowls on their heads. Either Tommies or Yanks. It doesn't matter, for I am both.

Our bayonets are fixed. We cross smashed trenches on a red hotel carpet. Artillery shells passing overhead shake my bones. A walking barrage.

Dogs in field-gray tunics bound away from us. They stop and turn to see if we will follow. When we do, they lope into the trenches ahead and disappear through gated elevator doors.

There is no sound but my heartbeat.

The smell of cut grass fills me with terror.

Where is Wilson? He should be here.

I catch a toe on a shattered root and tumble to the floor of a crumbling trench. Barbs on broken wire snag me. I pull and twist but can't get free. I'm trapped on the wet duckboards. Before me, Armistan sits in an armchair in the door of a dugout, wearing a top hat and tails. His mouth moves but I hear nothing. His words taste and smell vile. Bitter and putrid. Behind him, a shadow that is Reynolds lurks.

The walls of the trench waver, and shells shake the chandelier as they pass overhead.

The sensations fracture. Light, smell, and sound comingle and are inseparable. The visions before me lose their depth. Reality is two-dimensional flat and quivering.

It seems like it takes days for me to reorder my senses, to move my sight to my eyes, my hearing to my ears, touch to my skin. As time passes, depth returns to the room around me.

MY HOTEL ROOM WAS DARK. I WAS ON THE FLOOR, LOOKING AT THE nightstand lamp, which was lying broken next to me. The nightstand was shifted away from the bed. I tried to push myself off the floor, but my movement was restricted. I looked down at myself with dread. Was I again strapped to a table? Relief flooded into me as I realized my jacket and the pistol harness underneath had been twisted halfway down my chest by thrashing I didn't know I'd done. Judging by the nightstand and lamp, I must have rolled about wildly during my hallucinations.

"How was that for you, you bastard?" Tippy asked. He was sitting on the bed above me.

I managed to sit and pull my arms free of my coat and the harness. I stood, using the bed for balance. My hand passed through Frederickson's leg with no resistance.

I was shaking and weak. In my mind, the thin light coming into the room from the street flickered. Indistinct images crowded the edges of my vision but didn't overwhelm it. The effect of the mescaline had faded. The dosage the young woman had dumped into my whiskey was not nearly as potent as the massive, repeated doses Dr. Plöchner had given me intravenously in Basel.

I looked at my watch. The luminescent hands told me it was nearly five o'clock in the morning.

I stumbled to the bathroom, turned on the cold tap, and thrust my head under the jet of water.

"Drowning yourself?" Tippy called from the bedroom.

I stayed under the faucet for some minutes. I wasn't exactly sure how long. I scooped cold water into my mouth. I was surprised at how thirsty I was. Eventually I straightened with water running off my head, soaking my shirt.

The bathroom mirror told the story of my night. I had circles under my eyes so dark they looked like bruises, and my pupils were so big they confined the muddy color of my irises to the edges of my eyes, exaggerating my perpetual haunted look. I looked like I felt: rode hard and put up wet. I had three hours to clean myself up before meeting with the First Lady. I didn't know if I could, but I had no choice but to try.

I used the room telephone to order a pot of coffee.

18

―――――――

Goldfish Kissing

By the time I stood outside the east gate of the White House a few minutes before eight, I was about as squared away as could reasonably be expected. I had consumed the entire pot of coffee when it arrived. I'd also ordered a ham-and-spinach omelet, but one forkful convinced me that my stomach would violently revolt at the taste and the texture. I spit the lone bite back onto the plate to keep from vomiting. I tested the toast and found I could keep it down if I ate small pieces. Buttering it was out of the question.

I found that the advantage of an expensive hotel wasn't just the room service, but having an attached bathroom allowed me to take a long, hot shower with no other guests complaining. I gave myself a shock by turning off the hot water tap and standing under a spray of cold water for several minutes. By the time I dried off and dressed, the figures, canine and human, had retreated fully from my awareness. I pulled the knot of my tie tight. I believed I could function well enough to deliver Wilson's letter to the First Lady and escape the White House without any problem. I was wrong.

Outside the White House gate, I was distracted by the scent or perhaps the sound of the leaves beginning to turn with the coming of fall. The same officer was on duty from my first visit. He had seen me striding down the path between Treasury and the White House grounds and had used the call box to announce my arrival.

As I awkwardly greeted the policeman, Mr. Wood came out from the east door and waved me to him. The officer nodded, and I passed through the wrought iron gate and onto the White House grounds.

"The First Lady is eager to see you, Major," Wood told me. He didn't wait for a reply, which was good because my brain was too dulled to think of one. He hurried me down a long colonnade to the main building of the White House.

"As you would expect, she's staying close to the president. He's very tired from his travels. You've been to the White House?"

The change of topic caught me off guard. I was hot. I couldn't get enough air. My mind was having trouble keeping up with events. I felt the same numbness that had enveloped me when I'd been trapped in a dugout enduring prolonged shelling.

"No," I finally managed to say.

"This is the East Garden Room," he said as we passed through a ballroom with two huge chandeliers and benches lining the walls.

After that description, the tour was over because we were into a long hallway that extended the length of the house. The house itself was as quiet as a church. Unsurprising, given the hour.

Wood guided me up a broad staircase on to the second floor and stopped on the landing.

"Second door on the right," he said, pointing down the hall. "The First Lady will meet you there." I was confused. "Good luck, Major." He turned back down the stairs.

The thickness in my head made my thinking slow, and I didn't understand why he didn't take me directly to the First Lady. I was in the White House, unattended, with only the barest of instructions. I felt dizzy. My recent encounter with Fuchs and the woman at the bar had been profoundly unsettling.

"You're fine, Jack. You're fine," Tippy Frederickson whispered.

I knew I wasn't fine. If Tippy sought to reassure me, something was dreadfully wrong. Unfortunately, I was committed to wherever this course would take me. With a deep breath, I walked down the hall past the first door on the right. It was open, and inside was a circular room with windows overlooking the south lawn. It was set up like the parlor at my parents' house: couches, chairs, useless little vases.

I stopped at the second door on the right. It was closed. My brain felt disconnected from my body. Disconnected from my surroundings. My body was operating automatically. The feeling wasn't new, and it wasn't welcome.

Up and down the trench, officers blow whistles signaling the attack. Men in muddy khaki swarm up the ladders. I follow. Not thinking. Just doing. The barrel of my Enfield knocks my helmet down over my eyes as I top the ladder. My mind refuses to accept the reality of the hammering Maxim guns chopping down the men in front of me. It's loud. So loud. Shouting. Whizzing bullets striking flesh, belt buckles, rifles, helmets, and dirt. The wails of the wounded. As I run forward, the sticking mud slows my boots. I am breathless and terrified.

The door remained closed in front of me, waiting for me to have the courage to knock. I watched my arm extend and my knuckles rap on the wood before me.

Mrs. Wilson cracked the door, recognized me, and pulled me by the arm into the room.

"Major, thank you for coming. So you got my note?"

We were in a sitting room. A blanket and a pillow were thrown on a settee, which stood between the window and a door leading off to the right. Mrs. Wilson was alone, and despite my muddled brain, I understood from her rumpled clothes that she had slept on the couch. I dreaded what was on the other side of the door, but part of me, the part that was born in the Swiss basement, rejoiced that she was alone. I wasn't myself. Why would I be pleased she was alone?

Suddenly I understood everything. A mescaline-hangover epiphany.

Fuchs had braced me on the bus because he wanted to remind me of the horror of the Basel cellar. He wanted me to recall the images and emotions of Wilson produced by Plöchner, the drugs, and the pain. He gave me a small refresher of the basement training and then sent his agent to drug me one last time. He was relying on my previous overexposure to Wilson to awaken the fear and hostility created in Basel.

His meeting with me on the streetcar and my meeting with the girl in the bar were part of Plöchner's nefarious regimen of persuasion. German intelligence still believed I was a threat to Wilson. Fuchs, and no doubt his boss Schragmüller, expected me to kill Wilson.

That was why part of me was pleased. I was right where Schragmüller's scheming wanted me to be, and the horrible, twisted part of my brain was happy. The Germans had broken my mind in Basel, and they hoped that Fuchs's reminder and another drug-induced horror show would finish the work.

But I wouldn't kill the president. I knew in my bones he slept on the other side of the closed door, but I wouldn't kill him.

"Major?" I hadn't answered Mrs. Wilson. What had she asked? Oh yes, her note.

"Yes, ma'am, I got your letter at the Hotel Pennsylvania in New York, but I needed to come to the White House in any event on other business," I managed to say. "I trust the president is resting after his campaign on behalf of the treaty."

"Mr. Wilson has exhausted himself in the effort. I am doing the best I can to limit the demands on his attention. Time will only tell whether I have succeeded. Do you need to see the president in person? He needs to rest."

"No, no, I don't need to see him in person." A part of me was on the edge of panic at the thought. But not all. I didn't know what would happen to me if I saw the president. "I have a letter for him from the British Secretary for Air and War, Winston Churchill." I took Churchill's letter from my coat and handed it to her.

She took it automatically, glancing at it briefly. "The tour promoting the treaty taxed the president's energy. He needs rest. I trust this letter can wait."

"I know the minister was eager to see it delivered, ma'am. More than that I cannot say."

"Good. That's good. I'll see that the president gets it at the appropriate time."

Unfortunately for Mr. Churchill, his letter to her husband was not important. Only her husband was.

"Major, I called you here because I need your help."

"Ma'am?"

"I need someone I trust. A war hero. Someone who loves America. I need you, because you are a patriot and have no interest in or connection to partisan quarrels."

Schragmüller had needed me for the same reason. "You are an American hero. You love America," she had told me.

"Major, I have become most uneasy with the president's cabinet and the staff. They do not protect him as they should. They gossip. They force upon him consideration of the most mundane matters, when neither his fragile health nor the appropriate use of his time call for his attention to such minutiae. Even more worrying, I am convinced that clandestine efforts are being made to do him harm. I am sure these have resulted in his present incapacity, and that is why I needed to see you. I need your help."

Her face seemed to pulse with the passion of her mission.

"People are trying to kill the president?" I asked. "Have you told the Secret Service? His staff? The police? Who's trying to hurt him?"

My questions bubbled out in a single sentence. Did she know about the lifetime I spent in the Basel cellar? Did she suspect the

Germans and me of a plot to kill her husband? My vision began to tunnel. I forced in a deep breath.

"I am a woman, and I have no firm evidence. No one would listen to my *hysterics*. But I was independent for many years before I met Mr. Wilson. I know the world. I know how it works and how it should work. On the trip west, the little things that gnaw were always wrong. Laundry not completely dry, no heat in an auditorium dressing room, spoiled milk for our breakfast coffee. It is the small comforts that Mr. Wilson most appreciates, and these were often missing or flawed. Someone who knows him well is engineering these lapses. The campaign against him is subtle, but it is happening."

She studied me, expecting to see doubt or scorn. Unfortunately, she was right to fear for the president. I didn't know what to say. Did she somehow sense the German plot? My skin prickled at the possibility. Schragmüller and Fuchs weren't working to kill the president using spoiled milk, but they were working to kill him just the same. The First Lady read my belief on my face, and she smiled with relief at having found at least one ally.

"I need you to find those responsible and stop it. The president is too weak for it to be allowed to continue."

"Mrs. Wilson, I'm not a policeman. I don't know exactly what I would do to discover and reveal such a conspiracy."

"I don't care if it is revealed. I just need it to stop," she said fiercely. "Where are you staying?"

"The Washington Hotel," I said automatically.

It occurred to me that for her, her husband was more important than the presidency. I was there to help her husband. Not America. I needed to escape. I needed to be as far from the Wilsons as I could get.

A knock on the door interrupted our discussion.

"Come in," Mrs. Wilson commanded.

Wood looked in and said, "I'm sorry, ma'am, but Sir William

Wiseman[1] is on the telephone. He would like to arrange a meeting with the president as soon as possible."

"Oh bother," Mrs. Wilson huffed. "I do dislike that man. Major, please wait. I won't be a moment."

She hurried out of the room and down the hallway, and dread enveloped me. Here was the opportunity that the Boche and Schragmüller had planned for.

I stared at the closed door, the door that led to Woodrow Wilson. This was where the Germans had wanted me. They had succeeded by dumb luck. Their hoped-for assassin was just a few steps away from the president. But I wasn't their killer.

I opened the door without knocking. The curtains over the two tall windows on the south wall were drawn, but enough light leaked in to see the president. He rested on his back under the bedclothes of a large, dark carved-wood bed. An enormous oval-topped headboard rose above him, and he looked insignificant under it. His eyes were closed and his breathing shallow. He looked pale and old. I floated into the room and stood over him with a pillow in my hands. I wasn't sure where the pillow had come from.

His eyes opened. He saw me and reached for his wire-framed glasses on the bedside table. He perched the spectacles on his muzzle.

"Oh, Major Griffin. Edith told me you might be by."

I didn't speak. Something in my head didn't work.

Wilson pushed off the covers and swung his hind legs out of the bed. He moved like the old dog he was. With his hind legs on the ground, he leaned forward and rubbed his temples as if he were in pain.

"Sorry. I need to use the water closet. I'll be right with you." He stood and took a robe from the foot of his bed. He pulled it on and shuffled toward a door that had to be the toilet.

---

1. Sir William George Eden Wiseman. February 1, 1885–June 17, 1962. British intelligence agent and liaison to Woodrow Wilson.

He was just an ill old man.

He reached the bathroom door. I put the pillow down where his robe had been and accidently knocked a knuckle against the wooden footboard.

The president's head cocked slightly, and the ear nearest me rotated to point toward the sound. Just like a dog's would.

With three long strides I crossed to the president. The thick carpet covered the sound. Without hesitation or thought, I slammed my palms between his shoulder blades. Despite his height, he was frail and did not weigh much. He flew into the bathroom, across the tile, and his face struck the bathtub plumbing. He collapsed hard to the floor.

I stood in the doorway. My pulse pounded in my ears. He was a goddamn dog!

Wilson looked over his shoulder at me in confusion. There was no recognition in his eyes. Only pain. A long cut across his temple and snout bled freely. He pushed up to his knees and tried to stand. The long yellowed nails on his hind feet scrabbled at the tile. Just as he was nearly up, his left leg failed. He collapsed back to the floor like a falling marionette.

He lay on his back on the tile. He didn't look like a dog now. He looked like a deflated, dying man. His eyes were unfocused and vacant. He tried to speak. His face twisted in a grimace, and his mouth made weak gumming motions like a goldfish kissing the inside of its bowl. Drool ran from his mouth. Only half his face worked. The other half seemed flaccid and dead.

I needed to do something, but I couldn't think of what.

Finish him.

I would get help.

But not yet.

Whose voice whispered to me?

Elsbeth?

I whipped my head around to look back into the bedroom. I was still alone with the president.

Panic threatened to overwhelm me. I could feel my heartbeat pounding in my neck against my shirt collar. What had I done?

I ran through the bedroom and sitting room and out into the hallway. Mrs. Wilson was just arriving at the top of the stairs.

"Mrs. Wilson, hurry! Come quickly! The president fell. I heard a noise and went to check. He's hit his head!" The words came from my mouth, but they weren't mine. Tippy cavorted around me merrily.

"Oh no!" she exclaimed. She hurried to the president. "My God!"

He lay on his back, eyes closed. Both her hands went to her mouth in horror. He had lost control of his bladder, and urine mixed with the blood from his head wound and spread a red pool across the bathroom floor. He was unconscious. Hell, he might have been dead.

I bent down and felt for a pulse in his neck. It was there, but weak.

"He's alive," I said with amazement.

"Help me get him off the floor," she instructed, taking hope from my words.

Despite the mess, Mrs. Wilson didn't hesitate to help her husband. Together, we half dragged and half carried the president back to the bed.

She tried to wipe the blood from his face with a hand towel, but the wounds on his forehead and across his nose were deep. She thrust the towel at me.

"Here take this. I'll be right back. I need to call for help." She hurried from the room. I stared at the president's slack, lifeless face partially hidden by the cloth I pressed against it.

Finish him. Use the towel. Was it Sarah who spoke?

I realized there was a telephone on the nightstand where the president had placed his glasses. I wondered why Mrs. Wilson didn't use it, but I couldn't focus on the thought. I needed to get out of the White House. The president wasn't quite dead, and he could wake up and reveal me as an assassin.

And I had tried to kill him! My mind was still having trouble accepting that truth. I wasn't in control.

Finish him. It *was* Sarah.

I could put the towel over his mouth and just pinch his nose shut.

The First Lady returned.

"Mr. Hoover is bringing Doctor Grayson. Oh God, I hope he hurries."

I didn't know who Hoover was, and I didn't care. I needed to get out.

She took the towel from my hand and gently pushed me aside. "You should go. People will ask why you were here, and I don't want anyone to know you are looking into this. But please, Major, help me find those responsible for doing this to my husband. I will leave orders so that you can contact me day or night. Go. I'll take care of the president."

I didn't have time to respond as she pushed me out of the bedroom and into the hallway. I heard the door lock click behind me.

An odd elation took root under my heart.

Had I just gotten away with murdering the president? The thought was horrifying, yet an unwelcome feeling of triumph filled me.

"You're the dead man now, Griffin," Tippy told me. "The Yanks will figure out what you've done. You'll have nowhere to run."

I wasn't so sure. The First Lady was more worried about the president's staff finding out they were being investigated than suspecting me of murderous intent. She wanted me away so that she had a secret ace in the hole. Not that I was much of an ace. I had no intention of investigating Wilson's staff, especially when I was the one guilty of harming the president.

Did I really just attack the president? It seemed unreal. Impossible. I was glad Mitchell wasn't with me. He would be dismayed and disgusted even though he knew what I'd endured in Basel. At some point, I would have to tell him what I'd done. I dreaded seeing the inevitable condemnation in his eyes, but I hoped that he would understand.

I hurried from the White House grounds. With the president possibly dying by my hand, I needed the pistol I'd left in my room. Tippy was hopeful the Secret Service would piece together what had happened to the president. If they did, they would come for me. The First Lady knew where I was staying. Stupidly, I had told her.

"You'll be happy to know, Tippy, that if they come for me, they will have to kill me," I said as I increased my pace once I was out of sight of my friendly policeman at the east gate.

"That will make me happy, indeed, but I do hope they don't kill you quickly," Tippy said optimistically.

Once in my room, I armed myself. The trench knife went into its sheath at the small of my back, and I put on the shoulder holster, silently thanking Marie, who'd given it to me. I worked the slide of the pistol, chambering a round and then eased the hammer down. With the safety on, I topped off the magazine and slotted it home. I holstered the pistol and put on my suit jacket.

I looked into the mirror above the bureau. I hardly recognized the glowering man looking back. The red scar stood out against my too-pale face. I looked haunted, but I told myself I looked like a dangerous man. Yes. I was dangerous. I was ready if they came for me. I was unhinged, but the fear that roiled in my chest didn't show. Only Tippy and I knew it was there.

I left the hotel and returned to the tavern on F Street. Back to the English room.

I insisted on a table in the back and sat on a bench against the wood paneling studying the room. The pretty girl with the sharp tongue and hallucinatory pharmacy in her corset was nowhere to be seen. It was just as well. I already had one attempted murder under my belt for the day, and in my current state, another wasn't out of the question. The arsenal under my coat made it all too possible.

19

___

A Masterful Job

I had some time to kill before my noon appointment with Billy. I ordered a beer, hoping it would reduce my dismay at my attack on the president. I prayed for either the girl or, better yet, Karl Fuchs to appear. They would give me an outlet for the fragmented, violent thoughts crashing about in my head. Neither did. Fifteen minutes before the agreed time, I left for the park to meet Billy. I had difficulty remembering why I was seeing him and where he had been.

Lafayette Square was adjacent to the White House, and I was reluctant to go near the grounds. After my assault on the president, I was certain the police and Secret Service would be as busy as bees in springtime, but to get to the park, I had no choice.

Once more, I walked past the Treasury building. The soldiers there seemed no more alert than previously. Nearer to the White House, two motorcars were parked in front of the guard shack at the east gate, but no additional policemen or soldiers were in evidence.

I strolled into the park and sat on a bench not far from Jackson rearing on his bronze horse. The bench faced the White

House grounds. I could see no frantic activity. It certainly didn't look like a manhunt was underway for the president's murderer.

Perhaps the president wasn't as badly injured as he had appeared. I found that difficult to credit. He looked near death when I left, and I certainly had seen enough dying men to judge.

I turned my face to the sun and closed my eyes. I was drained. The drugs, the sleepless night, and fear had sapped all the energy from me.

My God, I just wanted to rest. To sleep.

Billy strolled past the statue, studying the White House.

"Jones!" I called.

"Ah, Jack. Good to see you. What an interesting, modern town this is. Part Paris, part London yet wholly American."

"Well, you Brits did your part to help modernize the berg," I said, hoping the joke would conceal my drained and nearly broken condition.

He gave me a questioning look.

"The British burned down the first White House, Billy."

"Yes, but that was years ago. Now you have streetcars, motorcars, modern buildings. The hotel I'm in has a bathroom en suite. No walking down the hall to the WC. It literally has a *peacock walk*. It's lovely, if a little crowded with foreigners." Jones said the last laughing, as he stepped out of the path of a group of drunk sailors. "You look awful, Jack. Are you all right? You look like you haven't slept for days."

So much for fooling Billy.

"I've been busy, and it's tired me out. Let's have lunch. I know a place that's not too far."

I took Jones back to the same tavern I'd just left, and we were seated at the same table.

"I've delivered all the letters, Billy," I told him.

"What? That was remarkably fast, and I am sure Sir Basil wanted me to accompany you."

A white-jacketed waiter took our drinks order. Washington had faster service than Paris.

I shook my head at Billy's comment. "Kell and Churchill picked me because of the relationships I've developed. You'll have to trust me when I say you wouldn't have wanted to be at the White House this morning. I delivered House's letter yesterday morning at his office. Yesterday afternoon, House took me to see Senator Lodge, and I delivered his. This morning I had an appointment with the First Lady, and through her, I got to the president. You know he's worn himself out promoting the treaty. She barely let me in."

"Yes. I've seen the newspaper. Well, I suppose that's all to the good. How were the letters received?"

"House remains committed to ratification of the treaty. Lodge was interested in the Bolshevik angle, and he might actually share Mr. Churchill's view that stopping Bolshevism is more important than ratifying the treaty as it currently stands. The president didn't tell me his views, but given his efforts over the past month, I'd be very surprised if he has time for anything beyond the treaty," I opined. I didn't tell him that I would be surprised if the president had time left for anything at all.

"I suppose that's all to be expected." He sounded disappointed that he hadn't gotten to meet the American luminaries I'd been sent to contact.

"What have you been doing since you got here?" I wanted to divert him from continued discussion of my mission. I didn't like lying to Billy, but I had no choice. I couldn't tell him that I experienced drug-induced visions resulting in my unplanned, and possibly fatal, assault on the president. It wouldn't help Great Britain's relationship with the United States if the Secret Service burst into the pub and found Billy Jones having a drink with the assassin. I wished there was a way to keep Billy out of the complications that threatened to escalate because of my mental state.

"Who would have thought you'd give any consideration to the welfare of your mate? It's so unlike you, Jackie," Tippy Frederickson said in my ear.

His lips were so close to my ear that I jumped at his words. I could feel his breath on my neck.

Fortunately, Billy was studying the bar and didn't notice. He looked back at me, leaning closer.

"I've had several meetings with Sir William Wiseman," he said in a low voice. "He has come to the capital from New York. He works with Sir Basil and Captain Mansfield Smith-Cumming and has a very close relationship with Colonel House."

"Sir Basil's CID, but who is Smith-Cumming? Never heard of him." I pretended to look around the bar as well. Really, I was looking for Tippy.

"John, mum's the word, but he runs the Secret Intelligence Service. Has done since before the war. In early 1914, together with Colonel Kell they rounded up dozens of Boche spies in Britain. Since then, he's assisted you Americans identifying anarchist and revolutionaries here. He's a very effective fellow."

I'd never even heard of the Secret Intelligence Service, but I saw no point in admitting my ignorance. I wanted Billy to keep talking. I didn't want him to question the need to educate me.

"And Wiseman?"

"Again, you can't mention it outside of the highest circles, but he's the head of the SIS in the United States. As I said, he's a confidant of Colonel House and knows the president well."

I nodded. That explained why Wiseman was calling the White House for an appointment with the president.

Damn him! If he hadn't distracted the First Lady, I would have never been in a position to harm Wilson.

"I've been briefing him on your mission. He'd very much like to meet you."

"We need to get back to England, Billy."

"Of course. Now that you've done as Churchill asked, I'll have the embassy staff arrange our return, but I'm sure the next ship won't leave for several days. We have plenty of time for you to meet Wiseman."

I nodded. Fine. What was one more British bigwig? What I

really needed to be doing was investigating Armistan and the Thomas Reynolds's connections, if any, to the War Industries Board.

That thought gave me pause. A man as well placed as Wiseman might know quite a bit about the WIB. Hell, he might even know Reynolds and Armistan.

"Okay, Billy. I think I might enjoy meeting Sir William."

"Excellent. He is staying at the Willard where I am lodging also. We can try to see him when we're done here."

We consumed our lunch of oysters and beer and then walked down the block to E Street and the Willard Hotel.

When we entered the lobby of the Willard, I found it to be more opulent than either the Washington Hotel or the Pennsylvania. Columns, palms, and end-of-the-century gilt trim made clear that the Willard was a hub for the powerful who visited Washington. I sat in an armchair in the lobby while Billy called Wiseman's room. He returned after a few minutes and told me Wiseman was on his way down.

"Sir William suggested a drink in the bar."

"Of course."

We made the short trip to the hotel bar. Instead of a long, traditional wooden bar top I'd expected, a circular bar dominated the room. Two white-jacketed bartenders were working in its center. Small mostly unoccupied round tables surrounded the bar. Simple green carpet and paneled walls gave the place a warm, cozy feel in contrast to the hotel lobby.

We took one of the tables. I sat against the wall on an overstuffed leather bench. Billy perched on one of the matching leather chairs, watching the door for Wiseman.

In a short time, Wiseman arrived. It could only have been Wiseman. Neat. Well dressed. A lampshade mustache trimmed to the edges of his mouth. He looked like a young, fleshy Colonel House. Despite his receding hairline, I judged him to be only a decade or so older than Billy and me. He quickly picked out Billy's wave, and he came straight over.

"Sir William, thank you for joining us," Billy said formally. "Please meet Major John Griffin of whom I've spoken."

We shook hands.

A bartender came to take our order.

I stuck with beer while Billy and Sir William ordered mint juleps.

"The house specialty," Billy told me.

"Major, it is a true pleasure to meet you. I understand you've done very fine work for your country and ours in France and Germany," Wiseman said with an approving nod.

Either he'd been in contact with London or Billy had fully briefed him about me. Likely both.

"Thank you. Much of it was luck. And fortunately, some of that luck has continued here. I've accomplished the task that brought me to Washington. I've delivered the letters as requested."

"Why that is excellent," Wiseman said. "I've contacted the White House to get an appointment with the president, but I haven't yet heard back. My intention is to follow up on the contents of the letters with President Wilson directly. I can now contact Senator Lodge and Colonel House as well."

"I must warn you," I said. "The president was just about done in by his trip promoting the treaty. He's exhausted himself. I would expect that getting any time with him will be very difficult. Mrs. Wilson is extremely reluctant to let anyone see him. I only saw him by happenstance. She's very worried about his health."

"Because you smashed her husband's head into the plumbing, you bastard," Tippy growled.

I shrugged in answer.

Wiseman took it as a comment on the emotional nature of women.

"Yes, she often seems put out with me as well. She is the most protective of wives."

"Sir William, I have a question for you, if you don't mind. Not directly related to my work for Mr. Churchill. Something I am pursuing separately. It's a simple question really."

"Of course! You've done exactly what has been asked of you. I am happy to answer what I can."

"What do you know about the American War Industries Board and its membership?"

His eyes narrowed. He sat back in his chair and sipped his drink to give himself time before answering.

"Your War Industries Board and our Ministry of Munitions had the very difficult job of ensuring the lifeblood of the allied war effort was delivered from the factories and workshops of the combatant nations. Resources, finished goods, ships, cannons, munitions. All of it. Without the American WIB, the allies would have lost the war. The board coordinated delivery and payment terms for the massive amount of material needed to conduct the war successfully. The president dissolved the board in January. Bernard Baruch was the last chairman. He had several assistants as well."

"How were the members selected?"

"I believe they were patriotic volunteers from all the key industries. Really quite admirable. They did a masterful job. And, as I said, the WIB is defunct. I know from my close relationship with Colonel House that he would view any inquiry of the board as a waste of resources."

Wiseman assumed that I was asking on behalf of Wilson, and he was trying to discourage me.

"I'd hardly say anyone is doing a formal investigation. I'm sure the president has people for that sort of thing. I'm just doing as directed, Sir William. What is Mr. Baruch's expertise?" I asked, pressing him.

"He's a financier. I believe he has gone back to work on Wall Street as he did before the war. If you have questions about Mr. Baruch, you could ask Mr. Churchill about him. I understand they are close," Wiseman volunteered. He had dropped both Churchill and House's names in a matter of seconds. The whole thing was starting to smell. Armistan was a financier. I'd bet that Thomas Reynolds was too. And now Baruch. At a minimum, Armistan and Reynolds would know Baruch.

"Thank you, Sir William. If I get the chance, I will do that," I said. "One more question. Do you know or have you heard of Thomas Reynolds or Harry Armistan? I think they're both also in finance in New York."

Wiseman looked from me to Jones and back. I hoped he didn't blame Billy for my impertinent questioning.

"Why are you asking, Major? Why would President Wilson investigate the WIB and these two men? I've met both men. Reynolds is an honorable, patriotic man who served with distinction on the WIB. Armistan. Well, his reputation is not as stellar as Thomas Reynolds's, but I know of nothing untoward in his business dealings."

"And his personal life?"

"I don't gossip, Major."

"Of course. But both men are well connected?"

"Mr. Reynolds's connections are of the highest order. I can't comment as to Mr. Armistan's."

"Does Mr. Reynolds have any relations working in Europe? I met a Morgan Reynolds in Paris. Are they related?"

"His son," Wiseman confirmed.

I nodded.

Billy Jones was watching our discussion as he would a tennis match. He was enjoying himself.

"And what about you, Sir William?" I asked. "With the war over will you remain in the United States or return home?"

"I've a home in New York and a position at Kuhn, Loeb & Co., a banking concern. And I've many friends here. I'll be staying."

Another banker. I should have known.

This was all too much of a coincidence. His opposition and attitude gave me the seed of an idea, but I needed to be careful how I prepared the ground for it to succeed. I was beginning to suspect that he would report the conversation to House and possibly Churchill. Neither would necessarily be bad for my purposes.

By the time I was done probing Wiseman about the WIB, we had finished our drinks. Sir William seemed much less happy with my company by then. I offered him a second mint julep, but he claimed another commitment, and I was happy to see him go. I had learned what I needed from him, and it wouldn't be bad if he started spreading rumors about presidential investigations.

"Let's go somewhere lowbrow and drink to the coming of Prohibition, Billy," I suggested deadpan.

He glanced at me and laughed. "My God, you can look horrifying when you want to. I like the suggestion. Unfortunately, I don't know any truly vulgar places that would embarrass me to be seen in."

"I might." I told him about Ninth Street, and he was all too happy to drink cheap watered beer and ogle prostitutes from afar.

As we left the Willard, I couldn't resist confiding in Billy enough to get his unwitting help in spreading the myth that Wilson wanted to investigate the wartime procurement apparatus.

"Billy, I have to say, all these old bastards who sent us off to war have come out of it smelling like roses. It wouldn't surprise me if they all made a killing off it. Hell, the guy in charge of wartime procurement for the United States was in finance."

"Jack, many of the gentlemen in banking and finance were naturally the ones put in key positions in wartime procurement, and it should come as no surprise that they are of the Hebrew persuasion," he said dismissively.

"Perhaps, but surely you can see why the president might want to look into it?" I said.

He gave me a sidelong glance. "You *are* investigating the WIB," he said, half accusingly.

I looked back at him. "As I told Sir William, I do as I'm directed."

We ended up at the Acropolis café, one of the two bars flanking the Gayety Theater. Billy loved the location and thought the Greek lettering used on its signage showed an unexpected sense of satire about America's level of education. I thought it was just owned by a bunch of immigrant Greeks who couldn't be bothered to use English. Billy's viewpoint showed a graciousness of spirit that I had lost somewhere or perhaps never had.

It was still early, and we managed to find a small round table with four dangerously fragile chairs. I expected the crowd would pick up once work let out, but we still had an hour or so until then.

We ordered mugs of beer and talked about our dead friends. We reviewed their lives, short as they were, and then their deaths. Inevitably, the talk brought their ghosts crowding around the table.

"I heard you were with Tippy when he died," Jones said sympathetically.

"And Bert Williams as well. Although I was actually talking to Frederickson when he was shot. Bertie, well, he had been newly assigned to the FSR. I think it was his first time leading his platoon on the attack. The Somme, of course, but not until August."

"That must have been ghastly," Jones exclaimed.

We both sipped our beers and shared unspoken morbid thoughts.

"When you decided to join up again, why didn't you go back to the Rifles? I'm sure they'd have taken you back." He seemed genuinely curious and not accusatory.

"I never even thought of it, Billy. It was just easier to join in the United States. And I'd be damned if I was going to go back and fight for Haig. I'm still convinced he's the reason all our friends are dead. Of course, I didn't know that Pershing wouldn't be much better, but at least he was a change."

Jones nodded as if my explanation made sense. The truth was, I had no desire to face my English comrades in the First Surreys.

I didn't want to explain to them why it took the American declaration of war to get me back in the fight.

Eventually our talk petered out, and we just sat and watched the bar fill.

I was exhausted. The mescaline had robbed me of all meaningful sleep the night before, and the events of the day had crushed my spirit.

"Billy, I'm gonna head back to my hotel. I can come by the Willard in the morning for breakfast, if you're interested."

"Nine?"

"Sure."

My return to the hotel was a blur. If Reynolds's boys had come for me during that walk, they could have finished me. Gun or no gun.

When I collected my room key, the clerk delivered two handwritten notes with it. One, on Army and Navy Club letterhead, was from General Neville. He invited me to breakfast in the morning at the club at eight o'clock. It looked like I might be late for my breakfast with Billy.

The second note caused my heart to thump and my fatigue to disappear.

John,

I have seen the evening papers. We need to meet soon for a chat. I'll send someone to contact you.

KF

I hadn't bothered to look at the evening edition of the Washington newspapers. There were some papers hanging on the rack in the lobby, and I hurried over to check them. Unfortunately, none were the late edition. I asked the concierge where I could find a final edition of the *Washington Times*. He promised to have one delivered to my chambers.

With my key and the two notes, I returned to my room and locked the door. I sat on the end of the bed. I intended to read both notes again, but I couldn't pull my thoughts from the second.

KF. Karl Fuchs. Goddamn him.

A knock on the door pulled me off the bed. With the pistol in my hand, I unlocked and cracked the door.

"Evening paper, mister," the young delivery boy said. I gave the kid a nickel, shut and relocked the door, and sat back down on the bed.

The first line on the front page read "President's condition not good at all today, Grayson says."[1] Grayson. The doctor Mrs. Wilson had called to the White House to attend the president. The main article was in the second column and stated that a specialist in nervous ills had been summoned to see the president. It also noted that, although Mr. Wilson had had a restful night, his condition was not at all good in the morning.

"It most certainly was not good after you saw him," Frederickson said.

I glanced up to see Tippy lying on his side on the floor in front of me with his shattered head propped up on his elbow.

The article stated that the nerve specialist was coming in from Philly and that an eye doctor might be called as well. Oddly, the tone of the column was optimistic. Grayson apparently felt that only time was needed for the president to recuperate.

A feeling of distress bubbled inside me. I had thought he was dying. I realized as I sat on the bed that I had wanted him dead. The German plan had worked. Somehow, through the drugs, the torture, and the absurd motion picture shows, Plöchner had convinced me I needed to kill Wilson.

"It wasn't the Germans, John," Sarah said with a parentlike patience. She now sat on the bed next to me. "You blame the old men for the war just like Horace and Gavin did. Just like I did. The difference between us and you is we tried to do something about them. You've done nothing. You've just wallowed in your

---

1. *Washington Times*, October 2, 1919. P. 1. Evening edition.

sham disgust of the old order and turned it into well-deserved self-loathing. You still march to the same tune you did before the war. Honestly, John, you're a bit pathetic."

I stared at her now. Unlike Tippy Frederickson, she didn't wear the wounds she'd suffered in the Paris apartment. Instead, she appeared as beautiful as the day I'd met her. Her raised brows, cocked head, and beautiful blue eyes confirmed the intended challenge of her words.

"I don't want to kill Wilson, Sarah," I said aloud. "You may think that's pathetic, but I never intended to kill him."

I was surprised at how painful I found her words to be. I didn't even think they were true, but they felt like betrayal.

"Oh, poor Jackie feels betrayed!" Tippy scoffed from his reclined position on the floor. "Welcome to the ball, you bastard. How do you think the rest of us feel?"

"It felt good when you pushed him, didn't it, John?" Sarah said.

She was right. It had felt good, and as I'd escaped from the White House, I had felt a surge of joy.

"See," she said, aware of the thought in my head.

"No. I felt that way because Plöchner's experiments on me created those feelings."

"In just a few days? Even you can't be that weak."

This wasn't Sarah!

I closed my eyes and took a deep breath. Whatever the origin, whether Tippy or my own deranged mind punishing me, these accusations weren't from Sarah. Not really. She hadn't wanted me involved in the plot in Paris.

It was some relief to realize it. The phantasm sitting next to me wasn't Sarah, wasn't real, and certainly wasn't sympathetic. I was sitting next to a reflection of myself.

"Sarah, it feels an awful lot like our honeymoon is over," I told the ghost.

Blood from her chest wounds began to leak through her blouse.

"Nice touch," I said, and I looked back down at Karl Fuchs's note.

How had he known where to find me? He or his people must have followed me to the hotel. Of course they had. I jumped up from the bed and went to the bureau. I distinctly remembered leaving the letters from Mrs. Wilson, Neville, and my sisters neatly stacked on its corner. The letters now lay in an untidy pile. The chambermaid might have done it, but my gut told me it was Fuchs. He or his people had been in my room. He had read all the letters. He had known I was going to see Mrs. Wilson. He knew where my sisters lived.

Goddamn Fuchs! He was the reason I'd attacked Wilson. I found that believing the Germans were to blame for my attack on Wilson was much easier than accepting that part of me wanted to kill the president. If the cause of my assault on the president was Schragmüller, Fuchs, and Plöchner, I could forgive myself. They had tortured me after all. If the reason was my own deep-seated hatred of the president and all those like him, I was either going to have to put a bullet in my head or go on a bloody romp across Washington and much of Europe.

Wait a second. I'd already been doing that. Maybe I'd just been killing the wrong folks.

20

A Brainy Girl

I presented myself at the Army and Navy Club at ten minutes before eight the next morning. I was early, but I knew General Neville would already be there. He was the type of officer who thought five minutes early was late.

I wasn't sure what I would tell Neville about France, Clemenceau, House, and Wilson. I figured it would come to me once I stood before him.

The receptionist directed me to the dining room nearby, and the maître d' led me directly to the general's table. He wasn't alone.

Neville and another marine were seated with coffee cups in front of them and cigarettes already burning in the ashtray. I knew the other man was a marine because both he and Neville were in uniform. Neville saw me, and his stern face broke into a smile. My heart lifted at the sight. He was one of those men who could get the most out of you, even when the *most* likely meant your death. I didn't resent him for it. He was in the business of killing, and the price for success always meant a bunch of poor suckers, who believed in God and country or who just got drafted, ended up dead in a ditch.

Both men stood as I approached. As I got closer, I was able to see that the other officer was slightly junior to Neville in rank. He wore the silver eagles of a full colonel on each shoulder. Neville wore the single silver stars of a brigadier general. Surprisingly, the second officer wore the pale blue ribbon of the Congressional Medal of Honor just as Neville did. He was one of the tough old-timers I had described to the girl who had drugged me.

The other officer didn't smile. I didn't know him, and I wasn't sure I wanted to. His beady eyes protruded slightly from his unsmiling face. His hair was receding, and he had a raptor-like nose and manner. He cocked his head and studied me dispassionately. He reminded me of the hawks I'd seen in Texas perched on the barbed wire cattle fences looking for some damn mouse to eat. Emotionless yet always hungry. I felt like the mouse.

"Griffin, it is a pleasure to see you in one piece," Neville said, pumping my hand. "Colonel Butler,[1] I'd like you to meet one of the most remarkable, and perhaps luckiest, fighting men I've ever had the pleasure to command, Sergeant John Griffin."

We shook hands. I knew of Butler. Smedley Butler. The old salts in the marines spoke of him with reverence. He was a legend in the Corps. Old gimlet eye. I could see where the name came from.

"A pleasure to meet you, Colonel. As you can imagine, I've heard a lot about you," I said. He'd been in the same fights as Neville: China, Nicaragua, Panama, Haiti, and Mexico.

"Sergeant, Buck here has been singing your praises." Butler nodded toward Neville. *Buck?* A nickname I didn't know Neville had. It didn't matter. He would always be *General Neville* to me.

---

1. Smedley Darlington Butler. July 30, 1881–June 20, 1940. Two-time Congressional Medal of Honor winner, author, and speaker.

"That's very kind but not deserved, Colonel." Humble. I was going to be humble because I felt an unreasonable urge to tell Neville about my politically fabricated promotion to major.

"Sit," Neville ordered as he waved an arm at the colored waiter. "Coffee, eggs, bacon, sausage, and toast." The waiter hurried off.

"Griffin, I wanted to apologize. My contacts in France remain quite good, and I only returned stateside a few months ago. I heard that the job you did for Mr. Armistan ended badly, and I'm sorry. I wanted to apologize in person."

I realized if I played my cards right by just telling the truth, mostly, I could use Neville in my quest to undermine Armistan.

"General, if you have the time, I've got a story to tell. You may find it hard to believe, but I swear it's all true."

Neville looked at Butler, who shrugged.

"Sure. Let's hear it."

As we ate, I told the two men of my mission for Armistan, how he misled me, and of his plot to thwart the treaty and the peace. I focused on Armistan's involvement with the Bolsheviks. I told them of the weapons in Paris, the attack on Clemenceau, and the French refusal to believe it was the Reds and not Germans.

"I didn't tell the French that an American financier was involved," I said. "That would have hurt America, and I had no real proof. But Armistan wanted to extend the war. It was profitable. More profitable than any investment he could find in peacetime. I managed to stop the plot, which got me involved with the French, Colonel House, and now the English, but the main point, gentlemen, is that we had an American working to undermine the peace."

"My God, that's a tale!" Neville said as the waiter cleared the remains of our breakfast.

"And I don't doubt every word of it is true, Buck. You know all the darn fighting we've done these past years in support of *dollar diplomacy!*" Butler said passionately, not hiding his disdain for the concept. "It's an embarrassment. And I'm not sure this last war wasn't as much a part of it as all our previous campaigns."

"What are you doing about Armistan, Sergeant?" Neville asked me. It was clear that from his viewpoint, I was still serving the country whether I wanted to or not.

"Well, sir, I haven't finished the story. Colonel House appreciated my work in thwarting the Red scheme." That made my efforts in Paris sound less like a barroom brawl and more like a planned investigation. "He and the Department of State asked me to work with France's military intelligence on a mission into Germany."

"The Deuxième Bureau? In Germany? What were you doing for them there?"

"Spy hunting, sir. Of course, they didn't tell me that. Even so, I did manage to catch a couple. But in order for me to have the right profile for the job, the French and the Department of State engineered a promotion for me. To major. In the marines."

Both men sat back in their chairs with shock. They could believe the worst of Bolsheviks, French spies, and American financiers, but to abuse the Marine Corps promotion system was heresy for men who had spent their entire lives in the quest to climb the ladder of rank.

"I'm sorry, sir," I said to Neville. "I didn't ask for it, but if you check the Corps' records, you'll find that I'm now a major."

Butler began to laugh. After a few seconds, Neville gave a reluctant snort.

"Lucky indeed. Congratulations on your promotion, Major," Butler said. Neville could only shake his head.

"It did work out to some degree," I told them. "After my work for the French, probably because I was an officer with connections to House and the president, the British asked me to deliver some letters to Wilson, Colonel House, and Senator Lodge. I just finished delivering them yesterday."

"What do the letters say?"

"What connections to the president?"

The men spoke over each other.

"Colonel House introduced me to President Wilson in July. The president specifically asked that I go on the mission to help the French. He didn't explain why, but I suppose he thought it might benefit the relationship with the French. The English found out about this, and based on the fact that the president knew and trusted me, they wanted to use me as their personal transatlantic mailman. I haven't actually read the letters, but Churchill, the Secretary for Air and War, wrote them, and he said the letters warned about the importance of resisting the growth of Bolshevism."

"Churchill?" Neville asked rhetorically.

"So the empire can continue unchallenged," Butler added cynically.

"That is probably part of it," I confirmed. "He's worried about the Reds destroying the established order of things. Capitalism, freedom, the empire. Not necessarily in that order. Or at least that's the impression he gave me."

"Hell, I would have thought the past four years would have already done that. It's not like the Bolsheviks popped up for no reason," Butler said.

"I'm more worried about American industrialists and bankers undermining peace than I am the British Empire," Neville said. "You think this business goes beyond Armistan?"

"I do, sir. And when I was at the White House yesterday, I was tasked with investigating."

"You were at the White House yesterday?" Neville asked.

"Briefly. I saw the president very early, but from what I've seen from the papers, it seems like he fell ill sometime that morning." My words were all carefully chosen so I could tell myself that I didn't lie to Neville. If he believed I worked for the president, he would be a powerful ally.

"I hope he recovers quickly," Neville said.

"As do I, sir." I actually hoped no such thing. "In any event, the White House has given me a job to do. I think the War Industries

Board is involved somehow in the plot I found in France," I continued. "That's why I was eager to meet you today. I wanted to learn what you know about the WIB generally and Thomas Reynolds."

"Reynolds. You think he's involved?" Neville asked. "I find that hard to believe. He's a patriot who's been nothing but a friend to the Marine Corps. Hell, he belongs to this club."

"I don't know if he's involved or not, General, but I know his son is. I just don't have any proof yet."

Neville didn't like what I was saying.

Butler, however, gave a grudging nod. "The WIB did a good enough job, but the truth is, much of the war material they were tasked with delivering was only available after the fighting was already done. If we'd had to invade Germany, its work would have been one of the keys to victory."

"How were profits on the goods determined?" I asked.

"Well, that's one of the things the WIB did. It worked out the appropriate prices and fair but reasonable profits on everything produced, and it negotiated with workers, prevented strikes, that sort of thing," Neville answered.

"So there might have been an opportunity for unreasonable profit if the membership were clever?" I asked it as a question, but I was telling Neville that he didn't know if the US government had been milked by the rich civilians directing the production efforts.

He narrowed his eyes. "Were you always this jaded, *Major Griffin?*"

"General, in the past four months, I've gotten a bit of an education on how the world works. A few rich men seeking to get richer is hardly surprising."

"There would have been lots of ways for members of the WIB to benefit," Butler confirmed. "Steering contracts, colluding on prices, backscratching one another. War is big business. So yes, there were lots of opportunities to make a buck."

"And Thomas Reynolds was on the board?" I asked.

"He was. I don't recall which industries he represented," Neville answered. "I met him as part of his work. And he worked hard. I think you're barking up the wrong tree, Griffin. At least as far as Thomas Reynolds is concerned."

"He may not be involved, sir. There may be nothing to it, but as I've said, I've been tasked by the White House to run these suspicions to ground."

My implication that the president was directing me was, of course, a bald-faced lie. The White House, through the First Lady, had ordered me to find those interested in harming the president. I'd completed that investigation when I woke up this morning and looked in the mirror. She didn't know or care about my pursuit of Armistan and the Reynolds family.

So much for not lying to Neville.

The shade of Tippy Frederickson was chuckling in the back of my skull. "Nothing's sacred to you, mate," he said.

"Could you set up a meeting for me with Mr. Reynolds, General?" I asked Neville.

"He'll be in New York, but I can send him a telegram asking him to meet you. When can you be there?"

"I need to report back to the British. My ship will depart no later than next week. So pretty much any time before that."

"I'll see what I can do."

"I'm at the Washington Hotel. Please send word to me there," I told him.

"Of course." Neville stood and offered his hand. "Good to see you, Griffin. Stay lucky."

I was being dismissed. "I'll try, sir."

Butler stood as well.

"A pleasure to meet you, son, even if you were promoted to major twenty years faster than I was," Colonel Butler said with a smile. He looked much less predatory when he smiled.

I was forty minutes late for my breakfast with Jones. I hurried to the Willard and found him reading the newspaper in the dining room.

As I arrived at the table, I saw the headline of Jones's paper facing me. It read President is very sick.[2]

Jones noticed me, folded the paper, and placed it next to his coffee cup.

"Sorry I'm late, Billy. I got a note last night from my old commander in the marines. He wanted to meet earlier this morning. I thought I'd be done in time," I said, sitting down across from him.

"No worries at all. Coffee? No? Well, I had time to read most of the paper. Your president is not a well man. Three medical specialists. Must stay in bed. I don't mean to sound pessimistic, but he sounds near death."

"Maybe he is, but I'm pretty sure the First Lady will do everything she can to help him."

"When does your vice president step in?"

"I have no idea. I guess the doctors think it's too soon for him to take over, and I sure wouldn't want to be the one telling Mrs. Wilson that he is going to. Billy, I have to warn you. It could be that Wilson doesn't have much attention left for Mr. Churchill's letter."

"Perhaps not, but it's been delivered, and that is what was asked. I'll arrange our return. I assume you want to get back as quickly as possible."

"I do, but I might have one more meeting in New York City. Since we're leaving from there, I don't think it will delay our departure."

"That should be fine. Well, how was your old commanding officer? Reliving the glories of the war?"

"Hardly. He's more worried about the peace and the president's health."

---

2. *Washington Herald*, October 3, 1919. P. 1.

"Can't blame him for that. Based on the headlines, you were lucky to see the president before he fell ill."

"Yeah, lucky."

Jones stood and tucked the paper under his arm. "Sorry to leave you, Jack, but Sir William and I are meeting with the new British ambassador, Sir Edward Grey.[3] He arrived in Washington only a few days ago. Drinks this evening?"

"Sure. Back here?" I asked, standing as well.

"That's fine."

"Wasn't Grey the head of the foreign office before the war?" I asked as we walked together to the lobby.

"He was. He remains a man of noble thought and vision, the ideal emissary to convince your government of the need for the Treaty of Versailles and America's continued engagement with Europe."

I liked Billy and found his faith in good old English decency charming. Unfortunately, Edward Grey, as British foreign secretary for the decade before the war, had helped craft the web of relationships that resulted in the slaughter of the past four years. He was exactly the wrong person to convince the US Senate of the need to become further entangled in European affairs.

It was odd that Billy was supporting a meeting with Sir Edward, given that Grey's mission seemed contrary to, or at least not aligned with, the letters Churchill had me deliver.

"Why would you and Sir William meet with the ambassador about the treaty? I thought you came to make sure the president and Mr. Lodge understood Mr. Churchill's view that a Bolshevik Russia is the primary threat to peace."

"I serve many masters, Jack. Sir Basil wanted me to be able to report back to him on how your task went, and despite Mr. Churchill's concerns, His Majesty's government very much needs

---

3. Edward Grey, 1st Viscount Grey of Fallodon. April 25, 1862 –September 7, 1933. Politician.

America as part of the peace framework. Sir William and I are to do what we can to help Sir Edward secure the ratification of the treaty."

"Good luck. You might suggest to Sir Edward that he'll need to persuade Senator Lodge, and he'll have his work cut out for him."

Jones raised a hand acknowledging my suggestion as he pushed through the revolving hotel doors and was gone.

Despite my fear of being named a presidential assassin, the day passed quickly. I spent most of it in my hotel room, reading newspapers and trying to learn about the War Industries Board. I discovered little new about the board. Instead, I learned that several senators were traveling across the country, making speeches against the ratification of the treaty. I also found that scaremongering about the threat of Bolshevism had found its way across the Atlantic. Churchill wasn't the only one who believed in the threat of the Red boogeyman. The meatpacker, Swift & Company, had taken out an advertisement in the *Evening Star* bitterly complaining about the dangers of misunderstanding the benefits of American industry to mankind. The ad was titled ENCOURAGING BOLSHEVISM.[4] I wanted to spit as I read it. God forbid the average guy should think for himself. "Everything that falsely encourages unrest also encourages bolshevism," it read. Looked like the meatpackers remained concerned about their image since Sinclair's book. I thought of Joseph Flavelle and his wife. He might have been charming, but he was still one of the old bastards who were intent on keeping the noose of the prewar social order around our necks.

I tossed the newspapers on the bed. It was near time to meet Jones back at the Willard.

When I arrived at the bar, most of the small tables were taken. I managed to find one with two chairs next to a window overlooking Fourteenth Street. I ordered a whiskey and watched

---

4. *Evening Star.* October 4, 1919. P. 10.

the other patrons talking, laughing, and drinking. They were happy. The war was over. The Spanish flu had faded away. America felt like the center of the world, and Washington was the center of America. These men were going to milk America for all she was worth, and the women with them were happy to tag along for the ride.

I felt sick and turned in my seat to watch the people hurrying by on the street below.

"Is this seat taken?"

Standing above me stood the girl who had poisoned my drink.

My instinct was to grab her by the throat and shake her, demanding to know Fuchs's location. Unfortunately, the bar was full, and some chump would jump to her aid if I did. Hell, if I didn't know what she'd done to me, I was exactly the type of patsy who would try to rescue her.

I could see that she read the thoughts as they raced through my mind. She didn't seem bothered. Instead, she sat down, retrieved a pack of cigarettes from her little handbag, and knocked one out.

"Light?" she asked me.

"I don't smoke, and you're lucky I don't kill you right now."

"I suppose it would please Karl if you did." She gave me a coquettish smile. She wasn't afraid, or at least, she hid it well. I was impressed.

"Fuchs," I said in confirmation.

"Yeah. Charming Swiss fella. Pays well but not too concerned with my health. I have a feeling he sent me in here so you would attack me." She looked around. "But it's crowded, and I was willing to take the chance."

"He's not Swiss. He's a Kraut. He works for German military intelligence, but I guess you know all that."

She raised an eyebrow. "Really? No, I didn't know. But the war's over, so I guess I'm still a patriot. God bless America." She waved at the bartender, pointed to my drink, and held up two fingers.

"Do you know what you put in my drink the other night?"

"Who said I put anything in your drink?"

"If you knew, you wouldn't be sitting across from me now. You wouldn't have been willing to take the chance," I said, ignoring her question. "It was a drug intended to drive me crazy. I hallucinated all night. Hell, I'm having visions right now!"

Tippy, who was leaning against the wall behind her, nodded his mutilated head.

"Of loveliness, I hope." She smiled again. "Look, I'm just trying to earn a buck. I don't ask questions I don't need the answers to, and he didn't tell me what was in the little bottle he gave me. I'm sorry if you got a little loopy. I did what I was paid to do, and Karl wants me to tell you he appreciates your work. As far as he's concerned, you're all square. He wants to meet you. To tell you himself."

"Where is he now?" I asked.

Our drinks arrived.

"I'm sure he's around," she said as she swirled the ice and whiskey in her glass.

"I'd like to talk to him too." I was willing to take my chances with Fuchs. I would shoot him dead as soon as I saw him, and if the coppers caught me, I'd tell them he was a German spy and I worked for Colonel House and the president.

"Well, that's good. He wants to have a chat. That's why I'm here. He wants to meet at the cemetery across the river."

"Arlington?"

"Yes. Seven o'clock tonight."

"Alone?"

"He's got a few of his stooges with him. I'm sure they'll come too. They look like tough guys. Not quite as rough as you, mind you. My job is to make sure you go."

"And how exactly will you do that?"

"Well, Karl, having the well-refined soft touch of the

Germanic people, suggested that I threaten your sisters." She shook her head. "But seeing you, I think that's a dead end. Literally. So I guess I'll have to rely on my charm."

The mention of my sisters nearly snapped my self-control. I took a deep breath and turned away from her to give myself time to calm down.

After a few heartbeats, I turned back to her. She could tell she'd made me sore.

"Sorry, mister. I'm just doing my job," she said.

"You know he's going to kill you when you return to see him," I told her.

She didn't respond. Instead, she just watched me, calculating.

"He doesn't want anyone to know what he's doing," I said.

"And what's he doing?"

"He's trying to kill the president."

Her eyes widened at that piece of information. "What's he want with you then?" she said to cover her surprise.

"He thinks I've already tried to kill the president. He reads the newspaper, and he thinks the president's current health issues are my fault."

"Why would he think that?" she asked.

"No idea, but I know he'll want to tie up all the loose ends in his plot to assassinate the president, and unfortunately, that includes you."

"And you," she said with certainty.

"And me."

Just over her shoulder, Billy breezed into the bar. He took just a second to locate me. He raised an eyebrow at the girl's presence, but his manners were too refined for him to question me.

Lucky for him, he didn't have to. As he arrived at the small table, he looked at me for an introduction.

"Billy Jones, please meet a nameless German spy," I said.

"Pauline. Pauline Murphy," my druggist supplied. "And I'm not a German spy. I work for the Swiss embassy from time to time." She held out a hand, which Billy took with exaggerated care. From the gleam in his eye, I could tell he found her attractive. She was a very pretty girl, but his obvious interest made me uncomfortable. It struck me as being disloyal to Evelyn, and I'd thought better of him. I remembered that, at university, we both had been all too happy to chase the few girls we could find. Perhaps he hadn't changed with marriage.

"It is a pleasure to meet you, miss," he told her.

"*Not* a German spy?" I asked. I didn't bother to hide the disgust I felt at her denial.

"Look, mister. Griffin isn't it? The Swiss gentleman I work for is a charming man. He's got that special European flair that Americans just don't have." She said the last and glanced at Billy. "Sure, I work for him, but I'm not a spy. He pays well, and I need every penny I can get. I've got a family to support."

Billy noticed my disgust, but I could tell from the slight smile on his face that he was more moved by her comment about European flair and her fabricated sob story than my reaction.

"A family?" I said with disbelief.

"I've got a sister. She's younger. Fifteen. If I don't take care of her, she could end up on the streets."

"And your father, the marine?"

"That bastard's been dead for five years. As soon as my mother left, he gave up on us and on life. Good riddance." She was a swindler, and given Billy's focus on her, I could tell he was buying every word.

"Jack, what is all this about?" Billy asked.

"Billy, Miss Murphy and I need to make a quick visit to Virginia. I can meet you for dinner later."

"Nonsense, old friend," Billy said. "I'll come with. I've no plans for the evening."

He signaled the bartender just as the girl had. He pointed at our whiskey glasses and circled a finger for three more drinks. He then borrowed an empty chair from an adjacent table and sat across from me next to Miss Murphy.

I was shaking my head as he crossed his legs and pulled out a cigarette.

"Billy, Miss Murphy and I really need to go alone."

"I'd appreciate you coming, Mr. Jones," Pauline said, ignoring me. Despite her bravado in approaching me at the bar, she was afraid of being alone with me. She was right to be.

"Well, that's settled then," Billy answered.

She gave Billy a slight smile.

Annoyed, I reached across the table and took her purse, which she had placed near her elbow.

"Hey, give that back!" Murphy said sharply.

It took just a moment to figure out the clasp, and then I had the purse open.

"Jack?" Billy Jones was appalled by my actions. No gentleman would think of pawing through a lady's handbag.

Just one more disappointment for Billy. Well, he'd just disappointed me.

"Sorry, Miss Murphy, but after our last encounter, I'm taking no chances."

Among the lip stain, powder compact, key, cigarettes, and match box, I found a small automatic knife with the words FITCHBURG MUTUAL FIRE INSURANCE etched into the ivory handle. I slipped the knife into my pocket. I also found a thin, elongated stainless steel case capped on one end. I twisted the steel cap free. Inside was a small medical syringe held in place in a wooden frame.

The snakes inside my skull began to squirm.

The plunger of the syringe was partially withdrawn, and the barrel held a clear yellowish liquid. Maybe two tablespoons. Mescaline. It had to be. A small amount but maybe enough to drive a fellow around the bend.

Pauline shifted back in her chair away from the syringe and away from me.

"Jack?" I suppose Billy saw something in my eyes he didn't like. I inspected the syringe as if examining an interesting tool.

I then held up the device and looked past its glass barrel into Pauline Murphy's frightened eyes.

I wrapped the barrel in my fist and put my thumb on the plunger.

"Do you know what's in this, Pauline?" I asked sweetly. Neither she nor Billy were fooled by my tone.

"Jack," Billy said again, trying to pull my attention from what I held.

Pauline shook her head dumbly.

"You seem like a brainy girl. Take a guess," I said.

"Look, mister. I just do what I'm told."

"Were you told to give me a quick stick with this on the way to Arlington?" I leaned toward her. She tilted even farther back in her seat. "Were you going to jump out of the taxicab after you did? You had to have a plan to get away."

I grabbed her arm across the small table and pressed the side of the needle against it. I didn't pierce the skin, but a slight change in the angle, and the hypodermic needle would slide into her forearm with no effort at all.

She took a deep breath as if preparing to call for help.

"Go ahead, Pauline. Scream your lungs out. It makes no difference to me."

Billy started to reach for my hand. I looked him in the eye and shook my head.

"Once this is inside you, you'll wish you were dead," I told her.

"At the cemetery," she answered. "When Karl distracted you with his charming talk, I was supposed to sneak it out of my purse and stick you then."

"Insane war veteran kills president. Now that's a good headline," I said.

"Jack, what are you talking about?" Jones asked. His brows were knitted together in a frown.

I sat back and carefully replaced the syringe in its small carrying case. I slipped the case into my side jacket pocket.

"Billy. You should stay here. You don't want to be anywhere

near Arlington tonight. Sir Basil would not approve. I promise you that."

"What the hell is going on?" He looked from me to the girl and back.

"The gentleman we are going to meet in Arlington intends to kill Miss Murphy and me. He'd prefer not to kill me. He'd rather she was successful in injecting me. I'd be left a drooling husk, but he'll kill me if this fails." I tapped my pocket where the steel container rested. "And, in any case, he will certainly kill poor Pauline."

Pauline didn't want to believe me, but the worry I read on her face told me she did.

"Now I'm definitely going with you," he declared. Apparently Billy believed me too.

I shrugged. He wanted to save the girl, and I wasn't going to argue anymore. I'd walked in those shoes before. It had never seemed to work out well for me. I hoped it worked out better for Billy.

"Do you have a gun?" I asked.

21

The Amphitheater

Billy didn't have a gun, but he did have plenty of unhelpful advice about going to the police, the Secret Service, or the military. He really was a painfully decent fellow who was in over his head.

"Billy, either stay here or shut the hell up," I snapped as the three of us climbed into the back seat of the motorcab taking us to the cemetery. I hurt his feelings, but the closer we got to the confrontation I knew was coming in Arlington the more frightened I became.

The taxicab took us south around the Washington Monument and the Tidal Basin. Although a few streetcars accompanied us, traffic thinned as we crossed the highway bridge over the Potomac. Once in Virginia, the taxi turned north along the river, which was soon lost from sight. Fields dotted with a few trees bordered the road on both sides. We were out in the country far from policemen and soldiers. Good. After about ten minutes, the cemetery came into view.

"Where do we go, Pauline? It's a big place."

"The new memorial amphitheater," she answered.

"You hear the lady?" I asked the driver over the noise of the automobile.

He nodded.

The sun was nearly gone behind the heights to the west when the taxi arrived at an ornate red sandstone gate and low wall that marked the entrance to the cemetery. We rolled through the narrow archway, and trees enclosed us for a short time. There was not a headstone in sight. The road wrapped around the base of a hill and then up through some trees. It looked like an army of bulldozers had smoothed the hillside. At its top, a circular marble temple glowed in the last of the sunlight.

"There it is," the driver said unnecessarily.

"How close can you get us?" I asked, leaning forward from the back seat.

"Right in front. It won't be a problem. They just finished building it, and it's not been used yet. I'm not even sure you can get inside."

"Can you wait for us? We shouldn't be long." I reached a five-dollar bill past his shoulder where he could see it. "For you, once we're on the way back to town."

"Yeah, okay. I can wait, but don't take too long."

He stopped the taxi at the bottom of a long, wide staircase that led to the front of the colonnaded amphitheater above us. No other automobiles were in sight, and the broad, open ground below us gave an unobstructed view should a sniper be hiding in the woods. Unfortunately, if I wanted a chance at Fuchs, I would have to risk a marksman in the trees. I couldn't leave Fuchs wandering around Washington, threatening my sisters.

When I stepped out of the car, I realized that the temperature had dropped with the setting sun. My suitcoat wasn't much protection against the evening chill. I felt bad for Pauline. She had only a thin shawl. Then I remembered the night filled with hallucinations in my hotel room, and my sympathy died.

"Stay here, you two," I said.

"Absolutely not!" Billy declared. "I'm coming with you." Billy opened the door on his side of the car and climbed out before I could object. Pauline followed. Realizing it had turned cold, Billy took off his jacket and wrapped it around Pauline's shoulders.

What a chump.

The sky was clear but for a few scudding clouds, and only the glow of the city behind us hid the stars. It was a beautiful night.

"Listen, you two. I'm sure there are a bunch of bloodthirsty Krauts up that hill. They will have guns. There is absolutely nothing the two of you can do to help. Please stay down here."

"Sorry, mister, but to get paid, I've got to deliver you," Pauline said.

"Yeah, so you could stick me with the syringe while I was distracted."

She shrugged.

I took the Colt from its holster, moved the slide a little, and saw the glint of brass in the chamber. Time to go kill Karl. My stomach fluttered. Whether with anticipation or fear, I wasn't sure.

"Suit yourselves, but let me get up there first and speak with Fuchs. Even if you show up a little later, I'm very sure you'll get the payment Fuchs intends for you," I said. She understood my meaning.

I leaned in the passenger window of the taxicab. "Pull down the road a bit. We're going to meet some folks up there," I said, gesturing with my head to the theater above us.

His eyes were big, and he nodded nervously. He must have overheard my conversation with Billy and Pauline, or maybe he just saw the gun in my hand. He would drive off at the first shot, but I wasn't going to kill him to keep the motorcar.

"But the thought crossed your mind," Tippy noted accurately.

I started up the stairs.

I watched the landing above me closely. I expected at any moment Karl and his men to appear with automatic machine pistols. I would be happy to see them. Tippy would be too.

At the top of the steps, I found myself on a wide plaza standing before the columned templelike structure.

No one was around.

More steps led up to the building itself and a door, which was nearly hidden behind the thick columns. I took the stairs, and when I reached the top, I turned to see that Billy and Pauline had reached the plaza.

I raised my arm, hoping Billy would understand that I wanted him to stop. He did but then raised his hands at his sides in question. I raised my arm once more and then turned back to the building. If I could find Fuchs before Billy and Pauline caught up, maybe they wouldn't get hurt.

The heavy metal door was locked, and I worked my way around the right side of the building. The light from the city gave the marble around me an ethereal glow. Despite the chill, sweat trickled down my spine. I was afraid. It wasn't anticipation at all. My lungs were constricted. The fear, the cold, and the old phosgene damage were conspiring against me.

Goddamn Fuchs! I tried to muster enough anger to wash away the dread weighing on me.

As I rounded the end of the building, the amphitheater beyond revealed itself. Row upon row of marble benches slanted up from below me. I realized I was on a balcony, which circled and overlooked the seating. A colonnade of man-wide marble pillars ran along each side of the balcony on which I stood. At the back of the theater, which had to be nearly two hundred feet away, four men stood in the shadows of the columns behind the last of the marble benches.

I knew when they caught sight of me. They shifted, and like ruby fireflies, three cigarette butts flew off into the darkness. One man, less anxious than the others, took a long drag, flaring the ember giving his indistinct face a brief, sinister cast. He then dropped the butt to the ground and crushed it under his heel.

"Leave it to you to take the long way round," Karl Fuchs called to me. The pillars had concealed him. Five men. Terrible odds.

"Karl, it's good to see you out here in the country." I knew the acoustics of the space had allowed my words to reach him because his chuckle made its way back to me.

"I must say, John, I am tremendously impressed by your success with the president. We watched you enter the White House and watched you hurry out, but we had no idea of what had happened until the newspapers came out that evening. And we still don't know exactly what you did."

"I didn't do anything." The words sounded like a lie even to my ears.

"John, you should be proud. You are protecting your country. Just as Senator Lodge is. I know you've met with him, and he is certainly no proponent of the treaty."

"I'm not the assassin you want me to be," I said with as much certainty as I could muster.

"Sure you are," Tippy volunteered.

"I beg to differ," Fuchs declared. "But let's move on to tonight's business. Is the lovely Miss Murphy with you?"

"If your question is did she inject me full of mescaline, then the answer is no. She didn't manage that."

"A shame. This will not be as artful as I had hoped."

As we spoke, I worked my way along the columned balcony. I kept the pistol by my leg, but I knew Fuchs wasn't fooled. His men were armed, but with the dark and distance, I couldn't tell what they carried. It didn't matter. I was committed.

"*Tötet ihn! Schnell!*" Fuchs ordered. His tone sounded determined and left no doubt that they were committed as well.

Fuchs remained by the rear entry to the amphitheater, but two of his men started around the circular colonnade toward me. The other two started down the center aisle between the marble benches. All four paced themselves, trying to keep me in sight as they moved. The men allowed the distances between them to increase. They weren't going to do me any favors by bunching up.

I wished I'd asked Billy to create a diversion. I hoped he and

Pauline were coming into the amphitheater behind me. If they did appear, their arrival would distract the Krauts, however briefly. It might give me a chance. Unfortunately, Billy and the girl were the only surprise I had. If it happened, I needed to make the most of it. If they were still waiting on the plaza below, I'd be a dead man in a few minutes.

Empty theater-like boxes ran along the inside of the balcony. Each had steps down into it and a marble balustrade separating it from its neighbors. The columns on each side of me curved toward Fuchs and the two men on the balcony with me. I increased my pace until the men were hidden by the tall marble pillars. Then, once they were out of sight, I tucked myself against a double column, which had just enough space between each pillar for my pistol. I steadied the iron sights on the German descending past the benches toward the dais. He was the nearest goon to where Billy and Pauline would appear. *If* they appeared. The German was moving slowly, maybe a hundred feet from me.

"Jack," Billy called. He hadn't seen the Germans stalking toward him.

Both the Krauts among the benches spun toward the stage. They raised their pistols aiming at the shadows that were Billy and Pauline. All three of us fired at the same time. The boom of the shots echoed through the amphitheater and rattled my brain. I missed. The orange flare of my pistol shot reflected off the marble of the columns, giving away my position. I fired again. My target, the German nearest Billy and Pauline, dropped. A bullet smashed into the marble pillar above me. I squatted low and duckwalked around the balustrade.

The second man had turned away from Billy and Pauline, who were gone. He had fired wildly, and he was still looking for me. On one knee, I rested the Colt on the top of the stone railing and fired. I thought I'd hit him, but he didn't fall. I fired a second time. His hat flew off and his arms flailed out from his sides as he tumbled back.

I moved but not into the amphitheater. Instead, I hurried

along the balcony back the way I'd come. I wanted to make sure that the curving row of columns continued to hide me from the two men on my level. When I was sure they couldn't see me, I crossed the inlaid walkway and swung my legs over the low marble railing to stand on the outside of the amphitheater. A narrow marble lip ran along the outside of the colonnade that circled toward the two men advancing along the balcony.

From somewhere in the theater, the sound of a whimper bounced between the columns. I hoped it was one of the Boche and not Billy or Pauline.

I hugged the marble pillar that hid me and tried to control my breathing and my fear. The left side of my face pressed against the cool stone. I held the pistol in front of my chin. My brain began to worry about the weight of the gun, the narrowness of my perch, and the certainty that one of Fuchs's men would peer around the column and see me.

A very soft hiss told me the Germans were close. The slight shift of a shadow was my only warning before, not five feet from me, a man's head leaned between the columns to check the outside of the structure.

I extended my arm directly at his face and pulled the trigger. The recoil, the sound, and my surprise at his closeness knocked me from the ledge. The fall to the ground below was much longer than I'd thought when I'd climbed onto the outside of the structure. Pain lanced up from my left ankle when I hit. I tumbled forward and ended up on my back, looking at the sky. A second man's face peered over the balustrade, scanning the darkness and looking for me. Miraculously, I still held the pistol and hadn't shot myself. I brought it in line with the pale full moon of his face as quickly as I could and fired. The bullet hit the stone edge of the railing just in front of him. Shattered marble spalled upward, and the man shrieked as the fragments struck him. I adjusted my aim and fired again as he fell back. Another miss. The bullet shattered the marble facing above him.

I scrambled to my feet. I had just one shot left.

On my throbbing ankle, I limped along as quickly as I could toward the back of the amphitheater. Fuchs had to be there. I might have missed the first of Fuchs's goons, but if I hadn't, with his men dead or wounded, he would run.

I couldn't let him.

My twisted mind couldn't see beyond this moment. If he escaped, I would descend further into the hallucinations and succumb entirely to the madness that had been toying with me since Basel.

"Mad as a hatter, you'll be," Tippy assured me.

"Jack!" Billy Jones called.

In the distance, a motorcar started and accelerated away.

As I rounded the theater, I realized a road curled around the back of the structure. A Ford Model T was parked on the pavement. The departing auto must have been our taxicab racing away from the shooting.

A shadowed figure hurried down the steps from the amphitheater and ran to the Ford. Fuchs!

"Jack, I need help! Pauline's hurt."

"You'd better catch Karl, Jackie boy. He's getting away and with him your sanity." Tippy was just ahead of me urging me on.

As he neared the car, Fuchs looked over his shoulder and saw me. Panic flashed across his face. For the first time that night, I felt good.

I hobbled after him.

He ran to the front of the automobile and threw the crank. The engine coughed but didn't start.

I'd reached the pavement only fifty feet from the back of the car.

He turned the crank again. Nothing but a sputter. I grinned at the fickleness of automobiles. Fuchs hadn't had a lot of experience driving. I remembered his rough handling of the car in Königsberg when he arranged the ambush that had killed Johann Ditzel. Fuchs had forgotten he needed to make adjustments on the steering column before the motorcar would start for him, but he was terrified. He just kept turning the hand crank.

One more look over his shoulder at me and he gave up. He sprinted across the field away from the amphitheater and away from me. Tombstones and what looked like a large cross lay in his path. I realized with my ankle, I'd never catch him. I reached the car and rested the pistol on the bonnet. Carefully I lined the sights up on his bobbing back.

"Jack, Goddamnit! We need your help." Billy again. I had told him not to come.

Fuchs, knowing I was behind him, cut left and then right, weaving to spoil my aim. One shot. I just needed one good shot.

I put the front post of the pistol on the center of his bobbing suit coat. I inhaled and let out half a breath, focusing on the target.

I squeezed the trigger.

"Jaaack!"

Fuchs didn't stumble. He kept running. Past the cross. Dodging in and around the markers. He didn't know my gun was empty. I watched him until he disappeared over the hill beyond.

"Goddamn you, Billy!" I roared.

I fell back against the car utterly defeated.

Tippy Frederickson threw back his head and howled with laughter. Behind him, Billy and Pauline came down the steps of the amphitheater. She sagged against him. Billy was trying to support her.

I holstered the empty pistol and limped over to them.

"She's been shot."

"Let's get her to the car."

Together, Billy and I carried her to Fuchs's automobile and laid her on the back bench of the Model T.

"Hey, Pauline. How're you doing? Can I take a look at you?"

She nodded, and her frightened, painfilled eyes seemed to plead with me to make her better.

The right side of her dress was wet with blood. I took her

small automatic knife from my pocket and cut open her dress and underclothes from just below her breast down to her hip. Carefully I lifted the fabric away from her skin. Below her ribs blood welled slowly from a wound in her side. I took my handkerchief from my pocket. Thank God it was clean. I wiped away the blood. A small bluish hole with a white rim showed itself for just a moment before blood covered it. I felt around her back. No hole there. The bullet was still inside her.

I left my handkerchief covering her wound.

"You're gonna be just fine, Pauline."

She looked at me with big, frightened eyes. "Mary. My sister's name is Mary. Eighteenth and Bay."

"You're going to be okay."

Together, Billy and I arranged her more comfortably on the back bench of the automobile.

"Billy, is your handkerchief clean?"

"Of course! My God, I'd give my eyeteeth for a medical officer, a stretcher-bearer, or even just a damned dressing kit," Billy said, looking a little wild-eyed.

I thought of Mitchell. He'd be perfect for this situation even without the medical belt he was always complaining about. I was not, but I'd dressed enough wounds that I was better than nothing.

"Sit back here with her. Put her legs in your lap and try to keep her from moving too much as I drive. You need to press our handkerchiefs against the wound. Try to slow the bleeding. The ride will be difficult. I'm going to go as fast as I can."

"Where will we go?"

"I don't know where the nearest hospital is, but I know where there's a doctor," I told him.

"She'll never make it," Tippy declared.

"She'll be okay!" I snapped.

"I'm afraid Tippy's right," Sarah said.

"Goddamn it, she's going to be fine!" I snapped.

"Jack, I believe you. Let's just go!" Billy said. I'd frightened him.

"Okay. Hold on tight to Pauline."

I set the throttle and the timing by the steering column, went around the front of the car and gave it a crank. I jumped into the driver's seat, and with a quick adjustment, I smoothed out the motorcar's engine. I'd become quite good with automobiles, or at least better than Fuchs. The thought gave me a small measure of satisfaction.

With a last wistful look at the hill beyond which Fuchs had disappeared, I released the brake and put the motorcar in gear. We would go to Elle's house and pray that Burton could save Pauline.

22

———

Incongruous Slippers

I drove back into the city and kept an eye out for a hospital or a copper. I figured a policeman would know where the nearest hospital was. I didn't see a hospital, and despite driving like the madman I was, I didn't see a policeman. I must have topped forty miles per hour as some points on the drive, and Pauline and Billy were both tossed around more than I liked.

"She's cold, Jack," Jones told me as we turned onto Elle's street.

I stopped in front of my sister's house.

"Stay with her, Billy. I'll bring the doctor to her." I didn't bother explaining that the doctor was my brother-in-law.

I limped up the walk and pounded on the front door.

"Burton! Elle!"

Doughboy began to bark.

An electric light went on in the house.

"Burton," I called again.

The dog was going crazy.

The front door opened a crack, and the muzzle of Burton's 12-gauge shotgun peeked out at me.

"John, what the hell are you doing here? It's late."

The dog's nose appeared in the crack below the shotgun barrel, which fortunately had dropped.

"In the car. A bullet wound in the abdomen, just below the ribs. Twenty-five minutes ago."

He opened the door more fully and looked down at the car and back at me. The dog stopped barking and sniffed my ankles.

"Goddamn it, John, why didn't you take him to a hospital?"

"I don't know where any hospitals are. I don't live here. Hurry, Burt, she's hurting."

"Her. Well, shit!"

Burton turned and rushed to a closet under the stairs.

"John?"

Elle was awake. She was halfway down the stairs, holding our grandfather's giant pistol by her leg. The barrel alone was nearly as long as my .45 automatic. I was glad she wasn't pointing it at me.

"Elle, the Kraut I told you about tried to ambush me. There was a girl with me. She got shot."

"How the hell did that happen? And why was there a girl with you?" Elle asked.

With his small black medical bag in his hand, Burt ran down the front path in his slippers with his robe flapping around his shins.

I followed him without answering my sister.

When he arrived at the car, he moved Billy out of the way so he could examine Pauline. He wasn't in the car more than a few seconds when he called to me.

"She needs a hospital. Now!"

He dug through his bag and pulled out some tubing.

"What's your blood type?" he asked me. Before I could answer, Billy did.

"I'm O positive."

"You're sure?"

"Yes."

"Get back in here and put her legs on your lap," Burton ordered. "Roll up the sleeve on your left arm."

Burton assembled a tube with steel needles on both ends. He uncorked a bottle I identified as iodine by the smell. He splashed some onto Billy's arm at the crook of his elbow. He did the same to Pauline.

I didn't see any signs of life in the girl. I tried to tell myself I didn't care. She had drugged me after all. But I did care. I desperately wanted her to live.

"Looks like you've killed another poor lass," Tippy said into my ear.

"John, get in front and drive like a bat out of hell. Straight up Fourteenth. Don't stop for anything. I'll tell you where to go."

I ran around the car, set the levers, then gave it a crank. The engine caught.

Elle had come down the walk and was watching her husband work. Anna and Clara stood in the front door, their wide-eyed looks obvious even from the street. One of them, maybe Clara, had Doughboy curled in her arms, though the dog looked too big for the little girl to hold. Thank God the dog had stopped barking.

Burton slid the needle into Billy's arm.

"I'll meet you at the hospital, Burton," Elle called.

I got in the car and drove like a life depended on it.

Burton gave me terse instructions, and in just a few minutes we pulled around in front of a stately red brick building. Burton was out of the automobile almost before it stopped. He sprinted up the steps and returned not thirty seconds later with two burly orderlies carrying a canvas stretcher.

"Ease her out carefully. And you," Burton said to Billy, "keep your arm above hers and keep up with the stretcher."

Burton was no longer the easygoing man I'd come to know. He had transformed.

"Billy. His name's Billy," I said.

Burton looked at me without understanding. At that moment,

his brain didn't give a crap about me or the name of the blood donor or anything other than the girl on the stretcher.

Billy jogged along to keep up with Pauline. Burton hurried the group up the steps into the hospital. I followed. The awkward party raced down a long hall to a door held open by a nurse. Burton took everyone right through it. The nurse put her hand in my chest and stopped me.

"Operating theater. You can't go in."

I nodded. I didn't really want to be in there anyway. She pointed to another door down the hallway. A waiting room.

I sat down on one of the uncomfortable wooden chairs and put my head in my hands.

Four men dead or injured, Pauline shot, and not a goddamned thing to show for it.

"Fuchs is a clever lad. Too clever for you, Jackie." Tippy wouldn't leave me alone. He could feel my disappointment and despair at Fuchs's escape and Pauline's injury.

Billy looked into the room. When he saw me, something flashed across his face. Fear? Anger? Disgust? Something was roiling just under his proper English facade, but he hid it quickly.

"How is she?" I asked.

"How the fuck should I know?" he snapped. The facade was gone. Anger. He was angry with me for what happened to Pauline. I almost reminded him I had told him not to come, but that wouldn't have made anything better. He stood before me, quivering with rage.

"The Germans wanted to kill Pauline and me, Billy," I said in a reasonable tone. "I didn't cause this."

"That's a lie, Jack. You can tell yourself that if you want, but I saw your face at the Willard's bar. You were always going to go after the Germans, and you were always going to make that poor girl go with you. You could have run away, but you went there looking for a fight."

"They were Boche spies, Billy. They're trying to undermine the treaty ending the war."

"That's just your excuse. You were always planning on shooting them all."

That was likely true, but I still didn't think his version of the fight was fair. I wanted to shout at him, but I didn't.

"Billy, when you called my name, they shot at you. I didn't cause that. And yes, I shot at them. They were shooting at all of us."

"My God, what have you become? You were such a decent man before the war. Funny, empathetic, honest. Now? Now I don't know you anymore."

"I told you that in London, Billy. I told you and Evelyn both, but you didn't want to listen. You're wrong about what happened in Arlington, but you're not wrong about me. I am changed from the boy you knew. Just as you are. But I didn't cause Pauline to get hurt. Blame those who hurt her. Not me."

"I suppose I would if any were still alive."

"One's alive, Billy. The one responsible is very much alive."

WE STOPPED TALKING. BILLY REMAINED ANGRY. WHETHER WITH ME or the situation, I wasn't sure. I was angry that he was unable to see the truth. Tippy was overcome with joy that our old university chum was in his camp. We sat on opposite sides of the room. Billy smoked, and I listened to Tippy claw at my brain with mumbled words designed to strip away any hope of composure.

"Murderer, liar, cheat, coward…" I don't remember him repeating himself.

By the time Elle appeared, I was ready to burst.

"John, you look like you're ready to commit murder."

"That's because he already has and probably will again," Billy Jones said from his side of the room where he had started pacing.

Elle's eyes narrowed at his words. She looked at me and back at him. She wanted to know who he was.

"Elle, this is Billy Jones. I went to school with him in England. He works for the British government now," I said. I looked at Billy. "This is my sister, Eleanor Rusk. The doctor helping Pauline is her husband. Burton."

"Well, at least someone in your family is of some use," Jones said.

My sister swung away from me and charged across the room and into Billy's face. "Mister, I don't know where you got your manners, but just because my brother will listen to your biting Limey brickbats doesn't mean I will. If I need to knock some manners into you, I'll be happy to do it!" She was outraged. "He's worth ten of you!"

I hurried over on my aching ankle and put my hand on her arm.

"It's okay, Elle. He's worried about the girl. We all are."

Jones opened his mouth to deliver another cutting remark.

"Billy, stop talking. Now. You're annoying my sister, and I'm not prepared to put up with that. You've made yourself clear. You blame me. Fine. But you need to look in a mirror, *old friend*." I said the last with sarcasm. Our old relationship was gone. "You bear some of the blame for her getting hurt too. If you hadn't agreed to go to Arlington, maybe she wouldn't have been in the amphitheater. I asked you not to go, but you wanted to play the gallant knight. You have to live with that, and I have to live with her being there too."

With my words, Billy's stoic English mask fell away completely. My words had reached him, and his dismay at being partly to blame was obvious. He realized that his insistence on accompanying me into the amphitheater brought Pauline there too. Sure he was angry with me, but he was angry with himself as well.

I was doing my best to ignore the fact that I used both Billy and Pauline as a diversion so I could get the jump on the Germans. Given Billy's mood, I certainly wasn't going to tell him that I bore more than my fair share of responsibility.

"Of course you won't tell him," Tippy said.

I escorted my sister back to the other side of the room and sat her in one of the chairs. I ignored the knot in my stomach that my guilt created.

"You don't need to be here, Elle. You should be home with the girls."

"John, after what you told me at dinner and then showing up at our home with that woman, I had to come. Don't worry, the girls are with the neighbors. They're worried about you too. What happened, and what happened to your leg?"

"I didn't know where else to go. I knew I had to hurry. She needed help, but I didn't know where any hospitals were," I said, answering her first question.

"I'm glad you came to us. But how'd she get shot?"

"She was working for the Krauts. She says she thought they were Swiss, but they weren't. She was supposed to bring me out to Arlington to meet with the Kraut who chased me across Germany."

"That Fuchs fellow?"

"Exactly. Well, he and four of his men were waiting for us at the new amphitheater in the cemetery. They ambushed us. We ended up in a shootout, and Fuchs got away."

"And the others?"

"As far as I know, they're all dead, Elle."

She nodded. "Well, don't worry about the young lady. Burt is the best. He really is. He learned more in France about trauma surgery in a year than he did in ten back here. His commander in France wrote him up for a medal. He didn't get it, but he should have. He's damn good at what he does."

We sat in silence for a time. One of the nurses came in to get Pauline's name and information.

"Pauline Murphy. She and her sister Mary live near the corner of Bay and Eighteenth. I don't know the exact address. She might be from Fitchburg, Massachusetts, but I'm not positive."

After the nurse left, I turned to my sister.

"Elle, I need a favor. I need you to find Mary Murphy. She's fifteen. She's got no other family. Do what you can for her. I'll get you some money. I'm sorry to put this on you, but I can't stay around and find her. I've got to find Fuchs."

"Sure, John. We'll do what we can, and don't worry about the money."

"Hush, Eleanor," I said, using her full name so she would know I was serious. "I'll get you money. Enough to look after the girl. But don't give it to her. She's young and alone, and someone will take advantage of her."

"Okay. Fine."

It must have been a few hours before an exhausted Burton pushed through the waiting room door. His operating mask was pulled down around his neck and his operating cap tilted back on his disheveled hair. He still wore the gown he must have used in surgery. It was dotted with blood. The incongruous slippers remained on his feet.

He looked at me and then Billy. A cold wave washed over me, and I knew Pauline was dead. Billy did too. He jumped to his feet, gave me one last enigmatic look, and left the waiting room.

Burt watched him go and then turned back to me.

"I'm sorry, John. She had just lost too much blood."

"You did what you could, Burt. It just took too long to get her to you. Thank you though. It means a lot to me."

He shook his head, and Eleanor, indifferent to his bloodied clothes, wrapped him in a hug.

"You both need to get home. You need to see your girls," I said.

"He should look at your leg," Eleanor suggested.

"It's a twisted ankle. I'll get the doctor at my hotel to wrap it. You both have done enough."

Together, we walked slowly down the hall and away from the operating theater where Pauline Murphy's body lay. When we came down the stairs from the entrance, the sky through the trees to our left was just starting to show the pink of dawn. It was still cold, but it didn't compare with the chill I felt in my soul.

Another woman dead on my watch. I had used Pauline and Billy too. She was dead because of it. I blamed myself at least as much as I blamed Fuchs.

Billy was nowhere in sight, likely too sick of me to consider riding in the same automobile with me back to the Willard.

The doors to the Ford were open. In our rush, we had forgotten to close them. A four-door older Model T was parked behind me. I was suspicious and my hand crept inside my jacket, despite the fact that the Colt was empty.

My sister saw the motion and said, "I drove, John. That's our motorcar. No Germans will pop out of it." She gave me a smile, and I tried to return it. She shook her head gently. "You should go to your hotel and get some rest. Unless you want to stay with us."

"No. I need to see the authorities and warn them about the Germans. I'll sleep when that's done, but thanks, Elle. I hope you can find Pauline's sister. In any case, thanks for trying. Thanks for everything." I gave her a hug. I then shook Burton's hand, and without thinking, I pulled him into a hug as well. It was spontaneous and awkward, but it still felt right.

"Sorry," I mumbled. "And thanks."

"I'm sorry too," he said.

I started Fuchs's Ford and drove south toward the White House.

23

———

Empty Eyes

I decided that the first step to catching Fuchs was to use Colonel House and his contacts with the Secret Service or Justice Department. If I could convince them the president was in danger because of a German spy without implicating myself, they might do my work for me. They might not kill him, at least not right away, but they might toss him in the clink and keep him away from me. A part of my mind, the deep, dark animal part, rebelled at the thought of him surviving. It wanted to see him tortured and dead.

"More barbaric with each passing day, Jack," Tippy said.

"I suppose I am, Tipton. It's not like I don't have reason to be."

We were in the motorcar driving back to the Washington. It didn't feel odd talking to Frederickson when I was alone. Lots of people talk to themselves. Maybe not to an apparition that haunts them daily, but still, they do talk to themselves.

"Always with the excuses. You killed that poor girl, but *it's not my fault* you whine." He said the last in a mocking soprano voice. "It's that awful Karl Fuchs! He's the reason all these bad things happen."

I opened my mouth to argue but decided against it. I would just be arguing with myself. I *had* killed Pauline. Indirectly, perhaps, but I had. She probably deserved it. She was an amoral pawn of the Germans. Unfortunately, I remembered Marie. She too had been a pawn of the Germans. At one time, I'd thought her to be amoral as well. My heart dropped into my stomach with the thought, and Tippy gave a throaty laugh.

"Bastard," I said in reply.

The doorman at the Washington Hotel was surprised when I arrived in a motorcar. For a reasonable fee I paid him directly, he agreed to arrange for housing the automobile. Pauline's blood on the back seat had dried in the night, and I was confident that against the dark leather no one would notice it. I would keep Fuchs's car. He wouldn't claim I'd stolen it. He didn't want me talking to the authorities. He didn't want Germany blamed for Woodrow Wilson's health problems. A claim he knew I would make if arrested. Since I wasn't as crazy as he'd hoped, any interview by the authorities was too risky for him and his Teutonic masters. That was why he'd decided to kill me at the cemetery. As he'd said, it wasn't as *artful* as driving me completely crazy with a massive dose of mescaline, but me dead was a necessity. He couldn't leave any link between the president's failing health and Germany.

It was still too early to see Colonel House, and although I had washed up some at the hospital, I needed to change clothes after administering to Pauline in the back of the Ford. The sleepless night weighed on me. I needed to rest, but first I needed my ankle looked at.

There were a few early risers sitting on the couches in the lobby, reading the free newspapers. They'd probably slept for ten hours and already had breakfast. I hated them all.

I collected my room key at reception. Along with my key, the clerk also handed me a message and a thick envelope. The message was from Neville. I scanned it quickly. He had indeed contacted Thomas Reynolds and made an appointment on my behalf to see Reynolds at his New York City office in two days' time.

The envelope was from Senator Lodge. It contained his sealed response to Churchill. I tucked both into my inside jacket pocket.

I asked the night clerk about the hotel doctor. He assured me the doctor was always available. After a quick telephone call, I was told to meet the doc in his office on the third floor. "I also need to collect my things from the hotel safe," I told the clerk. I didn't know when I would be back at the hotel, and I wanted to get the money I needed to give Elle for the Murphy girl.

"You will have to wait until after eight a.m., sir."

"Unfortunately, I can't wait." I peeled a five-dollar bill off the roll in my pocket and slid it over to the clerk. His eyes flitted across the lobby and back to me.

"Follow me, sir."

In short order, I had the thick envelope of cash that I had collected from my various jobs for Armistan, Patricia, the French, and the British. I placed it in the jacket pocket opposite where I'd put Lodge's letter.

"The doctor is waiting for you on three, sir," the clerk reminded me with a smile my five dollars had bought.

I considered taking the stairs, but the thought of navigating my way up each flight on my bum ankle convinced me to take the elevator. I shared it with a colored attendant with the drooping eyes of a man coming to the end of a long night shift.

"Three," I told him.

He nodded, shut the doors, and punched the button.

"Long night?" I asked him.

"Yessir. They're all long nights."

"Off at eight?"

"Yessir."

I nodded.

As we arrived at the third floor, I asked him for the location of the doctor's office.

"Left off the elevator. It's at the end of the hallway near the stairwell. There's a sign painted on the glass. Says doctor," he told me.

"That's handy."

He was polite enough to reward me with a chuckle as I limped off the elevator and followed his directions.

As promised, just before the door to the stairwell was the doctor's office. The door was cracked open. I imagined the poor bastard hurriedly dressing so he could be available.

I pushed open the door, thinking I'd see the doctor, but no one was there. A rolling privacy screen hid part of the room.

"Doctor?"

I moved past the screen and froze.

The body of a man lay sprawled on the floor half under a gurney.

Several thoughts flashed through my head, foremost among them was that I was an idiot. The Germans knew where my hotel was! I had known that, but I'd forgotten in the horror of the night before. My delay at the hospital had given Fuchs time to rally his remaining men and get them to my hotel. They were here at the hotel, watching the lobby. They'd overheard my conversation at the front desk about the doctor. My delay in collecting my money from the hotel safe had given them time to get to the doctor's office. I'd walked into an ambush with an empty pistol!

I started to turn to leave the room.

A cord flashed down past my face.

Garotte!

I'd seen them used in the trenches. Perfect for quieting sentries during trench raids. Brutal, effective, and quick.

I shoved hard away from the cord and desperately threw up both my hands to protect my neck. Only my left hand got there in time. My attacker yanked back hard on the line, and it bit into my hand and the right side of my neck. It didn't cut. Thank God it wasn't wire. But it didn't matter. My hand, which was saving me from immediate suffocation, was pressed against my neck and was doing a good job of cutting off my air.

I was suffocating just like in the Turkish bath on the *Adriatic*, but I couldn't rely on a bath attendant to save me. I pushed back into my attacker to ease the pressure on my throat, and I felt the outline of the trench knife on my belt press into the small of my back.

The trench knife! My right hand clawed behind me for the handle. My fight to reduce the pressure on my neck also limited the space for me to retrieve the knife.

I lunged forward increasing the pressure on my windpipe but gaining the room to reach under my coat and grasp the handle. I rocked back and immediately thrust forward again. The knife came free. I spun it about in my hand so that the blade was pointing down and hammered it behind me at hip height where at least some part of my attacker had to be. The knife hit flesh. And bone.

An agonized growl escaped my assailant. He jerked away from me. He released the garotte and shoved me from him.

I spun to face him and flipped the knife around.

Shorter than me but heavier. Sandy hair, blue eyes. I'd never seen him before.

His right hand clawed under his jacket.

He had a gun!

I punched him in the chest with the brass knuckle guard of the trench knife knocking him back into the wall. He had the butt of the gun in his hand, and he tried to recover his balance by bracing one hand against the wall.

He swung the pistol toward me, but he was too late. Our eyes met, and we both knew it.

I drove the knife up under his ribs and, with a savage twist pulled it free, only to thrust it up again.

Surprise, denial, pain. All flashed across his face in succession, and then there was nothing. Empty eyes in a dead face.

I left the trench knife in the body and stepped back. I'd had him pinned against the wall with my forearm, and without my weight against him, his body collapsed to the floor.

I was careful not to step in the pooling blood. I kicked the door to the doctor's office shut.

I checked the other body in the room. It was the doctor. He'd been an older man, bald, thin, and short. A stethoscope was still hooked on his neck, which showed the raw marks of the garotte that had been used to kill him.

My heart thundered in the aftermath of the fight. I knew I didn't want to face the police. Being the only living witness standing among two dead bodies was a bad way to convince the authorities that Karl Fuchs and the Germans were scheming against Woodrow Wilson and the treaty.

I found the garotte on the floor where it had been dropped. I left it there. At a small sink behind the gurney, I rinsed the man's blood off my hands. I tried rinsing the bloodstains out of my shirt cuff, but even after running water over it, the cuff remained pink. Pink and wet.

Recalling the danger of fingerprints, I tried to remember what I'd touched. The office door. Unfortunately, my handkerchief was lost somewhere in Walter Reed General Hospital.

I searched the Kraut. I found his handkerchief and a metal case just like the one I'd taken from Pauline. Inside, I found another syringe. Fuchs had not given up on pursuing the plan of rendering me insane through the injection of mescaline. I wasn't surprised. That explained why the garotte hadn't been made of wire. With wire, it was certain my neck would have been cut and a real possibility that I'd have been killed at the first jerk by the assassin. With my escape from Arlington, Fuchs had reverted to his original plan. His man was supposed to choke me until I passed out and then inject me. If they had succeeded, I'd have been discovered in the same room as the corpse of the doctor the desk clerk knew I was coming to see. Anything I said, assuming I could talk at all, would be the incoherent, discredited ramblings of a madman.

I put the tube in my pocket with its partner I'd taken from Pauline and opened the door using the handkerchief. Bracing the door with my foot, I wiped down the door face. Carefully I squatted over the German corpse and wiped the handle of the trench knife. I then pulled the doctor's body close to the German stiff. I tried to wrap the fingers of the dead doc's right hand around the knife's hilt, but they wouldn't stay in place. Maybe some of his fingerprints did.

With the two bodies stacked together, I hoped it looked like the two had killed each other. Unlikely, but with no other explanation, perhaps overworked coppers would believe it.

I found a wrap for my ankle on the shelf and tucked it in my pocket opposite my growing hoard of mescaline-filled syringes. One last look around the room convinced me that few policemen would believe a man, who been strangled, could miraculously kill his attacker.

I shut the office door and hoped no one needed the doctor for a while.

I needed to get the hell out of Washington, but first I had to take care of Fuchs. I couldn't leave him behind me.

I didn't want to call an elevator, so I took the steps down to the ground floor. It seemed to take forever. The stairwell exited into a small alcove from which I could see most of the hotel's lobby. There seemed to be fewer early risers reading newspapers than there had been just a few minutes ago.

"That's your imagination, mate," Tippy told me.

I hurried across to the front desk. One of the men in the lobby saw me, stood, and exited the hotel. Another locked eyes with me but quickly went back to pretending to read his newspaper.

"Now you're just seeing ghosts." Frederickson didn't want me to recognize the threats around me.

Once at the front desk, a new clerk greeted me. He was an

older man, probably senior to the clerk who had sent me to the doctor. The other man must have just gotten off work.

"How can I help you, sir?"

"I'll be checking out this morning."

"Very good. I hope you enjoyed your stay. Room number?"

I showed him the key with the number on the fob.

"I'll just go upstairs and pack."

"When you return, your bill will be ready for you, sir."

"What was the name of the night clerk who was here a few minutes ago? Did he get off duty? I wanted to thank him. He got your house doc for me in a hurry. Your poor doctor had a line out the door. Another fellow showed up just as I was leaving. Busy man, your doctor."

"The night clerk is Jerome, sir. I'll make sure to note your comments in his file. I'm glad you were able to see the doctor quickly."

I took the elevator to my room. Once there, I reloaded the Colt, then changed shirts and took the trench knife sheath off my belt. I didn't know whether leather could hold a fingerprint, so I rubbed it down with my damp shirt. I'd toss the sheath bundled in my stained shirt into the first garbage bin I could find.

I packed up quickly, stuffing the shirt and sheath in the top of my case. Fuchs's men in the lobby would report that they failed to drug me in the doctor's office. Fuchs would try again or try to kill me.

Unfortunately, I had no real way to find him.

It dawned on me that I didn't need to find Fuchs. I just needed him to come to me, and I was certain he would.

24

___

Spoon Drop

When I returned to the ground floor, the lone remaining watcher was still there pretending to read his newspaper. I crossed the lobby with my bag and sat down across from him. He was young. Certainly younger than me. And less weathered.

His eyes flashed up from the paper and then back down. He wasn't sure what to do, and he was afraid. He knew what had happened at Arlington, and he could guess what happened in the doctor's office upstairs.

Finally, with no choice but to confront me, he lay the paper in his lap and met my eyes.

"Can I help you?" His English was good, but he had a slight accent. Almost like he was from Switzerland.

Tippy guffawed.

"Hey, Fritz, I need you to deliver a message."

"I am sorry, but you have the wrong person."

"Sure, I do. Look, I could shoot you right now." I opened my coat enough for him to see the butt of the pistol. "But that would leave you dead and me in need of another messenger."

His blue eyes widened.

"I'm going to the hotel restaurant to have breakfast. I want you to tell Karl Fuchs to meet me there. Tell him I'm going to the authorities once I finish eating. I need to see him first. Can you do that?"

"I don't know any Karl Fuchs."

"Sure you do. You're Swiss, right?" I asked with a smile. He paled and carefully folded the newspaper. He didn't appreciate my joke.

"Go find Fuchs. You'll tell him, yes?" I moved my hand toward the pistol.

He nodded and stood very slowly, leaving the newspaper on his chair.

"Hurry, I'm a fast eater," I told him.

I took his newspaper and returned to the front desk to finish checking out. While there, I borrowed a large envelope and a page of hotel letterhead from the clerk. Using my body to hide what I was doing, I took about a third of the money from the envelope in my pocket, wrapped it in stationery, and put it into the hotel's envelope. From my bag, I added the legal documents that my sister Midge needed to sign. I addressed the thick packet to Eleanor. She would figure out that she needed to send the documents on to our sister. I didn't know the exact amount of money I was sending her for Mary Murphy , but it was all in hundreds, and the stack was about a quarter-inch thick.

"How much to get this to Brightwood in an hour?" I asked the clerk.

"Fifty cents, sir."

"Here's two bucks. Make sure it gets there. It's important."

I left my bag with the bellhop. I instructed him to keep it close because I would be in a hurry when I returned to get it. I dropped a quarter in his palm so he understood I was serious.

At the restaurant, I told the maître d' I would have a guest joining me and we needed privacy. He brought me to a table with seating for four on the far side of the restaurant away from the other occupied tables. I also asked for the chairs across from me and to my left to be removed. I wanted Fuchs on my right side.

I ordered coffee and eggs and opened the abandoned newspaper. I had a little time to kill.

My heart jumped at the headline, which claimed that the president was getting better.[1] Sort of. Specifically, the statement of Wilson's doctor, Dr. Grayson, noted that the improvement of Wilson's condition was "slight but not decisive," whatever the hell that meant. It seemed to me Grayson was a better lawyer than he was a doctor. Perhaps the president wasn't going to die. Part of me was disappointed. The part created by Fuchs and Schragmüller, I hoped.

The front page also told me that the Reds had taken a third game in the Series and were up three games to one over the White Sox. The damn Sox pitcher had committed two errors—in the same inning! How often does that happen? For the first error, he fielded a grounder and threw the ball over the first baseman into the grandstands. For the second, the ball deflected off his glove and into the bleachers as he tried to cut off a throw from the outfield to home. What were the chances of that? Something smelled rotten. Still, in a nine-game Series, the Sox might have a chance. Sure they did. Just like Wilson had a chance to recover from the bashing I gave his head.

I had finished breakfast and was working on my third cup of coffee when Fuchs arrived. He couldn't have been far from the Washington. The server had cleared the table but left the cream and sugar in its center at my request. My cup sat before me with the folded newspaper to its right. I was ready for Karl.

Fuchs entered the restaurant with a smile. He took in the location of my table and the absence of nearby diners, and his smile widened. Two more men filtered in behind him. More of his Kraut henchmen. He was confident he could take care of me when we left breakfast.

---

1. *Washington Herald.* October 5, 1919.

He arrived at the table and extended his hand as if we were businessmen about to make a deal. I didn't bother standing, and I didn't shake his hand.

"John, where have your manners gone? None of this is personal you know. I work for the good of Germany."

"Pauline's dead, Karl."

"I am truly sorry to hear that. How did she die?"

"Your men shot her in the amphitheater."

"Your fault, John. You could have just gone along with the plan."

"And let you drug me into incoherent insanity. Karl, please. Don't treat me like one of your blockheaded troopers." I nodded toward where his two men were seated. "You were always going to kill Pauline. Whether at Arlington or later. She was a loose end you needed to clip."

He gave a delighted laugh. "You are like an old friend. You know me so well. And I know you. You are sorry she died even though she drugged you. This does not surprise me. You are a hard man, but the sacrifices we must make in our work still trouble you. I suspect it is a flaw in you Americans."

The waiter arrived, and Fuchs ordered a coffee.

"You have difficulty seeing the big picture, and emotion drives you," he continued. "I understand, but it is hardly professional."

"So you're not bothered by the men you've lost?"

"It is unfortunate." He shrugged. "My resources are not without limit, but since I am here with you now, I am not worried I will need more men."

"Planning to kill me here, Karl?"

"Not here, John. This is too public. Too obvious. When you and I are done talking, I will leave, and my two men will follow you and kill you—even if it means their own arrest and detention."

"Not going to bother drugging me?"

"Sadly, I have no mescaline left."

The server arrived with Fuchs's cup and a carafe of coffee. Once done serving Fuchs, the waiter topped off my cup.

With my right hand, I fiddled with my unused coffee spoon, tapping its end on the table. Fuchs smiled sure that I was showing my nerves.

My heart began to thump in preparation for the action about to come.

Fuchs took the sugar bowl from the center of the table and added a scoop to his cup.

As he leaned forward to return the sugar, I let the spoon drop off the side of the table between the two of us. I bent down as if to retrieve the spoon, but instead, I took one of the mescaline-filled syringes from where I had hidden it beneath my leg. With it held firmly in my fist, I rose up and then brought the syringe down on Fuchs's leg. The needle stabbed through his trousers and deep into the meat of his thigh.

He grunted as I depressed the plunger.

A look of understanding and then horror flashed across his face.

Without hesitation, I dropped the first syringe to the floor and seized the second from under the newspaper.

Fuchs tried to pull away from the table, but I grabbed his tie with my left hand, holding him in place. He shifted his hips in his seat to avoid the second needle, but I was too close. I jammed the needle into his leg and pressed the plunger.

He knocked his cup over and coffee splashed across the table.

His eyes were wide with terror. "*Mein Gott,* what have you done?"

"You still have some mescaline, after all, Karl. It's just all inside you!" I said with a cruel grin. I put the syringe back under the newspaper. I didn't know what the effect of the drug would be, but I wasted no time reaching inside his coat and removing the small pistol holstered under his left arm. I stowed it in my coat pocket.

I glanced at his men. They knew something was wrong, but

they weren't sure what. They were on the edge of their seats, ready to rush over, but there had been no gunshot. Their boss was still alive.

I reached across the motionless Fuchs and set his cup upright. Then I leaned back in my chair and took a slow sip of my cooling coffee.

"It takes a while to feel anything, Karl, and honestly, I have no idea how much of this stuff it takes to kill a person. I'm pretty sure I just injected you with about two ounces. You probably have a better idea of what that means than I do."

The waiter hustled over with a new cup and more coffee. I waved him off.

"We're fine," I told him. I retrieved the first syringe from the floor and put it under the paper with its twin.

Fuchs seemed frozen, as if any movement would hasten his end. The knowledge of what was coming overwhelmed him.

"You must get me to a doctor," he begged. "Please. Not like this. I can't end like this."

"A doctor? I understand the doc has an office on the third floor. I'm not sure he's seeing patients though."

I opened the borrowed paper, not bothering to hide the two syringes. Fuchs couldn't take his eyes off them.

I tapped the headline of the newspaper.

"Looks like Wilson is recovering." It was probably a lie, but seeing the combination of terror and defeat on Fuchs's face was wonderfully satisfying, independent of the president's prognosis.

"It's not personal, Karl. We're professionals after all."

I rolled the syringes in the paper, stood, and as I passed the waiter, I said, "My guest is paying."

Fuchs's men watched me hobble past. They had expected their boss to leave first. That had been their plan. It looked like Karl hadn't bothered to foster initiative in his men. As I left the restaurant, I glanced over my shoulder, and only then were the men standing to check on Fuchs. I didn't know what he would tell them or what they would do without orders, but it didn't matter. I just needed to make it into a taxicab.

I limped quickly to the bellhop, collected my bag, and tipped him another quarter. No one had followed me into the lobby.

Once outside, I took a taxicab to Union Station, keeping an eye out for anyone who looked like they might work for Karl Fuchs. It was a waste of effort, but it made me feel safer. During the ride, between glances outside, I removed my shoe and tightly wrapped my ankle with the doctor's tape. I also stuffed Fuchs's pistol in my suitcase.

At the station, I gritted my teeth, ignored the pain, and walked through the entry hall out to the tracks that were disgorging passengers from the morning trains. Once the flow of arriving travelers embraced me, I turned to join them. Under my jacket and trapped under my arm, I had the stained shirt, which I'd bundled around the trench knife sheath, and the two empty syringes again housed in their stainless steel containers. During the ride to the station, I had carefully wiped down the medical implements.

As I passed a waste bin in the arrival hall, I slowed long enough to let the bundled shirt slip into the trash. I then reentered the crush of people hurrying to leave the station. When I spotted a bank of lockers just before the arrival hall, I left the crowd.

I stored my bag and went to the taxi stand in front of the station. I hired a motorcab to take me to the Willard, where I left a note for Billy telling him that I'd gone to New York for a meeting and could be reached at the Pennsylvania. I still needed him to get me the sailing date for our ship back to England.

I then went out the back of the Willard via Peacock Alley and caught another taxicab, but this time, instead of Union Station, I went to see Colonel House at his office in the tempos.

25

———

Scot-Free

The soldier at the reception desk of Building A sent me up to House's office with barely a glance. Now that the war was over, no one seemed to take security seriously.

Fortunately, House was in his office and free to see me.

"Major, this is a surprise. I am sure you have heard about the president's health setback."

"I have. I saw Mrs. Wilson that very morning, but I had no idea the president was that unwell." I saw no point in hiding the fact that I'd been at the White House the morning the president had taken a turn for the worse. Any serious investigation would quickly reveal I'd been there, and I didn't want to look guilty by hiding the fact from House.

"You *are* guilty," Tippy noted.

"Yes," House answered, and for one horrible moment, I thought he was answering Tippy. "The president's condition still isn't clear. Well, clear to me at least. You didn't see him by any chance, did you?"

At his question, my heart jumped into my throat. I had told

Neville I'd seen the president. It was entirely possible, if unlikely, that he and House might speak.

"Only briefly, and he was up and about," I said. "I was actually at the White House to see Mrs. Wilson at her request. It's my discussion with her that has brought me back to you."

"Really? With Mrs. Wilson? What on earth could she have wanted with you?"

I was surprised to find myself liking the colonel. I hadn't thought much of him when I'd first met him, but he wasn't a bad fellow. He really was trying to do his best for the country and for the president, who no longer had any use for him. I could see that it bothered him that Mrs. Wilson was willing to see me, a battered, trumped-up major, and not him.

"Mrs. Wilson thought someone is trying to harm the president. I found it hard to believe her because she didn't have any proof or details. It just sounded like her imagination was getting the best of her. I suggested she talk to the Secret Service or the police, but she is sure they will think she was just being hysterical. She asked me to look into it. I thought it was just the worry of an overprotective wife."

"But...," House said, understanding that something more was coming.

"There is a plot. It is real."

"My God!"

"In some ways it's like Paris all over again. The Germans are here, posing as Swiss citizens. They want to undermine the treaty by harming the president and by stopping his campaign for ratification. Their leader, a man named Karl Fuchs, works for German military intelligence. He is in Washington. And, sir, last night, I tried to stop him. At the new amphitheater over in Arlington, there was a shootout. Four of his men were injured or killed, but Fuchs got away. A young woman, whom he'd duped into helping him, was also killed."

"My God!" he said again. "Five dead?"

"I don't know if the bodies at the amphitheater have been

found yet, but I rushed the young lady to Walter Reed. The Germans had shot her. Unfortunately, she couldn't be saved."

"This is horrible," House exclaimed.

"This morning, Fuchs and his men tried to corner me at breakfast, but I got away and came straight here. I'm afraid Fuchs is unhinged. He will likely stop at nothing to harm the president."

"You must go to the police. Tell them all of this. The Germans have to be stopped!"

"It might be better, Colonel, if we used your contacts with the Justice Department or the Secret Service. I'm afraid if I walk into a police station and tell them what I told you, I'll be arrested for murder."

The colonel nodded. "You probably would be. The story is fantastical. If I didn't know what you'd done in Paris, I'd find it hard to believe myself."

He sat back in his chair, thinking.

"Here's what we will do. I will set up a meeting with the Justice Department. Ideally this morning with Attorney General Palmer. You tell him what you told me, and I'll vouch for you as I did in Paris. We'll get the entire Justice Department looking for these spies and finish this whole conspiracy once and for all."

"That sounds good, Colonel. I'm scheduled to leave for New York today, so the sooner the better." I didn't tell House that I was leaving town no matter what.

It turned out House couldn't get a meeting with the attorney general. Palmer was visiting New York City, ironically enough. House didn't want me to meet with Palmer without him present. I thought it might be because he wanted to remain relevant, but it was also possible that he wanted to protect me, which I appreciated.

Instead, he arranged a meeting with a junior but up-and-coming lawyer at the Justice Department, who worked closely with Palmer. Since I hoped that Fuchs was dead or dying, I didn't really need the meeting to result in Fuchs's capture. I needed it as cover from the police for the dead bodies in Arlington.

House's motorcar took us to the Justice Department building at 1435 K Street. The receptionist on the first floor took security much more seriously than the soldiers at the tempos or even the police at the White House had, but he still didn't take it so seriously that I was searched. I kept my suitcoat buttoned to keep my pistol as inconspicuous as possible. He asked who we were meeting, took our names, and placed us on a bench in the lobby. The staff knew who House was, but they made us wait anyway.

House was unbothered by the delay and regaled me with stories of the president's diplomatic successes, including the Armistice and the vaunted fourteen points. It went unsaid that he'd engineered the majority of them.

After about twenty minutes, we were taken to a small office on the fourth floor. Our escort knocked and opened the door without waiting for an answer. He then gestured us in and left.

Inside, file cabinets lined one wall, and a young man was just standing up from behind a desk stacked with folders. He couldn't have been much older than I was. He had dark, piercing eyes and coarse dark hair combed straight back over a high forehead, which gave the impression of intelligence. He didn't smile in greeting, but he did come around the desk and shake Colonel House's hand.

"J. Edgar Hoover,[1] Colonel House," he said. "It is a pleasure to finally meet you, sir. I am the head of the General Intelligence Division of the BOI. Your request came to me because it deals with alien radicals on American soil." His tone was obsequious. He was clearly a political animal, yet his words weren't smooth. Instead, they rattled out like machine-gun rounds, fast with almost no pauses.

I had no idea what BOI stood for, and I wasn't going to ask. I was confident it would become clear at some point.

"A pleasure to meet you, Mr. Hoover. Thank you for seeing us. This is Major Griffin. He works for the White House and the

---

1. J. Edgar Hoover. January 1, 1895–May 2, 1972. Law enforcement official.

president directly. He discovered the information we are here to discuss."

I shook hands with Hoover and could almost hear the gears clicking in his head as he calculated my importance in the Washington, DC, hierarchy.

"Please sit." He pointed us to two wooden chairs placed before his desk. "I was told that there is a German and potentially Bolshevik group operating in Washington targeting the president."

I didn't know where he got the idea that Bolsheviks might be involved, but House looked at me, and I realized that Hoover's mandate was to investigate radicals. And radicals meant Bolsheviks. Hoover was apparently the only official House could get a meeting with on short notice, and he was interested in Reds. A lowly flunky with a fancy title in the bowels of the Department of Justice was the best Colonel House could arrange?

Goddamn it!

I was not impressed, and neither was Tippy, who began to laugh.

Ignoring the snickers of Frederickson tickling the hairs on the back of my neck, I launched into my Kraut song and dance anyway. I included some hints that the Reds were likely working with the Germans on the plot against the treaty and Wilson. Hell, if Hoover wanted Bolsheviks, I'd give him Bolsheviks. I didn't care whether Mr. J. Edgar Hoover thought Fuchs was a Red or not, just as long as his investigators found the crazy son of a bitch and put a bullet in him.

Hoover took notes and nodded as I spoke.

"At the president's request, I worked for the French on an operation to catch spies still working for Germany. During that mission, I came across a German military intelligence plan to kill the president. Prefect Raux of the French police has some of the details. He also believes the Germans attempted to kill Prime Minister Clemenceau."

At that, House gave a timely bob of his head, which Hoover noted.

"The Bolsheviks were involved in this plot, and it's likely the Germans were supporting them. When I came here to deliver letters from Mr. Churchill to the president, Senator Lodge, and Colonel House, I learned that one of the leaders of the German plot against the president was in Washington."

House again gave another timely nod in confirmation.

"The man's name is Karl Fuchs. He is masquerading as a Swiss national and operating out of the Swiss embassy. He knew I was aware of the plot and wanted to kill me so I wouldn't spill the beans."

"You could have come to us right away."

"I thought about that, but I didn't want Fuchs to escape, and I didn't know the timing of his plan." Now I was just making things up.

"Major Griffin has had tremendous success in thwarting just these kinds of plots," House said in my support.

"I agreed to meet Fuchs at the amphitheater despite the danger because I knew of no other way to find him. Only his dupe, the unfortunate Pauline Murphy, knew where he could be located, and the price for that information was to walk into his ambush."

"Not afraid to tarnish the reputation of a poor dead girl, are you?" Tippy asked rhetorically.

"You took an incredible risk," Hoover said.

"Yes," I said in answer to both. "But it was necessary. Unfortunately, it ended in Miss Murphy's death."

Hoover held up a finger to stop me. He picked up the telephone handset from the cradle on his desk, tapped the plunger switch twice, and then spoke quickly.

"Bring me the report on the murders at the Arlington amphitheater." After a pause, he snapped, "Right now!" He then gestured for me to continue.

I told him about the gunfight and the race to save Pauline.

"The last I saw of Fuchs was at the Washington Hotel. He had two other men with him. I was at breakfast, and he had the audacity to walk right up and sit down with me. He told me his men were going to kill me. He was acting crazy, like he was drunk. I went right outside and caught a motorcab to see the colonel, and he brought me here. It was his idea to get the Justice Department involved." I gave a grateful look to House.

I didn't mention the dead doctor or the dead Kraut in his office, and I hoped that by the time they found Fuchs, his heart would have already exploded.

"He came to me, and I thought of the Department of Justice right away," House said verifying his part at the end of the story.

I waited for Hoover to ask me why I hadn't stuck a butter knife in Fuchs's neck at breakfast. I wasn't sure what would come out of my mouth, but he didn't.

A tap on the door came just as I finished.

A middle-aged man handed a thin file to Hoover and left without a word.

Hoover flipped through the pages in the jacket, which included several photographs. He flipped one around to show me the body of a man, who was clearly dead. Dark stains had spread across what once must have been a white shirt. The sightless eyes were half-closed. The body was lying among the benches in the amphitheater.

"Is this one of the men?" he asked.

"Could be. Probably," I said nodding.

"Okay. We'll take it from here. My people will assume control of the investigation from the local police. With what you've just told me, we know much more than they do in any case. We'll find this Fuchs fellow and take care of him. You can assure the president that the General Intelligence Division of the BOI has this well in hand," he said to House.

"Excellent."

"Where can I find you if I need to?" Hoover asked me.

"I'm going to New York this afternoon and then back to

England to complete a job. I am not exactly sure when I'll be back in the United States."

"As he mentioned, he's acting as a courier between the president and Mr. Winston Churchill, who is serving in Lloyd George's cabinet," House reminded him.

Hoover smiled, and my stature ratcheted a few more clicks upward inside his brain. "I understand. I'd enjoy working with you again, Major." He smiled a political smile.

"If you need anything, you can send me word at the Pennsylvania in New York City or Claridge's in London," I told him as we stood to leave.

After a round of earnest handshaking, House and I found ourselves on the street outside the Justice Department.

"That went remarkably well. He's a very competent young man," House said, once we were seated in the back of his motorcar. "Not so different from you, Major, if a hair more sedentary. Would you like me to drop you anywhere?"

"Lafayette Square please. And Colonel, what the hell does BOI stand for?"

House laughed. "Why, it's the Bureau of Investigation, son. And unless I miss my guess, with Mr. Hoover in its ranks, you're going to hear a lot more about it."

<hr>

I DIDN'T TELL HOUSE, BUT I NEEDED TO SEE MRS. WILSON ONE last time. If I'd told him I was going to see her, he would have wanted to go with me. If he were with me, she wouldn't see me. I wanted to tell her that the BOI was investigating German assassins, that the bureau was taking her worries seriously. It was too late of course. I'd already nearly killed her husband, but she didn't know that, and I wanted to give her what comfort I could. Of course, it was guilt that made me take the risk to see her.

"You're damn right it is!" Tippy opined.

Sarah disagreed. "You want to ease her pain, John. You're a good man."

Whatever the reason, I found myself walking back to the White House. There were two policeman at the guard shack. Both were alert. I told them my name and that I needed to see the First Lady. They nodded, as if they'd been expecting me.

A call brought Mr. Wood back out to the gate to collect me.

"Thank God, you're back. The First Lady is frantic."

"Why?" I asked.

"After you left two days ago, the president had a setback, and she is highly agitated, which has stirred up the Secret Service and White House police."

My heart raced as we walked through the East Wing. Two policemen stood guard, and I was sure they knew I'd attacked the president. Yet despite some suspicious looks, they didn't arrest me. Instead, they took my name and welcomed me to the White House.

"Sir, you need to stay with your escort," they told me while looking at Wood to make sure he understood.

"Of course," I answered.

One officer held open the door into the White House central hall for Wood and me.

Wood brought me to a library with a window overlooking the north lawn and Lafayette Square. He left to get the First Lady. I supposed he didn't feel the need to stay with me despite the commands of the police.

I knew the stairs to the residential section were just outside the library door. Fifty or so steps, and I could be in the president's bedroom. In less than a minute, I could be standing over the president's bed with my pistol in my hand.

I shook my head. Those weren't my thoughts. Those were Fuchs's and Schragmüller's thoughts. The fact that my head was clear of mescaline meant I could control myself. Instead of pacing, I forced myself to stand looking out the window. Only when the door opened, did I turn around.

The First Lady entered in a rush, and Wood shut the door behind her. Once again, I was alone with Mrs. Wilson. She had dark circles under her eyes and looked like she hadn't slept since I'd last seen her.

"Major! Thank goodness. What have you found? Do you have any news?"

"I do have some news. It will be hard to believe."

"Tell me!" she demanded.

"You will recall the mission for the French that the president asked that I join?"

"Of course."

"During that mission, I discovered several French spies who worked for the Germans during the war. I also uncovered a plot to undermine the peace treaty. This plan was developed and orchestrated by two German military intelligence agents."

"What does this have to do with the efforts to harm the president?" she asked.

"One of those German spies is here in Washington, and he, with the possible support of disaffected Americans, is intent on assassinating the president. They might have been working to further this plan since before the president left on his trip out west to promote the treaty."

"Oh my God!" She drew her hand to her mouth in horror.

"I tracked the spy to Arlington last night, and I tried to foil the plot. I killed several of his men, but he got away. This morning I met with Mr. J. Edgar Hoover of the Department of Justice. He is the head of the General Intelligence Division of the Bureau of Investigation. He asked that I assure you and the president that he and the BOI are taking this threat very seriously."

"I knew the threat was real! I knew someone was seeking to harm Mr. Wilson. Oh, Major, thank you. Thank you so much!" She took my hands in hers. She had tears in her eyes. "We will take every precaution to protect the president."

"Will you tell the president what I've found?" I asked, dreading her answer.

"Absolutely not! The president needs no more stress than he is already under. It will be up to me and those closest to him to protect him."

"I am sure that is wise, ma'am, and I am also sure that Mr. Hoover will leave no stone unturned to find those responsible."

"Thank you again, Major. Is there anything we can do for you? Anything to show our thanks."

"Well, ma'am, I know it's a lot to ask, but perhaps the president could veto the Volstead Act and prevent this Prohibition nonsense." I said it as a joke, hoping to lighten her worries.

Through her tears of relief, she smiled.

"I'll see what we can do," she told me.

The First Lady left me then, and Wood returned to escort me from the White House grounds.

I no longer feared the Secret Service or the police. There was no manhunt for a presidential assassin. Edith Wilson believed she knew the truth, and she was satisfied. The only person in the world besides me who knew the president had been attacked was Karl Fuchs, and he was either dead or crazy as an outhouse rat.

I was scot-free.

"You're a dog, Griffin. An awful dog of a man!" Tippy told me.

I walked through the gate onto the path by the Treasury building.

"I am indeed, Tippy," I agreed.

26

———

The Ant Hill

I dozed most of the way on the train to New York City. I was too exhausted after two days of no sleep to reflect upon either my attempted murder of the president or the fact that somehow I seemed to have escaped responsibility for it. I didn't know if the president would ever recover from what I'd done to him, and I didn't know if he'd remember what happened if he did. I could only hope that time would pass and so would he.

My fight with the Kraut in the doctor's office, my final confrontation with Fuchs, and my manipulation of Hoover and the First Lady deepened the already debilitating fatigue. The bruises, residual fear, and uncertainty had sapped all remaining physical and mental vigor, leaving me numb. I stumbled to my seat and was unconscious before the train left the station. The sleep the train brought was a godsend.

As was the fact that Fuchs was gone. The lulling rocking on the rails embraced me. When a stop or a passing train would wake me, I would recall the look on Fuchs's face as the injection of mescaline went home, and I would tuck my chin in my chest and fall back into oblivion with a smile on my face. Sure, there were still plenty of Krauts to take up the fight for Schragmüller, but Fuchs had been good at what he did. He'd done well for German intelligence, but I was confident that the massive doses of mescaline had either killed him or so shattered his mind that he was no longer himself. It was a confidence borne of experience. I knew exactly how difficult holding on to one's sanity could be when doped to the gills with mescaline.

I didn't arrive in the city until after dark. As on my first visit, I had no trouble getting a room at the Pennsylvania. When I checked in, the desk clerk handed me two cables.

I sent my bag to my room with the bellhop and a dime and went to the Men's Café for a bite to eat. I ordered grilled fish and a beer and read the cables as I waited.

The first cable was from London. It read:

William awake healing but bedbound and worried Stop Patricia returned to NYC Stop Rachel.

Rachel? What the hell was she doing in London? She must have been the help Eugene promised me. I had hoped for Eugene himself or at least a man—Disney or Nungesser—to go to London. That realization made me snort out loud. Rachel was probably as capable as any man I knew. She could certainly bully those in the London medical system better than I could. She would get along well with the staff at Endell Street, and it didn't hurt that she carried a torch for Mitchell. She'd be a fierce guardian.

Also, having Wag McDonald's boys watching Endell Street gave me some comfort, but why the hell had Patricia returned to the States? She must have finally resolved the issues with her dead husband's estate. Damn her. Why couldn't she have waited until I'd returned? If she came back with Morgan Reynolds, she'd end up under her father's thumb again. I was sure of it.

Good old Morgan must have convinced her to return to square away her citizenship status. For a bright girl, I worried that she'd done something incredibly stupid.

The second cable was from Paris.

Eugene Bullard. He was unable to go to London so he'd sent Rachel. Or she'd volunteered. I would just have to hope that Rachel and Wag McDonald's lads were enough. With Armistan and Reynolds both in New York, I might be able to take care of them as I passed through. Unfortunately, Patricia was either on her way to New York or already there. If she was in New York with Reynolds or her father, it could complicate things. I would have to play it by ear. My first step would be to meet with Thomas Reynolds in the morning.

⋅⋅⋅⋙⋘⋅⋅⋅

I HAD NEVER BEEN TO WALL STREET. I KNEW IT WAS THE FINANCIAL center of the country, but I didn't know what that would look like.

It turned out it looked a lot like a battalion in a hurry to move up to the line to stop an enemy break through. A frantic whirl of people of all classes rushing to and fro nearly running over each other in their haste to do their part. Whatever their part was, it felt like I'd stepped into a stirred-up ant nest. Each ant seemed clear about its individual role and objective, but if viewed from above, the street would look like a mad scramble. Hell, it looked like a mad scramble from the sidewalk.

I reported to the address on Wall Street indicated in General Neville's note. I knew I was at the right place because REYNOLDS BROTHERS & CO. was displayed prominently in gold letters on the wall behind the receptionist, who received me with a raised eyebrow and a respectful nod. The lobby of Reynolds Brothers was a pond of calm after the chaos of the street outside. A second receptionist offered me a cup of coffee or tea while his companion called upstairs to determine if Mr. Reynolds was ready for me. He said *Mr. Reynolds* in a hushed, reverent tone that made me wonder if I had traveled to commune with a saint.

I declined the coffee and was shortly escorted to the great man's domain on the twenty-fifth floor.

In a large anteroom, a pretty, young woman sat behind a large desk that dwarfed her. She gave me a film-star smile of welcome. Women in a professional office still seemed strange to me, but given what I'd seen in England and now in America, it looked like the future. I decided I liked it.

"Would you like a drink while you wait for Mr. Reynolds?" she asked, gamely looking at my damaged face.

What the hell. "Sure. A whiskey please."

She nodded and crossed to a bureau, which I wouldn't have guessed was a liquor cabinet before she opened it to reveal the rows of bottles inside.

I recalled a time, before Paris and Germany, when I might have tried a smile, even if frightening, on the girl, but I wasn't that man anymore. He had died somewhere in the past few months.

"More's the shame your body didn't get the message," Tippy noted.

"Ice?" the girl asked.

I nodded my head in answer to Tippy, and the girl opened a cleverly concealed drawer in the bureau to reveal an icebox. She dropped some cubes in a glass.

She handed me the drink as the telephone on her desk buzzed.

"Mr. Reynolds will see you now."

I tossed back the whiskey, enjoying the satisfying burn down my throat. "For my head cold," I told her, which earned me a fake smile.

"Of course." She took my glass and opened the imposing wood door to her boss's office.

Thomas Reynolds bore little resemblance to his son. He was tall and thin with a shock of white hair and icy blue eyes, whereas Morgan was shorter, stocky and brown-eyed. He held his chin high, which gave the impression he was looking down on me. I suspected he *was* looking down on me. We shook hands in front of his desk.

"Major Griffin, it is a pleasure to meet one of General Neville's *chosen few*."

Chosen few? That was new. As with Neville and Butler, I would be humble, at least at the start of the meeting.

"I'm afraid I am no more exceptional than the thousands of other men the general commanded, sir, but I do appreciate you seeing me on short notice."

"I am sure you are quite exceptional, Major. General Neville wouldn't have wasted my time with just anyone. I understand you want to learn a little about my work with the WIB," Reynolds said.

"Yes. I've been asked to look into potential connections between the War Industries Board and activities of foreign intelligence agencies."

"Asked by whom?"

"The White House."

"I see." He frowned. "That's very disturbing to hear. You know the board was dissolved at the beginning of the year. Please sit." He pointed to one of two chairs positioned in front of his desk.

I sat, and he returned to the large swiveling chair behind his desk he had left when he greeted me.

"What would you like to know?"

"How were members appointed to the board? How were suppliers selected? How were prices set and profits determined?"

"Well, President Wilson established the board by executive order. The members were selected by the chairman and, of course, the president. At least at the outset. The founding members, in turn, recommended other men across the various industries key to warfighting capabilities. There were hundreds of these. Ultimately, members were attracted to the WIB because the work was important, and many of us were too old to serve any other way."

"What did the board do?"

"It is a complicated business to arm a nation to fight a war, and all the other powers had a head start on us. After three years of fighting, both our allies and the central powers had transformed their economies to wartime ones. We had very little time to do the same. The board's purpose was to speed up America's transition to a wartime economy. For example, where necessary, the board created new manufacturing facilities, identified sources of supply, or converted existing civilian facilities to military uses. It conserved and directed resources. It provided advice to the several purchasing agencies of the government with regard to the prices to be paid. It also determined, wherever necessary, the priorities of production and delivery, including when shortages meant that supply was insufficient, either temporarily or permanently. Finally, the board coordinated the purchases of all materials for our allies."

"Very tall tasks."

"Indeed."

"I'm most interested in the procurement aspects of the board. Who decided prices, what to buy, and how much to buy?"

"And the president is questioning all this? He set the board up himself."

"Yes, sir. This is a follow-up by the White House now that the board is no longer active."

"Well, the procurement varied, but generally the divisions— underwear, leather, steel, for example—gave input. The price-fixing committee would dictate prices where necessary."

"And was this necessary?"

"Frequently."

"Did board or committee members direct purchasing to their firms, friends, or affiliates?"

Reynolds didn't answer right away. Instead, his eyes narrowed, and he studied me.

"Is that what the president thinks? That patriots serving on the WIB were enriching themselves?" He was angry or at least pretending to be.

"How many served on the board and the committees? Hundreds?"

"Yes, of course. They were needed."

"And you believe they were all patriots? Not a self-serving soul in the bunch?" I challenged.

He wanted to defend the WIB and the work done, but the sheer numbers of men involved meant that at least some weren't the honest patriots he pretended they were.

"Obviously, there might have been some selfish, even greedy members, but their influence would have been overborne by the vast majority of honest, decent men who served."

Wilson's phrase "a war to end all wars" sprang to mind. He had borrowed the sentiment from a series of editorials by the fantastical writer H. G. Wells. In August 1914, I remembered reading Wells's editorials claiming that the war would "end war." Wilson had cleverly modified the idea and used it as a sales slogan for America's entry into the war and ultimately his League of Nations.

"Men who believed in ending war?" I asked with what I thought was a neutral tone, but Reynolds must have heard an unintended sneer in the words.

"That's Wilson's idea. We will never end war. There is a civil war raging in Russia at this very moment. And the European powers and the United States have an interest in the outcome, but our interest should be the security of the United States, not the peace of the world, which we will never attain."

I recalled Eugene Bullard noting that the United States had grown rich on supplying the allies' needs during the war. It was no wonder that Harry Armistan wanted the whole damn thing to continue.

"And there's money to be made in supplying those who fight," I said.

"Of course there is," Reynolds said without hesitation. "The sun will rise and set, and men will find reasons to kill each other. President Wilson believes his League of Nations will transform the nature of mankind. It will not. Many in America don't support the idea. It is contrary to American sovereignty, contrary to the Monroe Doctrine, and contrary to man's nature. But he's the president, and he's giving it a try. That is his prerogative. I know these views may get me in hot water with the White House. Well, so be it! We fought this war for America's interests. Not for the world's."

"Did you or your family serve in uniform?" I couldn't resist asking. After all, I knew Reynolds and his son hadn't fought any war at all.

"What? No. I'm an old man and my brother's older. We'd be no use in the trenches. And my son was exempted because his work in war finance was deemed to be essential for the maintenance of the military establishment."

"War finance. Harry Armistan worked in finance, didn't he?"

That question stopped him. A sudden chill descended over the room.

"Harry? What has he got to do with this?"

"You know him?"

"Of course I know him. My son works for him and Sebastien Lynch."

Sebastien Lynch?

"Did Mr. Armistan or Mr. Lynch serve on the WIB?"

"Harry didn't, but I am sure he was consulted. He's a respected financier, so it would have been natural."

"And Mr. Lynch?" I asked.

"Seb sometimes partners with Harry on deals. I believe he was an assistant to the board of directors of the WIB. To Mr. Baruch, in fact. Why the interest in Harry?"

"Did you consult Mr. Armistan?" I was pushing now. I wanted to drive a wedge between Armistan and any who might support him.

"I don't see what Harry Armistan has to do with any White House assessment of the War Industries Board."

"I'll come to that in a moment, sir, but I do need to know if you consulted with Mr. Armistan as part of your work for the board."

"No, but I would have if I'd seen the need."

"Do you know who might have consulted him?"

"Any one of ten or twenty men might have. He has connections, close connections, with the banking houses here."

"What type of connections?"

"He's very persuasive and has a talent for arranging capital from diverse sources. Some of which I am sure he negotiated with the larger banks here before the war."

"And these banks and their directors, where did their sympathies lie at the start of the war?"

"These men are American!" He was insulted by my implication that the banks or their leaders might have been disloyal to the United States.

"But America wasn't involved at the start of the war," I said in my most reasonable tone.

"Well, most are of German descent. And of the Hebrew faith. I suspect many were sympathetic to Germany, but that would have been as much because they loathed the Czarist government's treatment of Russian Jews as because of their German heritage."

"Jews?"

"Yes. As I said, many of America's most successful bankers are Jewish."

I didn't know that big banking in America was run by Jews, and I didn't know the Czarist government had mistreated the Jews in Russia. Unfortunately, we were straying beyond the topics I cared about. I was meeting with Reynolds to learn about Armistan and to turn Reynolds against him.

"There is concern that Mr. Armistan was an illegal war profiteer."

"What? That's absurd."

"Perhaps, but it has been confirmed that he had close ties to Bolsheviks in England and France." Gavin was his son-in-law, so this wasn't exactly a lie, and I knew that Armistan had conspired with Gavin to prevent the signing of the Treaty of Versailles. "It is also very likely he has connections with the Germans." I conjured up the German connection because of what Reynolds had just told me about the Jewish finance houses having German family links.

"That is preposterous!"

"Do you have ongoing business dealings with Mr. Armistan? Other than your son working for him, of course," I asked in what I hoped was a knowing, prosecutorial manner.

"What if I have? He is a legitimate businessman."

"Perhaps."

"I won't take part in a White House witch hunt, Major!"

I'd riled him up some. "I am just following the information where it leads me, Mr. Reynolds. Obviously, I'll speak with Mr. Armistan about this to clear up any misunderstanding. I won't take any more of your time." I stood quickly, which surprised Reynolds. He had expected the chance to persuade me Armistan wasn't a traitor or a thief. "You've been very helpful."

Armistan would know I was coming, but he would think I had the backing of the White House. I was gambling that the president would remain ill. If he did, no one would be able to get through Mrs. Wilson to check on my credentials with the president. It might keep Armistan from killing me outright. In which case, I could kill him.

It was very possible that Thomas Reynolds might contact his son and discover that I was not as well connected as I pretended. It didn't matter. I had kicked the ant hill where Armistan lived, and I'd hope to stir up enough turmoil that it gave me a chance to reach him. Or him to reach out to me.

I RETURNED TO THE HOTEL PENNSYLVANIA.

I had played all my cards. I'd seen Neville, House, and now Reynolds. I'd dropped hints, asked questions, and done what I could to poison the well against Harry Armistan. All I had left to do was wait.

However, waiting in New York was not an option. I found a note from Billy Jones when I returned to the hotel. He invited me to dinner that night and advised me that we were sailing for Liverpool the next afternoon. Unless the chaos I'd hoped to create happened immediately, it would occur without me around to watch.

Dinner with Billy was at Engel's Chop House on West Thirty-Sixth Street. He was already seated when I arrived. He finished his drink when he saw me and gave me a smile I didn't deserve. He also waved the waiter over and ordered two whiskies without consulting me.

"Billy, I didn't get to talk to you after Pauline... I'm sorry. I should have found a way to keep her safe," I said as we sat down.

"Jack, please. I overreacted. I was angry with you and horrified. I'd thought I'd left the blood and death behind when I'd left the trenches. The world has become a hard place. You were faced with a hard choice. She had sacrificed your good opinion when she drugged you. And you didn't shoot her. The Germans did that!"

"And their leader got away. I'm sure he'll be hunting for me," I lied automatically. I was pleased that Billy no longer blamed me for Pauline, and I wanted to keep his sympathy.

"Why does he want you so badly, Jack?"

I wasn't sure how much to tell him. I certainly couldn't tell him I tried to kill Woodrow Wilson. I didn't even know that I truly had. I just knew that I'd given the president a good shove in the back. Sure, he'd cracked his head on the White House plumbing, but that wasn't necessarily attempted murder. I had a sickness in my head that momentarily took control because of the drugs Pauline had given me.

"I foiled a German assassination attempt in the Rhineland," I said. "Afterward, they captured me. They tortured me, using the drugs like the one Pauline had and electric shocks. I guess they hoped to drive me insane. Honestly, sometimes I feel like they succeeded. Some associates freed me. Now it looks like Fuchs wants to complete what he started."

"That's bloody horrible. No wonder you were hard on Pauline."

"She didn't know, Billy. I shouldn't have forced her to go to Arlington."

"My recollection is she insisted on going, and I didn't help things."

I nodded. I was glad Billy had forgiven me, but I hadn't forgiven myself. It was all lies, and I was lying to myself. Sure, I was a crackpot. And maybe it wasn't my fault, but that didn't mean I hadn't accomplished exactly what the Germans wanted. I might have foiled the German's assassination of General Mangin, but I had prevented Mangin from supporting a Rhinish succession from Germany. That had been the ultimate aim for Schragmüller and Fuchs. I also knew the Germans had come incredibly close to assassinating Woodrow Wilson and entirely derailing the treaty ratification by using me as a weapon. I was probably the most successful American agent the Krauts had ever had, but Jones didn't know the truth, and he couldn't hear the details I omitted that would have revealed it to him.

"You're a lying sack of shit, Griffin," Frederickson informed me.

Perhaps I was, but I sat back in my chair confident that Billy was fooled just like everyone else I knew. We sipped our drinks, and having lanced the tension between us that Pauline's death had caused, we fell into easy discussions of the treaty, the Reds, the empire, and Billy's prospects in government. We did not discuss Pauline or Evelyn. I would not be a guest at the Jones's home when we returned to England.

Billy finished another drink before dinner and ordered a bottle of wine to accompany our chops. I had no desire to spend the next morning hungover, and I limited myself to one glass.

As we finished dessert and ordered coffees, I realized that a man at the bar had been watching our table throughout the meal. At times, he would watch us in the long mirror behind the bar. At others, he would turn on his seat and pretend to scan the room, but I wasn't fooled. He was watching us. He was a dark fellow with slicked-back hair. An immigrant? I didn't think he was one of Fuchs's squareheads. He was well dressed. Perhaps he was one of Reynolds's men. Or his father's. If Reynolds senior had warned Armistan I was in town, he might even be one of Armistan's goons.

"Billy, there's a gentleman at the bar, who is watching us. The Italian-looking fellow."

Billy turned in his chair to study the bar. The man's back remained to us, but I could see his eyes in the mirror.

"You think so? I'll go ask him." Jones was full of drink, and he thought it was a good idea to confront a potential killer. He stood.

"No." I reached across the table to grab his arm, but I was too late. He moved unsteadily through the tables directly to the man. He struck up a conversation. Jones took out his cigarette case and offered it. The man took a cigarette, and they smoked and chatted amicably while I watched.

Billy came back to the table with a smile.

"Sorry, Jack. He's just a poor sap like we used to be. He's waiting for a young lady, who has not appeared. He's not watching us. He's looking for her."

I nodded. "Okay. It's just that he's sure has spent a lot of time looking at our side of the room."

"Trust me. He's no German spy," Billy assured me.

We left shortly after, and the Italian-looking fellow didn't follow.

Jones was staying at the Waldorf Astoria, and the restaurant wasn't far from either of our hotels. I offered to walk Jones to the Waldorf. He was soused, and I didn't want to leave him alone.

Almost immediately after leaving the restaurant, I picked out shadows in the doorways across the street. They were watching us. I told Billy, but he just laughed it off.

"Honestly, Jack. You're seeing things. It's a big city, and people walk from place to place."

"Yes, Jack. It's a big city," Tippy agreed. "You're seeing ghosts."

I nodded, smiled, and pretended they both were right. We turned onto Fifth Avenue, and at least two men turned with us.

I left Billy at the Waldorf and turned west on Thirty-Third toward the Pennsylvania. The two shadows made the turn with me. I picked up my pace. I had my pistol, but I didn't want to face two men on the dark streets. I couldn't just blaze away without knowing their intentions.

I arrived at the Pennsylvania out of breath but unscathed. I waited in the lobby to see if I was followed in. I wasn't. At least not that I could tell.

I was glad to be leaving the city the next afternoon. I was sure the men in the street had been following me. If they were Armistan's men, they would be a danger to Patricia. I worried about her. I wondered if she had arrived from London, but I didn't have the time to hunt for her. I needed to get back to Mitchell.

I didn't sleep well that night.

27

Up in the Air

Despite a dockworkers' strike, our vessel left New York as planned. On the return voyage, no one attacked me, and with the dinner at Engel's as the foundation, Billy and I reconnected in a way I feared we had lost. It wasn't quite the same as before the war or before Arlington, but we enjoyed each other's company.

"Bridge tonight?" Billy asked me after dinner on our first night underway.

"No more bridge for me, Billy. Let's just sit in the lounge and mind our own business."

"Of course."

After we were seated with drinks in our hands, Billy asked, "How soon do you need to go back to America to finish your investigation for the president, Jack?"

"My investigation?"

"I heard you questioning Sir William Wiseman about two men: Armistan and Reynolds. It seems the president has some interest in these men."

"I really can't go into the details, Billy."

"War profiteering?"

I nodded.

"Once you finish that investigation, will you continue to work for House and the president?"

"I don't know. Honestly, I haven't thought that far ahead. I'm just struggling to get through today."

"I could talk to Sir Basil. He might be interested in having you work in the CID."

I laughed. "He thinks I'm a murderer. He won't want me working for him. He probably won't even want me in Britain."

"You might be surprised. When I tell him of your exploits in Washington and your connections, I think he'll be interested."

"Billy, do you really want me in England?"

"What do you mean, Jack?"

"Don't you think it would be awkward for your family? You and Evelyn and the child?" I asked reluctantly.

"Jack, there is not much certain in this world, but I am certain that I love Evelyn with all my heart. I want what is best for her. I would never let our relationship with you become awkward. I give you my word it won't be a problem. I can promise you that," he said with deadly seriousness.

"Okay, that's good to hear. I really do value you both. Seeing you and Evelyn again has allowed me to recover a part of my life that I'd lost," I told him sincerely. "I just don't want it to be uncomfortable for anyone."

"It won't be, Jack. I guarantee it."

The obvious love Billy had for Evelyn got me thinking about my relationships. Sarah, Marie, and Madeline. Sarah was dead, and other than her shade, which periodically haunted me, I really saw no future for us. I felt an undeniable attraction to Marie, but she was exactly the type of woman I needed to avoid. Mysterious, dangerous, broken. Madeline, on the other hand, was none of those things, and I discovered that I very much wanted to see her again. I didn't mention her to Billy. I didn't want to jinx the possibility of a future with her. I also remained aware of my fractured mental state. Tippy Frederickson was a constant reminder, but in hearing Billy's plans, I couldn't help but think about mine.

The remainder of the trip to England was speedy and much more restful than my previous voyage. When not with Billy, I would sit with Tippy in the lounge and read old newspapers without worry that anyone would discover my mental imbalance. I remained careful. I had not forgotten the attack on the *Adriatic*. Our vessel, the RMS *Baltic*, was her sister ship, and I knew the places to avoid to minimize the likelihood I'd be ambushed. I still exercised, but there was no Turkish bath to tempt me.

The evening before docking in Liverpool, Billy and I sat under the stained glass wall in the smoking lounge with whiskies and a cigar for Billy and discussed our plans after arriving in England.

"What will you do once you've reported to Mr. Churchill? I'm going straight home like a shot."

"I don't blame you, Billy. As soon as we arrive in London, I'm going to drop my bag at a friend's house on Aldford Street and go directly to the Endell Street Military Hospital. Churchill will have to wait."

"Endell Street! Why would you choose to go there?"

"The day before I left for the United States, my very good friend William Mitchell was struck by a motorcab. He was taken to Endell Street Hospital."

"That's terrible!" he said with shock. "I had no idea."

"He's been there the entire time I've been in the States."

"I'm so sorry, Jack. Well, it's a bloody good hospital," he said with certainty. "Run by two very particular ladies, I understand, but the care is excellent."

"That's what I was told. He's recovering, but I've been worried the entire time I've been gone."

"That's only natural."

"It's not just that he was injured, Billy. He was attacked. Pushed in front of the taxi. I saw it, and I saw the man who did it.

It was intentional, not some accidental bump on the street. I'll kill the son of a bitch if I ever see him again."

"Who would do such a thing?" Billy leaned forward with interest.

"It's a long story, but I'm sure I know who is responsible. A man named Morgan Reynolds. He works for William's girl, Patricia Kingsbury. She's a very rich widow. He wants Patricia for himself, and he hates both Mitchell and me. I've been worried that while I've been away, Reynolds might try again to kill Mitchell while he's laid up. It's been driving me crazy."

Tippy laughed.

"Well, now I certainly understand why you need to go to Endell Street." Billy patted me on the arm. "I'm sure your friend is safe, and I hope he recovers quickly," he said with more optimism than I felt.

"Me too, Billy, me too."

<hr>

Upon reaching Liverpool, Billy and I trained to London, which took nearly the entire day. It was dark when we arrived. I promised him I would see Churchill as soon as possible, but I reminded him that I intended to see Mitchell that night. We separated in the great arrivals hall in Euston Station with Billy going home to Evelyn and I to Patricia's house on Aldford Street.

Hackworth opened the door at my knock and showed no surprise at my presence.

"Welcome back, sir. Your room remains ready for you."

"Thank you, Hackworth. I understand Mrs. Kingsbury has returned to the United States. The house must seem empty."

"She has, sir, but we've had the pleasure of another guest. Before she left for America, Mrs. Kingsbury invited Miss Eisen to stay here instead of a hotel. They ran into each other at the hospital the day Miss Eisen arrived from Paris."

"Rachel's staying here? That's excellent."

"She should be returning from the hospital shortly. A very devoted woman. No sister could be more diligent than she in watching over Mr. Mitchell since Mrs. Kingsbury left."

"Yes, Rachel is very committed to William, that's for sure," I said evenly. Hackworth had apparently failed to notice Rachel's attraction to Mitchell, and I wasn't going to point it out.

"I'll take your bag, sir."

I let my suitcase go because it wasn't worth the fight to convince him I could carry it.

"Did Mr. Reynolds also return to the United States with Mrs. Kingsbury?" I asked. I thought I knew the answer, but I had to know for certain.

Hackworth hesitated. He was reluctant to share the private details of his mistress's travel.

"I'm sure he did," I added. "Mrs. Kingsbury cabled me in New York to let me know she needed to clear up her citizenship question. Since Mr. Reynolds was helping her with that, it would be logical for him to accompany her."

"Yes, sir, he did. He continues to assist her with the problem. They departed for New York City a few days ago."

"How was she feeling? When I last saw her, she seemed under the weather." I was fishing. Patricia had seemed tired and distressed but not ill. I wanted to see if Hackworth had noticed or if it was my imagination.

Again he hesitated. "She's been very busy, and it is entirely possible that she's been a bit fatigued. I am certain the injury to Mr. Mitchell has been a challenge. I know that his steady recovery has meant a great deal to her."

He had noticed, and his brief comments were as telling as if he'd let me read her mail. There was something not quite right with Patricia. Hackworth had seen it too.

"She say when she'll be back?"

"A soon as possible, I am sure. She will not want to leave Mr. Mitchell too long in Miss Eisen's care."

"I've no doubt you are right about that." Perhaps Hackworth wasn't blind to Rachel's infatuation with Mitchell.

Rachel returned to the house less than an hour later.

"Griffin! I'm so glad you're back! I don't know what you did before you left, but you're the only person I know who can stir things up and not even be around. There are all sorts of hoods hanging around outside the hospital. Dr. Murray asked me if I knew why all the tough-looking men were around. Even Dr. Anderson noticed, and she's usually so busy with patients she wouldn't notice Frankenstein's monster standing in the lobby."

"I arranged for the hospital to be guarded before I left. If there are men there besides mine, they'd be Morgan Reynolds's goons."

"They may all be yours. I never saw Reynolds, and Will's *sweetheart* left for the States not long after I got here." Rachel had known Patricia since before I'd met her, and she hadn't liked her even before her connection to William Mitchell.

"Yeah, she went to the States with Reynolds. They both are in New York by now. Hell, they might have been there when I was. They could be gone a while."

"I'm sorry to hear that," she said with a complete lack of sincerity.

"Rachel, is there any way to get in to see Will tonight?"

"I don't know," she said doubtfully. "At night, they close that place down tighter than a snail's shell. Everything's locked up. There's staff at the reception desk and, depending on the needs of the patients, some night nurses on the wards. It doesn't help that all those hard-faced thugs are standing on the sidewalks."

"I think Reynolds is responsible for Will getting shoved into traffic. I think he's going to try to kill him again. And me too."

"What? Reynolds? Nobody told me that!"

"Yeah. Patricia doesn't believe that Reynolds is responsible, so she wouldn't have told Will. When I wrote Gene, I was in a hurry and didn't mention it. But I saw the attack. I saw the guy who did it. It wasn't Reynolds, but I'm sure it was done on Reynolds's orders. Just a quick little push into traffic? It smells just like

Morgan Reynolds. I need to talk with Will. Warn him. Is his head clear?"

"God yes!" she said passionately. "He's bored out of his mind. His leg's stretched out above him and his arm is in a cast, but he's been awake for a while. And despite the surgery on his head, he still seems to be himself."

"I'm glad to hear it. Since women run the hospital, I'm sure he's got the staff wrapped around his finger."

"You have no idea! They love having him there. Now that the meatgrinder in Franch is over, fewer patients are coming in, and I think the hospital will close shortly. It doesn't hurt that he's handsome, charming, and funny."

"Handsome, charming, and funny, huh? How do you really feel about him?" I asked.

"Oh to hell with you, Griffin. You know I like him, for all the good it will do me with that damn fairy princess around."

I laughed at her honesty.

"What about getting into his room tonight? Any thoughts?" I asked again.

"You might be able to hop the wall, but the watchers outside will see you go in."

"They're probably the men I sent, but even if they belong to Reynolds and they sneak in behind me, that's okay. I'll be with Will, and we both will be armed."

"But John, remember, he can't move. His leg is still up in the air."

"I know, but the longer we wait, the more likely it is Reynolds will send men in to kill him. Especially once they find out that I'm back in London. I need to get him his pistol now."

"You're serious?"

"Damn right I am."

"Well then, let's go!" she said.

"No, Rachel. You stay here. I can't have you tagging along like a little sister."

"Griffin, I've been a tomboy all my life, and I promise you, anything you can do, I can do with a smile."

The urgency to get to Mitchell overwhelmed any further urge to argue. I'd hate myself if she got hurt, but I already hated myself. The scheming part of my brain agreed that three pistols were better than two.

"Can you shoot?"

"Sure. I'm not a great shot, but in France, when I was stationed near the front, they made all the nurses' aides learn in case the Boche broke through the line and tried to rape us."

"Christ, that's a good reason to take practice seriously."

We went to my room, and I took the Webley and a box of shells from my suitcase. I handed both to Rachel. The black leather sap I'd stolen from the killer in the Irish bar in New York sat nestled in my socks. I put it in my pants pocket.

"Rachel, can you see if Cook can whip up something for us to eat? I want us to go as soon as we can, and I don't want to go hungry. I'll meet you in the dining room."

I went to Patricia and Mitchell's room. Mitchell's suitcase was perched on a stand near the window. At the bottom, I found his Colt and the Luger with its shoulder holster that Marie had given him. He had ammunition boxes for both guns. I put the ammunition in my coat pockets. The bullets and the sap were heavy and pulled the suit coat mercilessly. I checked to make sure the chambers of both pistols were empty and carried them down to the dining room.

Rachel was already there talking with Hackworth.

"...exactly. Like a trench raid. We're going to sneak into Endell Street to give Will a gun," I heard her say.

"I'm afraid there is a complication," Hackworth told her.

I stepped into the dining room.

"What's that?" I asked as I laid the pistols out on the table.

"There are men on the street outside. Several. Hidden in the shadows, but they're there. If they see you try to leave, I'm not sure what might happen," he said.

"We could call the police?" Rachel suggested.

"Waiting for the coppers to come would mean a delay," I said. "And probably a long one. Plus the men outside haven't done anything yet. Keeping us here may be exactly why Reynolds has those guys outside. He knows Mitchell is alone now." An overwhelming sense of urgency was building in my chest. I knew we couldn't wait.

"I'll call the driver and have the car brought around," Hackworth said.

"Now that could work," I told him. He went out to the hallway to make the call.

"What pistol did you train with, Rachel?"

"That one." She pointed at Mitchell's Colt .45 automatic.

"Okay. That one's yours for the night."

I was reminding her how to unload and reload the automatic when Hackworth returned.

"The telephone is not working. I believe they've cut the line. I've asked Cook to watch the front in case they decide on a raid."

It hadn't occurred to me that they might actually attack the house. I was glad Hackworth had thought of it.

"With Cook watching the street, I'm afraid we will have to eat in the kitchen before we go."

"We, Hackworth?"

"I'm going with you. I couldn't face Mrs. Kingsbury if her guests were killed on my watch, sir."

I pushed the Webley and the box of cartridges across the table to him. I had no doubt he knew how to use the British pistol.

"I'm not going to argue, Sergeant." This time he didn't correct me for using his old title.

"I'll pack the pistols in a holdall," Hackworth said. "One can't run through London waving pistols about."

I wasn't sure that was true, but having a bag to carry everything was a good idea.

He went off to find a case for the pistols and ammunition, and Rachel and I went to the kitchen. When we got there, we found a steaming pan filled with shepherd's pie. I ladled it into bowls, and Rachel placed a glass pitcher of beer on the table. Cook must have had the dinner waiting for Rachel's return from the hospital. Hackworth carried in a canvas bag with a leather bottom and placed it on the table. He put the pistols inside. I handed him my boxes of ammunition and the sap, and he put those in as well. I didn't tell him about the Colt in my shoulder holster.

As we ate, we debated the various ways to escape from Patricia's house. Ultimately, because Patricia's automobile was stored too far away, we agreed we had to find a way to get a different motorcar to the front door of her house. If we made it into an automobile quickly enough, Reynolds's men wouldn't be able to stop us from leaving. If Reynolds had men at the hospital, we could also outrace the news of our escape reaching them. After some discussion and using Hackworth's knowledge of the house and the neighborhood, we agreed that I would climb out of the attic onto the roof and cross from house to house and return with a motorcar. We didn't get into the details of whether I would steal one or hire a taxicab. We also didn't discuss how I would get down from the roof. I didn't want to think about it. Tippy, on the other hand, couldn't stop nattering about how I'd fall and break my back.

28

———

Gate Crashing

"Good luck, sir," Hackworth said as he pulled the attic door shut, cutting off the light from the hallway. I crossed the attic to the small window looking out on the street, opened it, and climbed out. It was a tight squeeze. I twisted to sit on the windowsill far above the pavement below. The men waiting for us stirred in the shadows. We really were trapped.

My heart was in my throat. I wasn't particularly fond of heights.

"And it's a bloody long fall," Tippy reminded me.

I grabbed the cast-iron drain attached to the wall next to the window and pulled myself out of the house. Standing balanced on the windowsill, I could just reach the brick lip of the roof above the window. With both hands hooked on the brick ledge, I pulled myself up to the rooftop, ruining the toes of my leather shoes as I scrambled for purchase on the brick facing of the house.

I got my belly over the ledge and rolled onto the roof, which was still damp from the rain earlier that evening. I cursed softly, got carefully to my feet, and shuffled across the old shingles

339

moving south. As Hackworth had said, the roofs of the adjoining houses were all connected, and I worked steadily away from Patricia's home and the killers on Aldford Street.

After the third house, I came to an enclosed garden. I climbed from the roof to a window ledge and shimmied down a drain pipe to the garden wall. From there, I dropped to the street.

I hired a Model T town car outside of Claridge's.

"I need you to go to Number 2 Aldford Street and pull up as close to the stairs entering the house as possible. Stay in the car. Two people will join us. Then you need to get us out of there. Fast." From the back seat, I held a five-pound note under the driver's nose.

"Must be dangerous," he said.

"Yup," I said, holding up another fiver. "Don't drive up to the corner house on Aldford Street. Come up from behind it."

"On Rex Place?" he asked.

I didn't know the street names, but he seemed to understand. "Yes."

He did exactly as I'd asked, and we arrived at Patricia's only forty minutes after I'd climbed out the window. As he pulled to a stop in front of the house, Rachel and Hackworth bolted out the front door and down the steps to the taxicab. Across the street, several men bolted out from behind the black wrought iron gates guarding the basement levels of the houses across from No. 2. I kicked the backseat passenger door open, and Rachel and Hackworth dove into the cab with the canvas bag.

I considered pulling the Colt, but we were racing east down Aldford before the thought was complete.

"Five quid more if you get us near Endell Street Military Hospital in fifteen minutes!" I said to the driver as soon as the door shut behind Hackworth. I waved the bill over the cabbie's shoulder. In no time, we swerved off Aldford Street. Despite his speed, he still managed to check his wristwatch to confirm the time. To his credit, the cabbie drove like a madman, but my panic flared with each delay. The streets were still wet from the rain, and indifferent to the questionable traction, the driver raced through roundabouts and turns tossing us together in the back seat. At times, it seemed like we were driving away from Covent Garden and the hospital.

"Are you sure we're going the right way?" I shouted to the driver.

"Oh, don't you worry," he answered without looking over his shoulder. "I've taken the Knowledge, I have. I know every street from here to the city and beyond." He had a mad grin on his face, and I shut up and held on tight to the back of his seat.

I'd been right. The men outside Patricia's house were Reynolds's foot soldiers. They had to be. They weren't Krauts. I'd gotten pretty good at identifying the type of men who worked for Fuchs. Clean-cut, square-jawed Teutons, who, but for their civilian suits, looked like they should still be wearing feldgrau stormtrooper uniforms. The men watching the Aldford house were English. Pint-swilling, fag-smoking, hard-living Englishmen. They were unshaven, rough men likely recently mustered out of the service looking for a job. Not so different from Wag McDonald's boys. The Brits who'd walked into Hanley's pub in New York looked very much the same. Hell, they might have even been the same men.

The motorcar rocked to a stop.

"We're at the intersection of Endell Street, Long Acre, and Bow Street. The hospital's just three blocks up that way," the driver said, pointing north.

I turned to Hackworth and Rachel. "Get out here. Wait five minutes and then walk arm in arm up the street to the hospital. Go to the gate. By the time you reach it, I should be inside and able to let you in. If the gate isn't open, keep walking. Go back to Patricia's and wait for me there. I'll take the guns with me."

"Griffin," Rachel started to argue.

"No, Rachel. Do as I ask. I'll let you in if I can. Go! Don't argue!"

She nodded, and they both climbed from the taxi.

Hackworth thumped his hand on the roof of the car, signaling the driver that he could depart. As we sped up the street, I looked back and saw their pale faces huddled together as they grudgingly waited the required five minutes.

I passed the driver the fifteen pounds I'd promised him. "You earned it."

He smiled and tipped his cap.

At this time of night, I knew the gate to the hospital would be closed and the policeman on duty gone. If I pounded on the gate, even if the staff heard me, they would turn me away. Any of Reynolds's men watching would know I was there, and that could be disastrous. I needed to find another way to Mitchell's room.

Hackworth's hand smacking the hardtop of the cab gave me an idea.

"I've got one more request," I said to the driver.

He waited, holding the money and hoping for more.

"I need to get into the hospital. I've got a friend in there who's in some danger and needs watching day and night. If I pound on the doors, I know the old birds who run the place won't let me in. Would you mind pulling on to the sidewalk and letting me climb on top of your automobile? I'll be careful. I just need to get high enough to pull myself into a window. There's another ten pounds for you, if you're willing."

"All right, mate. Just point me to where you want me."

And I did. He motored down Endell Street right to the gate. I stayed low in the back seat, but I could see the gate with its white lettering reflecting the headlamp light from the taxicab.

"That window just beyond the gate," I said. He pulled off the street onto the sidewalk and got me right up next to one of the windows. I dropped a ten-pound note over the front seat and jumped out of the back of the automobile. Quickly I shoved the canvas bag on the cartop and climbed up next to it. With one leg on the window ledge and one on the car, I used Pauline's automatic knife to slip the lock on the window frame, then pulled up the sash. Without hesitating, I pushed the bag of guns through and dropped in after it.

I'd made it into the hospital!

The driver must have felt my weight leave the car because he drove off as soon as I was halfway through the window.

A desk, cabinets, and papers on every surface convinced me I was in an administrator's office. I hurried out the door and down a hallway toward what I hoped was the entrance to the hospital yard. I was in luck and found the lobby where Patricia and I had waited when Mitchell had first come to the hospital. No one was behind the reception desk. I unlocked the front door, went outside, and crossed the yard to the heavy iron gate. Fortunately, it included a pedestrian door that I could open quickly. I unlocked the bolt and opened the door as quietly as I could. I peeked outside.

Hackworth and Rachel, arm in arm, were twenty feet away walking slowly toward me. When they saw my face, they picked up the pace. I threw the door wide and pushed them into the yard.

Once we were all through, I slammed the door shut and shot the bolt.

"Is he in the same room?" I called to Rachel, but she was already running up the steps into the hospital. Hackworth and I followed.

A staff member called to us as we raced through the lobby. Rachel didn't stop, and Hackworth and I followed her down the hallway from which I'd just come. She led us up two flights of stairs and down another hallway to the door at its end. Rachel went through the door without waiting.

I followed her.

Mitchell was lying on the sole bed in the room. His left leg was suspended above him. He was smoking a cigarette, and our rushed entry earned us a surprised look.

"Can't sleep, huh?" I asked.

"Been waiting for you."

"I doubt that."

Hackworth looked out the lone window in the room. "Looks like there's a bit of activity in the street," he said.

I opened the holdall and took out Mitchell's Luger. I put it on the nightstand next to his bed along with Pauline's automatic knife. I had to move the ashtray to make room. When he needed to hide the pistol, I hoped he could just slip it into the nightstand drawer. I was also sure he was clever enough to keep the knife close.

I gave Rachel the .45 and Hackworth the Webley.

Rachel sat down on the end of Mitchell's bed and ratcheted a round into the chamber.

Mitchell's eyes flickered to her, the gun, and then back to me.

"We expecting visitors?" he asked.

"Reynolds has men outside the hospital. So do I, but mine aren't going to stick around if Reynolds's men have guns, and I'm sure they do."

"Why would Morgan have men outside, and where'd you get men?"

"Remember the gangster I met in Brixton? His boys," I said, answering his second question first. "And Reynolds is the reason you're here. One of his men pushed you in front of the taxicab."

Mitchell raised his eyebrows at the information. "Well, how 'bout that? I don't remember a damn thing about it. Reynolds you say? I suppose we'll just have to kill the son of a bitch."

"We'll have to go to New York to do it."

"I'm aware of that," he said. "I just think it's important to say your goals out loud. It helps make them feel real and makes achieving them more likely."

"Your mother tell you that?"

"She did."

"We have to survive the night first," I said.

He laughed. "I'm not worried about that, Griff. This ain't no Alamo. It may seem like we're trapped in here with no way out, but I'm sure you've got a plan."

It buoyed my spirits to see Mitchell alive and sharp-tongued. I didn't really have a plan, but I'd come up with one now that I knew Mitchell was armed and had Rachel and Hackworth with him.

"You three wait here. Once I'm out, lock the door and shoot anyone you don't know who tries to come in. I'm going to go out to improve the odds."

"See? A plan," Mitchell said to the others.

Rachel and Hackworth reluctantly followed my instructions.

With the three of them safe in the room, I was free to act without any encumbrance.

"Excuse me, you shouldn't be here!" a young woman dressed in the blue Endell Street uniform called from down the hallway.

I walked toward her.

"Of course, you are correct," I answered. "But I'm worried some men outside want to hurt my friend in there." I pointed back at Mitchell's room with my thumb. "I can't let that happen."

"I'll have to call the police if you don't leave," she told me.

"I wish you would."

The sound of an engine motor revving came from outside.

She glanced out a window to the front yard.

"You're about to have some guests. I think they are here to harm Mr. Mitchell. I'm going to meet them in the lobby. It's probably a good idea if you stay here."

"Why would they want to hurt William?"

Ah, another victim of Mitchell's charm.

"What's your name, miss?"

"Ada, Ada Phillips."

"Miss Phillips. Ada. I'm John. I'm a friend of William's. We work for the American government. Against Bolshevism."

From behind me, Tippy snorted in disgust. "My God, man! Is there no one you won't lie to?"

"The men outside are Reds. They're here for him, and I need to protect him," I said.

"But Daisy's gone downstairs to the front desk!" she said in horror.

"Daisy?"

"Daisy Shaw. She's on nights with me. We were checking the boiler, but then we heard you come in. I followed you, and Daisy went to man the front desk."

"Well, hell!" I said.

I took the pistol from my shoulder holster, pulled back the slide to put a round in the chamber, and started down the hall to the stairs.

"Stay up here, Ada! Go to William's room. Make sure you tell them who you are. I don't want you to get shot by accident. You'll be safe there," I called over my shoulder. "I'll get Daisy."

The racing car motor got louder as I descended to the ground floor. The sound of crashing came up from the lobby. Shit! They'd driven an automobile through the front gate!

As I ran into the lobby, I saw a petite young lady in the blue Endell Street uniform, who had to be Daisy, standing in the partially open front door. She was yelling at the men outside.

"Oi! What's the meaning of this! Ya can't just crash through our gate, you gormless bastards!"

"We're looking for a Yank." The call came from outside.

"There're no bloody Yanks here. Only patients. You'd better scarper before Ole Bill gets here. We've a telephone box, and we've called him." Daisy wasn't afraid of the killers on her doorstep. She also wasn't afraid to tell a lie. I was sure neither Ada nor she had called the police.

"We saw the Yank climb in one of your windows. He's in there. He's got an ugly scar on his face."

"I tell you, there're only patients in here, you bloody knob!"

"One way or the other we're coming in, miss. The man's a coward. A deserter. He's also a traitor."

I agreed with the first two accusations, but the last was a surprise to me.

"Tippy?" I asked Frederickson.

"News to me, Jackie. Wouldn't surprise me, mind you. I suppose assassinating your president is traitorous."

"Only you and I know that," I said.

"Hey! Who are you?" she asked as she slammed and bolted the door.

My discussion with Tippy in the hallway had caught Daisy's attention. Her back was pressed against the door as if she could hold it closed all by herself. She had a dash of freckles across her nose, and her fair skin was flushed from her argument with the men outside. Unruly mahogany hair was doing its best to escape from her uniform cap. She was a cute little thing and didn't seem to have an ounce of fear in her.

"I'm afraid I'm the Yank they're looking for," I told her.

"Well, shite!" she said with passion. "I just told the bastards outside you're not here, didn't I?"

"It was an easy mistake to make. You didn't know I was here. I snuck in."

"Well, you can sneak right back out!"

"If I go out that door, I'm pretty sure those men will kill me."

"Should have thought of that before you chose my hospital for your refuge. Maybe you should have chosen a church."

"My friend, Will Mitchell, is a patient here, and those men want to kill him too."

"William. A friend of yours? Are you certain? He is a Yank, but he's not your type of Yank."

"And what type is that?"

"The angry, arrogant kind."

The men in the yard continued shouting dire warnings about what would happen if Daisy didn't let them in the hospital.

"You shouldn't judge a book by its cover. Although your judgment is at least half right. Ada is upstairs waiting in William's room. Maybe you should do that, too, while I talk to your visitors." I waved the pistol in the general direction of the door.

"Not if you're going to shoot them!"

Someone tried the doorknob and shook the handle when it didn't open.

"You'd better let us in, lassie," a voice called from outside.

"I don't want to shoot them, but I won't let them hurt Mitchell," I told her.

They were banging on the door now. I walked closer to the girl.

Daisy's arms were crossed. I didn't think she was going to leave the lobby.

The car motor in the yard restarted, and the engine raced as someone fed it too much gasoline.

"You don't want to be here when they come in," I assured her.

Indistinct shouts and the roar of the car engine warned me of what was to come. I grabbed Daisy and pulled her into the shelter of the hallway as the motorcar slammed partially through the front door of the hospital.

"My God," Daisy said with something approaching awe.

I pushed the girl behind me as a man squeezed between the car bumper and the broken doorframe. I recognized him. Balding. Stocky. It was the man who had attacked me in the New York subway station and again in the Irish bar. The bruises delivered in Hanley's were well on their way to disappearing. His manner and confidence reminded me of Sergeant Cooper of my old British regiment. He had to have been some kind of noncommissioned officer in the war.

"Hello again, Sergeant," I called, taking a chance with the rank. "Still working for Reynolds, I see."

His head snapped toward me. He saw the pistol and the nurse.

"Don't know any Reynolds," he said. "We work for the Crown. We're here for you. I'm disappointed, miss," he added calmly, looking at Miss Ward. "I thought you said he wasn't here."

The Crown? What the hell was going on? Why would the Crown be hunting me?

"Because they know all about you, Jack. They always have.

They've been leading you down a primrose path to your own destruction," Tippy Frederickson answered.

"I didn't know he was," Daisy said, ignoring Tippy and answering the man.

I tried to shut out Tippy's words, and said, "I snuck in after all. You said you saw it yourself."

A second man squeezed through the gap into the lobby. He had a pistol in his hand.

"He's not supposed to be here, and neither are you," the girl stated.

"You know, Sergeant." He hadn't corrected me so I decided the title was proper. "I work for the Crown too. Well, for Mr. Churchill at least."

"You're a messenger boy, who is a known coward, deserter, and a traitor! The toffs are using you for their own bloody ends, but they won't give a shit when you're dead."

A deserter and a traitor? Where had he heard that? Was Reynolds telling stories under a different name? The sergeant believed what he was saying. I was certain of it.

"This is too good to be true," Frederickson said in amazement.

Were these men hunting me by mistake?

"What makes you think I'm a traitor, and why'd you attack Mitchell?" I asked him.

"Don't know any fuckin' Mitchell, but we know you, you murderous milk-livered rotter. We've got our orders. We've been told all about you, we have."

"Who told you this crap? Before you tried to kill me in New York, I'd never seen you in my life," I told him.

A third man slipped through the gap and into the lobby. He had a pistol as well. The two men now flanked the sergeant.

"But we've seen you. We'd been following you, but you're a lucky bastard. We pushed you into traffic, but somehow you survived. I nearly scragged you on the *Adriatic*, but the damn attendant saved you. You killed poor Collins when you pushed him into the subway train in New York." He said the last bitterly, as if it were my fault they'd attacked me in the station.

These men didn't work for Reynolds at all! Or Fuchs! They had been trying to kill me since I'd come to London. I thought about telling him they pushed the wrong guy in front of the taxi, but I didn't want to mention Mitchell again. Suddenly I realized I'd made a terrible mistake leading these men to the hospital where Mitchell was recovering. And I'd brought Rachel and Hackworth as well.

They didn't want Mitchell. They weren't hunting him at all.

They were hunting me! Ever since I'd come back to London. It was as if my nightmares had come to life. They'd wanted to kill me outside of Claridge's not Mitchell. The attack on him had been a mistake. The attacks in the Turkish bath on the ship, in the subway, and Hanley's bar had all been aimed at me. They were waiting for me at Patricia's house and followed me into the hospital hoping to kill me. Someone had convinced these men I was an enemy to England and a coward and deserter to boot. They were partially right, but I couldn't figure out who would do such a thing.

"Why the hell are you after me?" I asked, genuinely confused.

"Don't play the innocent. You deserted from the army. Pretended injury. A coward who ran away only to come back and work with spies for the Boche."

"Who told you these things? They're at best half-truths. Exaggerations." I couldn't bring myself to say that what he claimed were lies. I *had* run away. Marie *had* been a German spy, and I *had* shoved Woodrow Wilson into his bathtub plumbing.

How could he have known those things? Somehow the ghosts in my head were communicating with the living. In the lobby of the Endell Street Military Hospital, the avenging angels of my long-dead friends had cornered me. These avengers weren't from the First Surrey Rifles, but they were close enough substitutes.

Tippy was standing beside the last man to enter the lobby. His arms were crossed, and his eyes were locked on me. He had been waiting a long time for this.

"They're the truth all right," the sergeant said. "You can't deny it. You haven't even the stomach for that. The captain has all the information about you. He knows what you've done. And so do we. Well, you're not going to survive the night. We'll make sure of it." He moved aside his jacket and pulled a revolver that had been tucked behind his belt buckle.

The captain? I didn't know this man or the two with him. And I certainly didn't know any captain connected to them. I was going to end up shot to death by mistake. Yes, I deserved it, but it was all a mistake.

I almost started to laugh, but a fourth man squeezed through the opening into the lobby. I knew him. He was the man who had pushed Mitchell into traffic. He balanced on his hind legs.

It no longer mattered who they worked for or what they believed. It didn't matter if it was all a mistake. I was going to kill them all.

Mitchell's attacker took up a position next to Fredrickson. He wore a grin of anticipation. He had a pistol in his misshapen paw.

"Daisy," I said, turning my head just enough so she could hear my lowered voice. "I need you to go down the hall. Now. Hurry, and don't argue. Run to Mitchell's room. Tell them what you've heard."

"No, you…"

"Daisy!" I took a risk and turned to face her. I held out my left hand to stop her speaking. My turn had hidden the pistol behind my body. The men in the lobby couldn't see my right arm and hand. I brought the gun across my chest with the muzzle nearly even with my left shoulder.

"You need to go. *Now!*" I hissed at her, channeling all my anger, self-hatred, and fear. She understood what I intended.

She turned and ran, and I spun back around and brought up the .45. Five men. But not for long.

The balding sergeant managed a strangled cry of warning just as my pistol boomed.

I knew the shot was good. My conviction was confirmed when the head of the bastard who had attacked Mitchell snapped back. The Colt's heavy slug smashed through his forehead, throwing him backward into the shattered door and onto the checkerboard floor.

For less than a heartbeat after the echoing blast of the pistol, all four men froze. Then the three newcomers raised their pistols. I fired twice. Both bullets passed through Frederickson and shattered the stone wall behind him. He gave me a grin.

I threw myself across the corridor as their guns barked. I felt the whip of a bullet pass my face, and I skidded into the wall.

I rolled over and fired once more to keep them back. I needn't have bothered. They had hidden against the walls of the lobby. They had no angle to take a shot at me without leaning into the hallway.

As quietly as I could, I stood and backed down the corridor to the stairs that led to the floors above. I had three rounds left. I needed more ammunition, but it was all in Hackworth's carryall. To get it, I needed to go to Mitchell's room, but if I did that, I'd lead the killers directly to my friends. I couldn't do that.

The quiet ended with a round of obscenities shouted in the lobby. A pistol appeared at the end of the hall and fired blindly in my direction. The bullet gave me a scare as it whined down the hallway.

"You bastard!" The cry came from the lobby. "You're a dead man. I promise you. You won't get out of here alive." It was the balding sergeant. He was angry about the man I'd killed.

Well, fuck him!

He shouldn't have come to Mitchell's hospital, and they shouldn't have attacked Mitchell even if it was by mistake.

"He had it coming," I called, and I turned and ran for the stairs.

I raced to the floor above, taking the steps two at a time. My recently healed ankle performed without complaint. Once out of the stairwell, I hurried back in the direction of the lobby. I knew the building had other exits, but I'd only seen the front door that opened onto the yard. I needed to lead the killers away from my friends. Away from the hospital. My hope was to pass over the lobby and to find another set of stairs to take me back to the ground floor. I would circle back through the lobby and out into the night.

I crept down the hall past glass-fronted doors with numbers painted on the center of each. I found the hoped-for entrance to a stairway, but from below, I heard the sound of someone climbing toward me.

I turned back down the hall and tried the handle of the first door I came to. It was unlocked. I couldn't tell what was beyond the door, but I stepped through anyway. I pushed it shut behind me.

I was in a long, narrow room. At the end of the room, a small window let in the thin light from the streetlamps below. Sturdy shelving, which began on each side of the door, lined both walls from the floor to the ceiling twelve feet above. The shelves were divided into large square sections. Each section was numbered. A few shelves held clothing: military uniforms and boots in neat stacks. It had to be a storage room for the patients' belongings.

I considered going back into the hall, but shadows visible through the glass convinced me that someone was out there. I was trapped. Unless I could curl up on one of the shelves, there was nowhere to hide.

If I was going to lead these men away from Mitchell, Rachel, and Hackworth, I had to convince them I was outside the building or at least on the ground floor. That meant I couldn't shoot whoever was following me. I holstered the pistol and scaled the shelves until my head bumped into the ceiling. Once there, I stretched across the narrow walkway and braced myself between the sturdy wooden storage frames built against each wall. I was suspended just past where the door would open. My body was wedged in place, facing the floor below. As I settled into position, which I knew I wouldn't be able to hold for long, I remembered the blackjack in my pocket. I couldn't reach it and keep myself braced between the shelves. I'd have to climb down to get it.

It was too late.

The shadow in the hallway drew closer. Sweat dripped down my scarred cheek to my nose. I tried tilting my head, but the drop fell free to the floor below.

The knob turned, and the door cracked open.

I hoped there was only one man.

The door swung wide, and the barrel of a revolver led the assassin's way into the narrow storage space. He took a step into the room to look behind the door. He stood below me with his left hand on the doorknob and his right pointing the pistol toward the window on the back wall. A second bead of sweat ran off my nose to drop toward the killer below me.

I let go of my perch.

He heard the scrape of my shoes leaving the wooden shelf. He started to swing the pistol up, but my legs crashed across his arm, and his pistol flew off into the darkness. I fell back into the shelves, but I got one arm around his neck. He stumbled into me, and I locked my other arm behind his head. Just as I had seen Mitchell do to the doorman at Jean-Paul's grandmother's house, I pulled him close with his neck vised between my forearms. He slammed me into the shelves, and we tumbled to the floor. I wrapped my legs around his waist and hooked my ankles together. Our twined bodies thrashed about as he tried to escape the crushing force on his throat. He squirmed desperately.

I held the lock tight for a long time after he stopped moving. I had no choice. I didn't want him warning his friends or following me.

I kicked myself free of the body and stood on shaky legs. I wanted his gun, but I didn't want to take the time to find it. I needed to draw the remaining men out of the hospital. I peeked out the door. The hallway was empty. I hurried to the stairs and went down as quietly as I could. The corridor to the lobby was clear and so was the lobby itself. Only the body of the grinning assassin remained. Tippy was nowhere to be seen. I looked out the front door past the crashed motorcar. No one was in the courtyard.

I drew the Colt and fired a bullet into the dead body. Now the Limey bastards would hear the gunshot and know I was on the ground floor. I reholstered the pistol and squeezed through the gap between the automobile and the doorframe. Once in the courtyard, I looked up at the facade of the hospital. In one of the windows on the second floor, I saw the pale, enraged face of the balding sergeant. I smiled and waved a hand as I turned through the sagging courtyard gate out onto Endell Street.

The Covent Garden tube stop was a short walk down the road. I knew where I needed to go. It had been right in front of my nose since the beginning. There was only one captain it could be.

I would take the train to Knightsbridge. It was late, but the tube was still running. Time to visit some old friends.

29

Mystery Solved

A soft, golden light glowed through the window shade covering the glass front door of Twenty-One Hans Road. Someone was home.

I wasn't quite sure what I would say or do. The murderous rage I'd felt in the lobby of Endell Street had cooled to a twisting knot of disappointment and sorrow. And maybe a little self-pity. I was surprised my emotions hadn't drawn any comment from Frederickson, but I hadn't seen or heard from him since the bullets had flown through his incorporeal form at the hospital.

I welcomed his absence.

I tapped on the glass of the door. I didn't use the mechanical bell because I didn't want to hear its strident clacking ring. Shadows shifted behind the glass, and a woman's hand pushed aside the shade.

Evelyn.

Her eyes widened when she recognized me, but she smiled and unlatched the door.

"John, this is a surprise! I didn't know you were back from

America. Is Billy with you?" She looked behind me apparently hoping for a sign of Billy Jones.

"No. He's not. I'd hoped to see him here."

"He's not here, but you are welcome to wait. Please come in. Have a seat. Drink?" She led me into the sitting room and the couch where we'd made love.

"Sure. Whatever you're having. I left Billy at the dock and thought he was coming home. I suppose he must have gone to work and had to stay late."

She poured two whiskies, neat. She must have sensed something was bothering me because she filled each glass with at least three fingers of the amber liquid. Perhaps something was bothering her too.

She handed me my glass and reclined next to me on the couch with one leg tucked under her. She leaned toward me, resting on one arm. She wore no stockings or shoes. She had noticed my eyes stray to her ankles as she sat.

"What do you need to see Billy about at this hour after spending a whole transatlantic crossing in his company?"

"Believe me when I say, I'd rather not be here, but I've been given cause to pay a visit."

"I don't understand."

"How much did you tell Billy about us? About what it was like when I returned to England after being wounded?" I asked her.

"What do you mean? I told him we tried to make it work, but it was hard. You were blind, angry, and afraid of going back. And I was afraid. Afraid of your blindness. Afraid of you going back as well."

"Yes, and what else?" I was prodding her for more detail.

"Why is this important, John?"

"Humor me, Evelyn. I have a feeling you'll be able to clear up some confusion on my part." The confusion was about who was responsible for the attacks on Mitchell and me.

"Well… even before he began to court me, I made it clear that I had been deeply in love with you. I never hid that fact. I never hid the fact of our intimacy or my heartbreak when you returned to America."

"Heartbreak? Really, Evelyn? You were just as glad as I was that I went back to America."

"Glad? No. Relieved. I was relieved that you would live. But I *was* heartbroken. I loved you deeply."

I shook my head in disbelief. "That's not how I remember things."

"Anything that would have held you here you were unwilling to see. You were afraid. And I wanted you to be safe too. Billy knows that at the time I wanted you to go home. To survive. He understands exactly how horrible the war was and how unlikely it was that you would survive it. He was, and is, sympathetic to the desire to escape the horror of it all. So few of his own company made it home, and I know he is pained by every man he lost."

"Did you tell him that you thought my vision was already returning before I left for America?"

"Well, I told him the truth. You were blind. You couldn't fight, so you went home. I told him it was over between us when you left. This was before he had made clear his intentions toward me. I don't lie to Billy. Just as I don't lie to you. Well, mostly. I suppose I did let you believe I no longer loved you. That was a lie, but it was a necessary one for you to survive."

"So you told Billy about us, your desire for me to escape?"

"Well, yes."

"Did you tell him about my vision returning before I'd even left England?"

She nodded reluctantly. "I was still in pain, and he was an easy shoulder to cry on. It's part of the reason I love him."

"Did you tell him you still loved me when I left?"

"Yes. Yes, I did. John, what's all this about?"

"I just want to understand what Billy knows and how freely I can confide in him," I lied.

"He knows the truth."

"Whose idea was it for us to have sex so you could conceive a child?"

The blunt question shocked her. She uncurled her lovely legs and placed her feet on the floor. She leaned away from me.

"It came up when we returned home after we had dinner with you at Bentley's. We talked about how wonderful it was to see you. I said it was a shame you weren't living in England where we could see you more often. I'm sure I said something silly about you being a wonderful role model for a son should we ever be lucky enough to have one. I think we both jumped to the possibility of you fathering our child at the same time. He has always loved you like a brother. You're a great friend to us both, and Billy knows how desperately I want a child."

"And so you both decided to invite me to tea the next day?"

"Yes. Of course."

I shook my head. "You're still lying to me, Evelyn. You invited me to tea while we were still at dinner. Before you and Billy ever had the chance to discuss me fathering your child."

"What? That's not true. We decided to invite you to tea together."

"No, Evelyn. You didn't. You invited me to tea while we were still sitting at Bentley's having after-dinner drinks. *You* decided. Without consulting Billy. *You* planned on having me father your child. And then you convinced Billy that it was what you both wanted. Or at least you thought you had convinced him."

Caught in her lie, her fair skin flushed.

"I knew he would happily agree once we'd talked it through," she said. She was unapologetic. She wanted a child, and if she had to manipulate her husband and me to get one, so be it.

"You know Billy thinks you still love me."

"That's ridiculous. Billy knows I love him."

"I think it eats at him."

"You're wrong. He knows I love him unconditionally."

"But I'm not sure he knows you don't love me too."

"Well, of course I still love you. Part of me will always love you. But I love Billy. He knows that. He's my husband. I married Billy," she said, as if her marriage ended any dispute about the relative hierarchy of her lovers.

"I don't think Billy understands your distinctions in love."

"You're wrong. He understands very well."

"I'm not here to argue with you. Really, I'm not." I'd come to Hans Road for only one answer. I dreaded what it would be, but I had to ask. "Evelyn, what rank did Billy hold by the time the war ended?"

She was confused by the change of topic but answered immediately. "He was a captain. In the Warwicks."

I stood and placed my untouched drink on the end table next to the couch. "Please tell Billy I was here looking for him."

"I'm sure he'll be home shortly. You can wait. Have dinner with us." She felt the chill her answer had brought into the room, and I knew she hoped she just imagined it.

"Tell him he can find me tomorrow evening at the Wellington Pub near Waterloo Station. Tomorrow night at eight forty-five."

"John, what's going on? What's the matter with you? You're frightening me."

"All of us were changed by the war, Evelyn. You. Me. Billy. I'm not sure you know what Billy is capable of. Unfortunately, I know what I am capable of. You made a terrible mistake manipulating Billy and using me."

"What do you mean? Why?" Her fear was clear in her rising voice and the urgency of her questions.

"Remember. Tomorrow evening at the Wellington. And Evelyn, tell him if he doesn't turn up, I'll find him, and he won't see me coming."

I TOOK THE TUBE SOUTH ACROSS THE RIVER. IF I HURRIED, I COULD get to the Wellington before it closed.

I had to knock on the locked pub door to gain entry.

Fortunately, the bartender recognized me. He let me in with a frown, which only became deeper when I told him I needed to see McDonald again. He sent the young runner, who had been helping him and a blond waitress tidy up after closing.

He sat me in a booth and left me. The waitress kept glancing my way until he whispered in her ear. After that, she stopped looking and left my part of the pub uncleaned.

The boy returned and reported to the publican, who came over to me immediately. He was in a hurry to get me out of his bar.

"He's at a nightclub in Soho. Go up Shaftesbury Avenue from Piccadilly Circus. Take a left on Denman Street. Number 26. Basement door. Tell them you're looking for Wag. Maybe they let you in. Maybe they don't."

I left the pub, and he locked the door behind me.

I found Number 26 Denman Street without any problem. There was only one door into the building, and it was unlocked. Inside, a cramped entryway was lit by a single electric bulb hanging from a wire overhead. The hallway had the sour smell of vomit and old cigarette smoke. Stairs climbed to the floor above, and I walked past the steps and followed a narrow hallway that led to the back of the building. When I came to a door with peeling black paint, I heard the faint sound of rag music.

I knocked.

The door opened, and the music got louder. The smell of tobacco smoke and spilled drinks wafted from inside. Fortunately, the smell of vomit did not.

"Who are you and what do you want?" The words came out as fast as J. Edgar Hoover's. The doorman was a big, beefy man with short hair and cauliflower ears. He was there to discourage the riffraff. His eyes widened slightly when he got a look at me.

"I was told I could find Wag McDonald here."

He stared at me just long enough to make clear that he wasn't afraid, then nodded.

"Near the dance floor. In the middle." He stepped out of the way.

At the bottom of the stairs, the room opened up into a nightclub not so different from Zelli's in Paris. Small round tables crowded the room right to the edge of the dance floor. A band played on an elevated stage, and couples gyrated right under the horns of the musicians.

It was dark, but I could pick out Wag, who was sitting with a woman. I worked my way through the tables.

Wag raised an eyebrow when he saw me, and he leaned over to speak in his companion's ear. She looked up, saw me, and gracefully stood. She didn't bother to smile at me. I didn't have the kind of face that invited a stranger's smile.

"Sit!" Wag shouted over the noise.

He waved a hand and a waiter brought me a teacup. I sniffed the contents. Whisky.

"You can call your boys off Endell Street." I had leaned across the table so he could hear me.

"Didn't have to come here to tell me that, but I'll pass the word." He was smart. He waited patiently for me to tell him the real reason I was there.

"I need another favor," I said.

"Good. I'm considering what I need you to do in return for my boys watching the hospital, and the more you owe me the less you'll whinge."

I nodded. I was going to do whatever he asked, and he knew it.

"It'll probably be some work for me in America," he said. "I've decided now that the war is over, expansion to America could be good for business, diversifying you might say. But it's still early days. I need to give it some thought."

"What would I do?"

"At first I'd probably just need someone local, who knows the ropes and can steer my people right."

At first. Perfect. One more boot on my neck.

"Sort of a tour guide?" I asked with a frown.

"Now don't be like that. You came to me, remember?"

He was right. I had.

"Sounds like a gas," I said half-heartedly. "When?"

"Not sure, exactly. I just need to know where to find you when your business here is complete. I wouldn't want you to forget about me."

The thought had crossed my mind, but I didn't want to be pursued by the London underworld.

"Leave a message at Claridge's or in New York at the Hotel Pennsylvania. Eventually I'll get the message."

"Easy enough. So what do you need from me?" he asked.

Speaking over the music, laughter, and the rumble of voices and drunken squeals, I told him.

He laughed when I was done. "Sounds easy enough," he told me.

"Until it isn't."

"True. Until it isn't."

I RETURNED TO PATRICIA'S HOUSE. THE WATCHERS WERE GONE. I went to my room and collected my things, including ammunition for the Colt. Then I took a motorcab to the Strand Hotel. Despite the late hour, the hotel had a room available, and I checked in under the name John Reynolds. I cleaned up and left the pistol and shoulder holster in the bottom of my suitcase. I put the blackjack in the suitcase as well. I suspected I was a wanted man again. A lot would depend on what Daisy Ward had told the police. It was nearly dawn when I took the short walk to Endell Street.

The hospital was crawling with coppers and the female medical staff, who must have been called by Ada or Daisy. I managed to blend in well enough to sneak through the lobby and up the stairs to Mitchell's floor. I slipped into his room.

Unfortunately, Detective Inspector Fair and Inspector Norton were there before me. Both men had watched me quietly close the door, and Norton couldn't help but smirk at my stealthy entry into a room holding two coppers.

Ada and Daisy were at the end of Mitchell's bed, looking protective. They were red-faced and likely angry. Given that the charming Detective Inspector Fair was in the room, I wasn't surprised.

In contrast, a serene-looking Rachel sat next to Mitchell on his bed. She was nearest the door and on the opposite side of his broken leg. Hackworth stood tall near the window. A Life Guard masquerading as a butler. The pistols were nowhere to be seen.

Of course, Mitchell hadn't moved. The inanity of the thought made me smirk. The look must have annoyed Detective Inspector Fair.

"Ah, the man of the hour," Fair said with false good cheer. "Happy to see us? I certainly never expected you back here in good old Blighty. I thought for sure you'd run off never to return."

"I'm doing a job for Mr. Churchill," I reminded him. "I still need to give him my report."

"Where were you earlier this evening?" Fair asked through his smile.

I looked at Mitchell and the others for a lead to follow.

"First time we've seen him," Ada Phillips volunteered. "Right, Daisy?"

Norton frowned. He'd caught my look and knew exactly what Ada was doing.

"That's right. Tough to forget that phiz," Daisy said with a wicked twinkle in her eye. They were getting back at Fair and Norton for the browbeating they had likely endured before I arrived.

"Perhaps we should separate the witnesses," he said to Fair.

"No point. Even if these two," Fair said, nodding at the Endell Street girls, "tell us they saw Mr. Griffin shoot the dead man in the reception in cold blood, Sir Basil won't allow him to be brought up on charges."

"That's very reassuring to hear," I told him.

"How long have you been back in England?" he asked.

"My ship docked in Liverpool yesterday."

"That long? And I've only got one corpse," Fair said ironically. They hadn't found the body in the storeroom.

"Well, give it time. You can't have looked everywhere," I said sarcastically.

Fair looked ready to burst. I didn't know what Mitchell and Rachel had told the two girls to keep them quiet, but whatever it was it was working.

"Time to go, Norton," Fair said. "Thank you for your time, girls."

Daisy and Ada nodded.

"Sorry to interrupt your recuperation, Mr. Mitchell. Glad to see it's going smoothly. Glad you didn't get shot," Fair said, glaring at me. He tipped his hat to Rachel and nodded at Hackworth.

"Detective Inspector, perhaps we should take a statement from Mr. Griffin," Norton said.

"Hah! No need for that. With him here, the mystery of who killed the man in the lobby is solved," Fair said. "Wouldn't you agree, Mr. Griffin?"

"I wouldn't know, Detective Inspector."

The inspectors left the room and shut the door.

I looked from face to face and waited for an explanation.

"Once you left, the gangsters left," Mitchell said. "It looked like they were following you and weren't here for me at all. We told Ada and Daisy as much as we knew, and they were kind enough to agree to say they'd never seen you before. Apparently, we all were caught up in a terrible shootout, and most of those involved escaped. No one's really sure why they came to the hospital. Given the trouble you were already in with the coppers, we thought it best you weren't mentioned at all. Oh, and the girls also hid the handguns."

"That's helpful. Thank you, ladies," I told them.

They nodded at me but looked to Mitchell for approval. He smiled. They smiled back. William Mitchell: Svengali in traction. Only he could have convinced honest, hardworking young ladies to lie to the police for a stiff like me.

"Well, I think the killers are gone from here for good. At least, I think they're done bothering you, Mitch. I have a meeting tonight that should wrap up this whole thing."

"You need to bring us with you," Rachel said.

"I agree, sir," Hackworth added.

"I've got all the help I need. Trust me on that. Really. Don't worry about me," I answered.

"As if we could do anything but," Mitchell said. The other four bobbed their heads in agreement, which was a little disappointing given that I didn't even know the two English girls.

30

———

Loose Ends

That evening, just after eight o'clock, I was in place in a booth at the Wellington. I knew Billy would appear. Of all the things he had told me, the one I believed without a shadow of a doubt was that he loved Evelyn more than life itself. He would come, if only to try to preserve his relationship with her.

The pub was full. Men leaned on the bar, talking and laughing. Others crowded the tables. Working-class blokes in cloth caps and worn clothes mingled with more prosperous middle-class workers in suitcoats and bowler hats. There didn't seem to be any class distinctions in the Wellington, or perhaps it was more accurate to say there were no class distinctions if you worked for Wag McDonald.

The bartender and the blond waitress were busy as beavers. She, of course, had to spend much of her time fighting off the hands of the patrons. The Wellington's little runner sat nearly hidden on a stool at the far end of the bar. I had to turn my head to see him.

The beer and whisky flowed without restraint. That was part of the price Wag had insisted upon. I had to pay for the drinks from eight to nine. Wag was a good friend to his people. By the time Billy was due, the clientele of the Wellington would be well and truly soused. They would certainly be unrestrained, which was fine by me.

At eight forty-five, fifteen minutes before closing and right on time, Billy Jones came through the door of the pub. At his shoulder was the balding sergeant and one of the two men who had broken into Endell Street. With the two dead at the hospital, I supposed Billy was running out of soldiers from his company willing to kill for him.

Despite the crowd in the public house, I sat alone. Wag McDonald had spread the word that I would need a booth of my own that evening.

Jones saw me as soon as he entered. He left one man by the door, and he and the sergeant came to my table.

Billy sat down across from me. His man stood at the end of the table. He'd be able to block me if I tried to get out.

"Billy, it seems I was right when I first saw you at Whitehall. You *are* a dead man," I said.

He laughed. "You seem to misunderstand what's going to happen, *old friend*. I've got you outnumbered and trapped. Yes, it's a public place, but it's a public place that's about to close."

I looked at the man by the door and up at the sergeant and then back at Jones.

"Perhaps, but why don't you explain to me why you're doing all this before you get two more of your men killed?"

The sergeant glowered at me. He didn't like my implication that I'd be the one doing the killing.

"Sergeant Major, wait at the bar. Keep an eye on us though. He's a clever bastard," Billy told him.

Billy's company sergeant major. I should have known. As solid a man as Billy could hope to find. Billy was a likable fellow and likely a good officer. He was brave, smart, and probably as careful with his soldiers' lives as any good officer was allowed to be. I wasn't surprised his men were willing to commit murder at his direction. Based on what the sergeant major had claimed in the lobby of the hospital, Billy had laid a solid foundation of lies for them to believe, and it didn't hurt that some of that foundation was true.

"Sergeant Major, I understand the drinks are free tonight," I said to the man. "Why don't you get one for your friend by the door while the captain and I have our chat?"

With one last look at Jones and a glare for me, the sergeant major went to the bar.

"It took you a long time to realize it was me, Jack. You were smarter before the war. Less of a paranoiac. But with all the lies you've told yourself and others, I supposed it is unsurprising." He reached into his coat for his cigarette case.

Jones had used my own fears against me, and the German torture had helped him. I was angry and disgusted with myself, but most of all, I was hurt by Billy Jones's betrayal. I'd confided in him. I had really thought he was my friend, and I couldn't understand why he'd want to kill me. Gone, yes. Away from Evelyn. But dead? It just seemed so extreme even for a man hardened by war.

Tippy eased into the booth next to Jones. He wore a frown. In his mind, I was supposed to be the bad guy. I was the cur who lied to people and ran away. Not Jones. Poor Tippy didn't like discovering that Jones was no better than I was. I felt no sympathy for Tippy. He'd made my life a hell, and I was happy to see him disappointed.

"Don't expect me to feel sorry for you," I told him.

Instead of Frederickson, Jones answered. "I don't. I should have realized you were a selfish bastard who would leap at the chance to have sex with my wife. It's my fault almost as much as yours." He took out a cigarette and tapped it on the back of the case.

"It is entirely your fault. Yours and Evelyn's, but we'll have plenty of time to talk about it, Billy."

"I doubt that, Jack. It's time you took your medicine. Come outside. We don't want to involve these good people, do we?"

He lit the cigarette. He was completely confident in his position and the outcome of our meeting.

I tilted my head back until I could see the end of the bar and the Wellington's young runner, who was watching our conversation intently. I raised my glass to him, and he jumped down and disappeared behind the bar. His hand appeared on the lanyard of a bell screwed into the wall between the mirrors backing the bar top. Two pulls and the clear rings stopped all conversation in the pub.

"Sure we do," I said into the lull.

I surged across the booth, knocking over my glass and splashing beer on us both. With my thighs hooked under the table top for leverage, I grabbed him by the ears and slammed his face into the runnels of the spilled beer. I pulled him through Tippy Frederickson's body off his bench and onto the floor. A revolver clattered to the floor with him. A Webley, of course. I put it on the table. Jones tried to stand, and I kicked him in the side. Anyone who's never kicked a man when he's down doesn't know what they are missing. It felt good, and I kicked him again.

By the time I looked up at the rest of the bar, Jones's men were trussed up like Thanksgiving turkeys and hooded under peck-sized fruit sacks.

At the ring of the bell, at my request, McDonald had ordered all the patrons of the bar, all of whom worked for his gang, to subdue whoever entered with Billy. I asked McDonald to make clear that I didn't want Billy's men killed, just overpowered and disarmed. They took Wag's direction seriously. It looked like both men had been wrapped tightly in yards of washing line.

I made a show out of looking at my wristwatch. "Only a few minutes of free drinks left, folks," I called out to the barroom.

That earned me a hard laugh from McDonald's crowd.

Two of Wag's bruisers rumbled over and bound and hooded

the groaning Jones. Once secured, they dragged him over to the other two by the entrance.

I followed, and Wag McDonald joined me there.

"The lorry's outside," he said. "We'll deliver you and your guests to the boat. There's a bargeman who will take you up river to a nice quiet place. He'll leave you there. There are two bicycles on board. He'll take one. The other's for you. Don't leave any bodies on the boat and clean up after yourself, if you get my meaning."

His words caused the sergeant major to struggle a bit, but a fist in the belly put an end to that nonsense.

"Thanks, Mr. McDonald. I appreciate the help." I held out my hand, and we shook.

"I'll miss you and your *misters*, Yank," he said. "Hurry back. We've work to do."

———

IN LESS THAN TWENTY MINUTES, MY GUESTS AND I WERE ON THE Thames chugging upriver past Westminster. The water smelled of sewage and dead fish. The rain earlier in the day had cleared, and some moonlight filtered through the overcast sky to show the muddy banks as we motored past. Our transport was a narrow canal boat McDonald had arranged. He had suggested that the Thames was the perfect place for a private talk with Billy.

The boat's captain was a squinty-eyed, pipe-smoking gent who had no time for chatting. That was fine with me. I had to decide what I would do with Billy once I reached whatever site the boatman chose for us.

The canal boat was no wider than a tall man, which made it seem deceptively long. The inside was cramped. When they had delivered us to the boat, I'd asked McDonald's men to separate Billy from his two soldiers. They placed Billy all the way forward in a room partitioned off from the rest of the interior. He remained bound, and they'd tied him to a sturdy wooden chair. He shared the space with an unmade bunk crammed into the bow of the boat. McDonald's boys had tossed Billy's two men on opposite sides of the low-ceilinged cabin taking up the remainder of the interior of the boat. I could see them from where I stood by the rudder. They had managed to sit up but were too far apart to communicate without shouting through their hoods. A few chairs were pushed under a built-in table, and a nearby counter held a sink and a tiny gas stove. A teakettle sat on its unlit burner. It would have been a cozy little nautical galley but for the two bound men on the floor.

After an hour or so on the water, the captain grunted. On each side of the boat, the banks were dark.

"We'll tie up here at the gardens." He adjusted the rudder to swing us right toward the north side of the river. "Battersea's across there," he said, pointing south. "Good current here."

He bumped the narrow boat against a landing. As nimble as a goat, he jumped across to the embankment. For a moment, I thought he was abandoning me to the Thames, but he brought with him a line, which was attached to a cleat at the front of the boat. He quickly looped the line over a thick wooden piling. The current pushed the back of the boat against the bank. The boatman waved to get my attention and pointed at my feet where I found a second line neatly coiled. He waved for me to throw it across to him, and I did. He pulled the line tight and tied it to another piling.

He jumped back in the canal boat and shut off the engine.

With the sound of the motor gone, the stillness of the night settled over us. The river softly lapping against the hull gave me a feeling of remoteness, from London, from civilization, from the decency with which I'd been raised.

"I'll be back at sunrise," the captain said. "I don't want no bodies on board nor any mess. There're plenty of lengths of chain right here and more under the benches down below." He spoke in a conversational tone and kicked the chains nearby. Billy's men had heard him because their bodies shifted and their hoods turned toward us.

"Understood," I answered. I had been given the perfect place to murder Billy and his men, and I was expected to sink their bodies.

The boatman carried one of the bicycles to the bank. Without a wave, he pedaled off into the night. I stooped under the low ceiling and moved through the boat to the cabin that held Billy. He was facing the back of the boat. I squeezed past him, and he flinched away. I sat on the end of the bed, staring at the back of his bound form.

Time to wrap up loose ends.

With that thought, I realized I was no better than Karl Fuchs. Fuchs had killed poor Frau Emma Vogt because she was extraneous. I would do the same to Billy and his men. They had tried to kill Mitchell. They'd tried to kill me. They were a constant threat that I couldn't allow, distractions from Armistan and Reynolds. I did, however, want to know why they'd made all the effort when it seemed unnecessary to me, and I had a few hours to find out.

"Jack?" He wasn't sure it was me in the space with him.

"Yes, Billy."

"What are you going to do with us?" Billy asked from under his hood.

"What would you do with me if you had me tied to a chair, Billy?"

He didn't answer for a long time, but I was in no hurry. I had all night.

"Let my men go. They're in this only because I asked for their help."

"They'll keep coming for me."

I heard them shift in the aft cabin. They could hear us speaking.

"I could order them not to."

I barked out a laugh. "I doubt very much that that would

work." Despite my answer, his suggestion gave me a thought. Perhaps there was a way to stop the killing. It would depend on what Billy told me.

I manhandled his chair around so he faced the bed and the front of the boat. Once I had him positioned where I wanted him, I pulled off his hood. His eyes quickly took in his surroundings, but all he could see was me, the grubby bed, and the tiny, narrow boat cabin. His eyes were wide with fear, but he wasn't frozen with it.

"Please, Jack. What would Evelyn think if you were to murder us all? Surely you haven't become so vicious as that."

"You can't get a man like your company sergeant major to stop, order or no order, promise or no promise. When I kill you, he'll have to come after me. He won't be able to help himself. And the poor sucker with him will follow. It really is a simple calculation. So I'll do what needs doing, and then you and I will have a chat."

"Jack, no! Please!" His voice rose with the terror he felt on behalf of his men.

I put the hood back over his head, not because I was afraid *he* would be heard, but because I didn't want him to clearly hear what *I* was doing.

I went into the aft cabin with the two soldiers. Despite their hoods, I could tell the difference between them. The sergeant major was nearest the back deck. He had his back against a bench, and his hooded head turned toward me as I approached.

"Sorry, mate," I told him.

"Fuck yourself, you bastard."

I grabbed him by the ankles and dragged him to the short ladder up to the back deck. He struggled a little, and I was forced to bang his head off the hatchway frame to quiet him enough to get him out of the cabin. The junior man gave me less trouble. I tumbled him on the deck hip to hip with his leader and rested. It was hard work moving the dead weight of two full-grown men.

"Please, mister," the younger man begged.

"Quiet, Sammy! There's no mercy in this bastard. No point in asking for any!"

I squatted down near their heads.

"That may be true, Sergeant Major, but I'm going to give you and Sammy here a chance," I said quietly. "You may know why the captain wants me dead, but I don't."

"Because you're a—" he shouted.

I cuffed the side of his hood to silence him. The blow to the head settled him for the moment.

"I don't care what your captain told you," I said softly. "I care about what he will tell me. I was his best friend once, and I want to know why he wants to kill me. It would probably be easiest to wrap you both in chains and push you off this boat, but I'd prefer not to do that. Of course, if you make this too hard, that is exactly what I will do. Nod your heads if you understand."

Both hoods bobbed.

Billy hollered something from the front of the boat, but I ignored him. I was busy with his men. I didn't want them working themselves free.

"Gentlemen, I'm going to have a talk with Captain Jones," I told them. "Once I have you settled, I suggest you stay still. You will be at the edge of the deck, and if you move around too much, you might just fall in the water. And if you make a single fucking sound, I will come back and kill you. That is a promise."

With the warning given, I dragged each man to opposite sides of the rudder. The boat had no bulwarks, and if they shifted too much, they would indeed plunge into the river. With them in place, I went to Billy. I tilted his chair back on two legs and dragged him from the front cabin into the galley space. He was still facing the forward bedroom. He would be able to hear the men on the deck, but that was a chance I would have to take. They would also be able to hear him.

"Say goodbye to your men, Billy."

"No. Please no! Jack, I beg you!"

At the base of the rudder lay the pile of chains. I collected one length, made a great deal of noise, and tossed it off the back of the boat. It hit the water with a loud splash.

"No!"

I repeated the effort, and Jones howled in misery at the imagined murder of his men.

"Now, Billy, with that little chore done, let's talk about why you've been trying to kill me and my friend William Mitchell," I said as I pulled off his hood. He whipped his head around and saw only an empty cabin. He couldn't see the stern where his men lay quietly.

"You've become a horrible brute of a man, Jack. I felt guilty about you, but now… now I only wish I'd succeeded in killing you."

"Well, Billy. Now you can tell me why."

"Why should I tell you anything? You're just going to kill me like you killed the sergeant major and Private Hoskins."

I rummaged through a few of the drawers in the galley until I found a small selection of kitchen utensils. I chose a paring knife with a promisingly sharp tip. I then pulled a chair around directly in front of him and sat.

"Probably, but if you don't talk to me, I will cut you with this until you do, and then I will think about visiting Evelyn."

Even in the dim light of the cabin, I could see his face turn ashen with horror at the threat.

"You'd never!" he croaked.

I chose to misunderstand him. I positioned the paring blade with my thumb a half inch below the point on one side of the edge and my fingers tight on the other side.

I leaned over from my chair and stabbed the exposed tip into his thigh.

His shriek was as much surprise as pain. I had all his focus.

"Goddamn you!" he shouted.

I supposed I'd have to clean up puddles of blood after all.

"I'm very serious, Billy. Talk. Why kill me? Why not just let me disappear from your lives?"

"For Evelyn, of course."

"Evelyn wants me dead?"

"No. I want you dead. I need you dead. When I found out you were here in England, I was so glad. So happy at the thought of seeing my good friend again. And then I told Evelyn. I told her I'd invited you to dinner. You should have seen her face. Part fear, part joy. Her cheeks flushed at the very thought of seeing you. I knew immediately that she still loves you. She's always loved you. At that moment, I knew she'd leave me. For you. I can't live without her. I wasn't going to let her leave."

I could only shake my head. He'd tried to kill me out of jealousy. I was disgusted beyond words. I had given up on Evelyn and all she represented a long time ago.

"My God, you're an idiot, Jones. All you had to do was ask me how I felt about her. Just a little honesty with me, and all your worries would have vanished. I don't want Evelyn. Hell, I ran away from her in '16. It was the two of you who concocted the plan to have a child. Not me. I didn't even want to have dinner with you."

"It wasn't my idea for you to father our child," Jones said. "I invited you to dinner before I knew she still loved you, before she told me of her hopes to get with child. I didn't know of her plan until after dinner. When she suggested you give her the child I couldn't, she confirmed everything I feared. She loved you. She would leave me, and I would be alone."

"I almost feel sorry for you, Billy. But you've gotten a lot of folks killed just because you're a jealous prick. You should have said something to her, told her how you felt. It isn't your fault you can't have a child, but it is your fault that you decided to become a murderer."

"But it is."

"What?"

"It is my fault I can't have a child."

"Why?"

"It wasn't the mustard gas. I told Evelyn that, but it was never the gas. It can cause sterility, but that wasn't what caused my problems. Yes, I was gassed, but it was gonorrhea that rendered me sterile."

A hiss came from the rear of the boat. The sergeant major had heard Jones's admission. Jones was so lost in his tale he didn't appear to notice.

"I got a dose in France. At one of those bloody French army whorehouses. You know the ones that the damned frogs certified. They were supposed to be clean." He was almost talking to himself now. "I didn't really notice any symptoms. God only knows when I became infected. I was only diagnosed after I'd been wounded. After the gas. Ultimately, the medical care for the gonorrhea was nearly as bad as the mustard gas. Months of lengthy, painful treatment with some supposedly miraculous drug. It was hell."

I sat back in my chair stunned.

"What a bastard," Tippy said.

I turned slightly to see him crouched next to me.

He shrugged at my surprise, which must have shown on my face.

"Oh, don't get me wrong. I still hate your guts, but he really is no better than you," Frederickson said.

I turned back to Jones.

"What about Mitchell? Why'd you try to kill him?" I asked.

"That was a mistake. It was the raincoat. My man was waiting outside Claridge's for you. I'd seen you in that buff-colored mackintosh the day you came to our home, the day you were with Evelyn. I described you and the raincoat to the sergeant major and Corporal Daggett. The weather was dreadful that morning, and Daggett followed the two of you from Aldford Street. He couldn't get a good look at your faces. He was waiting outside the hotel, waiting to see that mackintosh. He simply pushed the wrong man into traffic. It was supposed to be you."

I recalled when the attacker and I had locked eyes. I had thought the assassin was afraid because I'd seen him. But he wasn't afraid at all. He was shocked that he had pushed the wrong man.

"So you used the soldiers of your old company as your killers. What did you tell them to get them to agree to hunt me?"

Jones hung his head for a moment. When he raised it again, all the hatred and disgust he felt for himself and for me were apparent on his face.

"I told them you were a deserter. A coward. I told them you ran away from the war. From your mates. That you had no honor. That you were a traitor working against England. That you'd worked with spies in Germany."

I shook my head in amazement. After a moment, I started to laugh. Then Frederickson did too. Billy Jones had told his men much of what I had believed about myself since 1916. The very same things Frederickson believed about me. Yet when he said it, it sounded so unfair, so incomplete and unjust that it was quite literally laughable.

"Did you tell them I came back with the Americans and fought the goddamn Krauts again? At Belleau Wood, Soissons, Saint Mihiel? At the Meuse? Did you mention any of that?"

"No. Of course not."

"Did you forget to tell them that I got wounded again?"

He shook his head.

"Did you?" I shouted. I needed him to answer out loud so his men would hear him.

"No!" he shouted back. "Why would I?"

"Did you bother to tell them that I worked for Colonel House and President Wilson? That I saved that bastard Clemenceau and even the butcher Mangin?"

"I wanted you dead, and they were willing to do it. Why would I tell them those things? It was easy for them to believe you ran. We all wanted to run. You're a bloody Yank after all, and we'd all lost too many friends to allow a coward to survive and prosper."

"Goddamn you, Billy. I was one of those friends," I shouted. "I fought for two years with you bloody Brits. I came back! You lied to your men about me and nearly killed the wrong man. All because you couldn't keep your cock in your pants!"

He looked at me with such hatred I found it hard to believe we had ever been friends.

"I lied to my men because as long as you were alive, Evelyn would always love you more than she loved me. She wanted you to survive the war. She told me. She loved you so much she was willing to lose you so you could live. She loved you so much that when you reappeared, she wanted to have your child."

"You both wanted a child! You begged me to have sex with your wife so she could have the child you couldn't give her."

"I asked that of you because it was what she wanted. I'd rather be dead than raise your bloody get, Griffin."

And with that admission, I had no doubt as to how to deal with Captain Billy Jones.

I stood up so quickly I banged my head into the low ceiling.

"Goddamn it!"

I flung the knife into the little sink. I took off my hat and tried to rub away the pain, disgust, and anger as I made my way to the back of the boat.

I leaned over the sergeant major and pulled off his hood.

He studied me with watchful eyes.

"Did you hear all that?"

"I did."

"I'm sorry about your men. I'm sure they were good men, who didn't deserve what they got. They certainly didn't deserve to be lied to. Hell, we've all been lied to for the past four years."

He nodded slowly.

"I killed your boys, but I'm not the reason they're dead. He is." I jerked my head toward the cabin where Jones waited.

"Yes, he is," the sergeant major said, staring hard at Jones's back.

"Sergeant Major?" Jones called over his shoulder.

I pulled the bag off Private Hoskins's head.

"Private, did you hear as well?" I asked him.

"Yessir, I did." He looked at his sergeant major and then at Jones.

"I'm going to take a chance," I said to them. "I'm going to cut you two loose. In the morning, I'm going to the war office to report to Mr. Churchill. After that, I'll be back at the Endell Street Hospital sitting with my friend. If you want to kill me, that's where I'll be."

Both men nodded. They looked at each other surprised that they might live to see the morning.

I carried the one remaining bicycle to the embankment and leaned it against a tree. When I returned to the boat, I got the knife from the sink and cut the cords wrapped around both men. I wiped down the blade and left it on the narrow counter.

Jones shouted orders at the men, but they ignored him.

I waited on the embankment as they worked themselves free. I had collected my pistol from the hotel before going to the Wellington, but I didn't think I'd need it.

Both men stood and looked at me from the stern of the boat.

"What about him?" the sergeant major called over the gunnel in a hard voice.

"I'm going to leave Captain Jones with you. He's your man. You decide what's right to do with him, but I'd appreciate if you wouldn't leave the boat a mess. It's borrowed."

31

No Solace

I pedaled the bicycle east then north along the road that paralleled the river. By the time I arrived at Charing Cross, my watch said it was two in the morning. I turned away from the river and cycled the short distance to the Strand tube station. I left the bike leaning against a wall in a nearby alley that smelled of urine.

The night clerk at the Strand Hotel raised an eyebrow when I appeared at the front desk, but he gave me the key to my room without any fuss. I collapsed into bed and slept more soundly than I had in years. Jones's men might continue to hunt me, but I had done what I could. Oddly, I felt good about myself, and perhaps stranger still, Tippy Frederickson wasn't there in the morning to greet me. He would eventually appear, I knew, but I welcomed the solitude while I had it.

After breakfast, I went straight to the war office. I had no appointment, but I didn't really need to see Churchill in person. I just needed to leave the message that I had delivered the letters. If I saw his assistant Edward Marsh or even his secretary, that would be enough.

The civilian security passed me through with barely a glance. I went up the marble staircase and down the wide corridor, knocked on the anteroom door, and entered without waiting. The secretary recognized me. I had that kind of face. I wasn't sure she remembered my name, and to save her the embarrassment of asking, I said, "Major Griffin to see Mr. Churchill."

She picked up the phone on her desk and announced me.

"Go right in, sir."

Churchill was seated behind his desk, puffing away vigorously on a long cigar. He gave me a grim smile when he saw me.

"Please take a seat, Major. I'll be with you momentarily."

After a few final scribbles on the papers before him, he joined me in the sitting area.

"You look more rested than when we last met, Major."

"I believe I've finally taken care of some nagging problems, sir."

"Good, good."

Marsh joined us as coffee was delivered.

"Tell us about your trip, Major," Churchill ordered.

On the way to the war office, I had decided that I wouldn't tell Churchill that Billy Jones had spent the trip trying to have me murdered, nor would I mention my encounters with Karl Fuchs. Churchill didn't want to hear about either one, and I wanted to explore a different subject with Mr. Churchill. So, in response to his question, I explained that I had met with House and Lodge, and I gave Churchill a summary of both meetings. I also handed him Lodge's letter. He weighed the envelope in his hand before slitting it open. He quickly read the pages inside.

"Well, it seems my words have persuaded Senator Lodge of the risks we face. Of course, he promises nothing, and I fear he will use my concern as yet another reason to block ratification of the treaty." He put the pages of Lodge's letter face down on his desk as if shutting that diplomatic door. "And the president?" he asked.

"I did see him, and I delivered your letter."

"Did Mr. Wilson read it?" he asked.

"I don't know. He didn't read it in front of me. He seemed tired."

"When did you see him?"

"The morning he got sick. Other than his fatigue, he seemed well enough when I saw him, but I understand that later that morning he fell deathly ill," I answered.

"Oh, you sly devil. I wouldn't be surprised if they actually believe you," Tippy Frederickson said in my ear. It was all I could do to refrain from jumping when he spoke. I was surprised at the tone of approval in his voice.

"Yes, we haven't heard a word from him or his staff," Churchill said. "Our man in Washington, Sir William Wiseman, has been trying to get a meeting with him with no success. Was Jones with you when you met the president?"

Apparently, Churchill wanted independent confirmation that I'd done as he had asked.

"No. I got the appointment at the White House very quickly. I met Mr. Jones that afternoon, and Jones did introduce me to Sir William. I warned Sir William that the president was exhausted. I also warned him that the First Lady was very protective of the president's health. And this was before I'd discovered that the president's health had deteriorated that morning after I'd left him. I did suggest to Sir William that he might arrange for the new ambassador to meet with Senator Lodge."

"Sir Grey! A decent man, who is well past his time," Churchill scoffed.

"Yes. Sir, I don't want to take up too much of your time, but I do have a question for you."

"Yes?"

"During my meeting at the White House, I was asked to look into potential profiteering during the war. Specifically, I was directed to look into the operation of the American War Industries Board. Sir William mentioned that you knew Bernard Baruch, the chairman of the board. I was wondering if you had any thoughts on its operation or the likelihood of profiteering."

"Profiteering! Nonsense. Bernard ran a tight ship, and he wouldn't countenance any dishonesty whatsoever. What on earth prompted the president to even consider such a thing?"

"I'm not sure it's the board itself or its members, sir. Did Mr. Baruch ever mention to you the name Harry Armistan?"

"He did not."

"What about Sebastien Lynch?"

"I've heard the name, but I can't remember where."

"Thank you. I am sure the WIB is in the clear. But as a senior marine officer recently told me, 'war *is* big business.'"

"Well, they are certainly right about that!"

"I suppose that is why the president is concerned."

"Yes, but the world order is fragile. There are greater concerns than a few shop clerks stealing pennies."

Churchill's office phone rang. He went back to his desk and answered. "Good, yes. Send him in." He sounded happy for the distraction.

After one rap, the door opened, and Sir Basil Thomson entered. I had not planned on seeing Sir Basil. He didn't like me. He was convinced I was a murderer, and he was right.

"Major Griffin has returned with news from America," Churchill told him.

Sir Basil glanced at Churchill, then fixed me with a hard stare.

"Did William Jones return with you?"

"He did. We traveled back together and parted ways at Euston Station. He went home, and I went to check on an injured friend."

"Yes. At the Endell Street Military Hospital, where very early this morning my constables found a body in the lobby and a wrecked front door."

"So I was told. I spoke with two of your police inspectors at the hospital."

"And you haven't seen Jones since then?" Thomson asked.

"I haven't seen him since Euston Station. What is this about?"

"Yes, what are you getting at, Sir Basil?" Churchill added.

"Mr. Jones's body was found floating face down in the Thames this morning."

"My God!" Churchill gasped.

"What happened?" I asked with genuine curiosity.

"He drowned," Thomson said bluntly.

"But how? That's horrible. Has his wife been told?" I rattled off the questions, hoping I was the picture of a concerned friend.

"Not very bloody likely, and why should you be?" Frederickson said.

"We notified his wife this morning. Fortunately, she didn't have to see the body. We have plenty of men who could identify Jones."

"This is terrible. I had just reconnected with Billy and his wife," I noted.

"Yes, quite the coincidence. You appear and a month later Jones is dead and his beautiful young wife is widowed. Wasn't she your fiancée at one time?"

"What do you mean by that?" I did my best to muster a righteous anger. "Billy was a friend. Hold on! Billy was murdered? And you think I did it?"

"We don't know, but we know of no reason for him to kill himself."

"That you know of. If you'd been in France and seen what I'm sure Billy had seen, you wouldn't be so quick to doubt. You have no idea what was going on inside his head. Believe me, after that goddamn war, you've no idea what's inside any soldier's head," I said.

"You're bloody right about that!" Tippy chimed in, confirming my point.

"He's quite correct, Sir Basil, it was horrific," Churchill added.

"We are, necessarily, exploring all possibilities," Sir Basil insisted.

"Come now, there is no point in accusing anyone without evidence. Major Griffin has done great service to the allied cause. He has done exactly as we've asked, and he served in our armed forces and his own," Churchill said playing peacemaker.

"Well, if Billy was murdered, I hope you find the bastard who did it," I said. "Mrs. Jones will be devastated. If there was one thing I learned during my brief reacquaintance with the Joneses, it was that they were deeply in love."

I meant every word I said, but Billy's death was still good news. If he'd killed himself because he thought he was going to lose Evelyn, it meant he wasn't around to hunt me. And if his soldiers killed him, they must have blamed him for all their dead mates who died during the witch hunt Jones had convinced them to embark upon. They'd punished him for his lies and betrayal.

"Well, this is all a terrible shame," Churchill said, moving on from Jones's death. "Major, perhaps you would consider remaining in England and working with my office, in an unofficial capacity, of course."

I wasn't listening to Churchill. I was thinking about Evelyn. My reaction to Billy's death was pure selfishness. Evelyn would be heartbroken. She was alone. Perhaps pregnant. A widow. And I had allowed it to happen. Encouraged it.

"You had no choice, mate," Tippy said. "How were you to know Billy would need you and then would hate you for what you did?"

I shook my head at Frederickson's words. His recent support worried me. I didn't trust it or him.

"You've been hard done by, Griffin," Frederickson said. "I misjudged you. Seeing that Billy wasn't any better than you got me thinking. You know, maybe you could cozy up to Evelyn? Maybe you could have that life you left behind and a baby too?"

And there it was. The dagger in the back I could expect from Frederickson.

"Not likely," I said.

Churchill looked offended. I realized I'd spoken aloud.

"My apologies, sir. This news is difficult for me. It's given me a lot to think about. Perhaps working with your office is something I could consider, but for now I think I need some time to think about my future, here and in America. I trust I've completed the task you gave me?" I stood.

"Well, yes," Churchill answered. He had no choice but to stand as well.

Sir Basil didn't bother.

"Where will you be staying?" the hostile police chief asked.

"On Aldford Street. Your men have the address," I answered.

———

After leaving the war office, I walked to the Endell Street Military Hospital, thinking about Billy and Evelyn. I realized that I would have to see Evelyn. I had no choice. It was the only decent thing to do, but I would leave England immediately after.

When I reached the hospital, I found that the front gate had already been rehung, and workmen were toiling away on the frame of the lobby door. I told the receptionist that I was there to see Mitchell. Instead of being directed to his room, I was escorted by a blue uniformed orderly to Dr. Murray. It seemed they didn't want me on the loose among the patients.

"Ah, Mr. Griffin, thank you for coming. As you know, there was some excitement here last night," Dr. Murray said as I entered her office.

"Well, ma'am, I wouldn't know. I apparently missed all the brouhaha. I only learned of it from Miss Ward, Miss Phillips, and the police."

"No need to be coy with me, young man. Ada and Daisy have told me exactly what happened last night. I brought you here to thank you. I don't know what those men wanted, but both young women are convinced you saved them and William as well."

"I see," I said evasively.

"Daisy did feel you should have given a warning to the man

you killed in the lobby, but I explained that soldiers rarely give their enemies warning," she said. She seemed completely unbothered by the fact that I'd shot a man in her front hall.

"Yes, ma'am."

"Do you believe there is still a danger to William or the hospital?"

"No, ma'am, I do not. I think the issue was fully resolved last night."

"Good. I can't have my girls at risk. Can I?"

"No, ma'am."

"And I can't have them under suspicion by the police either."

"No. And I do understand the risk they took for me."

A tap on the door announced a second woman, who bustled into the office with such an air of enthusiasm that even Dr. Murray smiled.

"Flora, is this the devil the girls are twittering about?" the woman asked eagerly. Like Murray, she was older than the rest of the Endell Street staff, but she had an open, approachable air. She was deliberately teasing me about my face while complimenting me. Her bearing and delivery made it inoffensive. In fact, it made me feel like an ordinary young man in a hospital full of women, when I knew I was anything but. If she was a doctor, she had an exceptional bedside manner.

"Yes, Louisa. It is. Dr. Anderson,[1] please meet Major John Griffin."

"My pleasure, ma'am."

She seized my hand in both of hers. "Thank you so much for your help last night. Daisy was very concerned for her safety."

"She is one tough customer. She didn't back down from those fellows at all. I suspect I might have put her at risk."

"I know Daisy, and I am very sure you protected her from

---

1. Louisa Garrett Anderson. July 28, 1873–November 15, 1943. Physician and suffragette.

herself and those men," she told me. "For which I cannot thank you enough."

"The care you are giving Mr. Mitchell is more than enough thanks for me."

"Well, he is a joy to be around, and it is our job to heal, which he seems to be doing nicely. He does cause quite a stir among the staff."

I laughed. "I am sure of that."

"Come. I'll take you to see William."

Dr. Anderson escorted me to Mitchell's room at a pace that left me short of breath. She greeted Mitchell, took his pulse as a matter of course, patted me on the arm, and was gone in a whirlwind.

"She's a handful," Mitchell commented as I pulled up a chair next to his bed. I recalled him sitting next to mine in exactly the same way just a few months before.

"She is, and Dr. Murray is too. They both seem very competent and protective of the hospital and their girls."

"They are. That's why you got dragged to see Murray. She wanted to make sure there wouldn't be any more gunfights in her hospital."

"Can't say I blame her," I said.

"And?"

"What?" I didn't want to tell Mitchell what had happened, and I was going to make it hard for him.

"Will they be coming back?"

"No."

"Why were they trying to kill us in the first place."

"They weren't trying to kill us. They were just trying to kill me. They attacked you by mistake. You probably didn't even notice, but I'd borrowed your new raincoat the day I visited Evelyn and Billy Jones at their house. The killers followed me and saw me in your coat. The next day, when we went to breakfast, they thought you were me. I was the one they wanted to shove into traffic."

"What? Why?"

"It was rainy and the killer didn't get a good look at us that morning. It was my fault though. I shouldn't have taken your coat." I was evading his question. He wanted to know why they wanted to kill me. I couldn't bring myself to tell Mitchell the whole story. I couldn't tell him about having sex with Evelyn at the couple's request or that she might be carrying my child. I had no reason to mention Jones's gonorrhea. Those details were just too painful and bizarre. Instead, I blamed the whole thing on Jones's jealousy of my past relationship with his wife. I told him Jones had killed himself by jumping into the Thames, and I implied that in the night, I had killed everyone else involved. With my history, he had no reason to doubt me.

He smoked as I talked. I knew he sensed that I'd left out some details, but I distracted him with tales of some of my doings in New York and Washington. Pauline's death and Woodrow Wilson's fall never came up. I shouldn't have lied to him, but I didn't want to have to explain what was inexplicable. He was very interested in my meeting with Thomas Reynolds.

"I think I've gotten Reynolds wondering if Armistan was an illegal war profiteer. My hope is that Armistan won't have him or their other bigwig industrialist cronies as allies when push comes to shove, and it might create a problem for Morgan too. I also mentioned that same possibility to Churchill," I said.

"So you've already seen Churchill?"

"Yeah, I reported to him and Sir Basil this morning. It looks like I'm free to go."

"Well, I feel sick thinking about Reynolds and Tricia," he said. "We need to find her. You might have to go without me. I should be out of here in a month or so. At least that's what the doctors are telling me, but I don't think you should wait until then. You need to find her now, Griff."

"I agree. I'll go to Paris. Get the trunk full of guns and ship out for the States. I'll be at the Pennsylvania Hotel in New York, but you need to get well. I know Patricia wouldn't be too keen on all the time you're getting to spend with Rachel."

"What? Rachel and I are just friends."

"Sure you are, Mitch. Have you told her that?"

He looked thoughtful, and I didn't press him.

I patted his arm. "I'll get going. It'll be good to see Eugene and Kiki again. I'll tell them you fell down and hurt yourself. They'll both enjoy that."

"Bastard. That'll probably make Kiki happy anyway," he said, referring to his uncomfortable breakup with Kiki in favor of Patricia.

I stood.

Rachel breezed into the room. I glanced at Mitchell and caught an unrestrained smile, which disappeared as soon as he saw me looking.

"Perfect timing, Rachel. I'm off, but Mitchell will explain to you what's been happening," I said, kissing both her cheeks in the French fashion.

"Sounds good, John." She pulled the chair closer to Mitchell's bed. He saw me notice and just shook his head.

I sent a note to Evelyn's house, asking if I could visit her home and pay my respects the following morning. She agreed. I was afraid, but I refused to let my cowardice prevent me from seeing her.

I had lied to Sir Basil about my residence. There was no way I was going to make it easy for Fair or Norton to find me, and that night, I stayed at the Strand again. I had the hotel clean my suit and shine my scratched-up shoes. I didn't have time for a haircut, but in the morning, I shaved carefully, not that anyone would spend a lot of time studying my face.

It was a beautiful day, cool and clear. Exceptional weather for early fall in England. I took a motorcab from the hotel. I dreaded the meeting to come, but I knew I had to see Evelyn. It was the only decent thing to do. I was in danger of feeling good about myself for not running. I would have to lie to her, of course. Unfortunately, I'd have to tell her most of what Billy had done. I supposed I could leave out his disease. It wasn't much, but it was probably the best I could do.

"That's the Jack I know and love," Tippy said.

"Shush, Tipton," Sarah chided. "He's doing the right thing."

"Thanks, Sarah. I don't see any other choice," I said.

She put her hand over mine, but I couldn't feel it.

The steps up to the Hans Road house looked innocent enough, but I took them slowly. My heart was racing, and I felt the disconnection I had felt so often going into combat. At the door, I knocked lightly. Shamefully, I hoped no one would answer.

The door cracked open enough for me to be recognized.

"Ah, Jack Griffin. Evelyn had told me you were back sniffing around. You look even worse than Evelyn described." Evelyn's mother, Sandra Williams, was holding the door. I hadn't seen her since before I'd been blinded. She'd never really approved of me. I was an American and therefore not worthy of her daughter. She was right. I hadn't been worthy of her daughter, but it didn't endear her to me. I wasn't sure she was going to let me in. I was reminded of the intimidation I'd experienced in dealing with Mrs. Williams when I was a nineteen-year-old boy pursuing Evelyn, but that boy was gone. The slaughter of the past four years had erased him.

"*Sandra.*" I made certain the resignation and disappointment in my voice was obvious. "Is Evelyn able to see me?"

"I don't know why she should. Every time you appear, terrible things happen."

"As I recall, they sometimes happened to me."

"But I'm worried about Evelyn and not you, aren't I?"

"Is she available?"

She opened a narrow gap in the doorway, making clear her reluctance to allow me entry.

"She's upstairs in her room. I'll tell her you're here."

"Thank you."

I waited in the large sitting room, looking out the front window at the street. The cheerful light streaming in through the drapes seemed a perverse contradiction to the purpose of my visit.

Soft footsteps in the hallway alerted me of Evelyn's approach.

She was in a nightgown under a tightly wrapped robe. Her arms were crossed over her breasts and her eyes were swollen.

"Wait upstairs, Mother," she said. Mrs. Williams had followed her into the room.

"I don't think you should be alone, dear."

"I won't be. Jack is here. If I need anything, he can help me."

"Well, I'll just wait in the kitchen."

"Upstairs, Mother. You will wait upstairs," Evelyn said with iron in her tone.

"Very well," Sandra answered with a sniff.

We didn't speak as we listened to her mother's passage to the floor above.

"I knew something was wrong. Your last visit. You were so cold. I know Billy must have done something to anger you, but I didn't think you would kill him."

"I didn't kill him. I could have, but I didn't."

"What could he have possibly done that was so horrible, John?" She didn't believe that I hadn't killed him.

"I'll tell you what he did, Evelyn. He tried to kill my friend. He tried to kill me, and he used men from his old regiment to do it. He told them lies about me to secure their help. He convinced them I was a coward, a deserter, and a traitor."

"Now to be fair, you actually are all those things," Tippy noted in a reasonable tone.

I continued undeterred. "I only found out the truth when I

spoke with you. I questioned the men who tried to kill me. They were all English. They referred to a captain who knew the truth about me, who gave them their orders. I knew of no *captain*. It took me a long time even to suspect Billy. He was a good friend after all. It was only after you confirmed his rank that I knew for sure."

"That is ridiculous. Why would he do that?" she asked with a sob. "He loved you like a brother."

"He loved you more. He did it because he was jealous. He knew you manipulated him. He wanted to have a child, but he never wanted me to father it. That was too much to bear. Knowing about our past, our engagement, and then you asking for me to give you a child was simply too much for him to accept. The only way he could square what had been required of him was for me to die. If I were dead, I suppose he thought it would be easier to raise my child." That was a lie. Billy never wanted to raise my child, whether I were alive or dead.

She collapsed onto the sofa, put her head in her hands, and began to cry. I didn't move to comfort her. I wasn't going to take the chance of touching her. I had already abandoned any future with Evelyn.

"I'm sorry. I confronted him at the pub. We were both angry, but when I left him he was alive. I told him I had seen you to ask about his rank. I think that bothered him more than my accusations. I'm sorry," I said again. I hoped she believed that Billy had killed himself. I supposed it was even possible he had, but the look in the sergeant major's eyes told me that was unlikely.

"Oh God! This is all just so horrible I can't believe it's actually happening," she wailed.

I didn't tell her that I'd felt that same way for much of the past four years. That was a bit of empathy that would provide no solace at all.

"I'm going back to America shortly. I won't be seeing you again," I told her.

She looked up at me with tear-filled eyes. She wouldn't ask me to stay. She was too proud, and I wouldn't offer.

"You're strong, Evelyn. Stronger than you know. You'll get through this. I know you will." I knew no such thing, and that was, perhaps, my most cowardly lie of all.

The image of Evelyn's face, despairing yet still beautiful, accompanied me down the steps from the house.

"She'll be fine," Tippy said optimistically.

I didn't answer. Instead, I walked with long, purposeful strides. Away.

By the time I reached the Knightsbridge underground entrance, Evelyn was once again part of my past. That was where she belonged. I glanced down Brompton Road from where I'd come and stepped into the station.

My thoughts had shifted to New York City. Armistan and Reynolds were waiting for me, and our meeting had been delayed too long.

AFTERWORD

A few comments on some of the history in Stalking Ghosts.

The footnotes are intended to help the reader understand which characters in the story are actual historical figures. I include in the notes some limited information about each character. Nearly all deserve more study than a few lines in a footnote provide.

In researching the story, I have read too many books to list. All contributed to the atmosphere and accuracy of Griffin's world. The *New York Times* TimesMachine archive was invaluable in finding exactly what people were told or believed in 1919.

I have tried to remain close to times and dates of actual events. Perhaps the most crucial date for this book is that of Woodrow Wilson's stroke—November 2, 1919. With the exception of Griffin's presence, the book does describe the events of that morning relatively accurately. This is thanks to Ike Hoover's book *Forty-Two Years in the White House*. Irwin H. Hoover was the Chief Usher at the time of Wilson's stroke, and I have tried to faithfully mirror his description of that morning in this book. Rebecca Boggs Roberts book about Edith Wilson, *Untold Power*, was also helpful, both for the events of that morning and in developing my understanding of the First Lady. Daniel Schulman's book, *The Money Kings*, was helpful in providing an understanding of the importance of German Jewish immigrants to Wall Street and the close relationships between the banking families.

The opinions and words I attribute to Vernon Kell, Basil Thomson, and Winston Churchill are either taken from newspaper articles from the time (many footnoted) or biographies of the men. The antisemitism of Thomson and the perceived link between Bolshevism and Jews was very much an attitude of some at the time.

Also, Churchill's hostility to Bolshevism is as accurate as I could make it.

Smedley Butler is a fascinating character, and Jonathan Myerson Katz's book, *Gangsters of Capitalism*, is a wonderful read. I tried to convey Butler's disdain for politicians and raw, unbridled capitalism. I am sure he had already developed this disdain by 1919.

Discovering Endell Street Military Hospital and Doctors Murray and Anderson was one of the chief joys of researching this book. I had no idea such a hospital existed or such women were alive and kicking in 1915. Both ladies were tough, passionate, and very good doctors. For anyone interested in more complete information on the hospital and its two remarkable founders, I recommend *Endell Street* by Wendy Moore.

When in doubt about all things etiquette related, Emily Post is still the go-to source. Her 1922 *Etiquette in Society, in Business, in Politics and at Home*, helped create the atmosphere of London, New York, and Washington, in my mind, if not on the page.

ACKNOWLEDGMENTS

Before acknowledging the gracious support I've had in writing this story, I must make clear that all the mistakes in language, grammar, and historical accuracy are mine and mine alone.

My children no longer live at home and have not had to endure the daily questioning of "what happens next?" that my wife, Michelle, has. She has remained patient and vital to the sausage-making of writing this book. Fortunately for the reader, she has been firm when, in her review, she discovers something knuckleheaded that I have written. She makes these stories so much better.

I remain indebted to my sister, Elizabeth Christy, for her crucial editing and timeline review. Her comments and corrections tremendously improved the quality of the book. Annie Sarac of the Editing Pen (TheEditingPen.com) has given this work a professional finish that would not exist but for her.

Finally, I have strived to keep the language and attitudes in the book consistent with the times. Sadly, some language and attitudes were unattractive then and now.

ABOUT THE AUTHOR

Alex Juden is the author of two previous Griffin Post Great War mysteries, *Red Tiger Hunting* and *Crossing Darkness*. He lives with his wife in Houston, Texas. Two of his three children remain in Texas while the third has moved to California (for college anyway). Prior to writing, he enjoyed a variety of jobs, including naval aviator, trial lawyer, and public company general counsel. Alex now has a small farm in Texas where the vineyard is dangerously close to thriving and the trees might actually bear fruit in the near future.

He studied history and political science at Rice University.

Alexander C. Juden (alexanderjuden.com)

ALSO BY ALEXANDER C. JUDEN

Red Tiger Hunting

Crossing Darkness